THE
DARK
BLOOD

A.J. SMITH

HEAD
ZEUS

THE
DARK
BLOOD

A. J. Smith has been devising the worlds, histories and characters of the Long War chronicles for more than a decade. He was born in Birmingham and works in secondary education.

CHRONICLES OF
THE LONG WAR

THE BLACK GUARD
THE DARK BLOOD

For Mum

SECOND CHRONICLE OF THE LONG WAR

MAPS
BOOK ONE:
THE DARK BLOOD

SECOND CHRONICLE
OF THE LONG WAR

BOOK TWO:
THE SHAPE TAKER

THE LANDS OF
RANEN

THE LANDS OF
RO

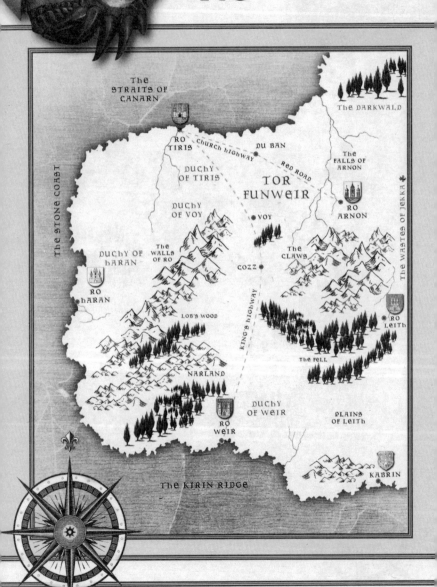

The Straits of Canarn

The Darkwald

Ro Tiris — Church Highway — Du Ban

The Falls of Arnon

Duchy of Tiris

Red Road

Tor Funweir

The Stone Coast

Duchy of Voy — Voy

Ro Arnon

The Wastes of Jekka

Duchy of Haran

The Walls of Ro

The Claws

Ro Haran

Cozz

Ro Leith

King's Highway

Lob's Wood

Narland

The Fell

Duchy of Weir

Plains of Leith

Ro Weir

The Kirin Ridge

Kabrin

THE LANDS OF
KARESIA

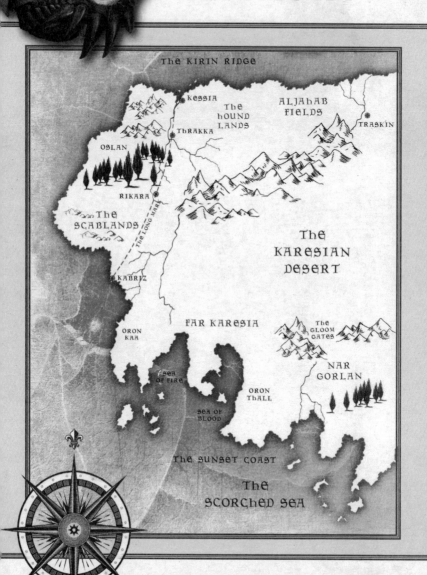

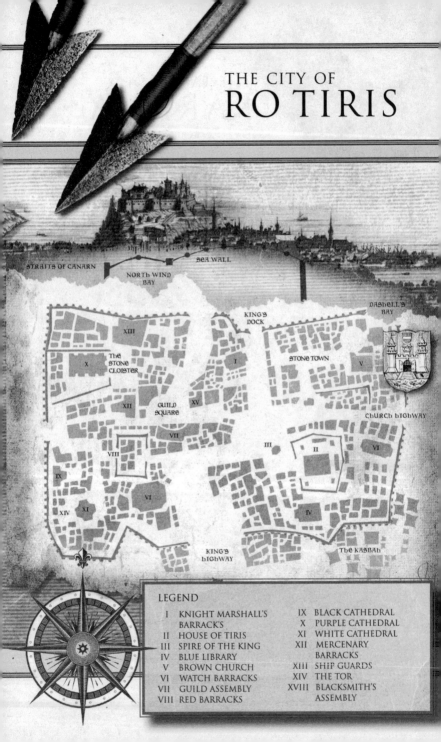

THE CITY OF
RO TIRIS

STRAITS OF CANARN

NORTH WIND BAY

SEA WALL

KING'S DOCK

DASHELL'S BAY

XIII

THE STONE CLOISTER

X

STONE TOWN

V

I

XII

XV

GUILD SQUARE

VII

CHURCH HIGHWAY

VIII

III

II

VI

IX

XIV XI

VI

IV

KING'S HIGHWAY

THE KASBAH

LEGEND

I KNIGHT MARSHALL'S BARRACK'S
II HOUSE OF TIRIS
III SPIRE OF THE KING
IV BLUE LIBRARY
V BROWN CHURCH
VI WATCH BARRACKS
VII GUILD ASSEMBLY
VIII RED BARRACKS

IX BLACK CATHEDRAL
X PURPLE CATHEDRAL
XI WHITE CATHEDRAL
XII MERCENARY BARRACKS
XIII SHIP GUARDS
XIV THE TOR
XVIII BLACKSMITH'S ASSEMBLY

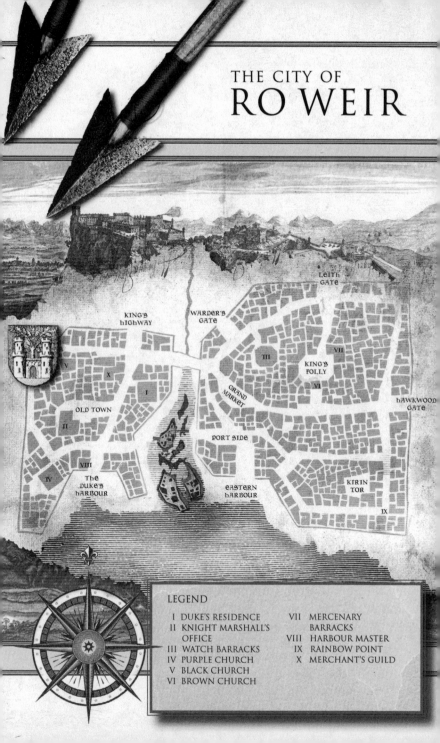

THE CITY OF
RO WEIR

LEGEND

I DUKE'S RESIDENCE
II KNIGHT MARSHALL'S OFFICE
III WATCH BARRACKS
IV PURPLE CHURCH
V BLACK CHURCH
VI BROWN CHURCH
VII MERCENARY BARRACKS
VIII HARBOUR MASTER
IX RAINBOW POINT
X MERCHANT'S GUILD

BOOK ONE

THE DARK BLOOD

THE TALE OF THE DEAD GOD

THE FOREST GIANT sat alone in his black and green halls beyond the world. His Dark Young were all dead or torpid, his Dokkalfar had betrayed him and the rampaging Ice Giant was near.

His hall, built over the nameless ages of deep time, was decaying and rotten as his power was slowly raped from him by the Fire Giant.

He waited.

The Long War had claimed more Gods and Giants than trees in his hall, and he knew his time was near.

The One had found him, Rowanoco would fight him, and Jaa would take his power, leaving him as nothing more than the memory of a once great God, a story to pass down through the coming ages of pleasure and blood.

When the end came, it was swift. Jaa had left him little with which to fight Rowanoco and the outcome was not in doubt. The God was laid low by the mighty swing of a mighty hammer and prepared for the void into which Gods disappear.

He sank into slumber.

But something happened. The God felt his power buckle and crack, but it did not break. The treacherous Fire Giant had stolen his power but not destroyed it. It was a thread of existence, but it was enough.

As strange beings called men appeared and spread across the lands, Shub-Nillurath smiled.

PROLOGUE

THE ASSASSIN SKULKED at the back of the tavern. It was a low-rent affair, nestled against the southern wall of Ro Tiris and catering for people who had been thrown out of most other places. He *did* fit in, even if he wished that he didn't, and no one had questioned his presence or doubted that he belonged.

The wine was vinegary and warm, probably gathered from various discarded half-glasses, and he pushed it away after a quick sniff. The Ro had only two kinds of wine, the excellent and the shit, and the assassin was not allowed in places that served the former. He hadn't tried the stew, usefully advertised as *cheap and brown*. He rarely felt hungry before killing a man.

The tavern was half full and, with another hour before midnight, it was about as full as it was going to get. The barman, a blotchy-faced pederast called Reginald, had paid the assassin handsomely to remove a local pimp who had been causing him trouble. He didn't like doing this kind of work for these kinds of people, but he needed coin and killing was all he knew how to do. Travelling, even travelling rough, was an expensive endeavour.

The target's back had been facing the assassin for about twenty minutes, as he poured more and more cheap liquor down his throat. He was standing with half a dozen other men, street scum by the look of them, and the assassin judged that none of them was fit for combat. The barman kept glancing over impatiently, not realizing that knifing a man in a crowded tavern would be foolish. The assassin mouthed the words *stay calm* across the smoky tavern, though it did little to mollify Reginald.

Another few minutes, and more vinegary wine, and the target shifted uncomfortably and took temporary leave of his companions. The assassin smiled and thanked the god of bladder control, and stealthily rose from his seat.

The target moved through the tavern, paying scant attention to those around him, and exited through a dirty fabric hanging separating the customers from the slit trench. He was a mid-level pimp, not the kind to have guards or friends in high, or even low, places.

The assassin wasn't one to moralize, but he thought child prostitution was a loathsome business. The fact that he was being paid by a disgruntled client, rather than an indignant parent, mattered little. He secretly planned to kill Reginald too before he left town.

The target made several unpleasant sounds as he moved into the trench and began to unbuckle his belt. The assassin momentarily lost sight of the pimp and across the tavern he could see unnecessary concern on Reginald's face. With a furtive glance, he entered the trench and swiftly replaced the fabric. Within was a long and unpleasant-smelling slit in the stone floor. At one end a steady trickle of water was pumped in from the city's supply and ran along the length of the trench, washing away the worst of the effluent. Another man was squatting uncomfortably and straining to relieve himself.

The assassin stepped close and said quietly, 'Leave, now!' He placed a small dagger against the man's throat and began to draw it across his skin. The man instantly forgot about his bowel movement and left with a flushed look on his face, holding up his trousers.

The target was drunk enough not to have noticed this exchange and was cheerfully urinating at the far end, whistling to himself.

With a swift movement, the assassin pulled back his head and dug his knife into the pimp's neck. He didn't cut his throat right away but let the man look back and see his killer's face before a swift jerk of the razor-sharp knife opened up his neck and let his blood flow down over his clothes.

'Shh, just keep quiet and let it happen,' he said calmly. 'There really is no business in selling kids to sweaty old men . . .'

The man died quickly and the assassin let him fall in an undignified heap into the slit trench. He smiled at a job well done and retreated into the tavern.

He skulked past the other patrons and stood by the bar. After a moment, Reginald came over to stand next to him. 'Is it done?' he asked in a whisper.

'Yes,' was the reply. 'Tell me, Reg, is there someone else that can serve this evening?'

'What do you mean?'

'Another barman to take over if you should happen to not be around for the rest of the evening,' the assassin said quietly.

'Well, I suppose . . . yes, we've got a few serving-boys in tonight.'

'Good, come with me,' he said with a disarming grin.

Motioning Reginald to follow, he strolled to the back of the tavern where a small wooden door led into a dark yard used primarily for wine storage. Once outside, he sat on a large barrel and waited for the barman to join him and close the door.

'Money,' said the assassin, holding out his hand.

Reginald smiled awkwardly and reached into his stained apron. 'Ten gold crowns, yeah?'

The assassin nodded and took the coin, placing it in his own purse. 'I'm afraid there have also been some expenses, Reginald.'

The barman was obviously uncomfortable and moved to stand closer to him.

'I was told that you were a man that gets things done, but I was also told ten gold crowns,' he replied guardedly.

'Relax, Reg, you and I are both businessmen.' He let his grin encompass his entire face. 'Who gave you my name?'

'A mobster called Kale Glenwood,' Reginald replied.

'The forger? Since when does he throw my name around?' It

was annoying that a streak of Ro piss like Glenwood was using his name.

'He said that you and him are good friends, and that you were reliable,' Reginald responded.

'Well, he was about a third right. Come here.' The last words were spoken quietly and with menace, and Reginald leant back to see if there was anyone else close by.

'Reg, before you think about leaving, be aware that I can kill you much quicker than you can get to that door.'

Reginald began to sweat and took note of the assassin's weaponry. He was not carrying his longbow, but his hand was casually resting on the hilt of a katana and a knife was sheathed across his chest.

'Okay,' said the barman, holding his arms wide in a gesture of submission. 'How do I get out of this alive?'

'I'm afraid you don't.' He moved his hand with lightning speed and threw the knife across the yard to lodge in Reginald's chest. 'I have little time for people that prey on children.'

The barman was momentarily surprised at the blade sticking in his chest, before falling to the dirty ground. Rham Jas stood up slowly and crossed to retrieve his knife.

'Okay, Mr Glenwood,' he said to himself, 'you and I need a little chat.'

* * *

Rham Jas Rami thought of the day everything had changed. He had been a hunter, a farmer, a husband and a father until the day, nearly fifteen years ago, when the Purple clerics of the One God had attacked his home. He had seen smoke on the horizon while out hunting. When he returned all he found was destruction. The Purple clerics had killed his wife and sold his son and daughter into slavery. By the time he'd returned to his farm, there was nothing left except anger, grief and vengeance. Though each of the clerics had since died in pain, he never had discovered why they had chosen to attack his farm.

What the clerics did not know, however, was that he was no normal Kirin. When he was a young man, before Keisha and Zeldantor were born, Rham Jas had repulsed a similar attack. He'd scared off a small patrol, but had ended up pinned by a crossbow bolt to a darkwood tree in an unremarked corner of Oslan. He had hung from the tree for hours, feeling his blood mix with the black sap of the tree, until he had finally managed to pull himself down and felt the world change around him.

Before he was a hunter, farmer, husband or father, Rham Jas was a dark-blood. The sap of the darkwood tree had altered him. He was stronger, faster and sharper than other men. The crossbow wound had healed within minutes and he had run the five miles home without stopping for breath or feeling tired. Now the feeling had become commonplace and the cynical Kirin had learned to trust his abilities. He was very hard to kill and he knew it. He was called Dark Blood by the forest-dwellers, *assassin* by the Ro, and *friend* by a select few.

Rham Jas smiled as he remembered the other advantage the tree had given him – he was the only man alive who could strike at the Seven Sisters. Men had tried, but without exception had been unable to raise a hand or fire an arrow. The enchantresses of Karesia were all but unkillable and, according to the forest-dwelling Dokkalfar, they were planning to exploit their invulnerability to raise the malevolent Forest Giant of pleasure and blood: the Dead God. Rham Jas was uncomfortable about being the sole man who could stop them, and had only agreed to become a soldier in the Long War because the Seven Sisters had bought his children from Karesian slavers.

He had much to do, and needed cash and time to do it. He had been back in Tiris only a few days, having spent a month in Canarn helping Brom and Nanon, the Dokkalfar, clear out the remaining mercenaries and assisting the other forest-dwellers settle into city life. More than a hundred had arrived during the time Rham Jas had remained there, and Nanon was sure more would come as the Ro continued their purges across Tor Funweir.

He had tried not to think of the Seven Sisters' last words to him. Ameira the Lady of Spiders had mentioned his son, the child he had lost fourteen years before, sold to Karesian slavers by the Purple clerics. The only consolation he could take from the news of Zeldantor's death was the hope that his sister, Keisha, might still be alive. If that were the case, the Kirin assassin had a better reason than just saving the world to hunt down and kill the remaining Seven Sisters.

PART ONE

CHAPTER ONE

RANDALL OF DARKWALD
IN THE TOWN OF VOY

HE WAITED. THE White chapel had doused its lights ten minutes ago and Randall had seen the last of the nightly congregation leave shortly afterwards, pausing only to exchange words with the cleric in residence. The white dove, symbolizing the One God's aspect of peace and healing, was displayed prominently either side of the simple wooden doors. Those doors were closed now and the churchman within would be shortly retiring to bed.

The town of Voy was small, with well-spaced estates around the edges and exclusive shops and boutiques in the centre. All the colours of the One God were represented within the town's walls, but the town was dominated by Oswald's Cathedral, the huge Gold church that acted as the bank of Tor Funweir.

Randall stood out here in his battered and dirty clothing, and found it easier to move around if he ventured out only after dark and stuck to the side streets. His cloak provided adequate cover but he worried about showing his face for fear of a Wanted poster.

In the month since he had left Tiris, Randall had descended further into lawlessness than he had ever imagined possible. He caught his reflection in a polished glass storefront and a hard and dangerous man looked back. His beard had thickened and become darker, and his hair was long enough now to need tying back. His eighteenth birthday had come and gone with no celebration. Neither of the young squire's companions had known the significance of the date, two weeks before, when he had got drunk for the first time. Utha was too frail to join him and Vasir, the Dokkalfar, did not understand why anyone should want deliberately to render themselves insensible.

The jewelled bell towering over the Gold church rang a muted peal, signifying midnight in the town of Voy, and Randall stepped out of the side street and towards the White chapel. The streets were well tended and empty, only an occasional figure moving between residences in the distance. His cloak cast a shadow across his face and he walked quickly, keeping his pace even and the sheathed sword of Great Claw out of sight. He reached the front of the chapel and paused. Seeing no one on guard, he removed the key he had stolen earlier in the evening and stealthily opened the door.

Randall had never broken into a church before, but without proper healing Utha the Ghost, Black cleric of the One, would surely die.

Their progress through the forested wilds of Tiris had been slow for the past month. For the first week Utha had not been able to walk or ride, and even after that he needed copious rest so as not to reopen his wounds. In quiet moments, while the cleric slept, Randall and Vasir had formed a plan to reach the forests of the Fell, far to the south. Vasir had assured him that they would be cared for in the Dokkalfar woods.

He stepped softly as he crept into the chapel. The lights were all extinguished and a ray of moonlight provided the only illumination. The cleric's sleeping chamber was separated from the main chapel by a simple white curtain, and Randall paused before slowly pushing it aside. The room beyond was simple: a low wooden bed, a fireplace and a water pump. He noticed a faint odour of expensive tobacco, likely the churchman's only vice. A small painting of a waterfront hung under the room's single window.

The cleric turned over in bed. He gasped as he saw the armed man standing over him.

Randall held a finger to his lips and slowly drew his longsword.

'I am a man of peace and there is nothing to steal here,' the cleric blurted out.

'I'm not here to hurt you or steal anything, brother. I need you to come with me,' Randall said quietly.

'What do you want of me?' the cleric asked.

'A friend of mine is dying and I need a skilled healer.' Randall moved to the doorway. 'Get dressed.'

The White cleric turned out of bed and, with shaking hands, reached for his robes. He was not a warrior or a knight, just a man who ministered to a common population of worshippers. A simple churchman was a welcome sight to Randall after months in the presence of the Black and Purple clerics.

'What is the nature of your friend's injuries?' the cleric asked.

Randall glanced behind. 'He nearly died a month ago from multiple sword wounds. He's strong and he pulled through, but one of the wounds has festered and he's fighting a fever,' Randall replied.

The cleric nodded. 'These theatrics really aren't necessary, young man.' He crossed over to his boots. 'I follow the aspect of healing and peace. It's my obligation to help those wounded by conflict.'

Randall did not respond. He knew he would never harm a cleric, but he needed the healer to think that he would.

The White cleric laced up his boots and retrieved a heavy fur-lined cloak and a satchel of healing supplies.

'What is your name, cleric?' Randall asked.

'Brother Hobson, originally of Haran, now of Voy.'

Randall nodded and motioned for the cleric to follow him. 'We need to hurry, Brother Hobson.'

He made less effort to be silent as he reached the outer door and paused, making sure that Hobson was close behind. The cleric still looked flustered, but at least he was cooperating. Scanning the dark streets, Randall could hear the slow and regular pace of armoured watchmen several streets away. He shepherded Hobson out of the door.

'This way,' he whispered, 'and be quiet.'

Randall knew the route well and moved swiftly, stopping only between buildings to check the streets were clear. As they moved further away from the centre of Voy the buildings became less opulent and, a few side streets from the northern gate, they entered a line of abandoned houses and shops. Randall was glad that not all of Voy was reserved for the rich.

'You didn't tell me your name, young sir,' puffed the cleric at his side.

'I'll tell you my name in a short while, brother,' replied Randall, looking out for Vasir's signal.

A glint of light appeared in the top floor of an old wooden shop. The building was in bad order, with no door or intact windows, but the structure was sound and it had given the Dokkalfar a good vantage point to keep watch on the surrounding area. Vasir signalled that the coast was clear and Randall ushered Brother Hobson forward. They entered the derelict shop and moved towards the wooden stairs within.

Hobson nervously surveyed their surroundings.

'You're in no danger for now, brother,' said Randall.

'It's the *for now* that I find concerning, young sir,' replied Hobson. 'Well, no sense crying about it now.' But the cleric followed Randall up the stairs without further comment.

The upper floor of the building was in even worse condition. Numerous holes in the wooden floor made it necessary to hug the wall for fear of falling through. Brother Hobson gasped as a tall figure appeared from a door at the end of the corridor.

'Calm, brother,' said Randall.

Vasir was approaching seven feet tall and his dark features were stark, even within the unlit building. His skin was grey, his ears leaf-shaped, and his hair jet black. He held a heavy knife in each hand and moved with inhuman grace.

'We have little time, Randall,' said the Dokkalfar.

'You associate with the risen,' said Hobson with wide-eyed fear.

Randall looked at the churchman coolly. 'Brother Hobson, there is your patient.'

On a bed, under a broken window, lay the shivering form of Utha the Ghost, Black cleric of the One God. The albino's skin was even paler than usual and clammy with sweat. They had fashioned a bundle of herbs into a poultice and strapped it across the worst of his wounds. Bandages covered his upper body. Randall hated seeing him like this.

Moving closer, the White cleric squinted at the injured man. Randall saw recognition come to Hobson's face as he examined the muscular albino who lay unconscious before him.

'I know of this man.' He turned back to Randall and Vasir. 'And I know of his crimes.'

Randall looked at Brother Hobson. He had not been able to find out what had happened in Tiris after they had fled; the brother was the first person of any note he had spoken to in the last month.

'You are the assassins of Prince Christophe,' stated Hobson. 'There is a sizeable bounty on your heads.'

Randall looked at Vasir. 'Do we have time for this?' The Dokkalfar shook his head and pointed at Utha.

'There you go, brother, we have no time for this.' Randall drew his sword. 'I don't want to hurt you, but I don't want to see this man die either.'

To hear that they had been painted as assassins was not a surprise. Prince Christophe Tiris had been killed by *something*. Exactly what was a question he had asked himself a hundred times over during the last month, and he was no closer to an answer. A Dark Young, a monster, the priest and the altar – none of these held the whole truth. Randall even doubted the truth would be believed, should he choose to tell it.

'Heal him and we can talk,' Randall said.

Brother Hobson was clearly terrified. Randall did not relish forcing this humble man to help someone he saw as a wanted murderer, but they had no choice.

'I will heal this man,' Hobson said reluctantly, 'but I will have to report your presence.' He smiled with grim resignation.

'I appreciate that you may feel the need to silence me, but I have an oath to the church.'

Randall considered. 'You're a good man, brother. I bear you no ill will.' He sheathed the sword of Great Claw. 'Heal him and you will greatly increase your chance of survival.'

Brother Hobson nodded. He placed his satchel on the floor and began inspecting the albino's wounds. The king's guardsmen in Ro Tiris had fought hard; some of the deeper and more jagged wounds had festered over the last week and needed immediate attention.

'What do we do when he's well?' asked Vasir in a whisper.

'We're still a long way from the Fell,' replied Randall, 'and I'd imagine that Purple clerics have been despatched to hunt us down . . . probably mercenaries as well.' He shook his head. 'We can gather some supplies and try to get lost in the wilds. Or we can trust in speed and take the direct route south.'

Vasir inclined his head. 'If the Shadow is fully healed, we will at least be able to move swiftly,' he said.

Trapped in the oubliette of Ro Tiris a month ago, Katja the Hand of Despair had called Utha the last of the Shadow Giant old-blood. The name seemed to hold great import for the Dokkalfar. From what Randall had seen, they respected the Black cleric more than any other man alive.

Brother Hobson turned from the shivering body. 'I am a servant of peace and as such I feel the need to tell you something, young man.'

Randall balked slightly at *young man*, but chose to let it pass. 'So, tell me.'

'There are mercenaries in town, dangerous-looking men. I don't know why they're here, but your presence seems a little . . . coincidental.' Hobson hesitated. 'I've heard them called *bastards*. Whether that's a title or a general description, I'm not sure, but they certainly seem to like the name.'

Randall considered the news. They had stayed off the roads, travelled mostly by night, and slept in abandoned or deserted areas. If the mercenaries were here for them, they could be just checking out Voy without any real idea that their quarry was present. His hand still shook whenever he had to draw the sword of Great Claw for combat and he was not eager to test his skills any further – especially not against anyone who voluntarily called himself *bastard*.

'Is that a Ro term?' asked Vasir. '*Bastards*.' He sounded it out in his strange accent. 'What does it mean?'

Randall thought about it. 'Bad men, killers, mercenaries, arseholes ... bastards. Technically, it means a man whose parents weren't married, but it's a term of abuse as well.'

Hobson looked incredulous, between Randall and Vasir. The propaganda of the clerics was doctrine in the lands of Ro. Even Utha had spent his life hunting and killing the risen. If not for an accidental encounter, during which one had saved his life, he would probably have continued.

Randall stared back at him evenly. 'Just tend to the patient, brother, let us worry about the mercenaries.'

* * *

Randall had never witnessed the healing powers of a cleric before. The voice of the One was gifted only to the White and a select few battle chaplains. Brother Hobson took his time, seeming to forget Utha's companions as he carefully tended the festering chest wounds. He used mundane items – ointments, bandages, poultices – but the true skill of his art lay in the magic he used. It started as a slight glow in his hands, flowing gently across Utha's body, rippling like water and moving straight to the areas of worst harm.

Vasir kept watch on the street outside and Randall slumped in a makeshift and broken chair. The young squire had filled out over the last few months and found his muscles aching. His right arm was sore from wielding the sword of Great Claw and both legs were stiff. The thought of a few hours' true rest was enticing, but he could not quite bring himself to trust Brother Hobson.

'Randall.' He heard urgency in Vasir's voice.

He crossed to the front room overlooking the town. 'What is it?'

Half in shadow, the forest-dweller was all but invisible and his gaze was focused on the street below. 'There are men below.'

'What kind of men?' Randall asked.

Vasir motioned Randall to join him by the window. 'See for yourself,' he said.

Only the barest hint of moonlight illuminated the street, but he could see several men – four or five at the most – moving slowly between the buildings. They wore mail armour and had a swaying gait that made him think they were the worse for drink, a thought confirmed when he saw a bottle of wine passing between them.

'We ain't gonna find shit in these fucking shacks.' The voice was slurred.

'They're just checking the town,' Randall whispered. 'They don't know we're here.'

'We're in a deserted building in a part of town being checked by mercenaries, Randall. It could be suggested that we are exactly what they're looking for,' said Vasir.

The mercenaries had stopped and were reclining against the opposite building. One was complaining about his feet and the others were swigging from a bottle of dark-looking liquor.

'We'll finish this line of buildings then turn in, okay?' One of them, slightly older than the rest, had decided they weren't going to find anything.

'We should kill them,' growled Vasir. 'If they check the building and find us, it is likely at least one will get away. If we strike first, we can silence all five.'

The Dokkalfar's cold manner chilled Randall.

'No killing,' he insisted.

'As you say, Randall of Darkwald.' The forest-dweller bowed his head respectfully.

Randall turned in time to see Brother Hobson appear by the doorway. 'My work is finished, young man.'

Randall pressed his finger to his lips, but the damage was

done. Below, the oldest mercenary was looking towards the building and had slowly unslung a heavy crossbow. His fellows followed suit.

'Shit,' muttered Randall, moving away from the window. 'Vasir, get to the top of the stairs – don't kill anyone until you have to.'

The grey-skinned warrior stood silently and, brandishing his blades, moved out of the room and towards the rickety staircase. Randall shepherded Hobson back towards Utha's room.

'I've done something foolish, haven't I?' asked Hobson, looking panicked.

'You didn't know, brother, but we may have some company.' Randall didn't blame the cleric. He should have told the healer to be quiet as soon as Vasir raised the alarm.

'The Ghost is healed. . . as promised. He should regain consciousness in an hour or two, depending on his strength.'

Randall moved into the back room, propelling the cleric before him. He glanced over his shoulder and saw Vasir standing in shadows at the top of the stairs. Below, the voices of the mercenaries and the sounds of chain mail and weaponry were all too distinct.

'It was definitely a voice,' said one, 'on the first floor.'

'Probably just someone the worse for drink looking for a quiet place to puke,' said another. 'I talk to myself when I'm in my cups.'

'So, we'll check and find out . . . clear?' barked the lead man. Randall heard him draw his crossbow, and looked down at the still-unconscious form of Utha the Ghost. The Black cleric was turned on to his side and facing away from them. His wounds had largely disappeared, replaced with more scars. Randall screwed up his face. Their attempt to heal him would all be for nothing if they were captured.

'Just stay quiet,' Randall whispered to Hobson.

The White cleric nodded. Randall swiftly drew the sword of Great Claw and stepped back into the first-floor corridor. The Dokkalfar was motionless on one side of the landing. Randall moved quickly to stand opposite him. He tried to lock eyes with his ally but the forest-dweller was focused on the stairs, blades held downward, and Randall could barely make out his grey skin in the darkness.

'If it's a drunk, I'm gonna kick him *hard* . . .' The voice was so close Randall held his breath. A step or two more and he'd be between them.

Randall held his sword tight against his chest lest its shine give away his location.

'You two . . . go and check that room at the back.'

Randall tensed. As two men wielding large blades stepped past the crossbowman, Vasir acted. The Tyr moved with phenomenal grace, slashing the neck of the first man before spinning to drive his leaf-blade into the throat of the second, sending twin sprays of blood across the wooden floor.

The calm night of Voy was broken. The three remaining mercenaries looked with open-eyed surprise at the huge forest-dweller.

'It's them,' one shouted. He wildly loosed a bolt down the hall and Randall stepped out, thrusting his sword towards the man. The point caught more chain mail than flesh and Randall overbalanced. Slipping on the pool of blood, he barrelled into the man who was feverishly trying to reload his crossbow. They fell together on to the stairs and Randall grunted in pain as his head struck wood before the two of them flew swiftly downwards, ending in a heap on the floor below.

The other two mercenaries had quickly regained their bearings and rushed up the stairs, swinging heavy maces at Vasir's shadowy form. The Dokkalfar danced backwards into the hall. Randall tried to stand, but his head was swimming and he could taste blood on his tongue. Randall's sword was stuck in the side of the man's chain mail and he swore as he tried to untangle it.

'I'm gonna fuck you till you bleed, boy,' spat the mercenary, elbowing the squire in the chest.

Randall reluctantly let go of the sword and wrapped his arms round the man's neck. As they wrestled in the detritus of the derelict building, Randall realized he was the stronger and began to exert leverage to keep the mercenary from drawing another weapon. He clung on, but a series of kicks and punches began to loosen his hold. This close, the man smelt terrible. Randall tried to manoeuvre on top of him, but lost his grip as a fist connected solidly with the side of his jaw. Randall went limp and the man rolled clear.

Randall tried to stand, but his legs weren't responding. The mercenary pulled the sword of Great Claw from his chain mail. The blade grated against the steel links and came away with a small amount of blood.

'Where's the Ghost, boy?' spat the mercenary through brown teeth. 'The cleric, where is he?'

The man levelled Randall's sword at him and grinned, a grotesque expression that showed missing teeth and stained gums. 'Answer me,' he shouted.

'That's my squire,' said a deep, gravelly voice.

The mercenary turned to see a broad-shouldered figure staggering uncertainly down the stairs, longsword in hand. Brother Utha of Arnon, a mask of rage on his face, stood bare-chested and covered with fresh scars, but pale-skinned, white-haired and terrifying.

The mercenary grabbed Randall by the hair. Pulled upright, the squire felt the cold metal edge of Great Claw across his neck.

'Your boy dies if you take one more step towards me.'

Utha stepped forward.

Randall felt the blade bite into his skin.

'Stop fucking moving,' barked the mercenary.

The cleric took another step forward and launched his longsword towards them. The blade flew end over end and lodged messily in the mercenary's chest, inches from Randall's own.

For a moment, Randall's laboured breathing was the only sound in the room.

Brother Utha of Arnon, last of the Shadow Giant old-blood regarded the room with a cool glare. 'Do we have any wine?'

* * *

The sun was beginning to intrude on the horizon and still Randall had not slept.

Utha sat by the window looking out into the twilight while Hobson examined Randall's head wound.

'I must say, you people truly don't appear to be the ruthless assassins you're made out to be. The news from Ro Tiris is that Brother Utha of Arnon is the most dangerous man abroad in the lands of men. A reckless traitor to be killed on sight.'

The White cleric raised his head and saw three sets of eyes glaring back at him. He smiled nervously. 'Of course, that's just hearsay. . .'

Utha snorted. 'Don't fret, brother, you're in no danger from us. We'll be out of your hair within the hour and you'll never have to deal with us again.'

'I must say, that is a relief,' replied Hobson. 'Though, as a fellow man of the One, I would ask you a question, Brother Utha.'

'I didn't kill the prince,' Utha said candidly. 'Though I can't tell you what did.'

Hobson shook his head. 'No, brother, I wished to know why you of all people, a man renowned for his skill as a crusader, would consort with the risen.'

The Black cleric stood and faced him. Though they were similar in height, Utha's bulk, muscle and demeanour spoke of his calling as a warrior; a sharp contrast to the aura of serenity that surrounded Hobson. As the two clerics – Black and White – looked at each other, Randall thought he could see a ripple of divine power as their eyes met. The back of his neck tingled.

Utha's face was stone. 'His name is Tyr Vasir. He is a Dokkalfar and no more an undead monster than you or I.'

As if to illustrate the point, the forest-dweller stepped into the room. Vasir was close to seven feet tall, and slender. His skin was a dusty grey and his hair and eyes were both jet-black. The White cleric stared at him. Vasir let himself be studied, reacting with nothing more than a slight twitch of his shoulders.

'I don't expect you to listen any more than the Purple, brother, but at least you'll have something to ponder once we're gone.'

Utha had repeatedly stated the futility of persuading other clerics that the Dokkalfar were merely a race of non-human beings, with culture, history and sophistication. Even Brother Torian, a Purple cleric that Utha and Randall had both admired greatly, was so influenced by the church's propaganda as to be almost blind to the reality.

'The Mandate of Severus has been church law for five hundred years,' said Hobson, mildly.

'It has never been a law of The One. It was a law of the Purple,' replied Utha. 'I don't think The One gives a shit about non-humans. Cardinal Severus did, that's all. And no-one questions it.'

'Well, your friend certainly doesn't seem. . . dangerous,' Hobson said hesitantly.

Utha laughed – the first good-natured sound he'd made in weeks. 'Let's not get carried away, brother, he is most definitely dangerous. But he doesn't eat children or abduct women, if that's what you mean.'

Vasir tilted his head at Utha. The forest-dweller didn't understand humour, but Randall thought he may have been aware that he was being teased.

'I will have to report that I have encountered you, Brother Utha,' said Hobson quietly.

Utha nodded his head. 'Would you give us the courtesy of a day's head start?'

'I'm sorry, no.' The old cleric bowed his head.

'I understand, brother.'

For a second, Randall feared his master would seek to silence the healer, but Utha crossed to the door and motioned for Hobson to follow.

'I would ask that you leave us now,' the Black cleric said, 'and I hope the One looks down on you with more kindness than he has shown me.'

Hobson bowed his head and the two churchmen shared a moment of prayer before parting.

'Brother,' Utha said as Hobson exited, 'at least walk slowly back to your chapel.'

The White cleric smiled and nodded before turning his back on the three of them. Randall regretted intruding upon the old man's life, but it was at least gratifying to meet another honourable cleric.

'Well . . .' said Utha. 'We're wanted by clerics, enchantresses and mercenaries. Apparently we killed Prince Christophe, and our odds of survival in Tor Funweir are slim.' He screwed up his face. 'I don't fancy going to Ranen or Karesia, so I'd say our best option is to get lost in the Fell.'

Vasir immediately began to gather up their belongings.

'You're keen,' said Randall.

'Indeed,' responded the forest-dweller, 'I am eager to assist the Shadow and will gladly give my life to see him safely to the woods of my people.'

Utha stood angrily. 'Stop fucking calling me the Shadow . . . I'm just a man.' He was almost shouting.

Vasir tilted his head and regarded the Black cleric before speaking. 'You are many things, Brother Utha of Arnon, but you are certainly not *just a man*. You possess the blood of the ancients, you are an old-blood of the Shadow Giants, and you are friend to the Dokkalfar – whether you wish it or not.'

Utha was silent for a moment and then slumped back into his chair. 'Seriously, do we have any wine?'

'Of course we don't have any wine,' replied Randall. 'I thought survival was more important than getting drunk.' He spoke with more venom than he had intended. 'Sorry.'

'I'll let it pass.' Utha said wearily. 'Let's just get out of Voy.'

* * *

Brother Hobson was not a man given to panic, but sitting tied roughly to his chair before Sir Hallam Pevain, he began to feel a sense of dread. Pevain was the leader of a large company of mercenaries recently returned from Canarn with a greatly diminished force. He carried a large warhammer of Ranen design and worked for a witch called Saara the Mistress of Pain.

It had been two days since Hobson had reported the presence of Brother Utha to the knight marshal's office and several hours since the mercenaries had begun questioning him. His bewilderment that a mercenary knight was hunting down the rogue cleric was matched only by his confusion that everyone seemed to be working for the Karesian enchantresses – or *our beloved allies* as they were frequently called.

'I'm getting sick of asking the same questions, brother,' said the black-armoured knight in a guttural growl.

'So stop asking, Sir Pevain,' responded Hobson.

'Utha the Ghost was seen two days ago in Voy and you insist that he was on his own.' Pevain was simple-minded but dangerous.

'I didn't say he was on his own,' responded Hobson. 'He had a young squire and a risen man with him.'

'Yes, yes, so you say – but no Kirin?' The knight had insisted that Utha must have been accompanied by a Kirin assassin. 'My mistress sent me to hunt down two men, Utha the Ghost and Rham Jas Rami. They are both evil men who consort with the risen and our beloved allies believe they will be working together.'

'I haven't seen a Kirin in Voy for many years.'

'I'll give you one last chance to tell the truth, brother.' Pevain leered.

'I saw Utha of Arnon, a young squire and a forest-dweller,' repeated Hobson; he could not keep his attention from Pevain's hammer.

'Risen man,' corrected Pevain, 'an evil undead monster.'

The White cleric shook his head. 'Whatever you want to call him, he was tall, with grey skin and black eyes.'

Pevain rested his hammer in Hobson's lap. 'And the Kirin? Fucked if I know why, but she places great worth on their capture . . . Utha *and* Rham Jas.'

Hobson forced a smile even as sweat began to sting his eyes. A noble knight would never harm a cleric of peace and healing, but Pevain was not noble and Hobson suspected the mercenary acted mostly on whim. 'I can only repeat the truth so many times, sir knight,' he said.

'That's a shame, brother.' Pevain pulled back his hammer and swung for Hobson's head.

The cleric didn't feel any pain and, after eighty years of life it might be said that Brother Hobson of Voy had lived a good life.

CHAPTER TWO

DALIAN THIEF TAKER
IN THE CITY OF RO WEIR

T HE WINDOW SILL was wide enough for Dalian to stand
on, but not so wide as to be particularly safe. The Mistress
of Pain had a scheduled meeting with her two hound
commanders and Dalian was eager to hear their plans. He risked
a glance inside. The enchantress was sitting at a desk reading an
old leather-bound book.

The Thief Taker was a man unmatched in his skill and devotion
to Jaa, but now he was a fugitive, falsely accused of treachery. He
was nearing his fiftieth year of life, and as he balanced precariously
seven storeys up from the ground, all he could think was that he
was too old to be clambering about outside buildings. Surely Jaa
wanted him to be reclining on a chair somewhere, within sight
of the sea, with a glass of wine in his hand.

He was not even sure which part of the city he was in. Ro Weir
was peculiar among the great cities of Ro in that its population
consisted of many Karesians and Kirin, men who were more
alarmed by the presence of the hounds than the native Ro. He
suspected that the foreign presence in the city was mostly of the
criminal variety – Karesians who, for whatever reason, could not
return to Karesia.

He had been here for over a month and had successfully lost
himself in the criminal culture of the city's port side, a near-slum
called the Kirin Tor. He had reluctantly thrown his black armour
into the sewer that ran the length of the city and had made an

effort to conceal both his face and his kris knives. The wave-bladed weapons were too distinctive in Tor Funweir, causing jagged wounds that an astute observer would quickly link to one of Jaa's faithful. He disliked having to conceal his presence and found subversion in general to be distasteful, but the Thief Taker was nothing if not pragmatic. He was in a foreign city that had willingly submitted to hound occupation under the guidance of a treacherous enchantress, and Dalian Thief Taker, greatest of the wind claws, believed himself to be the only servant of Jaa that could stop her.

'I'm doing my best, lord,' he said to the air, addressing the Fire Giant, 'but this window ledge is rather narrow and I am not as thin as I was.' He hoped that Jaa would hear him and cushion any fall to the cobbles below. *I won't doubt or fear, lord, but I still dislike heights.*

The spell of the Seven Sisters was strong. They had fooled the faithful into believing that they spoke the will of the Fire Giant. The Thief Taker had been framed for the death of a fellow wind claw. But, he thought, he had never been the kind of man to hide, and he hoped he was harder to kill than the enchantress and her thralls realized. Dalian had stowed away on one of the hound barges and travelled with them from Kessia. The faceless armies of Karesia numbered many thousand – he judged at least thirty – though they were spread out and chaotically organized. *I am one man against an army, lord. I hope they are ready.*

At a sound from within he crouched down against the stone wall the better to see through the dirty window. Saara's office was part of Duke Lyam's private rooms. She had somehow convinced the Ro noble that allowing an occupation force of hounds was a wise idea and, even now, small packs moved throughout Tor Funweir carrying out the Seven Sisters' bidding. The enchantress effectively ruled the city.

'My Lady Saara,' said a deep voice from within, 'we await your orders.'

As the speaker moved into his eyeline, Dalian recognized Turve Ramhe, a whip-master and Saara's second in command.

The hound commander was standing in black plate armour and wore an expression of disgust on his scarred face. Next to him stood a dark-haired woman in her early thirties. She wore identical armour and carried a two-handed scimitar across her back: Izra Sabal, a sadistic whip-mistress whom Saara had put in charge of maintaining order in Ro Weir. Both the visitors to Saara's chamber were unswervingly loyal to the Seven Sisters. They mistakenly believed that they were the highest authority of Jaa's will.

'Turve, Izra, please sit,' Saara said in her lyrical voice. 'Would either of you like refreshment?'

The hounds declined. Dalian watched them sit down awkwardly in wooden chairs barely big enough to contain them in their armour.

'Ro Weir is secured, my mistress,' Izra growled out of the corner of her mouth. Her jaw was slightly out of place. 'We have not had to immolate anyone for several days.'

Dalian's lip curled. His gaze was drawn over the roofs of buildings to the knight marshal's office where several hundred charred wooden stakes could be seen. The hounds were not accustomed to civil disobedience and would simply burn the perpetrators alive rather than lock them up. Prisons were a Ro concept that the Karesians had never adopted. Dalian knew he was far from a good man; he had immolated hundreds of people, but always in the name of Jaa. Izra, on the other hand, took wanton delight in any opportunity to make someone scream. And these were not her people. She had burned Karesian next to Ro next to Kirin.

'Excellent.' Saara laughed sweetly. 'A month to secure the second largest population in Tor Funweir. I would say that is rather impressive. Now I have other orders for you both.'

Dalian thought he could discern the hounds swell with eagerness to conduct further atrocities on Saara's behalf. Saara was an enchantress without equal; she had certainly wormed her way into the heads of Izra and Turve. Dalian was disgusted.

'We exist to serve you, mistress,' Turve stated proudly.

'I know . . . and I am forever grateful for your loyalty, Master Ramhe.' Dalian could only see the back of Saara's head, but he was certain she wore an expression of seductive serenity.

'Izra,' she began formally, 'you will take a force of two thousand hounds north. Your destination is Cozz and, more importantly, the merchants' wealth that the enclave contains.'

Izra's eyes began to sparkle at the prospect of more death and destruction. 'Am I to sack the town, mistress?' asked the hound commander.

'Only if necessary,' replied the enchantress. 'I imagine it will be sensible to conduct a few lessons in cruelty to keep the populace in line . . . much as you have done in Weir. But so long as Knight Marshal Wesson opens his gates for you, I see no need to destroy the enclave. After all, we need its wealth if we are to further our occupation beyond the south lands of Tor Funweir.'

'It will be as you say, mistress.' In Izra's eyes Dalian saw the telltale euphoria that marked those under the influence of enchantment.

'You will take twenty of the captive risen men with you, to be killed if you need additional forces,' Saara said quietly.

'They will not be needed, I assure you,' responded the whip-mistress. 'My hounds will be more than enough for a town of merchants.'

'You misunderstand,' Saara said, with a sinister note in her voice. 'I want you to birth more Dark Young.'

For a moment, Dalian thought he saw a trace of hesitation cross Izra's face, but then she bowed her head. 'It shall be as you say, mistress.'

Saara leant back in her chair. 'Turve, you will take a larger force – five thousand hounds should be sufficient – to the plains of Leith and the deep woods of the Fell. There you are to burn the risen men out of their home and capture all that flee.'

The whip-master's face contorted in what looked like violent pleasure. Dalian cared little for the non-human occupants of Tor Funweir, but was suspicious of all Saara's motives. There was a

32

larger game being played out by the Seven Sisters, and their final goal eluded him.

'And what of the old-blood and the dark-blood?' asked Turve.

'Pevain has taken his bastards north to find them. I believe they will ally against us, if they have not already done so, and we should all be wary. The assassin is a most dangerous foe, capable of causing great damage to our cause.'

'And the Ghost?' prompted Izra.

'He killed the prince of Ro. I think his own people will turn him in, given the chance.'

Dalian drew himself out of sight. He had made enquiries among the city's less-reputable populace regarding the identity and location of the Kirin assassin. Few were willing to talk about him and the Thief Taker was beginning to realize that Rham Jas Rami had a fearsome reputation. Most seemed afraid even to speak his name. The word was Rham Jas was friend to Al-Hasim, but even if Al-Hasim were in Ro, Dalian had no way to locate him. The Thief Taker had not seen his son for ten long years.

Dalian turned and began the climb back down to Kirin Tor.

* * *

The two hounds had been on duty for ten hours straight, as had Dalian, waiting in the shadow of Ro Weir's northern gate. He hoped they would be relieved soon. *I am patient, lord, truly I am. But I will need rest and food at some stage.*

He had arranged to meet a particularly paranoid information broker, a man of Ro who claimed to know something about the location of a Karesian scoundrel known as the Prince of the Wastes, which he recognized as his son's pretentious sobriquet.

The broker had insisted that they meet outside the gate. Dalian understood his paranoia and hoped the man actually knew something. He planned to leave Weir and travel north, another anonymous Karesian face among Izra's hounds. The merchant enclave of Cozz saw many kinds of business, he thought it the most likely place to start looking for Rham Jas Rami and

Al-Hasim. He hoped this broker would give him some valuable contacts in the city.

One of the two hounds on guard began to yawn and Dalian sensed an opportunity. It was early morning, not yet fully light, and the Thief Taker moved closer. He made little effort to remain hidden and trusted that his cloak and nondescript clothing would mask his identity. Timing was important – he had no desire to be interrupted by the relief shift. With a window of no more than a few minutes, he walked slowly but deliberately towards the gate.

The hounds moved to intercept him.

'Turn round,' said the first hound. 'This gate is off limits to common folk.'

Neither of the black-armoured men drew their weapon, and Dalian sauntered closer.

'Did you not hear me, Ro?' asked the hound.

'I'm not a Ro,' he said, smashing his fist into the throat of one of the guards and spinning to kick the other in the chest before he could react to the sudden attack.

The first guard fell to the ground and gasped for breath through his crushed windpipe. Dalian was quickly on top of the second man; he wrapped an arm round his neck and twisted until he heard it snap.

He stood up and stamped on the first man's head, crushing the man's skull.

No one had seen him and Dalian didn't wait to find out if anyone had heard the men die. He stole one of the hound's scimitars, tucked it into his belt and pushed open the inner door of the north gate. Before him the road was empty.

Thank you, lord, that went better than expected. The muster field was visible off to the east, sprawling across the fields of Weir, though the palisade and guard towers were far off, making it unlikely that anyone would see him leaving. To the west, a deserted sea of farmhouses and stables stretched to the coast, mostly intact, but all abandoned for the relative safety of the city.

Nontheless, he took pains to move between the deserted

buildings with stealth. He started when he heard the low crackle of a fire from a nearby stable. He slowed his pace and crouched under a wooden beam, between mismatched planks.

Putting his eye to a shard of light from within, Dalian saw a young man sitting in a yellow glow of fire, a bottle of wine in his hand and a crossbow resting next to him on the floor. He looked younger than Dalian had expected – barely twenty years old – and the Thief Taker, a man who had just murdered two of his own countrymen in cold blood, could not help but feel a moment of sympathy for a scared young man.

Taking less trouble to be quiet, he moved round to the front of the stable and paused momentarily, giving the man of Ro a chance to register his presence. The Thief Taker then stepped through the entrance and into the flickering firelight. The broker had his crossbow levelled between Dalian's eyes. 'That's far enough,' he said nervously.

Dalian stepped further into the stable and lowered his hood. 'I believe I am expected,' he said in thickly accented Ro. 'And that crossbow needs attention. The string is twisted at one end. I doubt the bolt would fly straight. Ordinarily, I would expect you to invite me in and offer me a seat. I have coin, you have information . . . if we like each other's currency, this exchange can be over within a few minutes.'

The youth's hand was shaking. 'Okay, but I'll keep you in my sights.'

'As you wish,' Dalian said, holding his hands wide and stepping slowly but deliberately into the stable. The cold had begun to creep into his bones and he was glad of the fire to warm his hands. In its light, he could see the young man opposite him had tufts of hair on his chin and his limbs were scrawny, a combination that made Dalian reconsider his original estimate of the boy's age.

'How old are you, lad?' he asked.

'What . . . why does that matter?'

Dalian leant back and sighed, keeping his hands extended in front of him. The lad was nervous enough to loose a bolt accidentally. With a lightning-fast movement, he snatched the crossbow cleanly out of the young man's hands. It was a well-practised manoeuvre and the Thief Taker implemented it perfectly, leaving the boy stunned.

'Now we can talk,' he said, placing the weapon on the floor and removing the bolt. 'Don't worry, young man, I don't kill people who aren't in my way. And you have information for me.' Dalian crossed him arms in front of his chest and relaxed. 'A fixer in Cozz?' he prompted.

The man of Ro took a swig from his bottle of wine in an obvious attempt to steady his nerves. 'Yeah, he's a blacksmith – knows everyone.'

'Might he know a Kirin assassin called Rham Jas Rami or a Karesian called Al-Hasim?'

'I've heard of the Kirin.' Again Dalian noted the reluctance to say the assassin's name out loud. 'He used to kill people for a mobster in Weir.'

Dalian had heard this several times since he came to Weir, but no one seemed to know when the Kirin had disappeared.

'And the Prince of the Wastes?' Dalian asked.

The boy nodded. 'Yeah, he's a Karesian . . . I think he's a pimp or something. The blacksmith would know him. I think he fixed him up with some women.'

Dalian could well believe that his son would make his living as some kind of low life – pimp, rainbow merchant, sword for hire, all these had occurred to him. He had not spoken to Al-Hasim since helping him escape Kessia.

'How do I find the smith?' Dalian asked, throwing three small gold coins on to the stable floor.

The lad leapt greedily on the coin, shoving it into his stained tunic. 'He's called Tobin. Ask for him in Culver's Yard.'

'What are you going to spend it on?' Dalian asked coldly.

The youth's hand was still shaking. 'Why do you care . . . you got the name?'

Dalian smiled for the first time in several days. 'I'm an old

36

servant of Jaa, young man. I've done hideous things in the name of my god, but I hate the sight of a young man wasting his life. Jaa detests the useless and, in my estimation, few people are more useless than a rainbow addict.'

The young man of Ro looked up sharply with a pathetic expression on his face. 'Ain't none of your business.'

Dalian frowned and slowly rocked himself forward into a standing position. He adjusted his cloak and made sure his weapons were well stowed. 'I do believe you are right, it is none of my business. You are a child of the One and not Jaa's to punish . . .' He paused. 'You are lucky that your god is ignorant and knows no better.'

The Thief Taker turned sharply, whirling his cloak across the fire and sending a shower of embers into the air as he marched deliberately out of the stable.

Once outside, he shook his head at the ignorance allowed in the lands of Ro. A level of casual lawlessness was tolerated in a way that would result in death in Karesia. The wind claws punished all transgressions against Jaa in as swift and brutal a way as possible. Jaa demanded fear from his worshippers and Dalian knew that nothing promoted fear like seeing your loved ones immolated before your eyes.

These people are strange, lord.

The Thief Taker had to confess that he was not against the principle of invading Tor Funweir, but he would have done it in the name of Jaa. Saara and her vile sisters were bringing war in the name of something else. They had turned from the worship of Jaa and stolen control of the Karesian faithful through enchantment and manipulation.

The wind claw pulled his cloak tightly around him and began the slow trudge north. Izra's hound pack was camped a few hours into the duchy of Weir, near to the King's Highway, and Dalian needed to join them before they marched in the morning. The whip-mistress would muster her men quickly. He was sure the people of Cozz would not welcome her efficiency.

Beyond the line of abandoned farmhouses lay an overgrown dirt track which connected the outlying farms to the King's Highway. Dalian was a lone dot in the lightening morning as he walked further from the city. Jaa willing, he would be able to melt into the hound pack. His face would be known to few below commander and so long as he stayed with the rank and file he should be able to remain anonymous.

* * *

Dalian arrived in Izra's camp just as the hounds were rising from their tents. He'd had to play the part of an alert warrior rather than a middle-aged man who'd been up all night.

I will fear nothing but Jaa. . . I will fear nothing but Jaa. . . As he walked through the large camp, Dalian was gratified that no one gave him more than a cursory glance. . . . *But a glass of wine or a warm woman would be welcome, lord.*

Izra's hounds were lean and ready for action. They each wore black armour, chosen for maximum anonymity, and a steel helm that removed any trace of individuality. On the camp outskirts, while its owner slept, Dalian had procured a set of armour and with his kris blades hidden he blended in seamlessly. He found the entire masquerade distasteful. The hounds were criminals convicted in Karesia and sentenced to this service. It was rumoured that powerful enchantments kept them in line and only the Seven Sisters and the viziers of Jaa could control them.

As he walked towards the corral in the centre of the camp, Dalian's head was full of Al-Hasim. Although he doubted his wayward son would greet him warmly, the prospect of reunion was still pleasant. Dalian had never been a good or a caring father and he had let his son do as he pleased from an early age. Al-Hasim had always been a precocious child and as he grew older he had become more and more rebellious, even going so far as to refuse to join the wind claws – his hereditary duty. Dalian had always ascribed that rebellion to Hasim's lack of a mother – his wife had died in childbirth – but privately the Thief

Taker was realistic enough to take some of the blame on himself.

At the corral, he raised the visor of his helm and looked around. A circle of guards surrounded a low wooden fence well away from the large iron cage at its centre.

Nothing in a cage is to be feared by men of the Fire Giant.

The cage was wide, but shallow. Within, the Thief Taker could see a number of seemingly dead bodies. He got as close as he could to the fence without arousing suspicion. A strange feeling began to rise within him, a disquieting shiver that ran down the length of his spine. 'You there,' growled a nearby hound. 'Get away from the fence.'

Dalian turned slowly and regarded the man, locking eyes for a moment and showing his confidence. Then he nodded in greeting. 'I think I may have missed a briefing, friend, why are we transporting dead bodies?'

'You don't need to know if you don't already, old dog,' replied the Karesian warrior. 'And they're not dead.'

Dalian smirked at the insult. 'Just answer the question and I won't have to tear your face off, boy.' Dalian took a step closer and smiled, letting the younger man know that he was outmatched.

'Yeah, watch the threats, this isn't a tavern.' The young hound relaxed a little. 'They're risen men, we're to kill them at Izra's command.' The hound looked uncertain. 'Supposedly they'll turn into a beast of some kind . . . if we need them.'

'Let us hope we don't need them,' replied Dalian conversationally.

The hound stepped in and spoke more quietly, as if indulging in gossip. 'I hear that the Mistress of Pain has already killed a few . . . you know, to see what happens.'

Dalian pushed down the uncomfortable feeling that persisted so long as he stood near the cage. 'And what did happen?'

* * *

Leagues away, Saara the Mistress of Pain rose slowly from her bed. The sky was just beginning to show the first signs of morning and the Karesian enchantress had much to do. The man lying face-down next to her was still snoring and seemed unaware that she was no longer in bed. She stood and crossed to the window, where her blue robe hung from a hook on the wall, and slowly covered herself up.

The morning air of Ro Weir was hot and sticky, but cool in comparison with Kessia. Saara found the stink of Weir all-pervading. Kessia had a constant perfume, maintained by slaves and well-paid incense craftsmen, making it seem cleaner and fresher than it really was. The deception helped the Seven Sisters claim that the capital of Karesia was the greatest city in the lands of men. But as Saara wrinkled her nose she was again reminded that she was far from Karesia.

Since the death of her sister, Ameira the Lady of Spiders, Saara had nursed a constant headache. The enchantments practised by the Seven Sisters were difficult to break and lasted as long as they desired. Now that Ameira was dead, her thralls had passed to Saara, and she found herself overwhelmed. Ameira had enchanted King Sebastian Tiris and several other lesser men, who now all fell to Saara. Her *phantom thralls* were making her mind more and more unfocused as the weeks went by. She feared what might happen should the dark-blood, Rham Jas Rami, manage to kill another of her Sisters. Each of the enchantresses held multiple men and women within their grasp, and for them all to fall to Saara could, she feared, drive her insane.

She breathed deeply and opened the shutters of her rooms. The breeze helped soothe her aching mind, but as she looked out into the twilight of Ro Weir she could not forget that she had enemies and that those enemies would not be idle.

'Come back to bed. It's still dark.'

'I have much to do, sweet Kamran,' she replied girlishly. 'You need not rise.' She crossed back to the bed and perched next to her consort.

Kamran Kainen was a wind claw of Karesia, a devout follower of Jaa, and one of Saara's closest allies in Tor Funweir. He had been here for several years, laying the groundwork for the occupation, and Saara controlled his heart and mind absolutely. He now struggled to think independently. Kamran was responsible for keeping an eye on Duke Lyam, and he spent his days intimidating any noble of Weir who spoke or acted out of turn. He was a tall and dashing man in his early forties, strong and well-toned for his age. As Saara cast her eyes over his naked body she felt a heat rise in her, but pushed it away. Much needed doing and, nice as it would be to return to bed and lose herself in sensation for an hour or so, she could not afford the time.

'I will return to you later, my love,' she said, stroking his back gently, 'but I am needed in the gardens this morning.'

Kamran stretched extravagantly and made a series of low growling sounds as he shook himself to full wakefulness. 'Surely the whip-masters can handle the details, my lady. The risen will turn as you have foreseen, they are caged and being transported, the dark-blood and the old-blood will be captured shortly . . . things are proceeding as you have predicted, my love.'

'Much has been accomplished, sweet Kamran, but much more needs to be done. I will say no more,' Saara responded with a sensual smile.

'Very well, my lady, I shall await your pleasure.'

He was a sweet man, but, in Saara's estimation, too devoted to the treacherous Fire Giant to be of much use now that the occupation was proceeding. She found herself requiring the services of Izra Sabal and Turve Ramhe and the armies they commanded, rather than lone warriors like Kamran. Each of her hound packs travelled with a number of captive forest-dwellers, ready to be killed should the Dark Young be needed. As a result, her military strength was greater than any of her enemies knew. The force of Red knights in Ranen was a significant loss to Tor Funweir and she had plans to order the Red cardinal, General Malaki Frith, to take the remaining knights north, thus neutralizing both the Ranen and the armies of the One God.

Her headache returned with greater intensity and Saara walked away from the bed. Her devotion to Shub-Nillurath was without question, but the Dead God's victory in the Long War was now far from certain and she knew that idle time was working against her, as was this near-constant pain. More worrying was the effect her lack of focus would have on her thralls. The king of Tor Funweir was engaged in her war from the southlands of Ranen. Could her pain unblance a thrall? At least Cardinal Mobius, Purple cleric and advisor to the king, was under the command of her sister, Katja the Hand of Despair.

Saara held her hand to her eyes, breathing deeply. She could feel each of her thralls as if they were a part of her, and each of Ameira's, unwanted interlopers intruding on her carefully ordered mind.

Give me the strength of the Forest Giants, my master. She hoped that the Dead God would sense her concern and lend her the power to combat it. She had made the same prayer each day since Ameira had been murdered, but Shub-Nillurath had yet to answer.

She left the bedchamber quickly and crossed the dark hallway to her dressing room opposite. Duke Lyam of Weir was a weak old man who had willingly given up most of his offices to the enchantress and her followers, and she had done her best to make them comfortable in the last month. The hounds she commanded needed little comfort, but the merchant princes and mobsters who had arrived demanded more opulence. Money was an important factor in her occupation and, until Izra secured Cozz, Saara needed the wealth of Kessia to keep her followers amenable.

She rubbed her eyes again and reached for a small hexagonal container on her dressing table. The gold and silver box contained a small amount of rainbow smoke. It did help, though the effect lasted only a short time.

She lit a small pipe, took a deep breath, and held the smoke in for a moment before breathing out slowly. She felt the effects flow through her body and her muscles relaxed for the first time since waking.

At the bottom of the duke's residence was a lush garden arranged across three levels. It was a well-tended area with beds of flowers and open lawns, with ornate fountains perched on plinths and marble steps linking the levels. Saara had had it cleared the previous evening. Now only a few trusted wind claws patrolled the peripheries of the area, a guard against curious eyes.

She had selected a large forest-dweller the previous evening and had the creature killed and left on the duke's lawn.

'My lady.' The wind claw Kal Varaz stood guard, holding his two ceremonial kris blades across his chest, with his pattern-welded black armour shining in the morning sun.

'Good morning, Kal.' Saara coyly fluttered her eyelashes. 'You have been on duty all night?'

'Indeed, my lady, though several of my brothers needed to leave once the . . . transformation began,' he replied. She thought she saw fear in his dark eyes.

Saara smiled warmly and touched the man's face. 'You are my strong right hand, sweet Kal Varaz. What would I do without you.' She let her hand linger on his cheek. Pleasure rose in her body as she used her power to calm the warrior. Euphoric compliance flowed across the man's face as his fear disappeared.

'I live only to serve the Seven Sisters of Jaa, my lady.' The words were stated with zealous conviction.

'I know . . . I know,' she replied. 'Jaa thanks you for your service.' It pleased her to deceive the wind claws and she made sure to keep them close to her now that the greatest of their number, Dalian Thief Taker, had escaped her influence. 'Show me the creature, Kal.'

The warrior nodded and turned sharply towards a tall water fountain and the statue of a noble-looking knight of the Red that dominated the top level of the duke's garden. At the base of the fountain, surrounded by a recently erected fence, was the corpse of the forest-dweller. No wind claws stood anywhere near the body and Kal Varaz shrank visibly as he approached the Dokkalfar, coming to a halt several feet away. Saara smiled. The creature before them, sprouting from the remains, had no disquieting effect on her.

Overnight, the body had folded itself in half, with arms and legs stretching up almost vertically. The creature's mid-section had begun to meld with the earth. The limbs had elongated and the Dokkalfar's flesh was starting to crack like bark. Its face, a mask of twisted horror, was fused with the flesh of its legs. The shape was impossible to imagine as a living thing, but to Saara's eyes the Dark Young was beautiful. Even Saara felt humble before the priest and the altar.

She planned to ensure they were seeded in every corner of the lands of men. From far Karesia to Fjorlan, the darkwood trees would enforce the chaos of pleasure and blood among the followers of the false gods.

She turned back to Kal Varaz. His eyes were cast downwards and he was making some effort to avoid looking at the monstrosity taking form before him. 'Sweet Kal Varaz,' said the enchantress, with tenderness, 'we will need to know how long the transformation takes. Please remain and observe.' She flashed a coquettish smile and touched him again, helping him focus through his fear. 'I need fifty risen prepared for a long sea voyage . . . and that takes preparation.'

'Of course, my lady,' responded the Karesian. 'It will take time.'

'Time we have,' she said. 'I'm sure the barbarians in the north can kill each other without Dark Young to assist them.'

Saara disliked Rulag Ursa, the Ranen lord of Jarvik, far to the north. She had relied on bribery rather than enchantment to secure both his loyalty and the death of Algenon Teardrop. Chaos in the north had been one of the more complicated elements of her plan, but she was sure that, with a few dozen darkwood trees, the foolish barbarians would bend their knee to the Dead God like every other man.

'Will I be accompanying them, mistress?' asked Kal Varaz. 'It has been many years since I visited the Freelands . . . and I have

44

never been to Fjorlan. I hear it is cold there.' The wind claw was smiling nervously, and Saara realized he was trying to distract himself from the darkwood tree.

'I will need men I can trust if the lands of Fjorlan are to be subjugated for the glory of Jaa,' replied the enchantress, stepping closer to the man and biting her lower lip. 'We have no army there, so the Young will be needed.' She traced a finger down the tall man's breastplate and smiled. 'But that is another day . . . the campaign in Ranen proceeds well, as does our pursuit of the dark-blood and the old-blood. We need not worry.'

Still, she mused on where Rham Jas Rami might be skulking.

CHAPTER THREE

KALE GLENWOOD
IN THE CITY OF RO TIRIS

KALE GLENWOOD HAD grown up in Ro Leith, a city
very different from Ro Tiris. Tiris was largely clean, well
policed and undeniably under the charge of the king and
his clerics. By contrast, the city of Leith was provincial, untidy and
green, with more trees and grass than the rest of the great cities
put together. Glenwood missed the open spaces of Leith and the
wooded glens that had formed his first art class. He was a skilled
artist by the age of fifteen and a talented forger by his twentieth
year. With the benefits of a moderately privileged upbringing, he
had had ample time in his youth to slide into lawlessness.

He had the golden hair of his family, which he hid under a
scarf when among Karesians, and aside from a pair of sparkling
blue eyes, Kale Glenwood was easy to overlook. Since coming
to the capital he had taken to wearing permanent stubble which
gave him a swarthy appearance that fitted in well with his image
as a rising mobster.

He didn't like Tiris, but he was forced to admit that his brand
of criminality would be pointless in Ro Leith. Being a forger meant
that you needed to have things to forge, and there was little in his
home city that needed forging. The duchess of Leith, a distant
cousin of King Sebastian called Annabel, was not overly strict
with the implementation of the laws of the One, and Glenwood
had found it difficult to make a living as a criminal in his home
town. Ro Tiris was different. It was a place of strict laws and

lethal punishments. However, as was often the case, the stricter the laws, the more opportunities for financial gain.

He lived outside the walls of the capital, so as not to rub the clerics' noses in his business, but he still received frequent visits from the watch, enquiring about some illegal transaction or other. He stood out for the longsword he carried – the mark of a noble – but he paid his bribes, kept his head down and tried not to rile the establishment, while quietly flouting the law and making as much money as possible.

Things had changed recently, however, and the mysterious death of Prince Christophe had turned Ro Tiris into a more tightly controlled city. With the installation of the king's cousin, Sir Archibald Tiris, as duke, the criminal underworld was now being watched closely.

The brothel where he made his home was called the Blue Feather and it had, up until recently, been owned by a Karesian mobster. Glenwood had killed the previous owner in his sleep and quickly begun using it as a base of operations. He didn't yet have a mob or a gang, but he was optimistic that his star was on the rise within the criminal underworld of Tor Funweir. He had begun to assemble a loosely connected group of associates who owed him favours, who would, he hoped, form the base of his mob.

A knock on the door caused the forger to look up from the king's guard seal he was working on. 'Busy, come back later.'

Another knock, slower, louder and more insistent than the first. He stood and moved round his table. 'This had better be good,' he said with authority.

The door was flung open to reveal the terrified face of Kaur, Glenwood's chief thug. The Karesian was not carrying his scimitar and he was holding a wounded arm protectively across his chest. He was sweating and a small blade was held across his throat.

'What the fuck!' said Glenwood.

A face appeared over Kaur's shoulder and the forger recognized the grinning face of Rham Jas Rami.

47

The Kirin assassin looked much as Glenwood remembered him, unremarkable in appearance, with lank black hair and an air of imminent violence. He carried a longbow across his back and a thin-bladed katana at his side. Slight in build, his slender figure made it easy to forget how dangerous he was.

Glenwood could see two of his men unconscious in their seats, knocked out without having been given a chance to stand. Rham Jas had entered silently, coming face to face with the forger with alarming ease.

'Kale, my old friend,' the Kirin said with humour. 'We need a little chat.'

'Err, okay . . . I don't suppose you thought of *not* beating up my men to tell me that,' the forger said ironically.

Rham Jas considered the comment. 'You know, actually, I didn't.' Emphasizing the point, the Kirin smashed the blunt end of his knife into Kaur's head, making the Karesian grunt and fall unconscious.

Glenwood considered fetching his sword and threatening the Kirin, but thought better of it and motioned for him to come in. 'Have a seat, Rham Jas.'

'Thank you, you're very polite,' the assassin replied, placing a small rucksack on the floor before sitting down.

Rham Jas Rami had always hovered around the line between friend and enemy. Glenwood was scared of him, largely as a consequence of his unnatural ability to kill just about anyone and never get wounded or captured or, indeed, lose his grin. He was the kind of man that Glenwood was glad to know, but frequently regretted knowing – a conundrum that led him to try and avoid the assassin whenever possible.

'Drink?'

Rham Jas nodded, pointing to the bottle of wine on the table. 'Is that actually Darkwald red or are you sticking the label on the normal piss you sell around here?' He didn't take his eyes from the aspiring mobster.

'It's genuine. I save the knock-off stuff for the punters. I try only to drink the best,' Kale replied, trying to cultivate an air of class that failed to impress Rham Jas.

The Kirin poured himself a large glass of wine and drank contentedly. 'Not bad. I've been drinking that white sparkling shit they have in Canarn for the last few weeks. This is a nice treat.'

Glenwood narrowed his eyes. 'Canarn? I heard things were a little unstable up there at the moment. Is Brom still alive?' He had picked up rumours about the occupation of the city and a strange attack that had taken place a month ago.

'Alive and well,' replied Rham Jas. 'Though he's quite busy at the moment.'

The forger smiled. 'I hope, in some small way, I helped. That Red church seal I sold him probably saved his life, wouldn't you agree?' It was a leap of imagination to suggest such a thing, but Glenwood was looking for common ground with the assassin.

Rham Jas raised his eyebrows. 'You mean that shitty piece of clay you sold him for an inflated price, that he was lucky to get away with?'

'It did the job,' replied Glenwood nervously. 'Got him out of the city.'

'Relax, Kale, I'm not here to give you hassle about your poor forging skills.' Rham Jas leant back on his chair and poured himself more wine. 'I wanted to know why you have been throwing my name around as an associate of yours.'

Glenwood pursed his lips and felt awkward. He'd hoped the assassin would take the job and not enquire as to where it had come from. Evidently, Reginald had a big mouth.

'Reg needed someone killed and I knew you were in town. You got paid, didn't you?' Glenwood was used to talking fast when questioned by the authorities. To employ the skill on someone like Rham Jas was rather different, however. A watchman would be unlikely to execute you summarily, whereas the Kirin assassin was more likely to than not.

Rham Jas nodded and Glenwood found it difficult to tell what he was going to do. His weapons were all stowed and no violence seemed likely to erupt, but the man was unpredictable and had been known to kill for little or no reason.

'The job was straightforward and I was paid well. That doesn't excuse you using me like your own personal fucking killer. You want someone dead, you come and ask me. You don't give my name to a sweaty old pederast and say that I'm a friend of yours.' His voice was ominously quiet.

'You're going to kill me, aren't you?' Kale blurted out.

Rham Jas was ice-cold and took a sip of his wine. He kept his eyes locked on the forger, then suddenly straightened up in his chair. Glenwood jumped at the movement, but saw no sign of the assassin drawing a blade.

'Rham Jas, things are different now,' the forger said, his hands held out submissively. 'The prince is dead – killed by a Black cleric, they say – and a Karesian witch is running things in Tiris these days. It's not safe for me to be seen dealing with you directly . . . and I fucking hate you.' He smiled, attempting to convey confidence.

He thought carefully before producing the Wanted poster he'd been given. It showed a likeness of Rham Jas Rami with the words *duty to do harm* emblazoned across his face. The Wanted sign had been posted around dark corners of Tiris in the last month, eliciting interest from plenty of street scum.

'My eyes are green,' Rham Jas said, with a cursory look at the picture, 'not black.'

'I think the black eyes are intended to make you look evil . . . or something.'

'Do you think I'm evil, Kale?' the Kirin asked. His grin was gone and the question hung in the air for a second as if a turning point had been reached in the encounter.

'Well, you do kill people for a living.' The forger had decided that, if he was going to die, he'd at least die without cowering before a Kirin scumbag. 'But I suppose morality can be fluid.'

Rham Jas smiled again and looked away. 'This Karesian witch you mentioned . . .' The Kirin had a knack of changing the subject.

Glenwood had never been sure whether this was a tactic to confuse people or a natural predilection for being an obtuse bastard.

'What about her?' the forger replied, narrowing his eyes.

'Tell me what you know of her.' His eyes flicked from side to side.

'I know what everyone knows, I suppose. Why do you give a shit?' Glenwood was confused as to the assassin's interest in Katja the Hand of Despair, but as long as the katana stayed sheathed he was prepared to tell Rham Jas pretty much anything.

The Kirin adopted a curiously professional manner. 'I'm going to kill her and you're going to help me, Kale. I hope that isn't a problem.'

It didn't sound like a joke and the assassin was glaring at Glenwood.

'Rham Jas, I accept that I'm not yet an actual mobster, and that you just beat up three of my best in two seconds, but I'm not your bitch.' He tensed, wondering if he'd gone too far. 'Look,' he continued, softening his tone, 'I'm sure you have a perfectly valid reason for wanting to kill an unkillable Karesian witch, but I'd just as soon stay here.' He knew little about the Seven Sisters, aside from their tendency to wear facial tattoos, to have scary-sounding names, and to be impossible to kill.

The assassin glanced around Glenwood's roughly decorated room. 'Do you have any clothes suitable for a noble, or does all your shit look like you rub it in mud each morning?'

Glenwood gritted his teeth.

'You are a noble, aren't you, Kale?' The grin returned. Again Glenwood realized just how much he hated Rham Jas.

'In a manner of speaking,' he replied, unsure where the conversation was heading. 'My grandfather was ward of the glen to the north of Ro Leith.'

Rham Jas screwed up his face. 'My knowledge of you Ro and your unnecessary titles is minimal. Where does it go in the great Ro hierarchy? Duke, baron, count . . . where does *ward of the glen* fit in?'

'At the bottom,' Glenwood admitted. 'Most towns and cities don't have them any more. Leith has always been a bit behind the times. Imagine a noble that no one gives a shit about and you have it.'

The dangerous Kirin nodded his head as if he'd made some kind of decision. 'Perfect . . . now, about those noble clothes?' The smile was broader now and Glenwood felt frustrated that he couldn't just punch the Kirin in the mouth and shut him up.

'Mobsters and nobles have very different wardrobes, Rham Jas, and I've had little reason to look like a noble recently.' He had taken to wearing toughened leather armour whenever he ventured out, usually hidden under a nondescript tunic and cloak. Currently, he wore common-spun clothing, chosen for comfort.

'I suspected as much,' said Rham Jas, unconcerned with the answer. He picked up his rucksack and emptied the contents on to Glenwood's desk, revealing a number of pairs of trousers, tunics, cloaks and some gaudy-looking jewellery. 'This is what Reginald's ten crowns of gold buy you in the Kasbah.'

'I acknowledge I may not want to know the answer to this question,' the forger began hesitantly, 'but why do I need to look like a noble?'

The grin that appeared on the assassin's face would have been too wide for a normal man's features. Rham Jas seemed blessed with more smile muscles than was usual.

'There's a little gathering at the knight marshal's barracks tonight and I need you to get me in,' he said through the maddening smile.

'*A little gathering*,' repeated Glenwood. 'You mean Lord Archibald Tiris's first address as duke?'

'If you wish to be formal, yes, I think that is the reason for the little gathering.' Rham Jas knew what he was asking and he knew how dangerous it would be for Glenwood to help him. 'You're a noble and I'm your bound man, couldn't be simpler. I hear many Ro lords have Kirin as servants. It seems to please your people to formalize your superiority over mine.'

It was traditional for a new duke of the city to address the other lords and clergy when he took charge. The death of the prince had caused a degree of chaos in Ro Tiris and so the address had been delayed. Tonight, at the knight marshal's barracks, the great and not-so-good of the city would gather to fawn over the family of the king. The enchantress would be there, as would a wealth of important Ro.

'You can get me in, yes?' asked the Kirin. 'You're a forger and a noble . . . everything I need.' Rham Jas threw a handful of clothes across the desk. 'Pick something classy – whatever the other Ro bastards are wearing at this time of year.'

The Kirin had spent the ten gold crowns wisely and purchased a good amount of genuinely upmarket clothing. The Kasbah of Tiris was notorious for selling expensive-looking items at relatively cheap prices. The clothes would fall apart within a few days, but until then they would do the job.

'What do I get out of this?' asked the man of Leith, becoming more resigned to his predicament. If he were to say no, Rham Jas would likely kill him and find someone else.

The Kirin narrowed his grin as if he thought the question a stupid one. 'My dear Kale, surely helping an old friend is all the payment you need.' The grin disappeared entirely. 'And, of course, I'll kill you if you say no.'

Glenwood puffed out his cheeks and sat back in his chair. 'Rham Jas, how do you expect me to play this? We both know you could kill me in a second, but I'm not a random whore you picked up in Ro Weir. So stop treating me like an idiot.'

He held his breath as Rham Jas considered his words. The Kirin contorted his face into a number of different expressions, each one more inscrutable than the last, until he turned his head sharply and narrowed his eyes. 'That's fair,' he said, 'you're not an idiot . . . so I'll pay you the courtesy of being blunt.' He poured himself another glass of wine and sat back, relaxing into his chair. 'I plan to kill a number of Karesian enchantresses – all of them if I can – and you're going to help me. I'm a scumbag . . . and, to make matters worse, I'm a Kirin scumbag, which means that certain doors are closed to me.' He took a deep drink of wine and showed a genuine smile. 'Kale, you can forge the documents I need, and the party invitations, and I can pose as your bound man, making my presence a curiosity at best.'

Glenwood tried to return the smile but it got lost around his eyes and came out as more of a grimace. 'And I would guess that not all of your marks are in Tiris?'

Rham Jas shook his head. 'Arnon, Leith, Haran and Weir . . . it'll be like a tour of your stupid country. But, don't worry, Kale, I'll make sure you get money . . . from somewhere . . . if that's what you care about.'

The aspiring mobster reached for the bottle of wine and took a deep swig, ignoring his glass and gulping down a large measure. Glenwood had often wished for a more interesting life, or for the opportunity to ally himself with a powerful individual, but to be the minion of an insane Kirin assassin as he went on a killing spree around Tor Funweir was not what he had had in mind.

* * *

The knight marshal's barracks of Ro Tiris was an impressive building. It sat within sight of the king's palace, next to the empty training grounds of the Red knights. The White Spire of Tiris still flew the banner of the king – a white eagle in flight – despite the fact that the monarch was currently waging a war in the Freelands of Ranen.

The streets in the royal quarter were clean and well maintained. This was only the second time Glenwood had been there and he felt out of place. Despite his current finery, the man of Leith was merely playing at being a noble. He had the longsword, the heritage and the charming banter, but the stink of criminality was difficult to wash off. Looking down at his blue tunic, embroidered waistcoat and leather riding boots, he knew he could look good when he needed to. He had shaved, wore his blonde hair loose to the shoulders, and had buckled on an ornate scabbard for his sword.

'I think you look splendid, Kale,' murmured Rham Jas. The Kirin had started walking behind Glenwood as soon as they'd entered the royal quarter. 'I barely recognize you.'

'Hopefully the watchmen on the gate won't recognize me either,' he replied.

'I'm not an idiot, Kale. I checked before I came up with this cunning plan. The guards will be king's men and Purple clerics – no one who'd have dealt with a small-time streak of shit like you.'

He glanced over his shoulder and saw an enormous grin on the assassin's face. Rham Jas had discarded all his weaponry, leaving it locked in Glenwood's brothel, and transformed his appearance simply by having a wash. He was still swarthy-looking, but, with his hair clean and tied back, and his face shaved, Rham Jas Rami looked completely different. Standing behind a noble, he'd be regarded as nothing more than a slightly exotic servant.

'How exactly are you going to kill a woman that can't be killed?' Glenwood asked, turning a corner and approaching the knight marshal's barracks.

'Don't know. I suppose I'll improvise.' It was not reassuring, but Glenwood knew that Rham Jas was not so reckless as to get himself pointlessly killed.

The streets of the royal quarter were lit by globed lanterns. The bottom level of the barracks was palatial, raised from the dusty training ground and approached by white stone steps. The title of 'barracks' was largely ceremonial and instead the building served as the administrative centre of the city, used by senior churchmen, knights and officials for conducting the daily business of Ro Tiris. It was also used for those occasions when formality required a sophisticated gathering of nobles.

Many bound men and servants could be seen swarming dutifully towards the barracks. Glenwood breathed deeply. As they came closer, he slowed his pace and began to sweat. Two Purple clerics were on guard at street level in front of the gates. Behind them, the white steps were flanked by ornately dressed king's men, standing in gold and silver armour and looking bored.

Glenwood pulled the forged invitation from his waistcoat and puffed out his cheeks, hoping that his forgery skills, coupled with his appearance, would be sufficient to get them inside. The old longsword buckled at his side was the closest thing he owned for proof of his lineage, and as he looked down it appeared dull in comparison with the finely crafted weapons carried by the clerics.

'Stop fucking worrying,' whispered Rham Jas from behind, sensing the forger's anxiety.

'I'll stop worrying when I'm back at home next to a warm woman,' he replied. 'What do I do while you're running from the guardsmen?'

Rham Jas chuckled. 'You just need to get me in, Kale. After that, I'd advise you to go and jump out of a window as quickly as you can.'

Glenwood glanced behind. 'Why didn't you tell me that two hours ago? I've been thinking this whole time that we'd be running back to the Kasbah together.'

The assassin raised his eyebrows. 'You need to stay clean, otherwise you're of no use to me. Just make sure you don't hang around. Once I kill the bitch, things might get a little . . . chaotic.'

Without really thinking about it, Glenwood said, 'Thank you.'

The Kirin's forehead creased up with confusion. 'I'm not certain I deserve a *thank you*. I'm sure I'll find a way to get you killed in Arnon . . . or Leith.' The grin flowed back across the assassin's face. 'Get your noble face on, Kale.'

Glenwood plastered on his best fake smile and flicked his hair back extravagantly. He'd need confidence as well as a longsword to pull this off. Casually holding the forged invitation in his hand, Kale Glenwood stepped before one of the Purple clerics. 'A nice evening, brother,' he said with confidence.

The clerics said nothing, surprised that a guest should speak to them. The forger took the hint and maintained his smile as he walked confidently past. Beyond, guests were making their way up the white steps or milling around the entrance, talking loudly in cultured tones.

He breathed in deeply as he saw the well-dressed nobility on display. Men and women in immaculately tailored outfits glided around the marble floor of the entrance lobby, with fake smiles on their faces. The gathering had an air of well-practised formality that Glenwood knew would be difficult to fake. The men wore fitted jackets and tight trousers and most had ceremonial longswords sheathed at their waists. The occasional noble – from Leith or Haran, rather than Tiris – wore a rapier or other exotic weapon, clearly designed to be a conversation point. Many had body servants or bound men fawning around them.

'Does he belong to you?' asked a guardsman, standing at the top of the steps and pointing to Rham Jas.

'Are you addressing me?' responded Glenwood, raising his eyebrows and making a show of formality.

'Indeed, my lord. Is that Kirin yours?'

Glenwood raised a hand as if to wave away the impertinent query and stepped past the guardsman. 'He is my man, yes.' He didn't look at the man as he spoke and pretended to be scanning the lobby for familiar faces. 'Tell me, sword-master, is Lady Annabel of Leith in attendance?'

The guardsman narrowed his eyes and scanned Rham Jas up and down. The Kirin had his head bowed and was playing his part well. After a moment of suspicion, the man simply shook his head. 'I don't believe the Lady Annabel will be here tonight, my lord. I understand that her husband is ill.'

'Ah, that is a great shame,' said Glenwood, still not looking at him. 'We provincial nobles need to stick together.' He contorted his mouth into a smug grin and chuckled. 'I suppose I shall have to endure all manner of comments upon my character from these nobles of Tiris. Is that not right, Kirin?' He turned his smugness on to Rham Jas and hoped that the assassin would think quickly enough to join in.

'Absolutely, master,' was his response. He was deliberately speaking with a pronounced accent and Glenwood was impressed at how unthreatening he appeared.

When relieved of his weapons and grimy exterior, Rham Jas Rami was a relatively short, slender man, with no sign of the bizarrely skilled assassin that lay beneath. The bound man averted his eyes both from the guardsman and from his own master, and Glenwood began to feel more confident.

Once through the enormous white arch that led into the lobby, they were confronted with a vista of ostentatious beauty. At least a hundred men and women of Ro stood in loosely clustered groups across the polished stone floor, chatting loudly, drinking wine from crystal goblets, soothed into a high-class trance by harp music. The white eagle of Tiris, woven skilfully into expensive fabric, flew from pillars and rafters. The women wore dark colours, with their hair either tied back or worn high on their heads – a sharp contrast with the rouged pieces of rough with which Glenwood usually consorted.

'Right, you're in,' whispered the forger.

Rham Jas got as close to his companion as he could without arousing suspicion. 'These are just the lesser nobles, knights and baronets. I need the big sharks, not the little fish.'

Glenwood frowned. 'Well, I don't know the layout of the place, so I'll leave you to it, yes?' It was a long shot, but worth attempting.

'No, you will not,' growled the assassin. 'You see that staircase?' He pointed to a set of grand, carpeted stairs leading upwards and arcing around the room to form high balconies that looked down on the lobby.

'That's where the high nobles are, we'll never get close,' murmured Glenwood.

'Why did you think I wanted to come here, Kale?' the assassin asked ironically. 'The bitch isn't going to be making small talk with random knights.' He paused and looked up for the first time since they had entered the barracks. He scanned the lobby and balconies. Little could be seen, but the occasional peal of silvery laughter indicated that the Karesian woman was in attendance. 'Why is it that her voice carries so?' Rham Jas asked.

'She's an enchantress. I hear that just the sound of her voice can sway men to her will,' Glenwood responded nervously.

'Well. let's shut her up then, shall we?' said Rham Jas, with the slightest indication of a grin on his swarthy features. 'When we get to the top of the stairs, you take a right and find a window to jump out of. I'll get it done and meet you back at the Blue Feather.' The assassin spoke confidently. 'Oh, and you'll be needing that invite to get up the stairs.' The grin on the Kirin's face was now back to its usual size and Glenwood glanced nervously down at his forged invitation. It was good work, but rushed, and he had little confidence that it would be accepted by the senior nobles.

Without further discussion, Glenwood strode across the lobby floor, pausing only to make fawning smiles and shallow bows to the assembled lords and ladies. A few regarded him with disdain, but most found the presence of a provincial noble a way of asserting their own superiority, thanking the One they'd been born in Tiris rather than Leith. Few people noticed the Kirin that walked behind him, and Glenwood was thankful that the high-born rarely so much as acknowledge the low-born.

At the base of the stairs stood two more Purple clerics. These were older than the men outside and, as the two intruders approached, Glenwood noticed that several nobles had already been turned away from the stairs. The churchmen stood beneath small banners displaying the purple sceptre of nobility, indicating that their church held almost as much sway in Tiris as the king's family itself.

'Show us your clay, my lord,' said one of the clerics, a look of haughty superiority on his face.

'Of course.' Glenwood attempted to look casual as he handed over the counterfeit clay tablet.

The cleric studied the invitation between suspicious glances at the man of Leith. 'Kale Glenwood?' the cleric prompted. 'Ward of the glen . . . that's not a title I expected to see at the duke's address. When did you arrive from Ro Leith?'

'Earlier today,' lied the forger. 'I expected to meet the Lady Annabel here, but I've been told her husband is still unwell and I'm expected to represent Leith on my own.' He let the nerves show on his face and hoped the story was believable enough, and his appearance unthreatening enough, to gain entrance. Name-dropping Lady Annabel of Leith had got him out of trouble in the past. The ploy was less likely to work on clerics than on the city watchmen, but currently it was the only trick in his arsenal.

'And your bound man?' the cleric asked, glancing up at Rham Jas.

'I expected to see more Kirin servants, to be honest. They are quite the fashion in Ro Leith.' He smiled smugly. 'It pleases Lady Annabel to show our dominance over the lesser races of men.' He spoke quietly and with a noble sneer on his face. 'I suppose such shows of status are less necessary in Ro Tiris, yes?'

The clerics showed no sign of amusement and the forger realized that two other people were waiting behind him, also hoping to be allowed up the stairs. If the queue grew much bigger, he guessed that those above might become suspicious and things would go rapidly downhill.

'We seem to be holding things up,' the forger joked. 'Could we hurry along? Our beloved ally in Ro Leith is eager to have her words delivered to the duke.' It was a bold, and possibly foolish, plan, but he was running out of options.

The clerics looked up sharply, with surprise on their faces. 'You are here with the Lady Isabel's words?'

Glenwood made a show of wide-eyed astonishment. 'Please refer to her as *our beloved ally*, my lord cleric, she dislikes having her name thrown around.' He gritted his teeth and glared at the churchman.

His gambit seemed to have worked. After exchanging a look, the two clerics parted and motioned for Glenwood to ascend.

He held his breath for a moment and felt every muscle in his body tense as he climbed the ornate staircase. It was only when he heard the clerics talking to the guests who had been queuing behind him that the forger breathed out. 'Fuck me, that was tense,' he said to himself.

'Did you even know her name?' asked Rham Jas in a whisper.

'Not until he mentioned it, no.' He knew how reckless he had been and could not yet allow himself to be impressed at his wanton deception. 'It got us in, didn't it? Stop complaining.'

'Wasn't a complaint,' replied the assassin. 'You're cleverer than I thought, Kale.'

'Fuck you, Rham Jas.'

The Kirin didn't respond.

The fact that the clerics knew his name and what he looked like made it unlikely that Glenwood would remain *clean* after Rham Jas had killed Katja. No other nobles had Kirin bound men and it would not take a great deal of investigation to deduce who had smuggled in the assassin. The forger did not particularly like Ro Tiris, but neither did he want to have to leave in a hurry with clerics and guardsmen after him.

At the top of the staircase, he glanced to the left. There were fewer people there, but they stood out more than those below. High-ranking Purple clerics resplendent in burnished plate armour stood toe to toe with gaudily dressed members of the house of Tiris and standing in the middle, the focus of much of the attention, was Katja the Hand of Despair. The Karesian enchantress was strikingly beautiful despite the distinctive wolf's head tattoo on her cheek. She stood on the lushly carpeted balcony beneath ornate tapestries depicting knights in armour and scenes of glorious Ro victories. Servants moved swiftly from side to side, offering drinks and small items of food. Katja had a strange, euphoric effect on those around her. Even Lord Archibald Tiris, flamboyant in his regal coat and golden circlet, fawned over the enchantress as if she were all he cared about.

'Wrong direction, Kale,' whispered Rham Jas. 'You go to the right and I go to the left . . . and stop looking at her, she'll twist your mind if you let her.'

'She's surrounded by armed men, Rham Jas. I know you're

hot shit, but this looks pretty much impossible. How about we forget this business and go have a drink?'

He felt the Kirin's hand on his arm. 'Let me worry about killing Katja. You find a window to jump out of. Once she's dead, events will move quickly, so you'd better get going.'

Glenwood took a last look at the nobles surrounding Katja before turning sharply and walking in the other direction, leaving Rham Jas alone at the top of the stairs. No guests stood on the other side and Glenwood was not interrupted as he walked towards several doors that led from the balcony. He was only a couple of storeys off the ground and he hoped that any random window would allow him to escape. A breeze came through the first door and he turned into a storage area for wine and silverware. The room had a large window which was slightly ajar and, after a quick look around, he was sure he wasn't being observed.

He moved to the window and paused. He disliked Rham Jas – hated him even – but leaving him alone to get killed made the forger feel bad. He was not a good man, far from it, but he hated these puffed-up nobles even more than he hated the Kirin assassin. With strained resignation, Kale Glenwood, wannabe mobster of Ro Tiris, returned to the doorway and peeked out.

He couldn't see the Kirin and his eye was again drawn across the carpeted balcony to the figure of Katja. She was tall, with a lush figure, and drew all eyes to her as she spoke. As before, her voice carried and each phrase she uttered was met with fawning approval and laughter from the nobles. Archibald Tiris stood next to her. The new duke's bearing was much less impressive. He had the high forehead and receding hairline common to the king's family and a look of vacuous euphoria on his face.

Just as he was beginning to think that Rham Jas had left after all, a slight movement caught his eye. Ironically, the presence of the enchantress worked in the assassin's favour because it meant that those normally observant men were sufficiently distracted to let the Kirin get close. He'd ghosted his way along the far wall, keeping away from the balcony's edge and making sure to stay behind the armoured Purple clerics. Glenwood knew how much Rham Jas hated the churchmen of nobility and he wondered if the Kirin would be tempted to kill more than one person before he left.

It was difficult to see Rham Jas now because he had hidden behind one of the tapestries. Then, through the throng of nobles, a hand reached out to a discarded drinks tray and took two crystal goblets. No one had seen this and Glenwood held his breath, waiting for Rham Jas to make his move. The man of Leith had one foot tapping nervously on the floor and he glanced back to assure himself that the window was close. He knew he should have left already, but curiosity had the better of him and he waited a moment longer.

Rham Jas appeared again, crouching behind a low drinks table. He lobbed one of the goblets into the air in such a way that its trajectory took it over the balcony's edge to smash loudly on the stone floor below. No one had seen where the goblet came from, and the nobles on the upper floor reacted with surprise before moving to investigate. Glenwood smiled. The duke and most of the knights and clerics left Katja's side to look down to the lobby. The enchantress herself appeared equally surprised by the sound but was far too demure to investigate what was, after all, merely a glass breaking.

When the assassin moved, it was with lightning speed. He sprang from cover with the second goblet in his hand. Two men either side, who had not gone to the balcony, saw the Kirin move forward but were helpless to react as he wrapped an arm round Katja's neck and rammed the goblet into the side of her head, just above the wolf's head tattoo. The glass drove into her temple and a high-pitched scream sounded out. Katja was thrashing around in pain, but Rham Jas didn't let go. He twisted the goblet, driving the jagged glass further into her head, until her eyes rolled back and the screaming stopped. Blood ran freely over her tattoo to fall on her limp shoulders.

Everything froze as the high nobles stared at the Kirin assassin and the dead body of Katja the Hand of Despair. A strange haze flowed over the assembled nobles and many of them involuntarily closed their eyes as months of enchantment waned in an instant. The haze was quickly replaced by murderous anger directed towards the assassin. Glenwood's hands shook and he was breathing fast, his feet now willing him to run for the window.

'Kill him!' shouted Archibald Tiris, with a crack in his voice.

Rham Jas grinned as fifty men drew their swords and advanced. He darted backwards and took a forward roll away from the dead enchantress, avoiding the clumsy nobles in their plate armour as he dived down the stairs.

Glenwood again lost sight of the Kirin as he sprinted in zigzag lines, avoiding the multitude of men trying to apprehend him. With shaking hand, the man of Leith closed the door to the side room.

He could hear shouting as he reached the window and, as he climbed out and hung from the window sill in the cool night of Tiris, a bell began to sound from the knight marshal's barracks.

* * *

Saara grabbed the sides of her head and cried out in pain. A dozen faces entered her mind and each one burrowed in further, causing a pain the like of which the enchantress had never experienced before. Each was a man whom Katja had enchanted, and each now belonged to Saara. She could feel the shadow of Cardinal Mobius, Lord Archibald Tiris, Animustus Voy and many others intrude upon her own thralls. Each of the men was now a little weaker, a little closer to the edge and a little harder to control. It might be a day, or a week, but if Saara didn't focus her thoughts, she knew that they would all begin to lose their own minds. With both Mobius and the king as her shadow thralls, the Mistress of Pain needed time to plan and to ensure that the invasion of Ranen took place as she desired.

'My sweet,' Kamran Kainen said gently from next to her, 'what has happened?' They were still in bed and the sun had yet to rise.

'I am . . . not myself,' replied Saara, 'please leave me.' The pounding in her head made conversation difficult and she wanted her lover to go while she accustomed herself to her new shadow thralls.

Kamran stroked her naked shoulder and kissed her neck tenderly. 'I can serve, my lady. As you like . . .'

She pushed the wind claw away and clenched her fists, attempting to shut out the pain. 'Leave!' she shouted; she had not even the strength to enchant the man. He frowned but rose quickly and pulled on a black robe to cover his muscular body.

Saara closed her eyes and held her head. Try as she might, she could not shut out the men enchanted by Katja. She was overwhelmed with fear, rage, frustration, pride . . . a hundred emotions felt by her new thralls.

As Kamran neared the door to her bedchamber, Saara felt a predatory urge.

'Kamran,' she said quietly, 'come here.'

The wind claw turned.

'I need you.' She looked up, letting the satin bedclothes fall from her naked shoulders.

Kamran waited a moment, letting a smile come to his face and his robe fall to the ground before he crossed the room to kiss her. She returned his kiss, then gripped the sides of his head and stared into his eyes.

The wind claw did not realize what was happening at first and continued smiling as Saara's grip became firmer, until Kamran's eyes betrayed a hint of anxiety. 'Shh, my sweet,' she whispered, 'I need your strength.'

It happened slowly. Kamran tried to move away, but he was helpless in her grasp. His face became a mask of terror.

'My lady . . .' His words were strangled as Saara slowly drew his life force into her, rejuvenating and cleansing her fractured mind. He flailed in her grasp as she slowly destroyed his mind. Blood appeared from his eyes, nose and ears, staining the white sheets. Saara cried with pleasure.

He died slowly and she used every morsel of the pain he felt to bring herself to the edge of ecstasy. She writhed in his blood and strangled every ounce of life from the man.

When Kamran Kainen had stopped screaming and lay motionless, Saara fell back heavily on the bed. Her head was clear and she felt focused again for the first time in weeks, though looking down at the desiccated corpse of her lover made her wince slightly. She was not squeamish, but she would need clean bedclothes before she took a new lover into her chamber.

Standing up and looking down at her body, wet with sweat and blood, her only thought was for her sisters. Those who were still alive would know of Katja's death, and they would also know that a new Hand of Despair would take years to train, like the new Lady of Spiders, a young girl currently being tortured into compliance at the abbey of Oron Kaa. At the rate the dark-blood was going, they could not afford to wait. The Mistress of Pain was patient, but the subjugation of the Ro had been meticulously planned and her scheme for the Freelands had been years in conception. If Rham Jas Rami could despatch the enchantresses so easily, a back-up plan would be necessary. Sasha the Illusionist was still in Kessia with the Kirin assassin's daughter. It would be wise to send for them both. She should also send for more hounds – five hundred thousand seemed a good number. With no enchantresses to keep the Ro in line, a more martial solution would be necessary.

CHAPTER FOUR

FALLON OF LEITH
IN THE RUINS OF RO HAIL

THE REALM OF Wraith was one of the more miserable places in the lands of men. Fallon had served on the front line of numerous conflicts, he'd slept in ruins, farms, under canvas, wood, leaves and, on one particularly memorable occasion, half-buried in mud. He was a knight captain of the Red, newly promoted after the death of his commander and friend, William of Verellian. However, all he could think as he stood, soaked in rain on the northern battlements of Ro Hail, was that he hated the lands of Ranen. Cold, featureless and permanently raining, he wondered why the Ro had ever bothered to conquer the place and, several centuries later, why they were bothering to do it again.

Fallon was thirty-two years of age and one of the finest swordsmen among the knights of the Red. He'd never known his match in combat, whether in a duel to first blood, a training exercise or a brutal encounter on a battlefield. The knight captain thought of himself as a fine example of his breed – tall, lean and well armoured in red plate, his dark brown hair cut close and his movements fluid. However, fifteen years as a knight had lent him a cynical and pragmatic edge that frequently placed him at odds with the more sadistic knights around him. Fallon was a true fighting man who valued honour, skill and duty. Unfortunately, he was all too aware that his superiors were mostly idiotic old men or pampered nobles. Verellian was one of the few whom he had admired, a man with both a sword and a brain, a combination that was sadly rare.

Currently, the Red knight was under the direct authority of a Purple cleric called Mobius, a cardinal of the One with the ear of the king and the heart of a warmonger. The cleric of nobility had adopted the position of general since Commander Rillion had been killed in Ro Canarn and King Sebastian had gone into seclusion. The knights had kept their displeasure to themselves as Mobius ordered them around and made his will known.

Fallon, who had endured a number of lengthy briefings, knew that Mobius's will included the subjugation of Ranen, or the *peasants and lesser men* as he insisted on calling them. The cardinal had even sent to Darkwald for reinforcements and the local yeomanry were apparently moving up to join the force of five thousand knights currently camped in Ro Hail. Fallon doubted he'd be there to greet them as he would be leaving on a scouting mission to the east within the next few hours.

'Captain, the men are at the ready.' The voice came from Sergeant Ohms, a man remarkable both for his skill with a sword and for his frustrating formality.

Fallon didn't turn his gaze from the northern plains. 'Where are you from, sergeant?'

'Sir?' responded the lesser knight in confusion.

'Where do you call home? When you're not part of an invasion force.' Fallon stepped back from the battlements and faced the sergeant. 'I lost my whole unit on that courtyard a month ago and I'd like to get to know my new men.'

A half-smile appeared on Ohms's face and he nodded slightly before glancing down into the rain-soaked courtyard. It had been in their hands for a little over a month, but a lot of men had died to secure it from Wraith Company.

The sergeant turned back to Fallon. 'Near Du Ban, a place called Old Ohms Bridge.'

'Nice place, is it?' the captain asked.

Ohms screwed up his face and shook his head. 'Not unless you like olives. There are a lot of olives.'

'I hate olives,' said Fallon, smiling.

'As do I . . . that's why I left.' The sergeant turned and walked slowly towards the stone steps that led down to the courtyard.

Beneath them was a great force of Red knights. Most were armed and armoured, but they had been largely idle for several weeks. The banners of the Red, two crossed longswords over a clenched fist, hung from a hundred tents. Although the purple sceptre of nobility was displayed prominently over the command pavilion, the army was decidedly Red.

The wait, as Wraith Company got further and further away, had been agonizing. Mobius had said little to the troops, leaving it to Knight Commander Tristram to give the occasional speech about duty to the One. Fallon had largely stopped listening, but he suspected that Tristram was merely a puppet of the cardinal, who in turn was probably doing the bidding of the king, whom Fallon had only seen once since he had been retrieved from the Fjorlanders two weeks before.

'At least we're rid of the enchantress,' Fallon said to himself, following Sergeant Ohms down the steps.

He'd read several reports about what had occurred a month ago in Ro Canarn and each had been slightly more ambiguous than the last. The gist of it, once filtered through a myriad otherworldly speculations, seemed to be that Bromvy Black Guard had returned to his home and killed Knight Commander Rillion. Quite how the enchantress had been despatched was one of many details that were unclear, but Fallon had been assured that Ameira the Lady of Spiders was certainly dead. Both Verellian and Fallon had seen the disquieting influence the enchantress had exerted over Rillion and, more worryingly, the king. The young knight was glad she was dead. Other news from Ro Tiris suggested that a rogue Black cleric had killed Prince Christophe, and this made the king's seclusion a matter of further concern.

'Knight Captain Fallon.' The voice was loud and came from one of Tristram's adjutants, a sycophantic captain from Tiris called Taufel.

'Men are ready,' Fallon responded quietly without turning.

'Later . . . now, the cardinal wants a word, captain.' Taufel was younger than Fallon and had, by all accounts, never seen combat.

'I'm a knight of the Red, like you,' Fallon responded, with just a hint of exasperation in his voice. 'Let the Purple talk to the Purple, I don't answer to the cardinal . . . and you shouldn't be running his errands.' Fallon glared down at the inexperienced knight and was aware that Sergeant Ohms was doing the same. 'If the knight commander wants to speak to me, all he has to do is order me to attend him . . . but Mobius is no knight.'

Captain Taufel looked offended, one of many indications that he was more than a little naive about the often stormy relationship between the Red and Purple aspects of the One God. The knights would follow orders only so long as Cardinal Mobius was filtering them through Tristram.

'Okay, captain . . . I suppose Commander Tristram awaits your attendance.' Taufel smiled thinly in an attempt to appear both professional and confident.

'That's better,' grunted Ohms.

Fallon banged his fist against his breastplate in salute and started across the courtyard. The sergeant was one step behind him and Taufel followed a moment later. They walked among massed knights and bound men, slouching around low-burning campfires. Whatever reason Tristram, Mobius and the king had for delaying their pursuit of Wraith Company, it was becoming frustrating.

Several old stone buildings had been torn down and the central courtyard of Ro Hail was a sea of military tents, with red pavilions housing the commanders and senior knights of the king's army. Fallon preferred to stay in the northern courtyard where the rank and file knights made their home and had only visited the king's ground for briefings and the occasional reprimand. In the month since he had been named captain, Fallon had been shouted at by his commander on several occasions and it seemed as if Tristram was regretting the promotion. However,

Fallon knew they were short of experienced knights and, with the loss of Verellian, everyone with battle experience needed to be in a position of command.

'I'm not sure I should be accompanying you, sir,' said Ohms as they moved between the red tents. 'I don't like the way the officers look at me.'

Fallon turned to his sergeant and smiled warmly. 'Officers are allowed to look at you any way they want, sergeant. Just make sure you don't look back.'

'All the same, if you'll not be needing me, I'll return to the men.' He was clearly uncomfortable on the king's ground.

'Very well, we should be leaving within the hour. Tell Theron to see to it,' Fallon replied, with a formal salute.

Ohms returned his salute and marched swiftly back to the northern courtyard, leaving Fallon and Captain Taufel to make their way to the commander's pavilion.

'You served under Captain Verellian, is that right?' asked Taufel, walking towards a line of guardsmen in ceremonial attire.

'I was his adjutant, yes.' Fallon preferred not to discuss his friend and disliked the fact that he was constantly being compared with the hawk-faced old knight captain.

'Is it true that he bested a dozen men of Wraith before they took him?' Taufel had the look of an excitable child as he imagined a heroic tale of battle.

'Nothing so grand, I'm afraid,' Fallon responded. 'We were outnumbered and everyone but me was killed on a rain-soaked courtyard, far from home. Verellian was still alive when I fled.'

'But it *was* a glorious last stand?' the young captain pressed.

Fallon stopped walking and faced the young knight. 'Have you ever drawn that sword with the intention of sticking it in a man's flesh?' he asked coldly.

Taufel spluttered and looked down at his pristine longsword. 'Well, no, captain, this is my first posting. I hope to see combat at South Warden.'

Fallon nodded. 'Okay, so ask me about heroics and glory once you've killed a few Free Company men. Things seem different when you have fresh blood on your face.'

He strode on without giving Taufel a chance to respond. Fallon was not a cruel man, but he had little time for the romance of chivalry and duelling that was still being taught on the training grounds of Arnon and Tiris. He had seen more than one young knight of the Red rendered catatonic by the reality of sword fighting.

'You're to go straight in,' Taufel said, rushing to catch up with him.

The line of guardsmen saluted in unison and the middle two men stepped aside to allow the Red knights entrance to Commander Tristram's pavilion. Once inside, the two men bowed respectfully to those within as the tent flap was closed behind them.

Knight Commander Tristram stood, alongside Cardinal Mobius and another Purple cleric named Jakan, around a central table, the contents of which were just being cleared away by bound men. Fallon saw the remains of a large meal, showing that those in command ate better than their subordinates. A stained map of Ranen was unrolled across the table and the commander raised his chin to direct a welcoming look at Captain Fallon. All three wore plate armour, but only Tristram's showed any sign of use. Cardinal Mobius had insisted on a fresh breastplate after he had fought the company of Fjorlanders a month before, and Fallon guessed that Jakan had never received a dent in his pristine armour. Purple clerics had a tendency to play at being soldiers. He felt their presence among so many good men and dutiful knights as an insult to the Red aspect of the One God.

'That will be all, Captain Taufel,' Tristram said, waving at his adjutant.

The young knight saluted enthusiastically and left.

The commander then turned to Fallon. 'Captain, you and I need a clarification before I send you out east.'

Fallon did not react. He stood at ease, waiting for whatever dressing-down he was about to receive. Cardinal Mobius was regarding him through narrow eyes and Fallon found himself wishing he could tell the Purple churchman exactly what he thought of him. For the time being, he kept quiet and returned the cardinal's glare.

'I do believe the young knight dislikes me,' Mobius said with a sneer.

'Captain Fallon will do his duty, my lord,' Tristram responded. 'And I don't believe he's required to like you.'

The young cleric, Brother Jakan, looked offended at the implication behind Tristram's words and seemed as if he were about to object. A hand casually raised by the cardinal silenced him.

'Indeed, but he will, I hope, do as he's told,' Mobius replied.

Tristram smiled tolerantly. 'That, you should never doubt, my lord.'

Fallon guessed that the commander's hands were tied. If the king wanted Mobius and the Purple in charge, then there was little the senior knight could do about it. It did, however, make Fallon feel better to see Tristram act as a knight should.

'Captain, you and your men – fifty knights, I believe – are to advance east until you meet resistance. At that point, you are to stop and fortify your position. Once you send a message back to Hail giving your location, we will advance on your position with the remainder of the army and the engineers will begin assembling the siege equipment.' Tristram was speaking formally and his strategy was consistent with an invasion. South Warden was no ruin and its capture would doubtless cost more lives than Ro Hail.

'Understood, sir,' replied Fallon.

'I believe the cardinal also wishes a word before you depart,' Tristram said in a voice that suggested he was unhappy about something.

Mobius came to stand before Fallon. He was a large man, though shorter than the captain by several inches. His face was shaved and his hair well groomed. Fallon, in contrast, had shaved infrequently over the last month and had the countenance of a toughened soldier. He was also without his red cloak, having lost it in Ro Canarn several months before, and despite Verellian's chiding he had not yet found a replacement.

'Do you understand the king's will in this matter, captain?' Mobius asked, sizing up the Red knight. 'You understand why we are in this barbaric land?'

'I follow orders,' Fallon replied.

Mobius nodded. 'You are a good soldier, captain, but the king needs loyal men as well as good soldiers.' He paused. 'Our beloved allies have provided intelligence that has led the king to declare a war of conquest against these . . . peasants and lesser men.' Mobius gestured to the map next to him, indicating the south lands of Ranen.

Fallon had heard the Seven Sisters referred to as *our beloved allies* on a number of occasions since he had left Ro Canarn and the term had bothered him a little more each time. 'Good soldiers are not idiots, Mobius, and I am not an idiot,' he responded.

Jakan widened his eyes. 'You will address the cardinal as *my lord*. I order you to show Lord Mobius the respect he is due,' he blurted out.

'I will address him any way I please, unless Knight Commander Tristram orders me otherwise.' Fallon's voice rose sharply, almost shouting the last few words. 'And you give me an order again, cleric, and I'll call you out and kill you. Understood?'

Both Mobius and Jakan stood aghast for a moment.

'Do you understand?' Fallon repeated.

'Yes,' stuttered Jakan.

Mobius, who had quickly regained his composure, took a step closer and spoke over his shoulder to Commander Tristram. 'Knight commander, please ask the captain to address me as *my lord*.'

The senior knight had thus far not reacted to the heated exchange. 'Captain Fallon, show the cardinal more . . . respect.'

Fallon smiled at Mobius and puffed out his chest, making his armour creak. 'Yes, sir,' he said. 'My Lord Mobius, I am both a good soldier and a loyal one.' He stopped smiling. 'And I know why we're in Ranen . . . if the king feels he needs a larger kingdom, who am I to argue?'

The cardinal smirked at Fallon's subtle disrespect and considered the Red knight's words. 'As long as your dislike is limited to the Purple, captain, and your loyalty to your king remains strong . . . I believe the king *and* the Purple can forgive your rudeness.'

Fallon shot a glance at Tristram, who raised his eyebrows before shrugging.

'Can the king not forgive me in person, my lord, or is he still recovering from being around the sweaty Fjorlanders?' Fallon was calmer now that Mobius had, in the captain's estimation, caved in under pressure.

'King Sebastian Tiris, scion of house Tiris and lord king of Tor Funweir, does not rouse himself to speak to knight captains,' replied Mobius.

'We're done here,' interrupted Tristram. 'Fallon, come with me.' The commander stepped past Mobius and motioned the captain to follow him.

Tristram coughed to alert those outside and the tent flap was pulled aside by a guardsman. 'I'll take my leave, my lord cardinal. Inform the king that our advance towards South Warden is under way.' Tristram banged his fist against his mottled breastplate and exited the pavilion.

Fallon waited a moment, still face to face with Mobius, before turning and directing a condescending wink at Jakan. He then showed the Purple clerics his back and followed his commander outside.

'You should watch your mouth, captain,' Tristram chided as the two of them walked away from the pavilion.

'Sir, may I speak freely?' asked Fallon.

Commander Tristram raised an eyebrow and motioned behind for two men to follow them in close guard. 'It's maybe a bit too late to be requesting such things. You did just threaten one Purple cleric and insult another . . . a cardinal no less.'

They were walking between smaller tents housing the officer corps and general staff of Tristram's brigade and both men received salutes as they walked.

'That's different, sir. I am a knight and I listen to other knights . . . the nobles of God have no place ordering around the warriors of God.' Fallon had seen at first hand what happened when pampered idiots commanded armies. Without exception, the results were disastrous. 'If you had been in command, sir, would you have left the king in the pavilion with so few guards while we assaulted Hail? Would you have allowed the Fjorlanders to capture him?'

Tristram wrestled with the question before slowly shaking his head. 'No, I would not.' He smiled. 'The point is a fair one – and, yes, if Mobius had not been in command, the king would not have been captured by the Fjorlanders – but you and I have other duties. Leave the Purple to questions of nobility and we'll handle the questions of war.'

Fallon was gratified that Tristram was not merely a puppet. Moreover, the captain suspected, he was the only man in the command pavilion who had not been manipulated by the Karesian enchantress.

'What are we doing here, sir?' he asked, now feeling more sure of himself with his new commander. 'In the Freelands, I mean. From what I've heard, Canarn is now in the hands of risen men and Tor Funweir is slowly being annexed by the hounds and *our beloved fucking allies* . . . And what are we doing? Engaging in a war of conquest, apparently?'

Tristram grabbed an apple from a nearby barrel and bit deeply. 'You're following orders, captain, that's what you're doing here. Everything else is for our betters to worry about,' he responded through a mouthful of fruit.

'Sir, I've never been very good at blindly following orders.' Fallon knew this was a massive understatement, but he also knew that without a friendly commander his cynicism would never be tolerated and he sought to bring Tristram on side.

'We are servants of the One God,' said the commander, with a shrug. 'I'd like to have some profound piece of insight for you, but alas, all I can say is that we are knights of the Red . . . we do as our king bids us.'

'And at what point does the will of the king conflict with the will of the One?' asked Fallon.

Tristram stopped walking and turned to direct a hard stare at the captain. He took a last bite of his apple and threw the core away. 'That's a dangerous question, young knight. He's your king and he speaks with the authority of the One.' He paused and placed a hand on Fallon's armoured shoulder. 'These questions make you a good soldier, Fallon, but they may also get you into serious trouble. Whether you like Mobius or not, he could arrest you, convict you and hang you, should he choose to.'

'He'd better send an army to arrest me, because I wouldn't willingly submit to his . . . justice. The first man that questions my honour gets bloody, the second loses his head.'

Knight Commander Tristram laughed, a good-natured sound that carried a distance in the still air of Ro Hail. 'Rillion was a fool, Mobius is a warmonger, Jakan is an idiot and only the One knows what the king is. You and I, however, we are knights, soldiers of Tor Funweir, and we will do our duty until it kills us . . .'

'It's not that simple, sir, and you know it.' Fallon shifted his sword belt and scratched his patchy beard. 'Why are we warring with the Ranen? If you can give me a reason . . . It doesn't even have to be good reason, just give me a fucking reason and I'll be polite to anyone you want. Until then, I'll give shit to any Purple cunt I please. Unless you order me not to, sir.'

Tristram laughed again. 'That's enough, captain. There is a line. Be careful.'

'Yeah, Verellian often told me that same thing,' Fallon replied. 'Recognizing *the line* is apparently not counted among my skills, sir.'

'Muster your men, Fallon, and assemble in the central courtyard before you leave.' Tristram adopted a more authoritative tone. 'The king wants to address the army – you included.'

Knight Captain Fallon of Leith raised his eyebrow and saluted slowly by banging on his red steel breastplate.

* * *

Fallon's unit consisted of fifty knights. All were good fighting men, seasoned warriors of the Red who did their duty without question. The knight captain had slowly become reconciled to the loss of his previous unit and was beginning to bond with his new company. His knight lieutenant, Sir Theron, was a young man of Haran who had served under the king's brother, Duke Xander Tiris. He rather idolized his new captain, frequently citing the famous duels that Fallon had fought and won. It was flattering at first to have his skill with the sword recognized by his adjutant, but after a while Fallon had come to find the man irritating. Sergeant Ohms was easier to deal with, so the captain left most of the practicalities of command to the haggard man from Old Ohms Bridge, who hated olives.

Between Ohms and Theron, the company assembled quickly in the central courtyard. With their swords, shields, armour and helms, Fallon's men looked as tough as any knights of the Red as they sat astride their horses and waited for the king's address. The captain himself had done little in the hour it had taken them to prepare, preferring to sit by and ponder their situation. He didn't like his orders and he liked the king's intention to take South Warden even less.

'Men at the ready, sir,' stated Theron formally. 'We ride at your order.'

The young knight of Haran was clean-shaven and had paid an unnecessary amount of attention to his long blonde hair. Fallon stood up from his perch on a barrel beside the horses and reached for his helmet. 'Make yourself comfortable, lieutenant. King Sebastian tends to go on . . . and on.'

Theron laughed politely. 'Very droll, sir.'

'Shut up,' responded Fallon without looking at his adjutant. 'I can have my cock sucked by a whore if I want, I don't need you to do it.'

Theron stuttered without forming any actual words and looked uncomfortable at his captain's brand of humour, before deciding to do as he was told and shut up.

Fallon pulled himself into the saddle and adjusted his armour. He had been putting off repairing his breastplate for the last month or so and an annoying dent had developed in his stomach area. The saddle held his round shield and a two-handed sword that he occasionally used. His longsword, the weapon he had used for ten years or more, was sheathed at his side. It had a worn leather band wrapped around the hilt and a simple steel pommel. It was the only thing he was sure to look after. His face could stay unshaven, his cloak lost and his armour dented, but his sword would always be sharp.

'Knight Captain Fallon.' The voice was loud and came from Sir Taufel. Tristram's adjutant was wearing his dress uniform, a pristine tabard and longsword, with a burnished red breastplate. His helm was of polished steel and finished with a high white plume made from the feathers of a dozen doves. 'Your men are to remain by the eastern gate and to ride when the king gives command.'

Fallon leant casually forward on the pommel of his saddle and raised an eyebrow at Taufel. 'Are we to be a part of his game, captain? Will his speech rise in a crescendo until he unleashes us eastwards?'

Taufel looked abashed at Fallon's cynical appraisal. 'I believe his highness wishes to emphasize his desire to defeat these peasants and lesser men.' The adjutant used Mobius's expression for the men of Ranen, and Fallon found himself disliking the term even more. 'He has decided that you and your unit will have the honour of being his first blow in the campaign.' His pious formality showed that he bought into the well-practised game of war.

Taufel saluted and marched away, heading towards the command tent on the far side of the courtyard.

'Is he as naive as he sounds?' asked Theron, showing more awareness than Fallon had credited him with.

'You'd know more about naivety than me, lieutenant.' The response was barbed, and once again Theron did not know how to react. 'Assemble the men by the eastern gate . . . let's do what the little prick says, shall we?'

Theron nodded, forgetting his customary salute, and turned to order Sergeant Ohms and the knights to follow. Slowly, Fallon's unit of fifty knights of the Red rode across the irregular cobblestones of Ro Hail towards the eastern gate. They were the only mounted men in the courtyard and many eyes followed them. Each was dressed for combat, their travelling packs filled only with the essentials and their personal belongings left behind. They received several half-hearted salutes from men as cynical about their situation as Fallon. By the time they had assembled in front of the gates, most of the knights had been ordered to stand in tight ranks, waiting for the king's address.

A bugle sounded and the senior knights barked at their men to come to attention. The noise of steel-shod feet echoed through Ro Hail and Fallon had to calm his horse at the sharp sound.

'Good to know someone else hates all this shit,' he said quietly to his mount.

From Tristram's pavilion, Fallon saw a small group of knights and clerics emerge on to a well-built dais, raised ten or so feet from the cobbles.

Cardinal Mobius appeared first, standing tall and proud in his spotless purple armour. Next to him were three lesser clerics, including Brother Jakan and an older noble called Rathbone of Chase. Knight Commander Tristram stood to the side, adopting a subservient position behind the Purple clerics.

All the men in the courtyard were silent now, as King Sebastian Tiris emerged from the command pavilion. The monarch looked terrible. His eyes were bloodshot, his skin pale and his hair greasy. He wore gold armour that didn't sit right on his shoulders, and a fur-trimmed cloak designed to make him look more bulky and muscular than he really was. At his side were two other clerics – his bodyguard, Cleoth Montague, and an elderly Black cleric called Aleister of the Falls of Arnon. The cleric of death was the army's chaplain. He seemed far too old for the position and Fallon thought he must have greatly angered his cardinal to be appointed at such an advanced age.

Mobius raised his hand. 'Brothers, you will salute your king.'

The five thousand knights and bound men banged on their breastplates in unison, again causing Fallon's horse to buck and paw at the ground.

Brother Cleoth Montague, a tough-looking Purple cleric and son to one of the richest men in Tor Funweir, stepped to the front. As a bodyguard he was largely useless, having been knocked unconscious by the Fjorlan axe-woman Halla Summer Wolf, but as a symbol of the king's wealth and nobility he was priceless. 'You will remember this day,' Montague announced in a clear and formal tone. 'For on this day, your king retakes Ranen.' He was a skilled orator, and as his voice rose in volume he encouraged the assembled knights to cheer. When they did not, several Purple clerics in the crowd banged on their breastplates until a slow cheer rose from the army.

Fallon shook his head. He had not cheered, neither had his unit. A glance across at Tristram showed that the knight commander was also silent.

Cleoth bent a knee in front of the king and bowed his head. 'My king,' he said, inviting Sebastian Tiris to speak.

Fallon narrowed his eyes as the lord king of Tor Funweir stepped on unsteady feet to the front of the raised platform. His eyes were wide and unfocused, leading Fallon to think that he had been drinking as well as not sleeping. A few knights made sniggering sounds or exchanged low murmurs of disapproval at the king's demeanour, but they were instantly singled out and ordered to remain silent by Mobius's clerics.

And then the king spoke. 'I will have order,' he began, in a quiet voice. 'I will have order and I will have obedience.' His words were slurred and Fallon frowned. Something was not right here. 'This land is mine by right,' he continued in the manner of a petulant youth rather than a middle-aged monarch. 'Our beloved allies have shown us the way . . . yes, yes, they have . . .' His eyes were wider now and a look of mania had appeared on his face. 'We will sack South Warden, we will bombard their city, burn their houses, kill their warriors and return these peasants and lesser men to their rightful place . . . as servants to the men of the One.' Again, the Purple clerics saluted and a murmured cheer was dragged from the knights of the Red.

'Brother Jakan of Tiris, step forward,' said the king, in a voice intended to be commanding.

'My king,' said the pompous Purple cleric, as he joined Cleoth on bended knee.

'Ten thousand men of the Darkwald yeomanry will arrive within days and I name you lord commander of their force.' Jakan's eyes widened in glee at his first command, and Mobius nodded with approval. 'You will form the vanguard of our advance, brother cleric.'

Fallon bit his lip at the pile of horse-shit he was witnessing. All around him he saw true fighting men with expressions ranging from confusion to anger. Whatever these men were, they were not simple, and to see an idiot like Jakan given command of so many men was distasteful to warriors of the One.

'Sir Fallon of Leith,' said the king in his cracked voice.

Fallon composed himself quickly and motioned his unit to follow. In formation, they rode across the cobbles towards the command platform and the eastern gate. 'My king,' said the knight captain.

'I unleash you as my first stroke in our war . . . ride now, my knight, ride for your king, for your God and for Tor Funweir.'

The Purple clerics banged their fists against their steel breastplates in a rhythmic accompaniment to the king's words. Fallon's salute was less than enthusiastic, but he saluted nonetheless.

'Sir Theron, we ride east,' he barked to his adjutant, before turning to see the eastern gates opened by bound men. He kicked the flanks of his horse and Knight Captain Fallon of Leith and his fifty knights of the Red rode in formation out of Ro Hail towards the realm of Scarlet.

* * *

Once out of sight of the ruined town, Fallon ordered his unit to slow down and within a few hours they were trotting leisurely across the featureless plains.

He had heard a certain amount of muttering among his men, mostly questioning the way the king had spoken or poking fun at Mobius and the other Purple clerics, but none of it was particularly insulting and Fallon decided to let it pass. Besides, he found himself agreeing with virtually every whispered word of dissent and a few of the comments even made him smile as he rode at the head of the column.

The main object of humour was the time the king had spent with the Fjorlanders, and what precisely they had done to him. Ohms joked that he'd been raped by a sweaty axe-man, while others suggested he'd been forced to bend the knee to Rowanoco. Fallon, however, was of the opinion that King Sebastian Tiris had been losing his mind well before his encounter with the men and women of the north. Also, he couldn't fully reconcile the honour the Fjorlanders had shown in releasing the king when they said they would, with the barbaric image he had been trained to associate with them. He didn't believe the same courtesy would have been shown if the army of Red knights had managed to capture a thain of theirs.

As the land began to look the same as far as the eye could see and the rain started to fall from the grey sky of Wraith, Theron of Haran rode to the front of the column and fell in beside his captain.

'Would you mind if we spoke for a time, sir?' he asked.

'What would you like to speak about?' Fallon himself found it infuriating when someone answered a question with a question, but he wasn't really in the mood to talk.

'When I was a boy in Ro Haran I heard a story about you

from General Alexander Tiris . . . I just wanted to know if it was true.' The young knight had a way of occasionally slipping into conversation the fact that he had served under Xander.

'What was the story?' asked the captain, prepared to humour his adjutant for the time being.

'You were called the Grey Knight for a time in Ro Arnon . . . is that true?' asked Theron.

Fallon smiled to himself. He'd not heard that story for a long time and had almost forgotten his old nickname. 'Yes, it's true. I've not been called that for a long time, though . . . I expect you want to know why?'

'The rumour was that you killed a Purple cleric and got away with it,' said the knight of Haran, unsure if he would cause offence.

'That's the general thrust of the encounter, yes, though, as with everything, there are nuances. It was a fair fight. I didn't jump him in an alley or anything.' Fallon dimly recalled the encounter. He could have been no more than eighteen at the time. 'Neither of us were where we were supposed to be, and neither of us was wearing armour or any mark of office. He didn't know who I was, and I didn't know who he was.'

Theron was leaning forward over the pommel of his saddle and listening intently. 'The general said you were one of the best swordsmen they had, even then.'

'That's maybe an exaggeration. I was good, but I knew it, and that made me cocky and arrogant. To be honest, I was lucky the Purple fucker didn't fillet me.' He raised an eyebrow at Theron, realizing that the young knight had asked him an interesting question for perhaps the first time since they had met.

'Did he challenge you?' asked the adjutant.

'No, nothing like that. He'd been in a brothel, I'd been in a tavern, and we bumped into each other – quite literally – in the street between the two buildings. He saw that I had a longsword, this one right here . . .' He patted the weapon at his side. 'And he was quite rude in his questioning of why I was wearing such a weapon.'

'Did he not wear a longsword?' pressed Theron, eager to hear more.

'He did, but I was a little drunk and didn't care,' replied Fallon. 'Well, not until he punched me. I don't think I answered his questions properly and he felt justified in striking me – quite hard – and so, when I stood up, I killed him.'

Theron gasped at the offhand way in which Fallon said this. His eyes widened as if he were about to hear the details of a long and heroic duel. 'Did he not fight back?' asked the young knight.

'Not really, I didn't give him a chance to. I suppose I expected him to draw his sword when I did. When he didn't, I thought I'd just stab him . . . as I said, I was a little drunk.'

'How did you get away with it?' pressed Theron.

'Well, that's where the Grey Knight thing came from. I was pulled up in front of Knight General Frith and a few Purple clerics, and they demanded that I be stripped of my Red armour. The general disagreed and said that I was wearing a grey cloak at the time and maybe I should be stripped of that.' Fallon smiled as he remembered the incident again. 'The general pulled my cloak off my back and threw it at the clerics and said: *There, he's a grey knight now and you have no authority over him*. I suppose the nickname stuck.'

'And what if you'd been wearing a pink cloak, sir,' asked Theron, displaying more of a sense of humour than Fallon had credited him with.

'I suppose I'd have been called the Pink Knight,' replied the captain, sharing the joke with his adjutant.

CHAPTER FIVE

HALLA SUMMER WOLF
IN HAMMERFALL

EACH TIME SHE rose from sleep and looked back along the rugged gullies, it seemed as if winter was chasing them. Halla and her company of Fjorlanders had slept for barely three hours and it was time to move on again. Rexel Falling Cloud, one of her captains, who hailed from the woods of Hammerfall, had insisted the weather would calm within days, but Halla remained sceptical.

They had no tents and for nearly a month now the two hundred battle-brothers and one axe-maiden had wrapped themselves in thick fur cloaks and huddled together in the snow. Several had muttered off-colour jokes about Halla being the only woman, but a few broken jaws had put a stop to that. Warmth was a rare commodity and Halla had slept close to Master Wulfrick for the last week. The huge axe-master of Fredericksand was the strongest, bravest and most honourable man she knew and having him as an ally made her believe they still had hope.

As the axe-maiden sat up and untangled herself, she felt the bitter wind strike her face. Her men were a line of black shapes, starkly outlined against the craggy white background. Her single eye burned for a second from the glare.

'Any regrets?' muttered Wulfrick, without opening his eyes.

She held up a frozen hand and replaced her eyepatch, scratching the deep scar as she did so. 'What am I suppose to regret? Are you still alive?' Halla said, without looking at the axe-master.

'I meant the king,' he growled under his breath, coughing slightly. 'We could have kept hold of him . . . or dropped him off a cliff.'

'I gave my word,' she replied with conviction, pulling her cloak tight around her shoulders. Seeing a clear blue expanse, with no sign of an imminent blizzard, she smiled.

'Halla,' barked Wulfrick, 'are you listening to me?'

'I said *I gave my word*. Did you want another answer?' Halla continued to smile and looked across at her men, most of whom were just beginning to rise from sleep. 'I won't miss the company of King Sebastian Tiris,' she yawned.

'I suppose it won't affect us too badly. I feel sorry for Wraith Company, though. Good men . . . good beer . . . no chance against those knights, though,' said Wulfrick as he sat up next to Halla.

They had seen Captain Horrock and the men of Wraith safely out of Ro Hail as they took the captive monarch north. As she promised, the king had been released in the low passes of the Deep Cross and they had seen an honour guard of Purple clerics pick him up. Since then, their path had been a difficult one as winter gripped the mountains. Luckily, they had now entered the lowlands and the ground was becoming more level by the day. Falling Cloud had insisted that they would sight a few settlements within a day or two, and Halla was looking forward to a bed and some hot water.

'Let's worry about Fjorlan right now,' said Wulfrick, mostly to himself. 'We have to find Alahan . . . if Rulag hasn't cut his head off yet.'

'He's a clever little bastard, from what I hear,' said Halla, remembering the few times she had met Algenon's son.

'Too clever for his own good. A bit more violent than his father, though,' elaborated the axe-master.

Halla saw her captains rise first and was gratified that they were happy to do the shouting for her. The axe-maiden disliked raising her voice unless it was absolutely necessary and she had established a quiet authority with her men over the last month, an authority build on intelligence and respect. She knew that her name, too, was a major factor. Her being a Summer Wolf, to whom Wulfrick deferred, had silenced most of the queries regarding her command, and the capture of the king at Ro Hail had answered any questions that remained.

Rexel Falling Cloud and Oleff Hard Head were invaluable to Halla as she tried to keep her men's spirits up. Oleff was the older of the two and had a curiously out of place ability with song. He was a grizzled man in his fifties who would break into song in a deep baritone at the slightest provocation, and his lengthy sagas of trolls slain and women bedded had been a constant background to the Fjorlanders' journey north. Falling Cloud was quieter, until angered, at which point he would erupt into a shout that demanded silence. Even Wulfrick and Halla were surprised whenever Rexel delivered a roaring reprimand to the men. Her third captain, a common man of Tiergarten called Heinrich Blood, had not stood out initially. However, as they travelled, he had revealed himself to be a novitiate of the Order of the Hammer and an aide to Father Brindon Crowe, a cunning old man of Tiergarten whom Halla knew well. Heinrich's gift was not shouting or singing, and Wulfrick had commented that he seemed slightly ill at ease in combat as well. Instead, what he offered the company was morale and an assurance that they were on a path laid down by the Ice Giant. His ability with the voice of Rowanoco was in its infancy, but he had managed to heal several wounds and stop several more from festering.

Between them, Rexel, Oleff and Heinrich had formed Halla's company into a well-drilled unit capable of moving swiftly and responding to a threat with brutal efficiency.

'*The dragons of Ranen were mighty and brave*,' sang Oleff, as a way of rousing the remaining men. '*Through ice storms and battles, fair maidens they'd save*.' His voice rose in volume until most men were either up or yawning themselves awake. '*With teeth and with claw the trolls they did smite*,' he continued. '*But when they met Oleff with fear they did shite*.' He elongated the last note and held it for a moment as the assembled men laughed.

'True story,' he whispered to Halla with a wink. 'Right,' he roared at the men, 'that's as much laughter as you lot are allowed today. Get up and get moving.'

The laughter died down quickly as Rexel took up the shouting and moved among the men, kicking them awake and querying the condition of axes, hammers and armour. Each man was responsible for keeping his equipment sharp, clean and well maintained, and Rexel took this duty very seriously indeed, chiding any man who neglected his weaponry.

'You can't kill a man with a dull axe, you useless troll cunt,' he roared at a sleepy-looking man of Tiergarten.

'Young Falling Cloud seems to have been blessed with the voice of the Ice Giants,' said Wulfrick, as he stood up and stretched his enormous frame. 'He scares the shit out of me with that roar of his.'

Halla looked to the sky again. 'Looks like we may stay dry . . . for today at least. And hopefully a warm bed isn't too far over the horizon.' If Falling Cloud's estimate of their location was accurate, she thought they should sight habitable land within a few hours.

The Deep Cross marked the traditional boundary between Fjorlan and the southern lands of the Free Companies, though the snowy plateaus of Hammerfall and Ursa were almost as rugged as the high mountain passes. The battle-brothers of Fjorlan were a maritime people, preferring to travel by sea or river, but their encounter in the Kraken Sea had robbed Halla's company of ships and men, rendering their journey a long and dangerous one across difficult land.

'Rexel,' Halla shouted through the press of bodies, 'when you're done, get your arse over here.'

The man of Hammerfall turned from his morning tasks and strode through the men to approach where Halla and Wulfrick stood. 'Morning,' he said cheerfully. 'Nice day for it.'

'Better than yesterday,' replied Wulfrick, as he retrieved his troll-hide armour and began to strap it on. 'Now, where the fuck are we, Falling Cloud?'

Halla raised an eyebrow at the axe-master and interjected, 'I'd settle for a rough direction of travel.'

Falling Cloud grinned at Wulfrick. 'She's a much better commander than you, big man . . . and that armour stinks.'

'And you're ugly, Rexel,' responded the axe-master.

'You can both shut up.' Halla's tone was sharp and she held her hand up to emphasize that she was serious. 'We can't keep trudging north. We need to have some idea of where we're going,' she went on more conversationally. 'And before you say anything, Master Wulfrick, I know we need to find Alahan Teardrop, but we're a long way from Fredericksand.'

Falling Cloud nodded and, shielding his eyes from the glare, peered north along the snow-covered gullies. 'The edge of the Wolf Wood can't be more than a few hours away and there are villages around there. We'll at least be able to get our bearings.'

Rexel knew Hammerfall better than any of Halla's company and had acted as their guide since they entered the low lands. His estimates had not always been accurate and they had stumbled into more than one encounter with trapdoor Gorlan, the large, unpleasant ice-spiders that were almost impossible to detect, but delicious to eat.

'Are we going to meet any trolls or spiders in these gullies?' asked Halla.

Falling Cloud considered the question, screwing up his bearded face. 'I'd say *no*, but I've been wrong before . . . the damn beasties don't stay still, you see.'

'To be absolutely fair,' said Wulfrick, 'if Rexel's directions had been any better, we wouldn't have so much salted Gorlan meat in our packs.'

Though he was joking, the point was a fair one. Supplies had been getting thin until they had begun to snare the ice-spiders and preserve them. The meat was tough and stringy, but surprisingly tasty after being cooked for several hours. Added to the roots and grain they had taken from Wraith Company, Halla's company had not had to starve during their tough march. With hunger defeated, they had only the cold to dampen their spirits, but these men were used to the cold.

'If you weren't so funny, Wulfrick, you'd be fucking useless,' replied Falling Cloud with a grin on his face.

'Yeah, yeah, just no more surprise Gorlan, okay?' said the axe-master of Fredericksand. 'Though I suppose Heinrich needs the practice with that bow of his.'

'Wulfrick, you're making me weary,' said Halla. 'Please shut up.'

* * *

The men were roused quickly and, after sharing a hastily assembled breakfast, they began to make their way further north. The journey was slow and the company was in relaxed mood now that the terrain was level and the sky clear.

From the north, where the eastern edge of the Wolf Wood met the plateaus of Ursa, Halla could see smoke. It was not the smoke of chimney or hearth but the slowly rolling smog of destruction. It rose in several black plumes and the acrid smell carried across the tundra. She raised her hand and signalled the company to stop, followed by a cacophony of shouts from Oleff as he relayed the order.

'What is it?' asked Wulfrick.

'Smoke,' was the axe-maiden's simple response.

The axe-master moved up to join her and peered north towards the smoke. Soon Falling Cloud had joined them, leaving Heinrich and Oleff to quiet the company of Fjorlanders.

'Rexel, what does that look like to you?' she asked the man of Hammerfall.

'That's no simple cook-fire,' he replied with concern. 'Looks like one of the villages of the Vale to me – farmers that serve the lords of Hammerfall.'

Falling Cloud's thain and many cloud-men of Hammerfall had died in the Kraken Sea, and as one of the few remaining lords he was now responsible for most of the common people of the area.

Wulfrick gripped the hilt of his battleaxe. 'Farmers? Not battle-brothers?'

Rexel shook his head. 'A lot of the toughest cloud-men were with the dragon fleet. Maybe there are a few left in the halls of the Wolf Wood, but that's a long way west of here.'

Halla stepped to the front and considered the possibilities. Behind her, Falling Cloud and Wulfrick considered the dishonour in burning the homes of common men and exchanged oaths of vengeance. She tried to tune out their swearing as she peered northwards to assess the situation. The nearest large town was Jarvik, the seat of Rulag the Betrayer, but that was a good way north and it was unlikely that the men of Ursa would come this far south just to burn a farm. Bandits were another possibility, but the cloud-men of the Vale had little of value.

'Rexel,' she ordered, silencing the two men behind her, 'take twenty men and see what's causing those fires.'

'My lady?' he queried.

'Did you misunderstand, Master Falling Cloud? Are you or are you not an axe-master of Hammerfall?'

'And proud to be so.' He stood taller and thrust his chest out. 'It will be as you say, Halla.'

Rexel turned sharply and pointed to the nearest squad of men, standing idly in the snow. 'You useless bastards have just volunteered to come with me. Light arms and armour, leave everything else with the column.'

They didn't hesitate before beginning to remove their chain mail and throwing their travelling packs on the floor. The men unslung their axes and moved into rough formation behind Falling Cloud.

'Right, there's smoke over there and Lady Summer Wolf wants to know what's causing it.' He paused and let silence return for a moment before roaring, 'With me,' at the top of his voice.

Halla and Wulfrick both jumped at the ferocity of the axe-master's shout, before exchanging a smile. As Rexel and his men broke into a dead run and moved swiftly towards the edge of the wood, Wulfrick asked, 'What do you think, Halla . . . bandits?'

She shook her head. 'Unlikely,' she said, still focusing on the north. 'Get the men ready. I have a bad feeling.'

Wulfrick stepped forward and she felt the wind drop as his enormous frame acted as a windbreak. 'I've had a bad feeling since Algenon died,' he responded. 'And I imagine I'll continue to have one until I find Alahan.'

'I gave you an order, Master Wulfrick.' Halla didn't yet feel totally comfortable giving orders to the fearsome axe-master of Fredericksand, but she tried to disguise her unease whenever she had to appear commanding.

'Yes, you did,' he said with a smile. 'You know, you're getting quite good at this, one-eye.'

She glared at him. 'I've castrated men for calling me that . . . and Rexel's right, that armour stinks.'

'So do I . . . we belong together.' His smile was now very broad.

'Wulfrick,' she said, in a disapproving tone of voice.

'I know, I know – get the men ready.'

He strode back a few ranks until he was standing within the company of Fjorlanders. Oleff Hard Head came to join him and a few words were exchanged between the two before Halla's orders were carried out. Almost in unison, the company began to heft axes and hammers and to fan out across the snowy ground. They had emerged from the rocky gullies a few hours previously and the ground was now level enough for them to form up properly. Oleff, Wulfrick and Heinrich Blood emerged through the line of battle-brothers and took their places next to Halla.

'What needs killin'?' asked Oleff, with a violent look in his eye.

'Not sure yet,' replied Halla. 'Let's hope, nothing.'

She turned to Heinrich. The young novice of Rowanoco was holding a fur-wrapped short bow and, at Wulfrick's urging, had stopped attempting to use his axe. 'Will you stand, Master Blood?' she asked.

'At your shoulder every step of the way, my lady,' he replied. The words were spoken with conviction, though the young man's hands shook as he nocked an arrow to his bowstring. 'Though

I wish old Father Crowe were here.'

Wulfrick snorted with amusement. 'Brindon would already be running at whatever's up there, swinging his hammer and frothing at the mouth.' A low murmur of amusement rippled through the men, most of whom either knew Brindon Crowe or had at least heard of the old priest of Tiergarten's fearsome reputation.

'Let's concentrate on those men who *are* here,' said Halla, silencing her men. 'If we make it to Tiergarten, you can all tell Crowe how much you missed him. Until then, keep your mouths shut.'

They waited. Halla looked along the line of men – two hundred armed battle-brothers, each looking meaner and angrier than the next. Word of the situation had spread quickly and the few cloud-men of Hammerfall in the company were vibrating with anger at the plumes of smoke rising from the Vale. The rest stood with weapons drawn, waiting for the order to advance or for Falling Cloud to return with news. Rexel and his twenty men were now out of sight and had entered the tree line of the Wolf Wood.

'Death comes to us all,' muttered Heinrich, largely to himself. 'But we need not fear. Rowanoco the Earth Shaker sits in his hall beyond the world to welcome his fallen warriors. We will drink with the Ice Giants before we feel fear.'

Halla and Wulfrick both looked at him and nodded with respect. 'We will drink with the Ice Giants before we feel fear,' they repeated together.

Then a sound reached the axe-maiden's ears. It was distinctive and left little room for doubt. She heard a blade shearing steel, immediately followed by a death rattle, the unpleasant gurgle that signified the end of whoever had been struck. It was a distant sound, but it was all Halla needed.

'Forward!' she roared.

The company of Fjorlanders erupted into a sprint and, with Halla and her captains at the front, they approached the burning village. She kept her eye open and her wits about her, ready to assess the situation as it developed. As they reached the tree line, the source of the smoke became all too apparent and her men gasped. Strung up against hastily erected pyres were the charred remains of several hundred men, women and children. Around them, the buildings of their village had been all but destroyed, with the flickering remains of wood and thatch showing how recently the attack had taken place. No cattle or crops could be seen, leading Halla to think that whoever had assaulted the village had done so in order to take supplies. A clatter of armour came from nearby, but the sight of the burning Ranen pushed other thoughts from her mind.

'The banner of Ursa,' growled Wulfrick, pointing to a pennant hanging over the largest pyre.

Halla blinked and focused beyond the fires to take in the thick fabric banner. The heraldry consisted of a bear's claw on a red background and indicated who had been behind the attack. Why the battle-brothers of Jarvik should have assaulted a village so far from their home was a mystery to Halla but, before she could puzzle it out in any detail, she saw Falling Cloud and his men. Several were already dead and the remainder were retreating quickly across the snowy ground. Behind them charged a sizeable force of Fjorlanders, wearing the same bear's claw heraldry on their tabards.

'Rexel,' roared Wulfrick. 'No need to run.'

Falling Cloud grinned at the presence of his friends and held up a hand to signal his men to stop retreating. The battle-brothers of Jarvik numbered around a hundred warriors and showed no signs of backing down at the sight of Halla's company. A quick look at her men told the axe-maiden that they were equally prepared to fight.

'This is the land of the high thain,' shouted a man of Jarvik, 'and we claim it in the name of Lord Rulag Ursa, Bear Tamer of Fjorlan and killer of Algenon Teardrop.' The man's voice carried far.

Wulfrick, whose massive stride had taken him to the front of the company, began to roar unintelligible sounds of anger and foam appeared at the corners of his mouth. The axe-master had been Algenon's friend and his closest ally, and he had not yet forgiven himself for letting his thain die. Halla sped up alongside him and saw an unknowable, depthless rage in his eyes.

Then came a colossal roar as the battle frenzy of Rowanoco entered the axe-master. The ground seemed to shake as the rest of her men joined in, roaring and sending a shiver of pride down Halla's spine.

'You die for that,' shouted Oleff.

'And for the betrayal of your master,' offered Heinrich in as loud a voice as Halla had ever heard from the young novice.

'We fight for Fjorlan.' The last words were roared by Halla just before the two forces clashed.

The battle-brothers of Jarvik were outnumbered and out-matched, though their ferocity showed they were no mere raiding party. Many carried glaives, long-handled weapons with serrated axe blades, the signature weapon of Jarvik.

Halla's first axe blow severed a man's arm, her second opened another's stomach and her third cleaved in a skull. Wulfrick quickly moved beyond her until he was amidst the press of enemies, swinging his two-handed axe from high above his head, killing men as if they were unarmed children. Soon, a wide channel of snow had turned red as Halla's company cut through the battle-brothers of Rulag the Betrayer.

Falling Cloud was quick and deadly with his two hand-axes, using speed rather than strength to deflect blows and cripple enemies. The axe-master of Hammerfall severed more legs and arms than heads, and a trail of maimed bodies lay behind him. Oleff Hard Head, the old chain-master of Fredericksand, was more brutal but no less effective as he employed head and elbows along with his axe. Heinrich Blood stood a little way past the others, killing men from a distance with his short bow. The novice of Rowanoco was becoming a good bowman.

Oaths were shouted from both sides – swearing and guttural growls of challenge and vengeance, but the outcome was not in doubt. Halla spared a glance to her side to take in the efficiency of her company as the men unleashed weeks of pent-up aggression. Their last serious fight had been against the Purple clerics and king's guardsmen outside Ro Hail, and these men of Jarvik were easy foes in comparison.

Then they broke. The battle-brothers of Ursa, fearsome and violent though they were, began to realize there was little but death awaiting them should they continue to fight. A few at first, then more, until the remaining men of Rulag the Betrayer turned and attempted to flee.

'Don't run,' growled Oleff, 'we wanna be friends.' He punctuated the last word by burying his axe in the skull of one of the fleeing men.

Wulfrick showed no sign of stopping the fight and used his lengthy stride to run down the nearest retreating foes. Other members of Halla's company roared their victory to the skies as they mopped up the remaining warriors who had not escaped.

When the sounds of battle had ceased, it turned out that fewer than a dozen had got away, and they were being pursued by the frenzied figure of Wulfrick.

'Let him go,' Halla said calmly to Heinrich who was following the huge axe-master. 'He'll burn himself out of his rage soon enough. In the meantime it'll do him good to release some anger.'

Panting and bloodied men stood all around her and she was gratified to see that fewer than ten of her company had died. Falling Cloud had a nasty cut down his cheek and several others carried superficial wounds, but their victory had been an overwhelming one.

'Oleff,' she shouted, 'get over here.'

The old chain-master was sweating heavily and picking chunks of enemies' flesh from his matted beard. 'Good bit of afternoon exercise, Halla,' he said cheerfully. 'Almost made me forget about that.' He pointed to the smouldering corpses of the villagers.

'Round up any prisoners. I want a little chat with our brethren from the plateaus of Ursa,' she said through gritted teeth. 'Let's find out why they chose to slaughter women and children.'

Oleff screwed up his face into a look of mischievous relish and nodded. 'At once, my lady.'

'For Teardrop!' Falling Cloud roared in victory. 'And Summer Wolf.'

Rexel was using his voice to good effect, keeping up the men's morale as they looked at the bodies both of their own fallen allies and the treacherous battle-brothers of Jarvik. Whatever else those men might have been, they were still Ranen, and that gave the conflict a bitter aftertaste.

When Rexel had finished shouting calls of victory and honour he returned to stand by Halla, leaving the rest of the company to kill the wounded who couldn't survive and to assemble the supplies that could be salvaged from the dead.

'I wasn't aware you held such goodwill towards my house, Rexel,' Halla said, querying his use of her family's name.

'Like it or not, my Lady Summer Wolf, this is your company. You've pledged for Alahan and the house of Teardrop, yes?' It had never been explicitly stated.

'I've pledged for Fjorlan,' she stated proudly, 'and will not accept Rulag the Betrayer.'

Falling Cloud nodded. 'That's close enough . . . until we find Alahan. Then you might find you need to offer a more definite oath of support.'

He was probably right. She had met Alahan Teardrop a few times and he had never struck her as the kind of man to accept half-hearted support. However, try as she might, Halla could not forget that Algenon Teardrop had killed her father.

She turned back to the man of Hammerfall. 'Rexel, get those bodies taken down and have Heinrich check the buildings for survivors.'

He nodded with a thin smile and went about his duties, leaving Halla Summer Wolf, axe-maiden of Rowanoco and heir to the hall of Tiergarten, to ponder her situation.

Her company did not pause to rest and she inferred they were deliberately occupying themselves in order not to have to think about the killing of Ranen by Ranen. The stakes to which the common folk of Hammerfall had been tied were disassembled, the dead collected together, and the few surviving battle-brothers of Jarvik tied up and closely guarded. They had eight prisoners in various states of injury, from missing limbs to light bruises, and Halla kept them waiting under the watchful eye of Oleff Hard Head before she deigned to interrogate them.

Wulfrick returned quickly, a look of exhausted confusion on his face as he came out of his battle rage. He carried several dead men with him, dragging them casually behind him as he trudged back to join the rest of the company. His eyes still showed his anger at the situation in Fjorlan, the death of Algenon, the loss of the dragon fleet, and the treachery of Rulag Ursa.

'Halla,' barked Oleff from where he guarded the prisoners. 'The hairless cunt on the end wants a word. He's an axe-master of Ursa apparently.'

She peered across to where the man sat. He was completely bald, with no hair or beard, and his appearance stood out among so many hairy-faced Fjorlanders. Halla glared at him for a moment, before striding deliberately across the shell of a village.

'Speak,' she said plainly.

'I speak to men, one-eye. Who is commander of this company?' The man of Ursa had a number of minor wounds but was otherwise unhurt. He had requested to speak with whoever was in command and was taken aback now by the presence of a woman.

Without waiting for an order, Oleff smashed the hilt of his axe into the speaker's face, breaking his nose and sending him sprawling to the ground. 'She is Halla Summer Wolf, you treacherous bastard.'

'Thank you, Oleff Hard Head,' she said with a smile. 'Now, I'll say it again . . . speak.'

The axe-master of Ursa did his best to straighten himself, but the pain of his newly broken nose made him look up through watering eyes and he did not attempt to stand.

'The Bear Tamer of Fjorlan, High Thain Rulag Ursa, has claimed these lands. By what authority do you kill his men?' He spat out the words and Halla could see he was a fanatically loyal follower of the Betrayer.

'Your master is a traitor to Fjorlan, to Rowanoco and to the houses of Teardrop and Summer Wolf. That is all the authority we need.' She glared down at him.

'What's waiting for us at the Bear's Mouth?' asked Oleff with a lighter blow from his axe's hilt to emphasize the question.

The Bear's Mouth was a fork in the river that marked the southern border of Jarvik. It was a naturally defensible position in a narrow gully which was almost impossible to bypass.

The man of Ursa grinned, showing bloody gums and missing teeth. 'Grammah Black Eyes awaits you,' he stated with confidence, 'the new thain of Hammerfall.'

Halla was glad that Falling Cloud was out of earshot as she had no doubt he would take exception to Rulag appointing a new thain for the realm of Rexel's birth. 'Rulag too busy to bring his law personally?' she asked.

'The Lord Bear Tamer sits in the high thain's hall in Fredericksand, one-eye. His son hunts down the son of Teardrop and he leaves the lands of Ursa and Hammerfall to the governance of loyal men.'

Halla and Oleff exchanged a look. 'He's been as useful as he's going to be, I would guess,' she said.

Oleff grinned and, without hesitation, buried his axe in the man's head, killing the axe-master of Ursa instantly and sending a spray of blood across the ground. The other captives winced at the sudden display of violence and looked at Halla and her captain with terror in their eyes.

'I can put up with one insult,' she said in a commanding voice, 'but two gets you killed.' Halla made sure that all of the prisoners had heard her, before continuing. 'This streak of troll piss tells me that your lord is in Fredericksand. He tells me that the Betrayer has claimed the realms of Teardrop, Ursa and Hammerfall.' She was shouting now, letting her voice carry to her own men as well as the prisoners. 'I am Halla Summer Wolf, heir to the hall of Tiergarten, and I say that Rulag Ursa is a murderer, a coward and I name him Betrayer.' She growled the last word. 'The realm of Summer Wolf does not recognize this new high thain and we will die before we put down our axes and bend the knee to Rulag.' Her last words were directed at her own men and she received a cheer of approval for her bluster. Wulfrick had a look of determination on his face as he listened to the axe-maiden. Halla spat on the ground in front of her to seal her oath and turned sharply away from the remaining prisoners and the pool of blood spreading from the dead man.

'Strong words,' said Wulfrick respectfully, as she approached. 'Your father had a silver tongue as well.' The warrior was bloodied and his skin pale and clammy. Halla surmised that he was hanging on to hope by the thinnest of threads. 'You know what loyalty is, Halla?' he asked quietly.

'What is loyalty, Master Wulfrick?'

'Fighting for the son of the man who killed your father . . .' he paused, 'because you know it's the right thing to do.'

Halla was not yet fully reconciled to where her loyalties lay. She would oppose Rulag with her last breath – having seen his treachery first hand in the faces of a thousand drowned men of the dragon fleet – but she knew that Algenon had killed her father for no other reason than to secure the rescue of his brother, Magnus, from Ro Canarn. If Algenon or his son were worthy of her loyalty, they would have to prove it, and one of them had died without doing so.

'I fight for Fjorlan, Wulfrick, as I hope you do. That's where our loyalties lie and that's why we'll carry on fighting.' Deception was not in her nature and, of all her captains, the axe-master of Fredericksand was the one she needed most. She would not lie to him or pretend that she would readily swear service to Alahan Teardrop – but luckily they were a long way from having to decide.

'That's fair,' said Wulfrick. 'But I swore loyalty to the house of Teardrop and I am Alahan's man until my last breath.'

Halla nodded as she saw how deeply the words were meant. She knew that his father had turned against Ragnar Teardrop and had lost his family name as punishment. Lars the Enraged's son, Wulfrick, had been allowed to remain alive provided he swore a lifetime's service to the family of Teardrop. Oaths of this kind meant everything to the battle-brothers of Fjorlan, and Wulfrick's commitment had led him to become axe-master of Fredericksand and friend to the late high thain.

She tried to smile. 'Those also are strong words, but we need to keep these men alive a while longer. At least we know Alahan's still alive. If he escaped Fredericksand and can get to Tiergarten . . .'

'He's still alive,' interrupted Wulfrick. 'Yes, that seems to be quite good news.' The huge warrior closed his eyes and for a moment Halla thought she saw a tear. They remained silent as the men around them cleared away bodies and put out fires.

Halla had to form a plan. As they were travelling north from the south lands and through the Deep Cross, her mind had been kept busy with simple questions of survival and morale. Now that they had reached the woods of Hammerfall and were in Fjorlan proper, she needed to consider other things. If they continued northwards, they would have to pass the Bear's Mouth and the new thain – this man called Grammah Black Eyes – before they would reach Jarvik, the seat of Rulag Ursa. That the Betrayer was not there made it more of an attractive destination, as did the likely presence of a cloud-stone, but the city of Ursa would still be hostile to Halla and her company. If they travelled westwards to her own home of Tiergarten, they would have several months of difficult travelling through woods infested with trolls and Gorlan, and there was no guarantee that Alahan would still be alive when they got there. It was a difficult choice.

'Halla,' growled Falling Cloud from nearby, 'there's a new thain of Hammerfall, apparently.'

'Yes, I had heard,' she replied, still deep in thought.

'One of those bastards said he's rounded up any axe-master that wasn't with the dragon fleet and cut his hands off.' Rexel was angry, and Halla secretly wished that she could get away and take an hour or two of quiet to think things over.

'What the fuck are we going to do about this?' he barked, rather more disrespectfully than he had intended.

'Rexel,' interjected Wulfrick, 'remember who you're talking to and what she's done for us.'

'It's okay,' said Halla. 'Anger is not bad . . . especially when it's warranted.' Rexel Falling Cloud breathed in deeply and composed himself before he spoke again. 'Sorry . . . I am true to you all, you know I am, but this is Hammerfall. I was born here, I grew up here and, if I'd stayed here, I'd have had my fucking hands cut off.'

Most of the rest of the company were close enough to hear Rexel and Halla saw agreement in many of their faces. She was not unsympathetic, but they were a mere two hundred men and passing the Bear's Mouth seemed foolhardy. However, the alternative was no better and so she decided to harness their passion and force a way northwards. There was always the chance of finding more survivors of the dragon fleet along the estuaries of Hammerfall and, though they were few in number, the axe-maiden knew that her company was fearsome indeed.

She stepped closer to Falling Cloud. 'Our road goes north. We make for the Bear's Mouth.'

He nodded and a smile came across his grizzled face. 'Very well, Lady Summer Wolf, we'll finish checking the village and move out in an hour . . . with your word.'

'My word is given, Master Falling Cloud,' she responded with authority.

Rexel backed off a few steps and turned to the rest of the company, issuing the order to check the remaining buildings and assemble the dead.

Wulfrick stepped behind Halla's shoulder and spoke quietly. 'You should have slapped him.'

'He's bigger than me,' she responded with a smile. 'And I agree with him.'

Wulfrick frowned. 'Most of Ursa's men won't be at Jarvik, but the Bear's Mouth will be impossible to pass. We have two hundred battle-brothers. We're tough, but we are not that tough.'

'There's a cloud-stone in Jarvik, yes?' Halla posited. 'Old Father Crowe has one in Oreck's Spire in Tiergarten. We need to know if Alahan is alive and it's the quickest way.'

The axe-master's frown increased and he moved round to face Halla. 'Clever,' he said. 'Stupid, but clever.'

'Shut up,' Halla responded with irritation. 'It makes sense. It would take months to reach Tiergarten, but we can be in Jarvik within three weeks if we move quickly.'

'And the Bear's Mouth?'

'Grammah Black Eyes will see if he is worthy to be thain of Hammerfall.' It was spoken with aggression and Wulfrick responded by narrowing his eyes and gritting his teeth.

'Strong words again, one-eye,' he said.

Halla had been called the name a thousand times since she first lost her eye and every time she heard it she wanted to punch the speaker. On this occasion, she decided to let it pass. 'Go and help Falling Cloud,' she answered drily.

* * *

The weather stayed fair as funeral pyres were built and the common folk of Hammerfall were laid to rest in traditional Ranen fashion. Heinrich Blood had his chance to shine and the young novice of the Order of the Hammer did not disgrace his god or his company as he spoke the words for the fallen. He had a small token, given to him by Brindon Crowe – a hammer pendant, finely honed out of the deep ice of Fjorlan. The young man clutched it tightly as he spoke of the ice halls beyond the world where the dead would go.

Rexel cried, but he was not embarrassed. Oleff stood next to him, glaring at anyone who might think of making an insulting remark. Halla's company had several men of Hammerfall and each took the death of his people extremely hard. The realm had no city and had always been in the shadow of Teardrop, Ursa and Summer Wolf, although its people were extremely proud to hail from Hammerfall. Falling Cloud seemed to exemplify the stubborn spirit of these Fjorlanders, which made them shake with emotion at the funeral pyres.

'The Bear's Mouth is our death,' said Heinrich, letting his voice rise, 'we give our lives to Rowanoco if he gives us vengeance in return. If two hundred honourable men . . .' he looked at Halla, 'and women of Fjorlan have a place in the ice halls beyond the world . . .' The company was as one, looking at the novice with wild eyes and rapt attention. 'Then let us die with our enemies' blood on our faces and their hearts in our hands.' A low growling cheer began to form. 'I pledge to you all that death is our right and we will take it . . . we will rip it from the limbs of any man foolish enough to face us.' Heinrich's voice grew louder with the accompaniment of two hundred warriors snarling into the air. Halla felt her breathing quicken. 'We are the chosen of the Ice Giants. We are the instruments of death for those betrayers . . . and we will . . . not . . . fear . . .' The last words came out at the top of Heinrich's voice and he spat with the emotion he experienced at delivering the words of the Order of the Hammer. The company roared their agreement and the sound carried far in the cold air of Hammerfall, hanging for a moment over the funeral pyres, as each man pledged his death in the fight against Rulag the Betrayer.

PART TWO

CHAPTER SIX

ALAHAN TEARDROP ALGESSON
IN THE REALM OF TEARDROP

H E KICKED OPEN the door and strode inside, drawing a
light hand-axe as he did so. He always carried two small
throwing weapons on his belt and a large double-headed
axe across his back. He hoped that the larger of the weapons
would not be necessary within the hunting lodge. The weather
outside had become progressively more hostile, and Alahan had
decided to find some respite from the snow. If he were to die, it
would not be the weather that put him down. He was the bearer
of his father's name and his strength of body and mind was equal
to any task, but he was pragmatic enough not to challenge the
driving snow to a duel.

The lodge looked deserted and he replaced the axe. The young
warrior threw back his thick hood and shook the snow from
his cloak, feeling better as the warmth returned to his body. He
was shorter than his father, at just over six feet tall, though his
shoulders were large and well muscled. He had inherited the jet-
black hair of his family and wore his beard long and braided in
silent tribute to his uncle, Magnus Forkbeard, priest of Rowanoco,
killed in Ro Canarn.

At twenty-six, Alahan was the youngest high thain of Fjorlan
ever to sit in the halls of Fredericksand. But, as he moved further
into the small hunting lodge, he was painfully aware that he had
not yet sat in the halls of Fredericksand, having been attacked on
the day he learned of his father's death. The treacherous lord of

Jarvik had betrayed Algenon Teardrop and his battle-brothers swept through Alahan's home, killing any Ranen still loyal to the house of Teardrop. The traitor's idiot son, the lordling Kalag, had been sent after the children of Teardrop and his men had closed in on Alahan, despite the snow. They had already captured his sister, Ingrid, though even now the little wolf of Fredericksand was likely conspiring a way to escape from their clutches and find her brother.

Watching Ingrid taken away in a dirty net and knowing he was helpless to assist her had been the hardest thing Alahan had ever had to endure, but he knew that he had to stay alive. If Rulag dared harm Ingrid, he would never keep the Order of the Hammer on his side. The priests of Rowanoco would not intercede if Rulag declared himself high thain after killing Algenon, but the lore masters of Fredericksand forbade the killing of children.

He puffed out his cheeks and was planning to get some rest when he heard a sound from further within the lodge. His hand went quickly to his battleaxe and he darted forward, crouching in readiness. The noise was a rhythmic shuffling from the next room – a room that was dark and, when Alahan entered, had seemed empty. Now he saw a shadow cast on the wall as he advanced into the room.

The man he saw was hunched over a low wooden table, scuffing his feet firmly against the floor and grunting in the manner of a wild bear. Alahan stopped when the man didn't turn to attack him. The stranger was a brute of a man and wore no armour on his torso, where vein-filled and swollen muscles strained against his mottled skin.

The hunting lodge provided protection against the worst of the storm, but it was still cold and Alahan wondered why the man had so readily discarded his wolf-skin cloak. There was no indication that the young thain of Fredericksand had been observed, and the stranger seemed distracted by whatever was causing him to tense his body and grunt with exertion.

'A cold night,' Alahan said quietly.

The stranger growled, sounding even more like a bear, and spun round to reveal a bare, tattooed chest and a ferocious face. Alahan did not step back, in spite of the man's grotesque, misshapen head and his vibrant blue tattoos.

'There's no fight here for you, berserker of Varorg,' Alahan stated.

For a moment the man stood, glaring at Alahan as a beast would glare at its prey. His eyes showed that he was fighting the urge to roar out and attack the young thain, but his padded and clenched fists made it clear that the berserk rage was unwelcome to him.

'You're a long way from the Low Kast,' Alahan offered, in as even a voice as he could muster. 'Why is a berserker of Varorg in the realm of Teardrop?'

The man closed his eyes and bared his teeth, each of which had been filed to a sharp point. Breathing heavily, he exerted a considerable effort to maintain control. 'Not . . . of Varorg . . .' he spluttered out. 'Not . . . any more.'

He turned away from Alahan and sat down heavily on the floor with his back to the young thain. It was a pose struck by a hundred stroppy children every day, but it looked strange when adopted by a monstrous berserker of the Low Kast. His arms were crossed and he huddled forward, rocking slowly and muttering unintelligible sounds to himself.

'I'd offer to come back later,' said Alahan, 'but it is cold outside and I'm being pursued.'

The berserker didn't respond. The frozen wastes of the Low Kast were home to the chieftains of Varorg and their ferocious berserker tribes, men who followed no banner and answered to no priest. To see one of their number so far west was strange, to see him huddled up like a petulant child was stranger still.

'Conversation is, by all accounts, not counted amongst your people's skills,' said Alahan, 'but I am stuck here until the storm lets up, so don't be offended if I keep trying to talk to you.'

He sat down wearily on a rickety wooden chair and surveyed his surroundings. The hunting lodge had clearly been home to the berserker for some time. Several sacks of dried meat and fruit were stored in the corner and a rudimentary bed had been set up next to the empty fireplace. Alahan had lost his bearings in the snow and wasn't sure exactly where in his realm he had ended up. East of Fredericksand was the best he could come up with, but to find such a man living here made him think he must have strayed off the trail in the storm and stumbled across a long-forgotten lodge. The berserker had a single lantern to provide illumination, but otherwise the lodge was dark and it was unlikely it would be seen unless a traveller should happen across it as Alahan had done. This seemed a welcome development because it made it less likely that the lordling Kalag would be able to locate him, at least until the storm abated.

'Do you have any firewood for that?' he asked the berserker, pointing to the empty hearth.

The man remained hunched up with his back to Alahan and simply pointed to a pile of broken furniture in a basket.

'Well, if you don't mind, I'll get a bit of heat back into the place.' Alahan stood up and threw an armful of splintered wood into the open hearth. He then took a flame from the low-burning lantern and slowly coaxed a fire into life.

He was worried that the smoke might be seen, but weighing up the advantages of the warmth against the remote possibility of a thin plume of smoke being spotted through the driving snow, he thought he could risk it. He was exhausted and shifted his weight uncomfortably in the chair, before moving it out of the way and slumping down on the floor instead.

Alahan blinked several times, trying to stay awake. The berserkers of Varorg were unpredictable and he did not want to fall asleep until he had got at least a few sentences out of the man.

'Name is Timon . . . I'm called the Butcher.' The words came out of the berserker's mouth as a hesitant growl.

Alahan wondered if the man had been reading his mind, or whether he was simply aware of the effect his people had on the other men of Ranen. 'Pleased to make your acquaintance, Timon.

I'm Alahan Teardrop. This is my land . . . well, Rowanoco willing, it will be my land some day soon.'

Timon the Butcher rolled around on the floor at the mention of the Ice Giant. 'I'm sorry, Varorg. I am weak,' he wailed.

His head was more readily visible now and Alahan could see his skull through wide splits in the skin. Bumps arose at odd angles and the man had wrapped leather strips around his forehead to stop his head becoming too misshapen. The young thain had never met any of the servants of Varorg before and the descriptions he had heard clearly did not do them justice. Even curled up and crying, the berserker was a beast of a man.

'I'm sure the Ice Giant will forgive you. I don't think he's that easy to annoy.'

Alahan had heard the legends of Varorg. His uncle had spoken of Rowanoco's first appearance to the men of Ranen. The story told how an enraged Ice Giant had appeared in the Low Kast and how, in his guttural growling as the rage took him, the primitive men of Ranen had discerned the sound *varorg*. Magnus used to say that Rowanoco later regretted his first appearance and kept his rage in check. However, the truth remained that the berserkers of the Low Kast were the oldest followers of Rowanoco, whether they called him Varorg or not.

Timon had stopped wailing and sat up in a cross-legged position. He hunched forward and looked at Alahan, before mumbling out some words. 'You are thain?' he asked, spitting less than before.

'I am . . . though my hall is currently in the hands of a traitor,' responded Alahan, starting to remove his weapons and to make himself as comfortable as he could.

'Not looking for me?' Timon's face was expressive and he seemed relieved.

'No,' Alahan shook his head. 'I think I may have stumbled upon your lodge. I'm a wanted man in my own lands, it would seem.' He extended his arms and rubbed his hands together in front of the fire.

113

'You are tired,' mumbled Timon. 'Sleep . . . I will think clearer when you wake.' The berserker was wrestling with an inner turmoil and still shuffled violently as he sat.

Alahan reclined as best he could and felt his eyes become heavy. 'I think I may have to do as you say, friend Timon. But yes, I would like to talk when your mind is clearer.'

* * *

Alahan Teardrop Algesson slept fitfully. His dreams had been vivid and disturbing ever since he left Fredericksand and his sleep in the hunting lodge was no less interrupted. He enjoyed the images of his father, standing proudly in front of the Ranen assembly in his black bear-skin cloak, his axe near at hand and his glare fierce. Alahan gained comfort from remembering Algenon Teardrop's face, but he knew that his dreams would progress and that he would soon be turning violently in his sleep.

His father slowly disappeared, his face difficult to recall, as the dark woman intruded upon the young thain's mind. Her face was never distinct and the writhing tentacles that sprang from her mouth gave her a terrifying visage of chaos. Alahan had never dreamt her name, or who she was, but he knew, somehow, that she was his enemy. The terror he felt at seeing her and the dark shadows that loomed behind her were mitigated only by the presence of his uncle. Father Magnus Forkbeard always appeared when Alahan was at his most terrified. When the tentacles extended, writhing in his mind, from the mouth of the dark woman, Magnus always swept in and brought Alahan back to Rowanoco.

Alahan had never been a pious man, leaving questions of faith to the priests, but he found that the presence of the Ice Giant within his mind had grown stronger since the death of his father. On some level, deep within his mind, Alahan heard his uncle saying something. He had heard it each night since he had fled his home, and each night he had tried to make sense of the words. Magnus's voice always seemed to have to travel a great distance to reach him, but within his dream Alahan Teardrop heard that he was

114

the exemplar of Rowanoco. He did not know what it meant; he only knew that it meant everything.

* * *

He woke abruptly and felt warmth against his face. The fire was blazing brightly in front of him, the hunting lodge was quiet, and the air was still. He yawned several times and flexed his sore limbs. His legs were tense and didn't like being moved. His arms were more cooperative, but on the whole the young warrior felt terrible. He wasn't sure of the time or how long he'd slept, and Timon the Butcher was nowhere within sight. Alahan hoped that the berserker of Varorg was still in the lodge because he was genuinely interested in the man's story. That it was a distraction from his current predicament was undeniable, but he could do little anyway, tired and sore, hidden in an unknown corner of his realm.

'Do you need food, friend Alahan?' Timon's voice made Alahan jump. The berserker was stealthier than he appeared.

'I think . . .' Alahan interrupted himself with a loud cough, realizing how dry his throat was. 'Sorry about that,' he apologized. 'Yes, I think I could do with some food.'

'I have meat and roots,' said Timon. A huge hand reached round the door and offered a fistful of dried meat and raw vegetables. 'Eat. I have had my fill.'

Alahan took the food from the berserker's hand, taken aback by its size. He inspected the food and decided that he was hungry enough to eat it. The meat was tough and overly salty, the vegetables were hard and with little flavour, but Alahan found the food comforting and ate gratefully.

'You seem calmer today,' he said, with a mouth full of unidentified meat.

Timon the Butcher, berserker of the Low Kast, stepped quietly round the door frame and stood before Alahan. The man was less intimidating now. His face was no longer a mask of suppressed rage, and he stood in a relaxed fashion, warming his hands before the blazing fire. Whatever inner turmoil he had been undergoing before had passed for the time being.

Alahan was confused by the man and was trying to remember the things he had been told about the followers of Varorg. All he could think of were the condescending words of his uncle – words that painted the berserkers as a necessary evil, left alone only because of tradition.

'Who pursues you?' asked Timon.

Alahan sat up and immediately winced at a sharp pain in his back. Sleeping on a wooden floor was stupid, no matter how tired you might be. 'A lordling of Jarvik. Kalag Ursa.' Alahan growled the lordling's name and a vengeful sneer appeared on his face. 'He has a small army and I seem to be out of options.'

Timon nodded. 'And you are the rightful high thain?' the berserker enquired in a strangely gentle tone of voice.

Alahan nodded. 'My father was Algenon Teardrop.'

'I have heard of this man. Honourable, from what I've heard. But you are far from Fredericksand.'

'I am trying to reach Tiergarten. I have friends there.' Alahan knew the family of Summer Wolf were allies of Teardrop and, if he could reach the city, he would at least have stone walls between himself and his enemies. 'If the snow has cleared I might be able to get my bearings. Last night I could have wandered into a family of trolls as easily as I wandered into your lodge.'

The Butcher turned to face Alahan and attempted a smile. The berserker's mouth was oversized and his lips slightly swollen, giving a comical edge to the expression. 'Family of trolls . . .' he repeated to himself, as if Alahan had inadvertently made a joke.

'I'm glad I amuse you,' Alahan responded with a straight face.

Timon chuckled to himself. Evidently there was humour in the mere idea of a family of trolls.

'What brings you so far west, friend Timon?'

The berserker stopped chuckling and sat down opposite Alahan. Both men were large, but Timon made Alahan feel small.

'Aleph Summer Wolf,' was the simple response from the man of the Low Kast.

'What about him?'

Timon shrugged. 'He is thain of Tiergarten, yes?'

Alahan shook his head. 'Not any more. He died in Fredericksand a few months ago. His daughter is technically heir, but she's missing as well.'

Timon pursed his lips and his brow furrowed in an exaggerated display of thinking. 'This is unwelcome news,' he said, looking at the wooden floor.

'Indeed,' said Alahan. 'The list of thains grows small in the lands of Fjorlan. The lords of Jarvik claim responsibility for many of them but . . .' Alahan considered whether or not to inform Timon of the circumstances of Aleph's death and concluded that nothing would be served by deceiving him. 'The thain of Tiergarten was killed in the Ranen assembly. An axe was cast by my father.'

The berserker knew what this meant and did not look as if he were about to erupt into violence at the news.

'Aleph was your friend?' Alahan asked.

The berserker considered the question as if its answer was a complicated one. After a few moments, he shook his head. 'I have never had friends . . . Aleph . . . was once kind to me and I sought to repay him.'

'I'm afraid that will have to wait until you are side by side in the ice halls beyond the world, friend Timon.'

'His daughter is grown?' the Butcher asked.

'She is.' He nodded. 'She's an axe-maiden of Rowanoco and, by all accounts, as fearsome a warrior as Fjorlan has produced.'

Timon again seemed to be wrestling with something. 'Then I will seek out the Daughter of the Wolf,' he said, standing sharply.

Alahan raised his eyebrows. 'She may well be at the bottom of the Kraken Sea, and Aleph had no other heirs.'

This news did not concern the berserker. 'If she is dead, I will find another to seek out. Until then, I have a goal.' The berserker was noticeably happier now and the young thain found the man's strange sense of conviction refreshing.

'Is there also a story attached to why you looked as if you wanted to skin me alive when you first saw me?' Alahan probed gently.

Timon showed a slight embarrassment and looked guiltily down at a small woven pouch attached to his rope belt. 'I am . . . not myself sometimes. The rage of Varorg passes only reluctantly.' He spoke clearly and with more awareness and intelligence than Alahan had expected.

'Then perhaps we should travel to Tiergarten together. I know a priest there who will help us. I can't promise the journey will be uneventful, but I'll swear to guard you when you are . . . not yourself.'

A childlike grin appeared on Timon's face and he eagerly leant forward. 'Will you help me find Summer Wolf?' he asked.

Before Alahan could answer, a sound came to his ears. The berserker raised his head, showing that he, too, had heard the noise, and both of them rose quickly from the wooden floor of the hunting lodge.

'A dog?' asked Timon.

'More than one, I'd say.' Alahan had heard a distant cacophony of barks and the sound was growing louder. 'Sled dogs,' he said through gritted teeth, glancing around the room. 'Do you have an axe . . . or a hammer, maybe?'

The berserker gripped the sides of his head and shook it rapidly from side to side. The suggestion bothered him greatly, and Alahan began to think Timon was not going to be much use in combat.

'Okay, well, let's hope it's just a scouting party ahead of the main army. Come with me.' Alahan picked up his two throwing-axes and holstered them on his belt. He hefted his battleaxe several times to get the blood flowing through his arms and strode towards the front door of the lodge.

Light was coming through the front windows and the wooden building was bathed in sun. No wind could be heard and the snow had stopped. Alahan hugged the wall and edged next to a window. He rubbed away the condensation and peered outside to see two sledges approaching from what he believed to be the west. The visibility was good and the hunting lodge must have stood out against the featureless white of the realm of Teardrop.

'Maybe eight men,' he said to Timon, who was standing behind him, looking nervously at the floor. 'They got lucky. They were probably sent off the main path when they lost my trail.'

'Friend Alahan,' Timon said tentatively. 'I . . . cannot shed blood.'

The young thain raised his eyebrows and turned back to the window, checking that he'd counted correctly. Each sledge was pulled by a team of black and grey dogs and held four men. As they drew closer, Alahan could make out tough, bearded faces and a variety of glaives and axes. They wore thick bear-skin cloaks and leather armour. Unfortunately he had not miscounted – there were definitely eight of them.

'Well,' said Alahan wearily, 'I suppose they won't be Kalag's best if he's sending them out here.'

Eight men was a push, even for a warrior as skilled as Alahan Teardrop. He could probably fell two of them quickly with his hand-axes, and staying in the doorway would increase his odds of survival, but he would still rather have the berserker of Varorg watching his back.

The warriors pulled back on the dogs' reins and stopped their sledges in front of the lodge. They wore the tabard of Jarvik – a black bear's claw on a red background – and each hefted a two-handed weapon as they carefully stepped from their transports. Most held axes, but Alahan also saw two glaives and a massive war-hammer. The glaive was the signature weapon of Rulag Ursa, a vicious-looking blade attached to a long spear, designed to keep an opponent at a distance. None of the men was young and most looked decidedly overweight. Alahan thought he could win, but that was more optimism than strategic thinking.

He shot a look at Timon and placed a finger to his lips to indicate silence, as he stowed his battleaxe and stepped towards the door. He breathed in deeply and drew his throwing-axes. He could now hear the gruff voices of the men as they approached the lodge and he tried to slow his breathing and concentrate. His axes had lacquered wooden handles and had been sharpened less than a week ago, making them deadly at close range.

'I hope you don't die,' whispered Timon the Butcher.

Alahan spared him a smile and turned, flinging the door inwards. The men outside were taken completely by surprise at the presence of an armed warrior and for a moment they didn't move as Alahan lunged forwards, putting as much power as he could into his first throw. The axe whistled quickly towards the closest man, striking him on the chin and shattering his jaw. He cartwheeled back, his head split down the middle. Alahan then spun round and threw his second axe.

The warriors of Jarvik reacted slowly and by the time the second throwing-axe had lodged itself in another man's chest, they were all shouting unintelligible words of alarm. Weapons were drawn, but two had died quickly and the remaining six looked panic-stricken.

Alahan turned back into the lodge and stood rigid against the inner wall, pulling the door closed behind him. He breathed out deeply and locked eyes with Timon. 'You can't shed blood, but can you break necks?'

The berserker looked confused for a moment until a broad smile appeared on his face. 'That is funny, but alas . . . no, I cannot kill.'

Alahan returned the smile. 'Okay, well stand there and look mean while I go and kill six men.' He drew his battleaxe with a shrug of his shoulders.

'In the name of High Thain Rulag Ursa and his son Kalag, you will surrender,' shouted a voice from outside.

'In the name of Teardrop, you can go and fuck yourself,' was Alahan's roared response.

He heard shouted commands and then men approached the door. The young thain held his breath and felt his knuckles tighten on the haft of his axe. He had never named his favourite weapon and wondered if a battle against eight men was significant enough to warrant a title.

The door was pushed tentatively inwards and Alahan saw a hand appear at the edge of the wood. He grabbed the door and pulled it roughly. The man on the other side grunted and lost his balance on the snowy doorstep. He was greeted with a powerful downward swing of Alahan's axe as he tried to regain his footing. The blow split his bear-skin hood and dug several inches into his skull, killing him instantly. Alahan rose quickly and assessed his remaining opponents. The five looked tough but scared. As he had hoped, the initial ferocity of his attack had rendered them slightly stunned.

The grim reality of his situation only dawned slowly as Alahan realized that he could not afford to let any of them escape. To make matters worse, Timon was once again wailing at the sight of the dead man on the doorstep, his hands clamped to the sides of his head.

'Please stop testing me, Varorg . . . I am weak,' cried the berserker.

Alahan had to admit that the roaring was also likely to cause alarm among the remaining battle-brothers of Jarvik. He let them assume the worst for a second or two, before stepping out of the lodge and on to the snow. He kicked the dead body from the doorway and tightened his grip on the haft of his battleaxe.

'You're outnumbered, boy,' barked one of the men of Jarvik. 'There are five of us.'

'You should have brought more men,' replied Alahan as he attacked.

The nearest man raised his glaive, using the wooden shaft to parry the axe blow. Alahan put considerable strength into the swing and split the glaive's handle down the middle, lodging his weapon in the man's shoulder, at the angle where it joined his neck. The remaining four moved to encircle Alahan and the thain lost the advantage of surprise.

'You're quick, boy, but now you're fucking dead,' spat a man swinging a large war-hammer.

'So come and kill me, you treacherous troll cunt,' was Alahan's reply.

The remaining men numbered two axes, a glaive and the hammer, whose wielder seemed to be nominally in charge of the squad. Alahan let them assemble round him, each keeping his distance and showing grudging respect for the man who had quickly killed half their number.

Two men moved at once, swinging from above their heads and attacking him from flanking positions. He darted forward and deflected one blow with his axe while dodging under the other. He spun round and swept the legs from under the man he'd parried, before killing the other with a single-handed upward swing into his ribs. He quickly moved to smash the hilt of his axe into the fallen man's neck.

'I don't feel fucking dead,' he barked at the two remaining men. 'Maybe Kalag should send better men after me.'

The realization that they were fighting the son of Algenon Teardrop slowly dawned on the two battle-brothers of Jarvik, and both looked ready to run.

With a grim look on his face, Alahan moved cautiously to where one of his throwing-axes was lying. Without taking his eyes from the remaining men, he picked up the weapon and took a step towards them. The dogs were beginning to howl loudly and Alahan was glad he could no longer hear Timon's wailing from within the lodge. Maybe the axe did need a name, he thought to himself.

The man with the hammer looked more willing to fight than his companion and so Alahan focused on him. 'I take no pleasure in killing fellow Ranen, even treacherous bastards, but you have to die,' Alahan growled.

The man of Jarvik held his hammer warily and adopted a defensive pose. 'Come on then, boy.' His words were confident, but his hands shook against the handle of his hammer.

Alahan moved quickly. Taking one hand from his axe, he extended his arm and rammed the crosspiece of his double-headed weapon into the man's nose. He'd struck just as the battle-brother had stopped talking and the older man had no chance of getting out of the way. Alahan then repeated the manoeuvre, ramming the crosspiece into the man's stomach and sending him sprawling on to the snowy ground, his nose broken and his breath coming in short gasps. He didn't take his eyes from the remaining warrior as he casually sliced the fallen man's throat with a single swing of his axe.

Alahan did not enjoy killing these men. They were not skilled opponents and their deaths served only to keep his location secret. Nevertheless, as he killed the last man, Alahan Teardrop, high thain of Fjorlan, felt that a line had been crossed. Ranen fighting Ranen was commonplace, axe-masters, chain-masters, even Free Company men, all were used to seeing men die. But this was different. As he cleaned his axe and returned to the hunting lodge amid a cacophony of barks and howls, Alahan realized that this was now a civil war. His father had been convinced that a Karesian enchantress was behind the problems in Canarn and Fjorlan, and Alahan, too, was beginning to believe that only sorcery could have torn apart the men of Ranen in such a fashion. The dark woman who appeared to him in nightmares was ever in his thoughts and he feared that more than his hall in Fredericksand was at stake.

* * *

Alahan and Timon had been running for most of the day, at a pace that made it just about possible to carry armour and weaponry and not die from exhaustion. They had stopped briefly around midday for some hastily eaten dried meat and unidentifiable roots, but otherwise the day had been a long and tiring one. The sled dogs had been too afraid of Timon and even after an hour of coaxing had been unwilling to carry the berserker. Strangely, this made him apologize repeatedly. He'd said little as they ran, but Alahan had been impressed at Timon's stamina. The huge berserker never seemed to tire or to need rest and the young thain wondered if he had run to Fjorlan from the Low Kast.

The terrain of the realm was currently a sheet of white. Winter was approaching and the rugged landscape was covered in deep snow. Alahan knew that a river marked the traditional boundary between the realms of Teardrop and Summer Wolf, but he doubted they'd be able to see it beneath the snow. He thought the first indication they were travelling in the right direction might well be the city of Tiergarten itself, though Timon had insisted that they would run into trolls well before they sighted the city. Apparently, the early snows meant the Ice Men of Rowanoco felt more comfortable outside.

As they approached a rocky gully, not yet covered entirely in white, Timon stopped running. 'We should rest here,' he said in a low rumble.

'Really? Because I've only just stopped feeling my legs,' was the dry response from Alahan.

The berserker frowned, an exaggerated expression that made his face crease up. 'I cannot feel tired. You should say when you do. I do not want you to hurt yourself,' he said sincerely.

'You don't ever feel tired? That's a gift I'd gladly take.' Alahan was panting heavily and, though he was a fit man, a day of running in the snow had taken its toll.

The snow itself had stopped and, though a bitter wind flew down the gully, the temperature was not too bad for the time of year. They were not within sight of the sea and landmarks were few and far between, making the occasional rocky outcropping a significant reference point in the snowy wastes.

'You should rest, friend Alahan,' said Timon.

'Thank you,' panted the young warrior. 'I think I will. These rocks are decent cover, unless that snow starts drifting.'

Timon smiled as Alahan sat down with his back against rock. The ground was hard and flecked with snow, but with cover from the wind and his thick bear-skin cloak, the son of Teardrop thought he could find a degree of comfort.

'Do you mind talking, friend Timon?' he asked, as he shifted his position against the stone.

The berserker screwed up his face again and Alahan guessed the expression meant he was thinking. 'Not at all, though there are things I cannot say.'

'Such as why a berserker of the Low Kast won't kill? That is not your people's reputation.'

'I know,' Timon replied with downcast eyes. 'But I made a vow. You may ask me anything else.'

Alahan nodded and began to remove his stowed weaponry and to get as comfortable as he could, feeling waves of tiredness flow over his aching body. 'How did you come to know Aleph Summer Wolf?'

Timon lowered himself into a cross-legged sitting position. 'The thain of Tiergarten visited my village when I was young. There was pestilence and my mother had died in my arms. It was a hard time for my people.' He was looking off into the snow. 'The thain had many warriors with him. I think they were looking for deep ice to make their cloud-stones . . . or maybe jewels . . . I don't know.'

Alahan knew that Ranen cloud-stones were made from mined ice, but had never thought where the ice came from. 'You fought them?' he asked.

The Butcher nodded. 'My chieftain was a brutal old berserker and he ordered all men to give their lives to keep the Low Kast pure. He was no great friend to the Fjorlanders. Even with so many dying from plague, he kept attacking. Even when Aleph begged him for peace terms, he just laughed.' Timon's expressive features showed that he had not agreed with his chieftain's decisions.

'Who won?' asked Alahan.

'They did,' was the simple response. 'They won every time we attacked. We were outnumbered and most of my village were simple men, but the chieftain kept ordering us forward. Men died, hundreds of them. Those not killed by Fjorlan axes were killed by pestilence, until only a handful of my people remained and the chieftain had been gripped by insanity.'

Alahan frowned at the tale and looked with genuine sympathy at the berserker. 'How did it end?'

'I was barely a man at twelve years, but I was sent forward with my father to die,' he said, with an angry curl to his lip. 'But I acted without honour and refused. I had barely started to embrace the rage of Varorg, but I wouldn't see my father and mother both die before my eyes and so I challenged the chieftain.' Timon was sitting in the middle of the gully and snow was beginning to drift in front of him as he spoke. 'Aleph saved my life when I was defeated. He spared me and my father when he had no need to. His priest healed our pestilence and the few men who remained surrendered with honour. The men of Tiergarten killed the chieftain and let the rest of us live.'

Alahan raised his eyebrows. 'You view that as kindness?'

'We had been attacking him unceasingly, and he spared our lives. A man of the Low Kast would not have done that. Aleph Summer Wolf was the first man I ever saw show mercy.'

'I understand mercy, but why try to find him now?'

'I have nothing to offer the Low Kast . . . not any more . . . so I seek out the best man I know and pledge my fate.' Timon spoke with conviction, as if acting out an honour ritual of his people. 'He should see it as a privilege,' the berserker stated with pride.

'And his daughter?' asked Alahan.

The man of the Low Kast absently chewed on a fingernail. 'I will hope that she is worthy of my fate. If not, I will find another.' Alahan smiled warmly at Timon, accepting the berserker's simple world view.

The young thain yawned loudly and fell further back against the rocks, making sure he was under an overhang. He was exhausted and he found Timon's voice strangely soothing. 'I may need to sleep, my friend,' he said wearily.

'That is good.' Timon smiled broadly. 'I have enjoyed talking to you. We will have to do it again.'

126

Alahan laughed, a loud, good-natured laugh, and gave the berserker a comradely slap on the shoulder. 'We'll get to Tiergarten and both reach our goals . . . I'm sure of it.'

* * *

Alahan was tired enough that the cold bothered him little as he drifted off to sleep. He had no bedroll or camping gear and wished he had been thinking more clearly when he had fled his home. At the time, his head had been full of anxiety for his sister and indignation at the treacherous battle-brothers of Jarvik. He estimated that they were no more than a week from Tiergarten and, as he closed his eyes and felt his breathing slow down, he prayed to Rowanoco that he would find allies in the realm of Summer Wolf. He had known an old priest called Brindon Crowe and he hoped the man would still be there.

Timon was standing above him, watching the snowy tundra from the high ground. Alahan was finding the man of the Low Kast a most intriguing travelling companion and, despite his initial lack of conversation and strange ways of thinking, it was evident that the berserker was more thoughtful and intelligent than was typical of his people – though, as he felt sleep intrude, Alahan was aware that he had only his uncle's word for this.

Then a deep, rumbling sound travelled along the gully and caused his eyes to open. It was an elongated and guttural snarl, which echoed off the rocky terrain. Alahan sprang to his feet and picked up his battleaxe. Looking down the narrow gully he could see nothing but a bank of drifting snow. He glanced up, but Timon was no longer there. The sound continued and Alahan swore under his breath as he realized he was listening to the keening of a troll.

'Timon,' he whispered upwards, 'we need to move.'

There was no response from the berserker.

'Timon,' he repeated, 'it's a troll.'

Alahan had encountered the Ice Men of Rowanoco a number of times in his life – living in Fjorlan made it almost inevitable – but he had never had to fight one and, if stories were to be believed, a troll was easily a match for a dozen armoured battle-brothers. Magnus used to say that the Ice Men of Rowanoco were essentially eating machines that would devour rocks, trees and men with equal gusto. Their bellies were never full and they would attack an army as readily as a mountain goat.

He crouched under the rocky overhang and waited. His breath was slow and he dared not blink. He peered into the drifting snow and saw a huge shape lumbering forwards. Hugging the rocks as best he could, Alahan saw the beast emerge into the glaring white of the realm of Teardrop. It was bigger than the ones he had seen near Fredericksand, standing over ten feet in height, though its hunched gait made it likely that its full height was a good deal larger. He couldn't make out the creature clearly, but its bulk made Alahan's fist shake as he gripped his axe. Almost as wide as it was tall, the troll swayed as it walked, following a zigzag path in its approach to the gully.

The keening continued. The troll was enormous and, as it came closer, the young warrior saw the talon-like claws extending from each of its bulbous limbs. The beast was covered in thick black and grey fur and seemed bloated rather than muscled. Though vaguely human in shape, it walked with all four limbs, using its claws to gain purchase in the snow.

It was close now and the young thain was beginning to feel panic. He knew he couldn't run, as the troll would catch him before he'd travelled ten paces, and fighting was clearly out of the question. His only hope was that the troll would pass by without noticing him. The trolls of Fjorlan were notoriously dim-witted, with no real sense of smell, hearing or direction. Magnus used to tell his nephew stories about ancient Ice Men who would die when they chased troublesome birds over the edge of a cliff.

The keening stopped and Alahan held his breath. Chancing a look out from his place of concealment, he saw the troll standing no more than ten paces away. He could see its face now and had to suppress the urge to simply scream and run away. The beast had a small face compared with the rest of its body, and its jewel-like green eyes shone slightly in the glare. It had thick lips coated in spittle and two large tusks pointing upwards through the dense fur covering its face. Its forehead was wide and creased into an exaggerated display of emotion. Something had alerted the troll and it looked around the gully, rubbing its eyes with its enormous paws as a child might do when tired or confused.

Some stones from the outcropping rolled down the gully to stop in front of the troll, followed by the slowly moving figure of Timon the Butcher. The berserker was making no effort to remain hidden and he moved deliberately towards the troll. Alahan swore under his breath, but made no move for fear that he would be seen. He doubted that even a berserker of Varorg could best so large a troll.

The troll hunkered down on the snowy ground and looked at Timon. It made no move to attack, but looked interested in the strange being that had appeared before it. Timon had taken the leather strapping off his head and the misshapen bulges were bleeding slightly as he approached the troll. In their own way, both were beasts, and Alahan felt as if he had wandered into a bizarre nightmare. The berserker held a small pouch in his fist and the troll's enormous nostrils twitched, catching a familiar scent. Timon slowly untied the pouch and shook a small amount of a dusty crystalline substance into his palm, before placing the pouch back in his belt and stepping closer to the troll.

All was quiet for a moment as Alahan, Timon and the troll stopped still. Then, with slow movements, the berserker raised his palm to his nose and sniffed in a quantity of the crystals, immediately rearing up as if he'd had freezing-cold water thrown over him. The troll moved as well, but not aggressively, and Alahan wondered what the berserker had snorted. The two beasts regarded each other for a moment longer – Timon twitching and blinking rapidly, the troll clawing at the snow and crouching so as to be at eye level with the berserker. Then, in a gesture that nearly made Alahan laugh, the troll embraced Timon. It was a huge movement in which the berserker practically disappeared within the thick fur of the troll. As the beast playfully patted Timon on the head, Alahan realized that the troll thought of the berserker as one of its own kind rather than a man.

The two of them sat on the snowy ground, pawing at each other as equals. Despite their difference in size, Timon gave as good as he got, even going so far as to mimic the keening sound trolls habitually made when wandering.

Alahan relaxed as he watched the strange ritual before him and almost didn't notice the other shapes appearing out of the snow. He moved quickly back against the rocks as half a dozen more trolls appeared at the southern edge of the gully and slowly meandered towards Timon. The berserker had seen them and showed no sign of alarm as the family of Ice Men approached. The young man of Fredericksand turned away, feeling exposed in sight of so many trolls, but no violence seemed likely to erupt and so he moved slowly back along the gully, with a vague plan to circle round the encounter and continue south. Timon would have to catch him up when he'd finished pretending to be troll.

'What a strange week I'm having,' murmured the young Thain to himself.

CHAPTER SEVEN

TYR NANON IN
THE CITY OF CANARN

THE STREETS OF Canarn were dark, with just enough breeze to remind Nanon that he was next to the sea. He glanced above him and saw the tower of the World Raven close by, indicating that he was near to the town square. He'd turned off the Brown Road that led to Brother Lanry's chapel and had taken a number of quick lefts and rights until he was well and truly lost among the back streets of the city. The roads here were narrow and the buildings loomed in over the Dokkalfar's head, pleasingly reminding him of the forest.

He smiled – a thin expression that didn't quite reach his eyes. He was conducting an experiment that Bromvy, the new lord of Canarn, had assured him was *simply stupid* and the forest-dweller was determined to prove his friend wrong.

He took a short run-up and vaulted over a wall and on to a nearby rooftop. Crouching down, he surveyed the dark buildings of Canarn, looking for any balconies or flat roofs within jumping range. There were a few likely candidates, but most would leave him open to the sea breeze and with not enough cover to remain unseen from below. Above, the black raven provided an easy reference point, but Nanon frowned at the lack of other tall buildings in the town. The lord marshal's office had been destroyed a month or so before, but he had been assured by Bromvy that when it was rebuilt it would be a large building with all manner of climbing and jumping potential.

However, all that remained for now was a pile of rubble.

The Dokkalfar got as low to the stone roof as he could, before rolling backwards and landing within a walled garden. As his feet touched grass, he felt a wave of pleasure shoot up his slender body. It reminded him that these men of Ro were not completely oblivious to nature. They had a strange view of grass, trees and rocks, though, and considered nature their servant, something to be bent to their will. There were trees and green areas within Canarn, but all were well tended and lacking in natural beauty. Even with so many Dokkalfar in the city, the natives were reluctant just to let the grass grow, as if they feared it would somehow take over the town. Nanon respected this view up to a point – he knew how terrible nature could be when left unchecked – but he also lamented the loss of the wild within these stone walls.

His experiment had not, so far, been a success, and Nanon grumbled to himself. He would have to admit that the lord of Canarn was probably right – it was not possible simply to live in a town as you would in a forest.

He wasn't being, as Bromvy had put it, a naive idiot, but rather he was trying to find a way for his people to adapt to life in the city. He was more worldly than others of the Dokkalfar, and he felt an obligation to help them settle in. However, he had had limited success and, as he turned to exit the small garden, the Tyr saw dozens more forest-dwellers dotted across the rooftops and walls as they, too, tried in vain to adapt to Canarn.

He tilted his head and looked skywards. Nanon could feel his people's uncertainty flowing through the city, and each new Dokkalfar that came to Canarn added to their sense of confusion. The Dokkalfar shared a racial memory that allowed the more powerful among them to feel the pain and emotional distress of others, and Nanon was more attuned to it than most. The Dokkalfar had come here at the behest of their Vithar shamans to bolster Canarn's strength and to prepare the city to receive refugees from Tor Funweir, but they had adapted only slowly and found the pace of human life difficult to comprehend.

Nanon was different. He had spent much of his long life among men and, because of his short stature, had managed to blend in, in a way that the larger of his kind could never hope to achieve. He had learnt much from Bromvy and, before him, Rham Jas Rami, and he had become adept at understanding humans. He was even beginning to laugh at their jokes because he understood them, rather than pretending to do so in order to fit in. Tyr Nanon puffed out his cheeks, mimicking a human expression of weary frustration, and decided that he would walk back to the keep rather than jump across the rooftops.

It was a pleasant enough night and he found the smells of Canarn constantly surprising, a strange cocktail of odours, most of which he was unable to identify. Crossing back towards the Brown Road, Nanon saw the dark profile of Lanry's chapel next to the main square. The Brown cleric was not currently in residence, having been sent north by Bromvy in an effort to find news of his sister, Bronwyn, and of the progress Wraith Company was making towards South Warden. Bromvy had not yet made a decision about the long-term allegiance of Canarn, except that the city would no longer bear the prefix *Ro*. Bromvy did not call himself duke, preferring *lord of Canarn* when the need for a title arose. Nanon knew, too, that the young man of Ro was still uncomfortable with the title *Black Guard*.

Nanon strolled casually towards the town square, taking note of the newly rebuilt homes and businesses. Most were closed, but he knew the human citizens of the city were pleased to have Canarn back to something like its former self. The few taverns that were still open late at night were quiet, with only a scattering of patrons and no Dokkalfar. The forest-dwellers had no real concept of taverns, and the drinking of alcohol was a curiously human habit.

He moved across the square and headed for the lowered drawbridge which led to the keep. A month ago, when he had first come to the city, the square had been full of funeral pyres and was being used by the bastard mercenaries as a playground where they could indulge their passion for rape and murder. The square had now been cleared and a sizeable memorial was already half built in the centre. The statue would be of a longsword, a leaf blade and a hammer, all rising above the spread wings of a raven in flight, symbolizing the three peoples who had fought and died to reclaim the city of Canarn. The Ro, the Ranen and the Dokkalfar made a curious alliance, but Nanon was proud to be able to call an increasing number of humans his friends.

At the base of the drawbridge were two guardsmen, men of Ro elevated to positions of authority following the battle. They wore ill-fitting chain mail and held crossbows, but their demeanour was casual. Both men smiled warmly as Nanon approached and the Dokkalfar tried his best to mimic the strange expression.

'You're still not quite getting it, my lord,' said one of the men, barely containing his laughter at Nanon's attempt at a smile. 'It just looks wrong somehow . . . maybe it's the black eyes.'

Nanon enjoyed the playful familiarity with which the humans addressed him.

'Hmm, I think I just need more practice,' he replied, thrusting his hand out enthusiastically.

'And you don't need to shake hands with every man you pass, my lord,' said the second man. 'A *hello* is often enough.'

Nanon considered it. 'But I like shaking hands. It's a nice way to bond with people. We don't really have any kind of ritual touching like that, so it's quite refreshing.'

Both men baulked at the term *ritual touching*, before looking at each other and shrugging. 'Okay, my lord,' said the first man, 'let's shake hands.'

Nanon tried to smile again as he grasped each man's hand in turn and shook it vigorously. 'There we go, I feel like we're all becoming good friends.'

As he walked away, the Tyr heard confused comments from the men of Canarn and wondered how long it would take before the interaction between man and Dokkalfar became second nature. He liked them, but he had to confess that many of his people did not and that it would be a struggle to integrate the two populations of Canarn.

Within the keep, all was quiet and he was sheltered from the sea breeze as he walked towards the wooden stairs that led to the great hall. The courtyard had been the site of the funeral pyres a month ago, but the remains of the dead were now gone. Father Magnus, Tyr Rafn and two dozen Dokkalfar had been burned.

Nanon paused for a moment next to the blackened ground where so many had died and felt the spirits of the dead whirl and dance in the night air. He could sense each one of them, as if they were looking at him from far away, and he closed his eyes the better to commune with the spirits of his dead brethren. Each face came to him, followed by their names and the manner of their deaths. Most had fallen at the edge of a longsword, though some had been beaten to death or skewered with other weapons.

He breathed in deeply and raised his head to feel the breeze over his face, before opening his eyes and returning to the present. He felt guilty at not being able to feel the dead humans. He knew that many of them had died – certainly more than the Dokkalfar – in the initial assault to retake the city, and Nanon wished he could pay them all equal respect.

Across the courtyard, he walked up the steps and tried to clear the thoughts of the dead from his mind. The racial memory of the Dokkalfar extended beyond death and he could never truly lose the companionship of his fallen people. If he concentrated, Nanon could feel the thoughts, dreams and fears of every Dokkalfar and, the older he grew, the more beautiful the gift became. Most of his people tried to shut out the thoughts of others, but Nanon was old and valued the insight it gave him. Unfortunately, it was difficult to explain to Bromvy, and Nanon had resigned himself simply to saying *trust me* whenever he had revealed an impossible insight.

He walked quickly into the great hall. The outer doors were not guarded. Nanon knew armed men were in short supply and that few Dokkalfar had accepted the concept of guards. The hall was cavernous and empty during the hours of darkness and, despite

135

the warm red and green colouring and the low-burning fire pits, he found the vast space unnerving. The floor was of large flagstones, making this one of the least natural spaces within Canarn and a symbol of the craft of men. Even the woven banners and ceremonial weaponry sent a slight shiver up the forest-dweller's spine, as he crossed to a small wooden door behind the raised dais.

The corridors of the inner keep were dark, even in daytime, with few external windows. The stone walls held braziers at regular intervals, and Nanon ghosted from shadow to shadow as he made his way along empty hallways. He had already found the strange network of secret passages and covert balconies that honeycombed the keep, and had begun to train some of his fellows in how to move swiftly through Canarn without being detected. If the Dokkalfar were to assist in defending this place, and to think of it as their home, they needed to know all they could about Bromvy's keep. The young lord had not objected and had indeed relished the opportunity to venture back into the secret tunnels. The forest-dweller had sensed in Bromvy a nostalgic love for the secrets of Canarn, which reminded the young lord of happier times with his father and sister.

Two levels above the great hall, Nanon turned a sharp corner and approached the guard sitting wearily in front of a set of large wooden doors. The man was portly and red-faced, struggling to keep his eyes open. Nanon pursed his lips in place of a smile.

'Hello,' said the Dokkalfar in a loud and friendly voice.

'What . . . no . . . yes, I'm awake.' The man spluttered and blinked rapidly, looking in Nanon's direction. 'Oh, it's you, my lord. Sorry, it's been a long night.'

'No need to apologize,' responded the forest-dweller, before extending his hand and attempting another smile.

The guard raised his eyebrows, but hesitantly took his hand. 'Still shaking every hand you can get hold of, my lord?' he asked with humour.

The guard was called Auker and, as one of the few guardsmen to survive the assault, he had taken it upon himself to protect

Bromvy at all costs. Nanon suspected a touch of guilt motivated the old soldier because he had been living on an outlying farm when the Red knights had attacked.

'You're not the first to ask me that, Auker,' replied Nanon cheerfully. 'But I choose to continue anyway.'

The soldier yawned loudly and looked around for a near-empty wineskin. 'Is it dawn yet?' he asked, taking a shallow swig.

'Nope,' replied Nanon. ''Tis still the dead of night.'

Auker rubbed his eyes. 'You really need to learn the human concept of night and day, my lord. I think your people have very different sleep patterns to mine.'

Nanon pouted, attempting to convey an apology for having got something wrong. He succeeded only in looking foolish and caused Auker to laugh.

'Was that a smile, my lord?' he asked.

'No, I was trying to say sorry . . . did I not quite manage it?' Nanon replied.

'Well, you look a bit like a guilty child, so . . . no, not really, no.' The old soldier was worldlier than many of his fellows and Nanon found himself liking him.

'I'll work on it,' the Dokkalfar replied with conviction. 'I wanted to speak to Lord Bromvy. Is he awake?'

Auker smiled again. 'I doubt it. He's in there with the Lady Hannah. They were certainly both *awake* a few hours ago, but I'd say they are having a well-deserved rest now.'

Nanon wasn't sure what Auker was insinuating. 'They've been spending a lot of time together recently. Are they good friends or are they mating?'

Auker spat out a mouthful of wine. 'Hannah is one of the few nobles left in the duchy, my lord. Her father owns three farms to the east and Lord Bromvy made a promise of marriage to him. Luckily for him she's quite an attractive young thing.'

The complex politics of the Ro was a complete mystery to Nanon and he screwed up his face, attempting to fathom the need to marry to secure alliances. Among the Dokkalfar you knew to whom you would be mated from a young age and, when the time came, you were bound together for life. Sex played very little part in a Dokkalfar union and, once a child was born, the match tended to be more ceremonial than loving. Nanon himself had one child and had not seen his mate for at least a hundred years. In fact, as he stood outside Bromvy's rooms, he confessed to himself that he did not know whether she was alive or dead, and even her name temporarily escaped him.

He looked up, mimicking the human expression of deep thought, before blurting out, 'Jasn. Her name was Shar Jasn.'

'What?' queried Auker.

'Sorry, I'd forgotten the name of my mate,' Nanon replied, with a tilt of his head.

'You're strange, my pointy-eared friend,' the Ro said, 'but I find myself liking you all the same.' He smiled warmly. 'Go on, wake him up. Just don't expect a smile.' He pointed over his shoulder to the large wooden doors. 'He's always moody these days, so a few hours' less sleep won't make much difference.'

Nanon nodded. 'You and I will be good friends, Sergeant Auker.'

He stepped past the guardsman and pounded loudly on the oak door.

'Of course, the more rudely you wake him up, the moodier he'll be,' said Auker with another chuckle.

A loud grunt sounded from within Bromvy's room. It was guttural and filtered through several layers of tiredness. Nanon pressed his ear against the door and listened. More grunts followed, mostly male, with a barely audible female accompaniment.

Nanon knocked again, quieter this time. 'Brom,' he whispered through the door.

'If that's you, Nanon, I'm gonna throw you off the battlements,' was the response from within. 'Go and sleep, we'll talk in the morning.'

Nanon tilted his head and wondered why he was required to sleep during the night if he wanted to talk to his friend. Dokkalfar required little sleep and tended simply to rest for an hour or two when tired. Nanon regularly went for days without closing his eyes.

He knocked again. 'Brom,' he repeated, 'it's Nanon.'

A roar of frustration carried through the door and echoed down the silent halls of Canarn. 'I know it's you, Nanon, you grey-skinned bastard. Leave me alone.'

The Dokkalfar smiled at Auker. 'I'll just go in.' He turned the door handle to the sound of muffled laughter from the guardsman. 'Brom,' Nanon whispered. 'Can I come in?'

'NO!' shouted the young lord of Canarn.

Nanon pushed the door open and entered the dark room beyond. Thinking it likely that his friend was teasing him in some way, the forest-dweller ignored the muffled cries of alarm from within and closed the door behind him. The light in Bromvy's chamber was minimal, a sliver of moonlight coming through the single window, but Nanon could see perfectly in the darkness.

Lord Bromvy Black Guard of Canarn was sitting up in his large bed, half-covered with a fur blanket and rubbing his eyes. Next to him, face-down and grumbling to herself, was Lady Hannah of the Eastern Marches. She was a tall and slender woman, with dark red hair and freckled skin. Their room was large and comfortable, decorated in dark wood with a bear-skin rug in the centre. Bromvy's sword hung above an empty fireplace. The room had the distinctive smell of sweat and bodily fluids, indicating to Nanon's sensitive nose that the young lord had been engaging in coitus in the recent past.

'Hello,' the Dokkalfar said cheerfully as he crossed to a chair by the window.

'In the name of any god you care to mention, if you wake me up once more, I'm going to cut off your pointy-fucking-ears,' said Bromvy blearily.

'What . . . what's happening?' mumbled Hannah, barely looking up.

Bromvy ran a gentle hand down the woman's back and tenderly kissed her shoulder. 'We're under attack from a particularly persistent foe, my dear,' he said quietly. 'Go back to sleep while I go and defend you from him.'

Bromvy rose up reluctantly from his bed and reached for a woollen tunic, leather trousers and thick fur cloak. 'Cold, cold, cold,' he muttered, covering himself up. 'Do you not feel the temperature?'

'Not the cold, no. I don't like too much heat, though,' replied the forest-dweller, taking a seat and making himself comfortable.

'What are you doing?' the young man of Canarn asked. 'Get up, we're not staying in here.'

'Okay.' Nanon was still being cheerful, though he suspected his demeanour was aggravating Brom. The young lord frequently wrestled with the need to appear dour and miserable. Or maybe he actually *was* dour and miserable, Nanon wasn't sure.

'Hannah,' whispered Brom, once he was dressed in his cloak, 'I'll be back as soon as I can.'

She made a contented, sleepy sound and wrapped her arms around his neck. 'Just don't wake me up when you do,' she said, with a tired kiss.

'Bye, Hannah,' said Nanon enthusiastically.

Brom pulled on his leather boots, instantly feeling better without cold feet. He opened his chamber door and glared at Sergeant Auker, who spread his arms wide with a helpless look on his face.

'He does what he wants, my lord,' said Auker. 'Do you want me physically to stop him next time?'

'I thought we were friends,' replied Nanon, surprised that Auker would suggest such a thing.

'He's joking, Nanon. Humour, remember. What did you call it . . . the last real war between us?' Brom had tried to foster integration as best he could, but, like Nanon, he still felt the differences keenly. 'No, sergeant,' he said to Auker, 'just suggest that he come back in the morning.'

'My lord,' replied the sergeant with a nod and a smile.

Bromvy returned the smile, further confusing the forest-dweller, before walking down the passageway towards one of the outer towers of the keep. Bromvy liked to be outside, watching the slowly rolling ocean of Canarn, while they sat talking.

Opening the door by its heavy metal handle, they were hit with a heavy waft of cold sea air. They were high up on a balcony, looking out over the rocky cliffs below. The wind was blustery and even Nanon felt a little uncomfortable. Bromvy walked down a set of stone steps that snaked their way round the outside of the tower. Nanon followed and they gained the cover of the balcony below. There were several chairs on the stone terrace and a brazier was kept alight by the household guards.

'It's not too cold if you sit right next to the fire,' said Bromvy, plonking himself on a wooden chair and huddling close to the brazier.

'Why don't we just sit inside,' asked Nanon, 'if the cold bothers you so much?'

Bromvy rubbed his hands together in front of the fire and smiled, letting his expression soften. He was still a young man and, despite the full beard and thick, curly black hair, the Ro noble remained capable of displaying boyish charm. 'Because, if we sat inside, I'd fall asleep listening to you,' he said through the smile. 'My father used to say that the cold winds of Canarn were a man's greatest advantage when listening to dull counsel . . . I think he meant idiot diplomats from Ro Tiris, but the same applies to you, my friend.'

Nanon tried to frown, to show that he wasn't sure whether or not he should feel hurt. 'I'm not dull, am I?' he asked.

'Not at all. You're just shit at time-keeping.'

The forest-dweller took a seat opposite Brom. 'I do actually need to talk to you, you know. I didn't wake you up for the inherent humour.'

Brom gave him a sideways glance and leant back from the fire. 'Why do you insist on pretending that you don't understand the humour of men?'

'I'm getting better, but it pleases your people and mine if I seem a bit dim-witted. My people prefer me to be more like them, and your people don't like me to be too human.'

'Okay, but between you and me, let us not play games, my friend,' said Brom sincerely. 'What was so urgent?'

'It's the Shadow,' said the forest-dweller. 'He may need my help.'

'The Shadow? You mean Utha the Ghost, the Black cleric that did this?' Brom tapped his broken nose and frowned. 'Where is he?'

'I'm not exactly sure. Somewhere south of Tiris. The Dokkalfar with him is young and a bit difficult for me to read at this distance.' Nanon was not even sure of the young forest-dweller's name, only that he was deeply afraid of Utha the Shadow even while trying his best to guide the old-blood towards the Fell.

'Young?' replied Brom, still smiling. 'You've still not told me how old you are.'

'Older than the Dokkalfar with Utha and the squire,' was Nanon's simple reply. 'I need to leave.'

'Why?' queried the young lord. 'Utha's a Black cleric, which means he can look after himself. It took Rham Jas to put him down.'

'He needs to reach the Fell and I'm not sure the two youngsters with him are enough. I don't know if *I*'ll be enough, but he's important.' Nanon was no longer trying to smile. 'He's the last old-blood, Brom, the last man with the blood of Giants.'

'Okay. I don't think I'll ever fully understand . . . but, okay. A Black cleric of the One God has the blood of the Shadow Giants.'

Nanon baulked at the term and involuntarily tilted his head to show his displeasure. 'Don't call them that. We call them *those we loved*.'

Brom was deep in thought but still had his eyes locked on the Dokkalfar. 'I swore I'd help you in any way I could. So, I ask you, my friend, how can I help?'

Nanon stood up and turned to look over the balcony's edge and out to sea. The inky black water was rolling quietly and the Dokkalfar felt a keen sense of confusion and fear from his people. Those in Canarn were the strongest he felt, but further afield, far across the sea to the south, Tyr Nanon could feel the steady heartbeat of a young forest-dweller looking at the sleeping form of Utha the Shadow.

The Vithar shamans that dwelt in the Fell would do their best to protect the Black cleric once he was in the forest, but until then he was vulnerable, with only his young squire and an anxious Tyr to protect him.

'You can't come with me, Brom,' he said, without turning. 'Your sword arm will be needed elsewhere.' He could sense something of the young lord's future, though the images were far off and indistinct. The more time he spent in his company, the stronger the impressions had grown and now, a month or more since meeting him, Nanon knew that Bromvy needed to remain safely in Canarn until the Red Prince came. He didn't know who the Red Prince was, and he had not mentioned this to Brom, but he knew that his arrival would be to the benefit of both their peoples. 'You need to remain in Canarn. There is work to be done,' Nanon said cryptically.

'While you wander the lands of Tor Funweir looking for a cleric in a wood somewhere?' Brom responded drily. 'I'm sure I heard a riddle about that in my youth.'

'Stop joking. I'm being serious.' Nanon was not in the mood to pretend he didn't understand. 'I wish I could help you know more than your own *now*, but I don't think a month is enough. The *now* of men is on the edge of a cliff with more than water to meet them at the bottom. I need to leave.'

Bromvy pulled his robe tight around his shoulders and scratched thoughtfully at his close-cut beard. 'Brother Lanry went to South Warden, Rham Jas went to Ro Tiris, and Magnus is dead . . . why shouldn't you go as well.'

'You're getting lonely,' stated Nanon, without thinking.

The young lord of Canarn narrowed his eyes. 'Perhaps . . . or perhaps I just don't like waiting here while my friends go to war.'

Nanon smiled at the last word and thought for a moment that Brom had understood something. 'Everyone you mentioned has something in common . . . with you and with me,' he said gently. 'We are soldiers in the Long War . . . you just have to wait a bit longer before you take the field. There'll be plenty of enemies left to fight when Lord Bromvy of Canarn marches to war.'

Nanon did not wait for his friend to respond. He turned back to the balcony, took two large steps forward, and leapt over the low stone wall. Brom shouted in alarm and rushed forward as Nanon flew downwards. He had not judged the jump particularly well and felt a little foolish at having succumbed to the need to show off rather than simply exiting the keep by the door. He concentrated as he fell, allowing his mind to slow and his body to change. Nanon had not taken the shape of a bird for over a century, but the feeling of feathers ruffled by the sea wind was as welcome as ever.

With a loud caw, the black hawk that had been Nanon pulled up well before the rocks and soared out to sea, leaving a stunned Bromvy, lord of Canarn, standing on his balcony. Nanon chuckled inwardly as he picked up a wind current and relaxed his wings. Only the oldest Tyr were gifted with the ability to take animal form, and most no longer used it. Nanon had to confess that he had done it mostly to surprise his friend Brom. As he began to enjoy the sensation of flying again, the Dokkalfar thought his type of humour was much superior to that of the humans.

As he flew south, Nanon grew worried. Things were moving quickly now and he felt the need of guidance.

* * *

Bromvy didn't get much sleep after Nanon had left. Not because the infuriating grey-skin had turned into a bird, but because the young lord of Canarn was deeply troubled. He had seen enough strange things since he had begun associating with the Dokkalfar that the discovery of Nanon's shape-shifting ability did not surprise him that much.

He smiled and rolled over in bed as he realized how worldly he had become in a few short months. Bromvy had been a well-travelled noble and, on occasion, a virtual vagabond, but only recently had his search for an interesting life really taken off. Since Canarn had been attacked by knights of the Red and his father executed, everything had changed. He saw a world open before him that he could never have imagined. A world of enchantresses, Giants and monsters. Nanon would simply say that Brom had seen *beyond the now of man to the forever beyond*.

He yawned and made one last attempt to sleep, trying to shut out the thoughts that kept him awake. Hannah rolled over in her sleep and lazily put an arm over his chest. He had accepted the need to marry her and judged her an attractive match, both as a wife and as a lover, but he didn't relish the prospect of staying in Canarn and producing children while the Long War – or whatever Nanon called it – was fought without him.

Hannah's father was a farm-owner to the east – or maybe the west, he wasn't sure – but he knew his allegiance would be important if Brom were to establish Canarn as an independent duchy, tentatively allied with the Ranen. He kissed her on the forehead and delicately removed himself from her arms. Standing up from the bed, he puffed out his cheeks and accepted that sleep was not going to come. Crossing to the dresser, he inspected the jagged scar than ran down his left shoulder. Brother Lanry was a skilled healer, but the blade of Knight Commander Rillion had nearly killed him and Brom quite liked having the ugly scar by which to remember the man. Rillion had also killed Magnus, and the lord of Canarn was just as keen to remember that. News of the death of the priest of the Order of the Hammer would have reached South Warden by now, and Al-Hasim would probably be getting very drunk as a result. The world seemed smaller without Father Magnus Forkbeard in it.

Autumn was turning into winter and a bitter wind blew from the straits of Canarn across the city, making it necessary to wear thick fur clothing outside. Bromvy kept his hall warm, but the common men and women of Canarn, who had already endured the occupation, now looked set for a hard winter.

The population had decreased greatly, but those that were left had shown strength of spirit as they helped rebuild the city and welcomed in the Dokkalfar refugees. Bromvy had worried that their visitors would not be welcome, but in fact their sacrifices for the liberation of Canarn had been much appreciated by the Ro. Nanon had helped greatly and he was now viewed affectionately as a comical diplomat.

Pulling on his fur-lined boots and heavy woollen tunic, Bromvy quietly left his chamber and shivered as he stood with Sergeant Auker on duty outside. 'How long till dawn?' he asked.

'An hour or two, my lord,' responded the guardsman. 'Can't sleep?'

'Not tonight, no,' Bromvy answered, with a tired smile. 'You know something, Auker, I saw Nanon turn into a hawk tonight . . . but it's the prospect of an arranged marriage that I can't stop thinking about.'

Auker nodded and screwed up his face slightly. 'A hawk, you say?' He thought about it. 'That doesn't surprise me.'

Brom chuckled as Auker echoed his own thoughts. 'Have we had word from South Warden yet?' he asked.

'You asked me that before you went to bed, my lord. I've got the same answer now as I had then. No, we've received no word from South Warden. Lanry must have got there by now, but it'll be a week at least until we hear back.'

Brom was barely listening and had asked the question merely out of habit.

'Lord Bromvy,' said Auker sharply, making his master suddenly become more alert. 'You okay?'

Brom nodded. 'Yes . . . sorry, I've a lot to think about.' He smiled at the guardsman. 'I'll be on the balcony if you need me.'

'Sunrise in an hour or so, my lord,' Auker said, as Brom loped off down the stone passageway.

CHAPTER EIGHT

RANDALL OF DARKWALD IN THE MERCHANT ENCLAVE OF COZZ

H E HAD GROWN used to the need to post a watch during the night, but still hated having to rise from slumber before the sun was up. He had managed to get the last watch most nights, in the mistaken belief that it was the easier shift, but he still spent most of the time fighting to stay awake.

The last watch of the night meant that he got to see the sun rise and the night turn into day. The sight was beautiful, but it had an edge of melancholy as well, as if the world wasn't quite sure that it deserved another day of sun.

He moved further behind the large tree, trying to keep as low to the ground as possible. Their camp was well off the King's Highway and there was a large area of open ground between the copse of trees and the road, allowing him to see southwards clearly.

The morning was crisp, with swirling winds travelling north across the open plains of Tor Funweir. Utha and Vasir were sitting round the remnants of their nightly cook-fire – now down to the smouldering embers with a pot of porridge slowly warming – while Randall had gone to investigate a distant sound. Utha was rubbing sleep from his eyes and was in a foul mood, whereas the Dokkalfar was as calm as ever, showing no signs of having been woken prematurely.

The trees and the distance gave Randall ample cover from whatever might be approaching, but he was still worried about the strange noise. It had started as a rhythmic clank of metal, too uniform to be just a squad of soldiers or clerics and too loud to be a single rider. As he looked, he had seen a cloud of dust appear. At first it was merely a gentle distortion in the air, maybe a trick of the morning light. However, the cloud became larger and the sound grew louder until a shimmering black line appeared to the south. It was irregular and indicated a large force of armoured men moving slowly in practised step.

The first rank of a large force was marching along the King's Highway, stretching a hundred feet or so either side of the road. The men wore black plate armour and strange, anonymous-looking helms, with no facial features visible. If it had not been for differences in size and height, the soldiers would have been completely indistinguishable from one another. A hollow drumbeat kept the men in time, a deep and regular accompaniment to the familiar sound of armour.

'Hounds,' said Utha quietly from behind, making the squire jump. Randall had got used to Vasir being stealthy, but frequently forgot that his master was not called the Ghost simply because of his pale skin.

'You shouldn't sneak up on me, master. I'm on edge enough as it is.' He turned back to the south. 'Do they all look like that?'

'They have no lives or individuality and supposedly they live only to serve Jaa. The armour is intended to make them act as one.' Utha was also peering at the approaching men and looked more concerned than usual.

'There are a lot of them.' As soon as he said it he realized he had stated the obvious.

'Numbers, my dear boy. When you don't have skill, you rely on numbers. The One values skill and Jaa values numbers.' Utha was holding his longsword and the weapon looked somehow wrong in his hand. When they first met, the Black cleric had used an axe, and since having it taken from him in Ro Tiris he frequently complained about having to use a sword. 'This is not a good sign,' said the cleric.

More hounds came into view as they watched. Five ranks of

black-armoured men were now visible with supply carts and what looked like cages. It was difficult to estimate how many hounds were approaching, but Randall guessed at several hundred at least – possibly an advance guard or a large scouting party.

'What do you think?' he asked.

Utha didn't respond. Then, as the dust cloud rolled closer, Randall saw a thin line of horsemen and several more ranks of infantry marching to the beat of the drum, alongside large wooden contraptions pulled by carthorses. There were now more men than he could count, arrayed across the southern plains and moving slowly towards Cozz.

'I hate being right,' spat Utha. 'That's two thousand men at least. And they have engineers and siege equipment.' Utha turned to look northwards where the morning sky was dominated by chimney smoke rising from the merchant enclave.

'Aside from the Gold church in Voy, Cozz has the greatest wealth in Tor Funweir.' Utha was talking mostly to himself. 'If I was invading, it'd be one of my first targets. Shit.'

Randall had heard only rumours from Ro Weir, but it was impossible to ignore the fact that Karesians had essentially annexed the city. With numbers on their side and the mysterious Seven Sisters orchestrating things, it was believed that the south lands of Tor Funweir were slowly falling under the authority of foreign forces. 'Why would the nobles submit to this?' he asked.

Utha shrugged. 'Who knows. Remember the effect Katja had on the prince and Cardinal Severen?' He was referring to the enchantress they had met in the oubliette of Tiris, a woman who had dominated the minds of the senior nobles of the city. 'Well, the duke of Weir is a fucking idiot, so I imagine he's a lot easier to enchant than a tough old bastard like Severen.' Utha was processing their present situation, his eyes flicking from the army of hounds to the smoke from the merchant enclave. 'We should move,' he said quietly.

'Will they have time to prepare if we warn them?' They backed off hurriedly into the trees.

'Warn them?' queried Utha. 'We're not getting involved. We need to move south before those bastards encircle the enclave and start killing people.'

Randall was a surprised at this. 'We can't let them sack Cozz,' he said with concern.

'I wasn't aware you had such strong feelings for the merchant lords.' Utha looked at the hand Randall had placed on his shoulder and raised an eyebrow. The young squire quickly removed it.

'I have no opinion about them, but that doesn't mean I want them killed or imprisoned.' He was not used to arguing with Utha and shrank under the withering glare of his master's pink eyes.

'Randall, we are wanted by virtually every authority in Tor Funweir. It's likely that that lot have been ordered to apprehend us as well, and you want us to backtrack to warn the marshal?' The cleric was not convinced. 'Marshal Wesson is a decent sort of man. He's no love for the church or the crown and I'm . . . sorry for the loss he's about to experience, but it's not our problem.'

Randall frowned. His master was not a cruel or an evil man, but he was pragmatic and that meant not doing things that would endanger him or his companions.

'I think it *is* our problem.' The voice came from Tyr Vasir. The tall Dokkalfar had appeared out of the trees and made Randall jump again.

'Am I the only person here that makes a noise when he moves?' Randall asked. He was becoming fed up with everyone else except him being naturally stealthy.

Utha raised an eyebrow. Vasir tilted his head. Neither of his companions had realized how frequently they made the young squire jump. But right now they had more important concerns.

Randall smiled awkwardly. 'Okay, not the matter in hand . . . sorry, carry on.'

Vasir came to the edge of the trees and looked south towards the approaching hounds. 'Do you see those cages, my friends?' he said.

Randall and Utha peered at the steel cages amidst the marching warriors. At first they'd looked empty, perhaps intended for captives. But as they stared, they saw that the cages were already occupied.

'Who are the prisoners?' asked Utha. 'There isn't a significant-sized town between Cozz and Weir . . . they'd have no reason to imprison anyone.'

Vasir bowed his head and began to hum quietly. It was a deep and echoing note that managed to convey extreme sadness and regret. The forest-dweller closed his eyes and composed himself before he spoke. 'The forever of the Dokkalfar tells of our gift from the Fire Giant.' He was speaking clearly and reciting a story or scripture of some kind. 'Our forms will burn . . . must burn . . . upon death.' Utha had once told Randall that the Dokkalfar burst into flames when they died. What it meant now, however, was a mystery.

Utha looked at Randall and then put a hand on Vasir's shoulder, making the tall forest-dweller open his black eyes. 'I know of this, but what does it have to do with them?' Utha's words were both caring and impatient as he pointed towards the cages.

'The maleficent witches have removed our gift. We no longer burn,' responded Vasir.

'So what happens if you don't burn?' Utha's eyes were narrow, and Vasir looked more and more uncomfortable.

The forest-dweller began swaying and muttering something under his breath. It was a chant of some kind but was not clear at first. As Vasir continued to sway, Randall and Utha heard the words he was repeating. 'The priest and the altar, the priest and the altar, the priest and the altar,' he said, over and over again.

They turned away from Vasir and focused back on the approaching cages. They were still distant, but the forms within were tall and, though some were evidently conscious and sitting up, others looked torpid or dead. Neither of them said anything, and Randall's hands shook as he made out twenty or so Dokkalfar prisoners being transported along with the army of hounds.

'If each one of them turns into that tentacled tree-thing from the oubliette,' said Utha quietly, 'Tor Funweir has a bigger problem than I thought.' He was silent for a moment. He looked at his two companions, then towards Cozz, and then at the approaching army of hounds.

'Master –' began Randall.

'I know, I know,' interrupted the Black cleric. He suddenly slapped Vasir hard across the face. 'Snap out of it.'

Vasir blinked rapidly, stopped chanting, and looked from his crouched position at the bulky albino standing over him. 'My apologies, Utha the Shadow, but the . . . *transformation* is the greatest fear of my people.'

Randall's head was full of images of the tree. He strained to conceive how a creature such as Vasir could change into such a madness-inducing monstrosity. 'They won't believe us,' he said, without turning from the cages.

'No, I don't think they will,' Utha replied, 'but maybe Wesson is wise enough to accept the danger of an army of hounds.' He puffed out his cheeks and Randall sensed that his master was going to embark on a course of action that he considered unwise. 'Right,' he said wearily. 'Vasir, figure out some way to get to those cages. Randall, you and I are going to have a little chat with the knight marshal.'

* * *

Randall had been to Cozz before, and his memories of the merchant enclave were not especially positive. The last time he'd been there it had been on the trail of Bromvy Black Guard and the encounter had resulted in Brother Torian's death from a Kirin assassin's arrow. Utha had also been present, but he was less perturbed by past encounters as they strode through the well-kept streets.

It had taken them two hours, moving at a steady run, to reach Cozz, and they had been allowed to enter with no questions asked, in the wake of a series of hard glares from the Black cleric. Utha had made little effort to remain incognito and Randall had been anxious that it was an ideal place for mercenaries on their trail to lie in wait. The cleric had shrugged off his concerns and evidently thought the merchant lords of the enclave would care little for a fugitive in their midst, even a fugitive accused of killing the prince.

'They don't answer to the crown or the church,' Utha said, as they entered the wide, circular market which dominated the enclave. 'Have I not explained this to you?'

'The last time we were here, Torian died. To be honest, master, I can remember little other than that.' They were still walking quickly and Randall frequently had to jog for a few steps to keep up with Utha.

'Yes, well, you shouldn't dwell on past battles . . . won or lost. I'm not armoured this time, so hopefully no one will recognize me.'

Randall raised an eyebrow, but didn't say anything.

The inner market housed the agents and stalls of the richest lords and were filled with exotic Karesian spices and expensive wine. The outer stalls were progressively less opulent, with a corresponding decrease in quality and price, though no less busy. The only kind of business that was not conducted in the central market was the enclave's metalwork, which was located in a number of open blacksmiths' yards, one of which had been the site of Torian's death.

The knight marshal, the man called Wesson, was responsible for the enclave's security and was the only true noble in Cozz. By all accounts, Marshal Wesson of Cozz was a pragmatic knight, from humble origins, whose only concern was the security of the enclave. He had, apparently, been squire to Duke Alexander Tiris, the king's brother, and was held in high regard in consequence. The great cities of Tor Funweir needed the wealth and trade of the merchants of Cozz much more than they were pleased to admit.

The markets were all open for business as usual, and there was no obvious sign that they were aware of the approaching hounds. 'Do you think they know?' Randall asked.

'They must have an idea at least. Two thousand men cannot travel quietly,' replied the Black cleric, with a puzzled look.

'Look over there.' Utha pointed to the lower level of the knight marshal's office, a squat building on three levels which acted as gaol, courthouse and central authority for the enclave. The cleric was pointing to a group of rough-looking men hanging around the steps. 'What do they look like to you?' he asked.

'Mercenaries, master.' Randall resisted the urge to say that he had warned Utha about this. 'Ten of them.' The men wore mismatched leather armour and carried knives, maces and crossbows, all of which looked to have been well used.

Utha pulled up the hood of his brown cloak and walked directly towards the wide steps that led up to the marshal's office. 'Let's see how observant they are, shall we?' Utha's words were spoken with a smile and, for a moment, Randall saw again the caustic and belligerent Black cleric he'd first met.

The mercenaries were blocking the way and, aside from disapproving looks from nearby watchmen, they were being left well alone. Each man was unshaven and, as they approached, Randall detected a definite similarity between these men and those who had attacked them in Voy.

'Get out of my way,' Utha barked at the nearest man.

The mercenaries showed surprise at the large man who had marched straight up to them. They stopped cursing at passers-by and turned to regard the newcomer. Their hands rested on their weapons, and Randall clenched his fists to stop his hands from shaking. Glancing at the watchmen, he was glad to see a dozen within earshot. They were the bound men of Cozz, charged with policing the streets.

'Nice cloak, sweetheart,' quipped one of the men with a sneer. 'How about you come over here and rub my shoulders for me . . . I'm a bit sore.'

The other men laughed. The way they looked at Randall made his skin crawl. 'You're a handsome little boy,' one of them said to the young squire. 'We should be friends.' Another round of laughter erupted.

Utha didn't stop moving forwards. 'I said *get out of my way*,' he repeated. 'I'm going into the knight marshal's office, and you're not going to stop me.' He hadn't raised his head and his pale face remained hidden under his hood.

The mercenary narrowed his eyes, but didn't step aside. 'We work for Sir Hallam Pevain,' he snapped. 'Now, show your face!'

Utha stepped to the side of the man and, almost as an after-thought, kicked him violently in the groin. A sharp intake of breath, a strangled cry, and the mercenary crumpled to the floor, curled up into an undignified ball. Without breaking step, the bulky Black cleric stamped on the man's head.

'Kill the fucker,' shouted another mercenary, drawing a steel mace from his belt.

'Very foolish words,' said Utha, pointing beyond the mercenaries to the watchmen, all of whom had drawn crossbows.

'No one dies in Cozz without the marshal's word,' said an old watchman wearing the shoulder flashes of a sergeant. 'Brawls are brawls, murder is murder.' Eight more watchmen warily regarded the mercenaries. Randall enjoyed the spectacle of ten men who were powerless to act against Utha. They clearly wanted to start a fight, but realized they were likely to be killed before they got the chance.

'I'm just on my way to see Marshal Wesson,' said Utha to the sergeant. 'I'll be sure to tell him that I'm guilty of brawling in the street.' The Black cleric didn't wait for a response. He turned away and walked up the steps. Randall followed hurriedly, with less style and confidence than his master.

'Was that luck?' he asked as they entered the lower level of Marshal Wesson's offices.

'Half of everything is luck, my dear boy,' responded Utha, evidently very pleased with himself. 'Those watchmen were look-ing for a reason to exert a bit of authority over the bastards. I just gave them an opportunity.' He smiled at his squire. 'Yes, Randall, it was mostly luck.'

The stone building was warm and homely, with paintings displaying caricatures of greedy-looking merchants and stiff-necked nobles. The floor was carpeted in light blue and made the entrance hall feel open and airy.

'Can I help you?' asked a young man seated by the bottom landing.

'I need to speak with Marshal Wesson,' Utha answered with authority.

'He's busy currently, my lord. Would you like an appointment?' The man was younger than Randall and looked with curiosity at the cloaked man before him.

'No, I'll see him now.' Utha didn't wait for the man's response. He marched up the stairs, ignoring the young man's spluttered objections.

Randall was a little way behind. 'Sorry, he's . . . very single-minded. Don't worry, he won't cause any trouble.'

The words were not very reassuring, but the man didn't give chase. Randall ran to catch up, his boots clattering on the wooden stairs. 'Politeness isn't always an inconvenience, you know,' he said, as they passed the first floor.

'No, but waiting for an appointment is,' replied the cleric. 'It's urgent, remember.'

They reached the third floor and turned from the stairs to walk along a carpeted corridor. More caricatures lined the walls and Randall guessed that Marshal Wesson had a sense of humour. A caricature of a Red knight was well executed in watercolours, showing a nobleman sitting astride a bored-looking horse, his crested helmet far too big for his head and his red breastplate falling from his spindly frame.

'Couldn't get away with stuff like that in any other city in Tor Funweir,' said Utha with a smile.

At the end of the corridor they entered a large seating area filled with comfortable-looking couches and low tables. The decoration was unpretentious, with warm wood and light-blue fabrics.

The waiting room was empty, though raised voices came from beyond a simple oak door. The area had several exits, leading to balconies that looked out over the central market.

156

'Where are all the guards?' Randall asked.

Utha glanced round the empty waiting room. 'Probably in with the marshal. I think those pricks outside are waiting for their master.'

The mercenary had said that they worked for Sir Hallam Pevain, a name unfamiliar to Randall. 'Do knights normally have mercenary attendants?' he asked. 'Sir Leon never had one.'

'Not normally, but this particular knight is different. Keep your arse clenched, boy, you're about to meet a rapist, a murderer and a man unfit to be called *sir*. Hopefully, Wesson's reputation as a fair and decent man is more than just rumour.' He looked concerned.

If Pevain controlled the mercenaries, then it was he who sought to apprehend Utha and his men that they had encountered in Voy. Cozz was the likely next place for them to search and Randall swore silently at having insisted they warn Marshal Wesson about the hounds.

The Black cleric pushed back his hood to reveal his face, gripped the door handle and pushed it inwards. Utha did not knock but, with his squire following him, he stepped boldly into the knight marshal's office.

Within was a large, simple room. A wooden desk dominated the space, positioned in the centre of the room. Behind, there was a wide, open balcony with billowing blue curtains.

The dozen men in the office all looked up sharply as Utha and his squire entered. Two were seated on either side of the desk, the larger of them with his back to the door. The one facing them was clearly Knight Marshal Wesson of Cozz. He wore a light-blue tabard with heraldry of an open purse, over a well-maintained chain shirt. He was a man in early middle age, with thinning brown hair, but still tough-looking and with a shrewd glint in his light eyes. Standing guard round the edge of the room were watchmen of Cozz. Each carried a loaded crossbow and made a movement to cover the door when Utha entered.

There were also three men in the office who were clearly not officials of the enclave. Two stood by the desk, glaring viciously, and the third was seated opposite the marshal, wearing black plate armour and carrying a strange war-hammer. Randall had to look twice at the two standing mercenaries before he realized they were twins, each slender and blonde-haired, with multiple hand-axes and knives poking out from their well-worn leather armour.

'It's clearly my day for interruptions,' stated the marshal, with an ironic lilt to his voice. 'And who would you be, my pale friend?' The marshal was not alarmed by their presence.

'My name is Brother Utha of Arnon, my lord,' stated the Black cleric confidently, causing the seated mercenary to rise and stare at him.

The man was tall, almost seven feet, and wore a full beard. His black hair was long and curly but greased back from his face, lending him the image of a man who was endeavouring to look presentable. Sir Hallam Pevain was a hard-looking man by any standards and Randall tried not to meet his eye. The twins both growled gutturally and reached for their knives.

'Enough!' shouted Wesson. He raised his hand at the watchmen, who levelled their weapons. 'You fight in my office and I'll arrest you all.'

Pevain's glare turned into a smile. He stood up and faced Utha. 'You're a bold one, Ghost.' He straightened to his full height and looked down at the shorter man.

'And you're a son of a whore, sir knight,' responded Utha. He didn't back off and showed little concern for their difference in height. 'I'm here to talk to Marshal Wesson, not to a sewer rat like you.'

'Brave words, pig-fucker,' said one of the twins, with a vicious look to his narrow eyes. 'I should open you up right here . . .' he glanced at Randall, 'and fuck your boy while you lie bleeding.'

Wesson stood up sharply. 'I said that's enough. If I have to say it again, bolts fly. Understood?' His watchmen dutifully took aim. 'I'm sure you're all very scary, but my crossbows aren't afraid of you, so sit the fuck down,' he barked with authority.

'Marshal Wesson,' said Pevain, without turning from Utha, 'this man killed Prince Christophe Tiris and is a wanted criminal. You have a duty to arrest him if you are able.'

Wesson laughed. The sound was relaxed. 'If I apprehended every man wanted in Tor Funweir, we'd have no merchants or clients left, Pevain.'

One of the twins spoke. 'He's a knight; you call him *sir*.'

Pevain waved away the mercenary's objection. 'Parag, just keep your mouth shut. Okay, Wesson, I'll buy into this. I hope you realize what will happen to you if you let this man escape.'

Wesson raised an eyebrow at the threat and sat back down. 'This is Cozz, not Tiris. As far as I know, this cleric has not committed any crime in my enclave. Until he does, you and he are equally welcome.'

Utha smiled at Pevain and motioned to the seat behind him. 'Sit down,' he said coldly. 'This won't end well if you don't.'

The two men sized each other up. Pevain was taller by nearly a foot, but Utha was wider and more confident. The mercenary's war-hammer looked to be of Ranen design and had ornate carvings around the metal braces. Randall didn't want to think about the outcome if the two should fight, but he knew his master was one of the most dangerous men in Tor Funweir.

Slowly, and without taking his eyes from Utha, Pevain took his seat and waved the twins to step back. Then he faced Marshal Wesson. 'I came here seeking assistance in hunting down a murderer. Now that murderer wanders freely into your office. So what do you propose we do about it?'

'Nothing,' responded Wesson. 'He's broken no law in Cozz.'

Utha chuckled to himself. 'Fascinating as it is seeing you flounder around, Pevain, I have urgent news for the marshal.'

'What news?' asked Wesson.

'My lord,' spat Parag, 'do we have to stand 'ere with this cunt and listen to his horse-shit?' The twins were itching for combat and Randall disliked the way they were eyeing him up. He guessed that they enjoyed violating people.

'Parag, Broot, both of you keep your mouths shut,' ordered Pevain. 'Wesson, I intend to make this man a captive. Our beloved allies will reward you handsomely for any assistance you can give.'

Utha snorted at the mention of the Seven Sisters and perched on the edge of the desk. 'We can deal with how you want to die later, sir knight. Right now there is an army of hounds marching this way.' The Black cleric spoke with conviction.

'I know,' replied Wesson. 'They come from Ro Weir. No need to fret, though. I've already sent riders to Voy and Tiris asking for aid. The Karesian dogs won't dare attack a town the size of Cozz. I'll go out and parlay with them and we'll turn them round in short order.'

Pevain smiled, clearly aware of the hounds' approach.

'My lord, this is not a scouting party. There are several thousand of them with siege equipment and . . . other weapons of war.' Utha referred ambiguously to the captive forest-dwellers. Randall was sure they would not be believed should they mention the true nature of these *weapons of war*.

'Brother Utha, your reputation is of a serious man, a man not to be trifled with. Whether you killed a prince or not, I will always respect the words of a Black cleric.' Wesson leant back in his chair. 'But Cozz is far from helpless. We have five hundred watchmen and many more yeomen can be pressed should the need arise. We also have high walls and solid gates. Only a military idiot would attack us.'

Utha nodded and was evidently searching for a well-reasoned argument to dissuade Wesson out of his overconfidence. He looked at Pevain – who was still smiling – then at the twins, Parag and Broot. Each of them was clearly concerned at the presence of the Black cleric, but showed not the slightest alarm at the news of two thousand hounds marching on Cozz.

'And you, sir knight.' Utha addressed Pevain, the title dripping with sarcasm as he spoke it. 'What do you know of this army?'

The mercenary shrugged. 'The same as everyone knows – they are our allies. The king has allowed their presence in Weir.'

'But not in Cozz,' interjected Wesson. 'They can occupy Ro Weir for as long as they like, but the merchant lords are guaranteed autonomy by decree of the house of Tiris.' He smiled at Utha. 'Have no fear, brother, I've talked my way out of worse situations. Hanging around with merchants rubs off on you after a while. I just need to explain to these . . . allies . . . that the blood that would be required to annex Cozz really doesn't make it an attractive proposition. Then we wait until Voy or Tiris sends aid.' The knight marshal was supremely confident that his riders would return with reinforcements. 'You're welcome to stay if you wish,' he said to the Black cleric.

Utha shook his head. 'I'm sorry to say that our path lies elsewhere, my lord. We only came to Cozz to warn you. I'm not sure you appreciate how serious the warning is.'

'And the warning is appreciated, Brother Utha, but we have the situation in hand.'

'You hear that, Ghost?' Pevain said with vicious glee. 'It's in hand. You can fuck off any time you like.'

Randall didn't think before he spoke. 'Excuse me, sir, but the hounds don't look like they want to talk, or parlay, or whatever you call it. I think –'

'Silence, boy!' shouted Parag, 'or you'll get a good spanking.' Both twins laughed and licked their lips suggestively. 'You ever been fucked?' asked Broot.

Utha glared across the table. 'Better keep your cock out of sight, shit-stain, you're likely to make us all laugh.'

'I won't tell any of you again,' said Wesson, gesturing to his crossbowmen. 'I won't have brawling in my office.'

'And outside?' asked the mercenary, gripping the hilt of his war-hammer. 'How do you feel about brawling in the street?'

'Don't push me, Pevain,' responded Wesson, more aggressively this time. 'I won't hesitate to lock up a knight, or a cleric.'

Utha shook his head. 'I'm sorry things have turned out so, my lord marshal,' he said with respect, 'but if our warning has gone unheeded, we need to leave.'

'Very well. Sergeant Jerome,' Wesson gestured to one of his watchmen, 'please take a squad of men and escort Brother Utha to the south gate. And make sure Sir Pevain and his men don't interfere.'

'At once, my lord,' responded the sergeant.

As Utha and Randall moved to the door, Pevain stood. 'See you soon, Ghost.'

'I'll be easy to find, sir knight.' Utha didn't turn. 'I'll be the one burying my sword in your face.'

* * *

They had left the knight marshal's office quickly. With five watchmen of Cozz in close guard, they headed south. Though Marshal Wesson had seemed friendly enough and had been respectful towards them, Randall was sure he wanted Utha out of the enclave as soon as possible. Unfortunately, they still had to wait at the gate as various important merchant lords had decided to leave. Evidently, they had learned that an army of hounds was approaching and did not share Wesson's confidence.

The watchmen said nothing as they waited. They stood close to the cleric and his squire, their crossbows ready. Randall wasn't sure whether the weapons were intended to make sure they left or to protect them from Pevain's men.

'How long do we have to wait?' Utha asked Sergeant Jerome. 'Your marshal seems keen on us not being here.'

'I'm escorting you, but I don't need to talk to you,' replied the watchman. 'We'll have you on your way as soon as possible.'

Utha didn't press the question and simply stood there, leaning on a low wooden fence that acted as a holding area in front of the gate. A number of people glanced across at them and Randall felt more exposed than was ideal. They were in plain view of everyone massed round the gate – merchant lords, common traders or mercenary guards. Several took a second glance at the bulky albino cleric and Randall heard the name *Utha the Ghost* murmured twice.

'We've been here too long,' Randall said quietly. 'You stand out, you know.'

'What?' asked Utha, oblivious of people's reactions to him. It was an infuriating trait.

'Your face, it is white. See mine, it is not. See all their faces, *they* are not. You stand out.' There was no hint of humour and Randall simply wanted the cleric to be aware of how exposed they were.

Utha glared at him. 'And if I punch my squire in the head? Will that make me more or less conspicuous?' The words were spoken without any ill intent and, for perhaps the first time, the young man of Darkwald did not feel afraid of his master.

He smiled to himself but said nothing further, content that they'd be on their way soon. Hopefully they could find a way to rescue the Dokkalfar – if they couldn't save Cozz from the hounds, they could at least lessen the odds by preventing the darkwood trees making an appearance.

Then he saw something out of the corner of his eye. A drawn crossbow appeared through the press of waiting traders and pointed towards them. No one nearby had noticed, and it was only the steely glint catching the morning sun that alerted Randall.

'Utha,' he snapped, grabbing his master by the shoulder and turning him round, 'crossbow.' Just as he spoke, the bolt was loosed, making a whistling sound as it flew towards them. The watchmen began to turn, but the bolt was well aimed and pierced Sergeant Jerome through the chest.

'To arms,' shouted another of the watchmen.

Screaming and shouting erupted from the crowd and people began to run from the scene. The open ground leading to the gate was a wide roadway. Wagons and horses started to scatter, with guards and traders wielding weapons or protecting their goods.

Randall and Utha ducked down behind the wooden fence and drew their swords in unison. A quizzical look passed between them. 'We've spent too much time together, young Randall. You've started to copy me.' Then another bolt flew overhead.

A second watchman was wounded in the leg and cried out in pain, but he didn't drop his crossbow. Randall peered out through the wooden fencing and saw the distinctive features of Parag. The mercenary was crouched low to the ground and had sneaked up on them through the crowd. He had a wild smile on his face and was dribbling slightly. Behind him, his brother and a dozen more of Pevain's bastards appeared from between the wooden buildings and approached. All of them had crossbows and were now starting to fire.

'Get down,' Utha shouted to the remaining watchmen.

Two bolts caught fleeing citizens of Cozz. Randall could no longer see how many mercenaries were approaching. The watchmen behind him seemed to die in slow motion as bolts thudded into them.

No more bolts had been fired once the watchmen were all down, and the mercenaries were giving the populace a chance to leave. Utha was hurriedly looking around. Behind them was a high wooden palisade that led to the enclave's stables. They had three sides of a solidly built wooden fence for cover, but no obvious means of escape.

'Ghost,' shouted a distant voice.

'Oh, fuck,' muttered Utha. 'I didn't think Pevain was that confident.' He smiled thinly. 'Well, Wesson won't let him back into Cozz any time soon.'

Randall frowned. 'You're not very good at motivational speeches, master. What do we do?' His sword hand had begun to shake.

Utha didn't respond straightaway. Instead, he got low to the ground and reached back to grab two of the fallen watchmen's crossbows. 'I think they want me alive . . . I hope so anyway.'

The populace had mostly left the scene and the sound of screaming was now distant. A few wagons and traders' carts were still being pulled clear of the gate or back into the enclave.

'This is what's going to happen, Ghost, you're going to get bloody . . . I'm going to fuck you up in ways you never dreamed of.' A chorus of off-colour jokes was directed at them from the mercenaries. 'But it's my mistress you should be worried about,' Pevain shouted.

'Another of the Seven Sisters,' Utha said to his squire. 'I'll bet you a bottle of Darkwald red that the pointless prick is talking about a Karesian enchantress.'

Randall smiled. 'If they take us, we'll find out.'

'They won't take us,' growled the Black cleric, in a way that didn't invite dissent.

He loaded the two crossbows quickly while the mercenaries shouted at the remaining innocents to leave. Then the Black cleric rose from behind the fence and levelled the first weapon. Randall couldn't see his target, but he heard a guttural shout as a mercenary was hit.

An answering bolt thudded into the fence, inches from where Utha stood. He quickly ducked back to join Randall.

'We need him alive, Parag. Knives and maces, boys,' commanded Pevain, his voice still distant.

Randall chanced a look through the fence and saw twelve men on the road. The one dead body, sprawled with a bolt protruding from his eye, had bothered the others very little and they eagerly hefted an assortment of large knives, heavy maces and cudgels.

'Okay, just this once, Randall, you're permitted to fight mercenaries.' Utha rose again and fired his second crossbow, causing another man to fall backwards. As he ducked behind the fence, the cleric breathed in sharply and discarded the crossbows. 'Your hand isn't shaking any more,' he said.

Randall looked down and saw a steady hand gripping his longsword. He tensed his body and pushed away the rising fear, hoping that the bastards' need to capture rather than to kill would enable both squire and master to escape. 'Okay,' he said to Utha, 'we make for the gate.'

The cleric smiled and nodded. They both moved quickly from behind the fence and Utha kicked open the gate. With the Black cleric in front of him, Randall stepped out on to the southern roadway.

'Take him,' shouted Pevain, making his presence known as soon as they moved into view.

The mercenary knight stood atop a cart on the opposite side of the road. The tall man was wearing black plate armour and held his Ranen war-hammer across his shoulders. Towards the southern gate of Cozz was an open roadway, with a few huddled people taking cover behind the enclave walls. Randall looked straight ahead at the grinning face of Parag as the mercenary banged two large knives together in front of his chest. He looked at Broot, the other twin, who was licking the blade of his knife and staring wildly at them. Lastly, he looked at Utha. His master wore a mask of confident rage and advanced towards the nearest mercenary.

The Black cleric roared a challenge as he swung his sword downwards. 'You should have retreated when you had the chance, Pevain.' His longsword was met with a risen mace that buckled limply. The mercenary looked shocked as the sword struck a second time and cut through his skull, releasing a spray of blood. It was a brutal statement of intent. The Black cleric had made no attempt to fight the man, he had simply killed him as quickly and efficiently as possible.

Utha picked up the fallen mace and stepped sideways towards the gate. Randall stood alongside him, the sword of Great Claw held steadily forward.

When the attack came, it was wild and uncoordinated. Two of the mercenaries lunged at them while Parag attacked from the side. Utha deflected the first lunge and kneed the man in the face as Randall ran the second man through, feeling a rush of blood to his head as he killed the mercenary. Parag had attacked Utha, but his knives met only air as the cleric dodged back and continued moving towards the gate.

'You okay?' Utha asked Randall over his shoulder, his words coming through quickened breath.

'He's not the first man I've killed,' replied the squire, 'and I really hate this lot.' Randall found that his dislike of Pevain's men was making it easier to fight them. His hand was still and he had found the strength with which he'd killed the man surprising, reminding him that the past few months had toughened him up.

Then the other mercenaries were upon them. They were not skilled and, so long as Randall concentrated on defence, he found the reach provided by his longsword a great advantage. The mercenaries smelt terrible and he could feel their breath upon him. Utha was concentrating on keeping the bastards away from his squire, swinging the mace he had acquired around his head to keep them at a distance while Randall feverishly parried lazy attacks.

'We haven't got all day, Ghost,' shouted Pevain, closer now, though Randall could not see the mercenary knight among the combatants.

Utha split a man's head and crushed another's ribcage, roaring at the top of his voice and appearing larger than any of Pevain's men. He was a trained warrior and, as he launched an all-out attack, he was too much for these men. Randall was in the cleric's shadow now, concentrating on covering his master's back rather than getting in the way.

Then Parag threw a knife and caught Randall in the thigh. It was a sudden move and caught the squire off guard. The pain was immediate and sharp, lancing deep into his flesh and making him fall to one knee. His head swam and his vision blurred, though he clung on tightly to the sword of Great Claw. He vaguely saw Utha kill a man with an upward swing of his sword, then leap backwards to stand over his fallen squire.

'We don't need the boy, Ghost,' said Pevain with an evil chuckle.

Randall focused sufficiently to see the knight aim a crossbow at him. Half of the mercenaries lay dead and Utha was not wounded. Parag, Broot and Pevain were still standing off to the side, leaving the job of dying to their men.

As the bolt flew from Pevain's crossbow, a strange sound came from beyond the southern gates of Cozz. It was a whistling noise that started distantly and became progressively louder as the squire followed the trajectory of Pevain's bolt. The sound was steadily growing to a roar as a dull pain erupted in his side. Looking down, he saw the bolt poking through his leather jerkin.

'Randall!' Utha was shouted his name, but the squire was beginning to lose consciousness as the whistling roar turned into a giant boulder crashing into the walls of Cozz. The palisade crumbled inwards, not far to their left, and now the tension of further catapults being armed could be heard away to the south.

'Get down!' Pevain roared, as more boulders were launched at the enclave and wooden splinters filled the air. 'Izra's started the festivities early, lads, we need to get the fuck out of here. The Ghost can wait.'

Randall could just make out the bastards laughing as they hurriedly left the roadway, but the last sound he heard before he passed out was Utha saying, 'You die when I die, not a second before.'

* * *

Randall woke abruptly, bright light making him squint and raise a hand to shield his eyes. He felt weak and his leg and stomach both throbbed with sharp pain. Reaching down, he felt grass underneath him and the rustle of trees made him think he was back at the camp south of Cozz.

'He didn't hit anything important,' Utha remarked from nearby.

'My leg and stomach are both important,' responded Randall weakly.

'You'll mend . . . and he hit your side, not your stomach.'

Randall tried to sit up, but he was only an inch from the ground before the pain made him wince and lie back down. A poultice made from grass and twigs was firmly tied to the wound in his side and there was another on his right thigh. Vasir sat next to him, carefully tying green roots together and rubbing them in a foul-smelling black substance.

The Dokkalfar looked up and tilted his head to one side. 'You are lucky, Randall of Darkwald, both for the mercenary's poor aim and for your master's broad shoulders. He ran here with you on his back.'

Randall stared at Utha, who turned away with a look of embarrassment on his face. 'You've saved my life twice, boy. Consider this half-payment.'

'How . . .' began Randall.

'Did we get out of Cozz?' supplied the Black cleric, and Randall gave a shallow nod. 'The hounds started throwing rocks at the southern wall. They've not advanced or made any demands. They're just out there, formed up for battle on the King's Highway.'

Vasir leant over Randall and poked at his wound, making the squire shrink away and gasp in pain. 'Careful, there was a bit of wood stuck in there a minute ago . . . it hurts.' He was light-headed and had to fight to stay conscious.

'I need to apply another dressing to your wound,' said the Dokkalfar, waving the sticky black roots in front of his face.

'He knows what he's doing,' offered Utha, with the slightest hint of a smile. 'I would have used maggots and torn fabric bandages.'

'Okay, get on with it.' Randall closed his eyes and tensed his body as best he could.

Vasir removed the poultice and began to rub firmly at the wound. The pain was intermittent, but fierce when it came, and Randall had to grab a handful of grass and mud to keep from crying out as the forest-dweller cleaned the wound.

'Just because he's a cleric of death, you don't need to kill me,' he said through the pain.

'I intend to stop the pain,' replied the forest-dweller without looking up from the wound. 'The salve should dull it sufficiently for you to travel. And the black roots will keep the wound clean.'

Utha began sharpening his longsword and Randall noted that his master had also kept the heavy mace he'd acquired in Cozz. The sound provided a distraction from Vasir's poking and prodding, and the wounded squire began to feel numb.

'I think,' he said weakly, 'I might pass out again.' Randall had rocked on to his side and was looking at his master.

'Well, young man, Vasir and I have an errand to run. You can have an hour's sleep. After that, you're over my shoulder again.' He frowned. 'Actually, you're a heavy fucker, you can go over Vasir's shoulder.'

'An errand?' queried the squire.

Vasir and Utha exchanged a determined glance. 'The hounds don't know how to protect their lines. They're pretty disorganized. The cages have just been dumped next to the road with a single keeper each.' He paused. 'They're at the back of the pack, while the others are shooting stuff at Cozz. We're going to stage a rescue.'

Randall wiped the sweat from his forehead and blinked a few times to stave off sleep. 'Has Wesson done anything?' he asked, finding himself as concerned for Cozz as Vasir was for the imprisoned Dokkalfar.

'Not that I've seen,' replied Utha. 'I think he's waiting for them to stop the bombardment so he can go out and talk to them. Assuming we get away with the Dokkalfar, the marshal should only have two thousand hounds to deal with.'

'We can't just rescue them and leave,' said Randall through a light-headed yawn, as Vasir finished tying the poultice to his thigh.

'We can and we will,' replied Utha. He resumed sharpening his sword. 'Sleep, Randall. We'll be in a hurry when you wake, so enjoy the peace.'

His eyes felt heavy and he soon gave in to sleep. He was a wanted man, travelling with other wanted men, and Randall of Darkwald was beginning to lose hope that he would ever experience peace again.

CHAPTER NINE

DALIAN THIEF TAKER IN THE MERCHANT ENCLAVE OF COZZ

THE WEATHER HAD grown cooler and the wind heavier, indicating to Dalian that the strange disposition of the Ro was most likely due to the poor weather. In Karesia, the heavy armour worn by the hounds was viewed as punishment as much as protection, while in Tor Funweir it was almost a luxury protecting them against the horrid weather. Dalian had heard stories of hounds boiling in their own sweat while refusing to remove their steel shells for fear of offending Jaa. He wondered if they would become soft in the lands of the Ro, or whether the upcoming battle would give them enough of a workout to remain useful.

The Thief Taker had travelled with the pack through several weeks of marching northwards. They had slept every other night, and the daylight hours had been a miasma of threats, punishments and strong drugs to keep the pack sharp. The hounds were not regarded as men and women but as the blunt instruments of Jaa, to be wielded as a wind claw would wield his kris knife.

Dalian prayed often – a common sight as the hounds made camp each night, but a ritual that had special significance for the wind claw. He was not a hound, nor was he an ally of Izra and the enchantress she followed. He was a true devotee of Jaa, an interloper amongst traitors to the Fire Giant. They did not know they were being led astray by one of the Seven Sisters, but that was not a mitigating factor in Dalian's eyes. If he could, the

Thief Taker would gladly immolate every single one of them for their betrayal.

They had been stationary for several hours now and, for a change, none of the hounds was interested in sleep. They had sighted Cozz in the early morning and, once within catapult range of the enclave, Izra had ordered a halt. Dalian had managed to get close to the front, another anonymous hound wanting to look at their goal, and he'd seen the whip-mistress dancing like an insane child as the first boulder thudded into Cozz.

The atmosphere in the camp was strange, and Dalian imagined himself elsewhere, to avoid listening to the hounds as they boasted about the children they would eat and the facial tattoos they would get. In his mind, the Thief Taker was on a distant coastline, with water caressing his tired feet and a glass of fine Thrakkan wine in his hand. He knew that Jaa intended more for him, and that having to endure the tedium of being around brutal idiots was just the precursor to victory.

The bombardment went on for hours, as Izra and her captains playfully targeted particular parts of the wall to amuse them-selves. Their intention, if rumour that ran among the hounds was to be believed, was to strip the town of anything valuable. Merchants were to be imprisoned, coins seized and buildings claimed. The whip-mistress would then order the death of the captive forest-dwellers. Exactly what would happen when they were killed was a matter of speculation among the pack. The Thief Taker himself knew what would happen and, if Saara the Mistress of Pain was right, the Dark Young that would sprout from the dead forest-dwellers would signal the end of Cozz. He had never seen one of the beasts, but he had listened to the enchantress's account of their power and her manic insistence that they should be birthed. Dalian knew that they were not of Jaa. Whatever god the Seven Sisters now followed, he knew that it was his enemy.

'Old dog,' grunted a voice nearby, 'up front with the rest of twenty-three.'

The pack was divided up by number. It was thought that to give a unit a name might encourage pride and individuality. Dalian had simply joined the closest group when he arrived. Twenty-three was a skirmisher unit, using light javelins.

'At once,' he responded in a monotone.

'The mistress is angry about something and wants you lot flanking her when she gives orders.' The words were devoid of emotion and conveyed the information in as simple a manner as possible, indicating that the man had been a hound for some time.

Dalian and the rest of twenty-three walked silently towards the front of the pack and he began to hear high-pitched shrieking. The voice was female and contorted itself into a bizarre spiral of half-formed notes which conveyed anger, frustration and other emotions that defied description.

'Someone's gonna die,' joked a nearby hound, a young cutpurse recently sentenced in Kessia.

'Hopefully you, you little pink cunt,' barked a senior hound, slapping the young man to emphasize the point. 'Mouths shut, dogs,' he growled to the rest of twenty-three.

The fifty-strong unit emerged through the front rank of hounds and on to the open fields to the south of Cozz.

The enclave was partially hidden behind a cloud of dust. Dalian guessed that the citizens of Ro had retreated to cover to wait out the bombardment. The catapults had ceased firing and the engine crews were now standing idle, awaiting orders. Nearby, Izra Sabal, the whip-mistress, was ranting at her senior hounds. Dalian recognized Kasimir Roux, an ex-wind claw, convicted of mass murder in Rikara.

'They weren't as helpless as they appeared, mistress,' Roux was saying to Izra. 'Once their cages were opened, the risen killed half a dozen men in as many seconds.'

'How did they escape?' shrieked Izra. 'Who opened their cages? Who would be so stupid?'

Kasimir, Izra and several other hounds had removed their helms – a luxury of command – and they stood out among the two thousand expressionless men and women. Dalian looked no different, and he smiled inwardly that he had been able to get so close to the hound captains. If it would have gained anything, the Thief Taker could easily have assassinated the commanders and melted back into the pack.

'A pale man of Ro and a risen, mistress. They killed the guards and released the captives.' There was a twisted sneer on Kasimir's face as he spoke and his dark eyes flicked constantly from side to side, as if he were searching for someone else to take the blame. 'I've sent men after them, mistress.'

Izra paused and for a second she stopped ranting and focused through her rage? After a glance either side of her to take in her captains, Izra Sabal drew her two-handed scimitar. It whistled from its sheath across her back and travelled quickly downwards. Kasimir didn't move as the blade sliced down his face, cutting into the skin from his forehead, across his nose, and down to his chin. It was not a deep cut and the skill it had taken not to kill the man was staggering, even to a warrior as experienced as Dalian.

No one moved except Kasimir, who slowly shuddered backwards and fell to the grass underfoot. He was bleeding heavily, but he did not cry out or ask for aid. He was a hound captain and to show weakness, even after so vicious a cut, would be to invite insubordination. If the hounds didn't fear their captains, drugs and enchantments would only go so far.

'Get up,' she sneered, 'and find me the commander of the unit that was on guard duty.'

Kasimir pulled himself slowly to his feet, gritting his teeth and clenching his fists. His face was a mask of blood. He stood defiantly erect in front of the whip-mistress, who smiled at his strength. 'What . . .' he began breathlessly, 'would you have me do to the dog?'

'Ears and nose, Kasimir,' replied Izra, 'and let him bleed.'

The ex-wind claw nodded weakly and staggered away into the press of hounds. He had not sought help for his wound, nor would he be asking for attention until he had carried out Izra's orders. Dalian was impressed at the man's reaction, though the wound would fester if not taken care of quickly.

Izra breathed in deeply and turned her gaze back to Cozz. The dust was beginning to settle and the walls could be seen clearly. Two whole sections, flanking the southern gate, had been destroyed and now lay in broken piles across the dusty courtyard, just visible through the gaps. A few Ro were hastily using the pause in the bombardment to move the wounded and clear some of the rubble, though they all kept an eye on the road south.

'Before we get back to these merchants,' said Izra to her remaining captains, 'fetch me the bastard.'

A hound replaced his helmet and walked away from the lines. *The bastard* was a mercenary knight of Tor Funweir, firmly under the sway of Saara the Mistress of Pain. What concerned Dalian was that this man was not enchanted, but rather he did as she asked because he enjoyed doing so. Such a man was dangerous indeed, and the Thief Taker wondered if Sir Hallam Pevain followed any gods at all and, if so, what they thought of his chosen profession.

The front line of hounds parted and a motley group of Ro emerged. They stood out among the dark-skinned Karesians, and the weapons they carried – an array of knives, crossbows and maces – seemed to have been chosen primarily for the fear they could induce rather than for their usefulness. Pevain himself carried a large war-hammer of uncertain design, and wore plate armour that was thicker and better made than that worn by the hounds and formed a sharp contrast to the piecemeal leather worn by his men. There were twenty of them and several carried recent wounds, though the vicious-looking twins who flanked Pevain were unhurt, as was the knight himself. Evidently, mercenary knights were not required to fight their own battles.

Izra strode with purpose towards Pevain, her captains and Dalian's unit closely following. 'You were supposed to have killed the Ghost by now, you useless Ro cunt,' she shrieked.

Pevain smirked, showing that he was not the least bit afraid of the whip-mistress. 'If you hadn't started bombarding Cozz, we would have done.' He stepped closer to Izra and glared down at her. 'Don't mistake me for one of your mutts, hound-bitch,' he spat. 'I don't work for you, I work for Saara the Mistress of Pain, so get away from me unless you wanna fuck.' He spoke quietly enough that only those close by could hear, and the hounds held their breath in anticipation of Izra's reaction.

The whip-mistress pursed her lips. Clearly, she was unable or unwilling to strike the mercenary, but her face revealed a woman with torture and death in her mind.

'Now,' continued Pevain, 'lend me some hounds and I'll hunt the Black cleric down.'

Izra said nothing. She waved at a hound standing next to her and clenched her fist.

'It shall be done, mistress,' said the man, turning to Pevain. 'We can spare fifty hounds, sir knight.'

'Should be enough,' replied Pevain, who was still smirking. 'Come on, lads, we've got work to do. Our road goes south.'

As the bastards pushed their way through the hounds, Sir Pevain turned back to Izra. 'Mistress Izra, I never did hear what crime you committed that saw you sentenced to life among the hounds.'

She looked at him with downcast eyes. 'I raped twenty-three men of Kessia with a burning poker.'

The mercenary said nothing and the two made eye-contact for a moment before Pevain marched after his men.

* * *

Several hours later and Dalian was again called to the front of the army. Izra had not resumed the bombardment and numerous crossbowmen were now visible on the surviving walls of Cozz. The rubble had been cleared and large carts were positioned across the open spaces in the walls. They had been able to see men of importance walking on the battlements and watchtowers, men who had counted the hounds and assessed the strength of the army arrayed against them. From what Dalian had heard, Cozz could muster a few hundred men-at-arms, but no clerics. Though its walls were high and well made, there was no way the men of Ro could withstand a dedicated attack with siege equipment.

All five of the hound army's skirmisher units were now at the front and Dalian was placed no more than fifteen feet from Izra and the captains. They had spied a white flag flown from the highest watchtower of Cozz and now, as the afternoon drew on, a guard of ten mounted men had exited the enclave and was riding towards their position. A horseman at the rear carried a pole flying the heraldry of Cozz – an open purse – and the man at the front was dressed as a knight.

Izra was calmer now that she had seen one of her men have his ears and nose cut off by Kasimir. Dalian did not expect a polite meeting with the officials of Cozz, but maybe they would leave in one piece. Maybe.

'By what right do you assault my town?' shouted the lead man of Ro, a hard-looking man with thinning brown hair and a light-blue tabard. His chain mail was well-worn and Dalian imagined he knew how to use the longsword sheathed at his side. 'This is an act of war.' His eyes showed extreme anger.

'And who are you, man of Ro?' asked Izra calmly.

'I am Knight Marshal Wesson, governor of Cozz and lord of Tor Funweir,' shouted the man, wheeling his horse sideways in front of the hounds. 'I have sent riders to Voy and Tiris. Reinforcements are on their way. I advise you to leave before you're up to your eyes in knights and clerics.'

The hounds were arrayed in columns and the two thousand warriors were silent as they awaited orders from their whip-mistress. Dalian respected the courage it must have taken for the knight marshal to speak with such fervour when faced with so many enemies. However, it seemed likely that his hope of reinforcements was misplaced. The Seven Sisters were nothing if not thorough and the Thief Taker suspected that neither Tiris nor Voy would go against *their beloved allies*.

Izra stepped close to Wesson's horse, followed by her entire pack. The sound of metal armour as two thousand hounds moved in unison was deafening for a second, before silence returned. The whip-mistress produced a piece of parchment from within her armour and handed it to the knight marshal.

'This is a decree signed by Duke Lyam of Weir, co-signed by King Sebastian Tiris. It states that any and all lords and knights of Tor Funweir must extend every possible courtesy to your Karesian friends.' Izra smiled as she delivered the news.

Wesson read the parchment and his shoulders sank as he saw the betrayal of his people. The nobles of Ro were no more than pawns in a larger game.

'This piece of paper doesn't mean you have the right to kill men, women and children, common people who have committed no crime and wronged none of you.' There was a look of desperation on the marshal's face as he continued. 'Most of my people couldn't give a damn for the rest of Tor Funweir. We're merchants and traders.'

Izra smiled, the expression of someone in complete control. She knew her opponent had no cards left to play. 'If you open your gates,' she said, looking past the marshal to the shattered walls, 'and surrender to us with no terms or conditions . . .' The smile became broad and toothy, accentuating her broken jaw, 'then we will cause no unnecessary suffering.' The term *unnecessary* was deliberately vague.

'Fuck you,' roared Wesson. 'Who do you think you're speaking to, hound-bitch?'

Izra's concentration didn't crack, though most of her captains growled at the insult. 'I think I'm speaking to a man with no choice,' she said quietly. 'You agree, or many of your people die. Any man that takes to his knees in front of us will not be harmed.'

The knight marshal was in a state of incandescent rage as he wheeled his horse left and right, gritting his teeth and holding on tightly to the hilt of his longsword. 'Is there not a man I can speak to, you Karesian whore,' he demanded, with no thought that the remark might well signal his death.

Izra Sabal, whip-mistress of the hounds, was a sadistic woman and however capable she was of remaining cool, the one thing she could not abide was reference to her gender.

'I was trying to be nice, Marshal Wesson.' Her face turned red with rage and she practically vibrated as she spoke. 'But I'm afraid you may have to be my first lesson to the people of Cozz.' She turned to Kasimir Roux, who stood next to her, a thick bandage over his new facial wound. 'Let us see how he likes it as a woman.' She gestured to her crotch.

A vicious smile appeared on Kasimir's face and the other captains swiftly drew their scimitars. 'Kill the others,' she shouted to the skirmisher units.

Dalian hesitated at the needless slaughter, but after a moment he joined the others launching their javelins at the marshal's men. Several missed, but the men were few in number and they received sufficient wounds to unhorse all of them, leaving Wesson alone.

Those still alive were swiftly beheaded by the hounds and the marshal found himself surrounded in a matter of seconds. He was not a young man, but the speed with which he drew his longsword spoke volumes for his experience.

With a downward cut, he split a man's head. With a wheel of his horse, he sent three hounds flying backwards and, for a moment, it looked as if he might escape. Then the swarming warriors of Karesia hacked at the horse's legs and Marshal Wesson of Cozz, knight of Tor Funweir, was pulled to the ground. He shouted out oaths of defiance and struggled as best he could against the gauntleted hands that grabbed at him. His sword was pulled away and his arms and legs were grasped until he was spreadeagled on the floor.

Izra and Kasimir moved to stand over the beaten man. 'Remove his armour,' whispered Izra.

Try as he might, Wesson could do nothing but shout and struggle as his chain mail was cut from his chest and the tabard of Cozz was unceremoniously ripped in two. His greaves and gauntlets were thrown to the ground and within moments the man of Ro lay bare-chested in simple cotton trousers. Two hounds held each of his arms and legs, and another held his head still, forcing him to look at those standing above him with evil intent in their eyes.

Dalian seriously thought about intervening to assist the man. He had done nothing to deserve death, but the wind claw thought better of it and simply joined the rest of twenty-three watching the spectacle. In the distance, men of Cozz feverishly moved across the battlements with loaded crossbows.

'Marshal Wesson, it is not easy being a woman in a man's world,' Izra spat with glee. 'I will show you what I mean.'

The whip-mistress crouched on the ground in front of the marshal and, amid shouted insults and oaths of vengeance, ordered her men to spread his legs wide. She then took a small knife from her belt and cut away his trousers, leaving him naked and exposed.

Wesson stopped struggling and spoke, through quickened breathing, 'There are brave men in Tor Funweir . . . strong men and honourable men who will make you pay for your actions today.' Then he smiled. 'Hound-bitch.'

Izra's eyes were wide and she had begun to drool as she looked at Wesson. 'I don't think you'll be fucking anything ever again, Ro cunt.'

Without further words, the whip-mistress placed her knife between the marshal's legs and drew the blade firmly across the base of his genitals. A strangled cry erupted as he was brutally castrated, lying on the King's Highway within sight of his home.

Izra howled with glee and pulled away a bloodied hand, discarding Wesson's manhood over her shoulder and dancing like a crazed Gorlan. Then she whirled round. 'Raze the town,' she screamed.

It was an act of pure spite. Without their leader, Dalian knew the people of Cozz would have no chance of resisting the hounds. Reluctantly, he joined in the cries that rippled through the two thousand hounds as they shook with battle-fervour.

'Any man or woman that bends the knee to us will be spared,' ordered Izra. 'Kill all others.'

The pack drew their scimitars and ran forward. With Izra and her captains in the lead, they moved as a sea of black plate armour and swirling blades towards the gates of Cozz.

Dalian spared a look through the press to where the naked body of Wesson still lay. He was twitching slightly, and blood was covering his legs and spreading in a pool away from him, but he seemed to be still alive. Loss of blood would take its toll, however, and the brave man would likely die on the road.

'Sorry I could not stop this,' he said to Jaa. 'The man was just trying to protect his home.'

Dalian was not a soft or emotional man, but he believed in the word of the Fire Giant, and Jaa had no interest in the lands of Ro. It was the word of the Seven Sisters that drove the hounds.

He made sure he was at the front of the advancing column, though his legs were not as sprightly as once they were. He was determined to get into Cozz and find the blacksmith before any of the idiots with him had a chance to cut anything off the man. If the man of Cozz whom he sought knew the location of Rham Jas Rami, the Thief Taker would gladly protect him from the brutality of the hounds.

He remembered Culver's Yard and he remembered the name Tobin, but nothing else, as he joined in the rousing cries of battle shouted all around him.

Dozens of crossbow bolts were fired from the walls. Those that were hit were shoved out of the way or trampled over. A large wagon had been wheeled across the open gates and within a moment the first line of hounds was swarming over it. Barrels of flaming pitch were rolled down at them, but few hounds were hurt and the rest flowed relentlessly into the courtyard.

'You lot, to the battlements,' shouted Kasimir to a nearby unit. 'You lot, to the marshal's barracks,' he barked at another. 'Numbers one and two, with me.'

The two assault units of the pack would accompany Kasimir

and Izra to the great merchant estates that lay in the centre of Cozz. Despite their battle-fervour, the captains had not forgotten that they were here to seize the wealth of the enclave.

The few watchmen brave enough to stand against the hounds were killed quickly, and the crossbowmen on the battlements were thrown from the walls to be despatched below. The rest of the pack fanned out into Cozz, looking for people to kill and wealth to plunder, flooding through the well-tended streets.

Dalian kept close to his unit at first, not wishing to appear suspicious by leaving them to seek out the blacksmith. He made sure not to be at the very front so as to avoid the worst of the violence, as the common folk began to run and hide or drop to their knees in terrified surrender. He saw a dozen men die within the first few minutes and many more mutilated or tied up for later amusement. Izra actively encouraged her hounds to rape and torture, and Dalian had to fight the urge to defend some of the weaker citizens. He felt a deep surge of hatred towards what was being carried out here and he knew that Jaa would be watching with equal anguish.

Sounds of slaughter, oaths of challenge, cries of pain and of surrender filled the air. Doors were kicked in and the occupants – mostly commoners – were brutally dragged from their homes and businesses, to be executed or tied up by the faceless hounds of Karesia. Dalian saw a young man of Ro attempt to defend a woman and have his head severed as a result. He saw the woman stripped and added to a growing number of trophies corralled by the gate.

With a deep breath, he turned from the spectacle in the central squares of Cozz. Despite the number of hounds, it was not a small town and he knew that it would take Izra's pack most of the day to cover the whole of the enclave. That gave him a chance. If he could locate Culver's Yard and find the blacksmith, he was confident that he could smuggle him out of Cozz and not be spotted in the chaos.

He turned sharply away from his unit as twenty-three kicked in the door of a jewellery shop and charged in to kill or steal whatever they found within. He paused, his back against a wooden wall, and waited for a moment to check if his absence had been noticed. When no one emerged to find him, the wind claw concluded that they were too preoccupied to worry about a missing hound.

He ran down the adjoining alley and away from the bulk of the pack. The noise of the rape of Cozz could still be heard, even as Dalian turned from the main squares and hurried along a tree-lined street that led away from the markets. To his left was a green hill that rose above the rest of the enclave, housing the majority of the merchant lords' estates. That was where Izra and Kasimir had taken most of the seasoned hounds. Within the hour, all the revered merchants of Cozz would be dead or imprisoned.

A watchman, armed with a crossbow, suddenly stepped out in front of him. The man was young and Dalian saw wide eyes and shaking hands as he fired his weapon wildly. He dropped the crossbow and fumbled at his waist to draw a short sword. Dalian stepped forward, punched him solidly in the stomach and grabbed him by the throat.

'Where is Culver's Yard?' Dalian barked. 'Tell me and live.'

The young man looked as if he were about to faint and the Thief Taker saw a steady trickle of urine beneath him. This was not someone who should have to fight for his life. He was a simple child of the One, and Dalian decided not to kill him. He relaxed his grip on his throat and allowed him to stand up straight. Then he removed his faceless helmet and glared at the man. 'I'm not a hound and I'm not here to kill or steal. Culver's Yard, where is it?'

The young man now looked every bit as confused as afraid, and he pointed weakly to his left, down the cobbled street and further away from the markets.

'More specific,' growled Dalian through clenched teeth.

The watchman stuttered over his reply. 'It's the third yard down. The biggest one,' he blurted out.

'I'd go and find a very dark place to hide in, young man,' said the wind claw. 'There are many men in this town who will kill you for holding a weapon. Consider yourself lucky that I am not one of them.' He left the young man in terrified silence and ran down the cobbled street.

He was startled momentarily as a serious of explosions sounded from the centre of the enclave. The watchmen of Cozz had shown that they were far from helpless, and Dalian smiled. Marshal Wesson's mutilation would be a spur to these common people to fight against the Karesians. Izra's pack would at least get bloody as Cozz was annexed.

He didn't slow down, though weeks of sleeping rough and tough living were beginning to catch up with him. Whatever it was the Ro were using to blow things up – Ranen pitch most likely – made his ears ring and he was tired and sore. Even the brief encounter with the young watchman had left him breathing heavily.

'Lord, I would have been much more use twenty years ago . . . when my feet weren't so sore.'

As he began to feel the pain of exertion in his side, he reached the bottom of the incline and turned away from the grassy hillock. In front of him, on level ground, were a dozen fenced-in yards containing open wooden structures and blacksmiths' equipment. Culver's Yard stood slightly higher than the others, flanking the grassy avenue that led back to the market squares. He turned abruptly into the dusty yard and stopped.

In front of him were anvils, forges and racks of freshly forged weaponry. The craft of the Ro was advanced compared with that of the Karesians, and Dalian paused for a moment to discard his hound scimitar and avail himself of two short swords. He preferred the feel of two lighter blades than one heavy one.

'Get away from those weapons, thief,' barked a voice from close by.

Dalian spun round and saw three burly men approaching him. They were all Ro and likely the owners of the yard. Each hefted a large hammer, more like smithing equipment than weaponry, but intimidating and well-handled nonetheless.

'Cozz won't fall without a fight,' said the largest of the three, a barrel-chested blacksmith with bright red cheeks.

'Which one of you is Tobin?' asked the Thief Taker, tucking the two short swords into his belt.

Two of the men looked at the barrel-chested smith, answering Dalian's question without speaking. He admired their willingness to fight for their home, but he didn't have the time to take them for a drink.

'I am not a hound,' he said, advancing with his arms spread wide in a gesture of peace. 'And I am here for Tobin. You can stay and die or you can come with me and live.'

Tobin the smith narrowed his eyes and relaxed his hammer. 'Who are you, Karesian?'

'My name wouldn't mean anything to you, but I seek Rham Jas Rami and Al-Hasim. I understand you know these men.' Dalian was pushed for time and could hear the approach of steel-shod feet, indicating that at least one squad of hounds was nearby.

'What's he talking about, Tobin?' asked one of the other blacksmiths.

Before he could answer, six anonymous hounds rushed into Culver's Yard. They made a quick assessment of the four men before them – one Karesian in hound armour and three Ro – and attacked.

'Stay back,' shouted Dalian to the three men of Ro. 'Let me prove to you that I'm not an enemy.'

The hounds were more surprised than the blacksmiths as the wind claw interposed himself between the two groups and drew his new swords.

'What are you doing, old dog?' asked one of the Karesians from behind his plain steel helmet.

The Thief Taker didn't respond with words. He thrust a short sword through the hound's throat, sending blood over the floor and the man to the ground. Then he wheeled round and severed the next man's leg, just above the knee. Dalian was impressed at the quality of Ro steel – and equally impressed that a tired old faithful of Jaa could kill two hounds in less than two seconds.

The remaining four all attacked at once, but succeeded mostly in getting in each other's way. Dalian sprang backwards and let them flounder for a moment. He then rolled forward, tripping up the first two men and forcing the other two back. He couldn't match them for youth or fitness, but he was clever and had killed more men than he could remember.

The two fallen men let out grunts of frustration as they tried to stand in their heavy steel armour. The last two died quickly, as Dalian parried a clumsy thrust and cut upwards between the first man's legs. Kicking the final hound in the chest, he finished him off with a downward thrust into his head.

Before he could turn, Tobin and the other two men of Ro had jumped on the two fallen hounds and were pounding them to death with heavy blacksmiths' equipment.

'More will come,' said Dalian between heavy breaths.

He was exhausted now and hoped he wouldn't have to do much more fighting. As he grew older, he had come to the uncomfortable realization that, although he was still capable of killing any man who faced him, he would likely need a rest before the next one.

'Who are you?' demanded Tobin, as he surveyed the six dead hounds.

'I . . .' he began, trying to slow his laboured breathing, 'am Dalian Thief Taker, greatest of the wind claws.'

None of the men knew what the title meant and they were none the wiser as to the identity of the strange man who had saved their lives. They looked at each other until the sound of more hounds approaching shook them out of their confusion.

'I need to find Rham Jas Rami,' repeated Dalian in a hoarse whisper. 'Can you help me or not?'

Tobin nodded and turned to his two friends. 'Help us get out of Cozz and I'll help you find the Kirin.'

'We can't just leave . . . I built this yard with my own hands,' said a second man of Ro. 'How do we know Wesson isn't kicking their arses at this very moment?'

'Wesson is dead,' replied Dalian simply, 'and your town is overrun.'

News of their lord marshal's demise hit all three of the blacksmiths hard and each looked at the floor with the sudden realization that Cozz would fall and would probably be razed to the ground.

'We need to leave,' said Dalian, standing upright and flexing his sore back. 'Get moving. We head for the eastern gate. They won't be there yet.' The men of Ro returned blank looks. 'Move!' he shouted.

As blacksmiths, they were built for strength rather than speed, and even a tired old warrior like Dalian could keep up with them as they ran east out of Culver's Yard.

The streets of Cozz were erupting in chaos. Men and women ran from their homes, clutching any belongings they could carry, as the hounds of Karesia stole anything they found and killed any that stood against them.

'Keep to the side streets,' said Dalian, shoving Tobin behind him. 'If you die, I'll kill your friends and join in razing Cozz.' He didn't mean what he said, but he needed the three men of Ro to be more scared of him than they were of the hounds.

Dalian poked his head out of the side street and could see the eastern gate a few streets away. Between them and the safety of the eastern plain were several dozen hounds. Izra's pack had spread quickly through the merchant enclave and now the scene before Dalian was one of violence and destruction. Men had died defending their homes and families, women had been dragged into stables and violated by several clumsy rapists at a time, and buildings had been set on fire. He flinched as he saw two female hounds rape a man of Cozz with their scimitars.

'They'll die for this,' growled Tobin from behind. 'This is Tor Funweir.'

'It was,' replied Dalian in a deathly quiet whisper. 'Now it belongs to the Seven Sisters.'

The Thief Taker ducked back down the street, grabbing Tobin as he did so, and turned away from the scene of slaughter. They quickly ran down three adjacent side streets until they reached the outer stockade of Cozz. The wooden walls were secure, but several small gaps were in evidence. Dalian ushered the blacksmiths behind him and stepped out into a narrow alley that ran along the length of the eastern wall. No hounds were within his field of vision, though the sounds of their assault echoed from all around him.

'Move quickly,' he said to the men of Ro, 'and try to keep quiet.'

With the wind claw in the lead, they moved from the side street and quickly reached a gap in the palisade. By moving two planks out of the way, it was a simple matter to squeeze through, though the bulky blacksmiths made the operation a slow one.

Dalian dragged the men through the gap, and they fled east across the grassy plains of Cozz.

* * *

As the sun went down and the smoke rising from Cozz faded over the horizon, Dalian allowed the three blacksmiths to stop for a rest. He had been planning to travel through the night and gain some ground on the assassin, but Tobin the smith had stubbornly refused to tell him anything until he'd had a chance to eat and sit round a fire.

Somewhere in the world, under a rock, in a tavern, or killing one of the Seven Sisters, was Rham Jas Rami, the Kirin assassin. Dalian was impatient, but he tried to keep his temper while the big men of Ro wheezed and complained, lamenting the loss of their home. The man of Karesia sympathized, even if he expressed it poorly because he was running out of time and needed to keep moving.

They had found a small forest directly east of Cozz, and now they sat within the tree line, huddled round a fire. The mountains of the Claws were just visible across the fields, towering over the eastern landscape, and Dalian was in unfamiliar territory, deeper into Tor Funweir than he had ever been, and far from the lands of Jaa. It was not especially cold, but the weather across the flat lands was temperamental and the wind never seemed to stop, putting the old wind claw in a foul mood.

'You should eat something, Karesian,' said Tobin, offering a bowl of Gorlan stew.

Dalian was not convinced of the blacksmith's culinary expertise. He thought the spiders he'd used had been far too small to make a flavoursome broth, and the men of Ro did not seem to understand the concept of seasoning. 'I'll pass, thank you,' he replied, as politely as he could.

The blacksmiths were in melancholy mood, ruminating on the destruction of Cozz, and on family and friends who were most likely captive or dead by now. Each had family elsewhere, however, and Dalian had heard a dozen plans as to where they would go and how they would finance their future blacksmithing endeavours. They were tough men, and the old Karesian admired their spirit, if not their stamina.

'How long do you need to rest before you'll tell me what I want to know?' he asked.

They each looked at him and exchanged concerned glances. None of them had asked him anything about himself or why he'd been in the merchant enclave in the first place, and it was evident they were simply glad they'd managed to escape. 'You saved our lives, Karesian,' said Tobin, nodding in subtle gratitude.

'I am a servant of Jaa, it was the Fire Giant that saved you,' replied Dalian. 'You should thank him.'

Tobin smiled. 'There isn't a god of blacksmiths. When they invent one, I'll follow him . . . but I'm not thanking a Giant for anything.'

The remark made Dalian chuckle ironically. He'd kill any man in Karesia who made a similar comment, but these were simple men, and the clerics of the One clearly allowed a more flippant attitude than the wind claws of Jaa.

'This country is strange to me,' said the Thief Taker with a smile.

'Never been to Karesia,' replied Tobin, taking a mouthful of stew, 'but I'm fairly sure that we'd find that place strange too.'

'Can I push you for some information, or would that be rude . . . given that your town was recently destroyed?' asked Dalian, trying to remain patient.

The three men of Cozz looked downcast, and it took a moment for Tobin to reply. 'You're after Rham Jas?' he asked.

'I am.'

Tobin looked at his fellows, who evidently did not know who Rham Jas was. 'He passed through my yard . . . maybe three weeks ago, with a mobster from Tiris. Glenwood, I think his name was,' volunteered the blacksmith.

'Tobin, you been fixing for criminals again?' asked one of the other blacksmiths in a judgemental tone.

'My steel isn't as good as yours,' replied Tobin. 'A man has to make a living.'

'But fixing for assassins? That's dirty work.' The other two were shaking their heads, and Dalian snapped his fingers to attract Tobin's attention.

'The assassin, where is he?' he repeated, more insistently. 'Or the Prince of the Wastes, a Karesian friend of his.'

'Yeah, I know them both,' Tobin conceded reluctantly. 'I've not seen Al-Hasim for a while, though. He was running bootleg wine out of Tiris a few years ago.' He paused for a moment and ate some more of his thin and watery stew. 'Rham Jas was on his way to Arnon and then Leith, something about some women that need killing.'

'Did he give you any names?' asked Dalian, hoping that the women in question were the Seven Sisters.

Tobin shook his head. 'I don't ask for names. All I do is provide food, steel, repairs, supplies . . . I don't ask questions.'

'How do I get to Ro Arnon?' asked the Thief Taker, planning to leave in pursuit as soon as possible.

'Why are you after him?' pressed Tobin with narrow eyes. 'Has he pissed you off?'

'I'm not going to kill him, if that's what you're asking,' replied Dalian.

Tobin chuckled to himself and looked unconvinced. 'I'm not worried about that. Rham Jas is a slippery fucker. You're tough, but I know people who think he's unkillable.'

'I've very glad to hear that.' Dalian looked to the sky. He estimated that it was approaching midnight. 'I'll leave in the morning.'

'You're better off heading to Leith,' said Tobin. 'You're a few weeks behind and you'll miss them in Arnon.'

'So how do I get to Leith?' he asked.

'Take the road east, towards Arnon. When you cross the river, head south past the Claws. You'll have to rough it a bit, but it's a pleasant enough journey.' Tobin was chewing on a stewed Gorlan leg, but remained suspicious as to why Dalian was looking for the assassin.

The Thief Taker smiled, content that he had the information he needed. 'Thank you, blacksmith,' he said. 'Find somewhere nice to live. Start a business, meet a woman, drink wine, eat food and raise children.'

All three men of Cozz looked at him and Dalian smiled. He was not unsympathetic to them and he genuinely hoped that the people of Tor Funweir would find a way to weather the invasion of the Seven Sisters. Unfortunately, these men were simple folk and knew nothing of the larger game being played out. They worried about their lost town, their dead friends and family, and their future. But they were not pious, or even afraid, and they lacked even the most basic divine awareness. They were not true children of the One any more than they were children of Jaa.

CHAPTER TEN

KALE GLENWOOD IN
THE DUCHY OF ARNON

THEY HAD LEFT Tiris is a hurry and, much to Glenwood's distress, had been sleeping rough ever since, without even an overnight stay in Cozz. An occasional night in a roadside inn was apparently too much to ask, and Rham Jas had resorted simply to ignoring questions that he didn't want to answer. It was an infuriating habit, but no less than Glenwood had expected. They had little to talk about, and the forger was just as comfortable in his own little world, trying to forget where he was and keeping busy with his sketch pad. He'd sketched mountains, rivers and skylines. He'd even drawn pictures of his companion, moodily hunched over in his saddle.

All Rham Jas had said directly to him, since they had crossed the river and entered the Falls of Arnon, was that their next sister would be Lillian the Lady of Death – who, in Glenwood's opinion, sounded absolutely lovely. Since then, it had been three days of silence as they ghosted along next to the Red Road that led to Ro Arnon, avoiding passers-by and spending their nights by the roadside. It was not a comfortable way to travel, the only break in the monotony being the occasional night when they found a small wood to camp in.

'Do you blame people for being afraid of you, Rham Jas? As far as I know, you can count your true friends on three fingers, no?' asked Glenwood, while he stoked the fire and attempted to get some warmth back into his aching body after a long day's travelling.

The assassin frowned and took a large gulp of wine. 'I'm just misunderstood.'

'No, you're not,' Glenwood shot back. 'Don't try that *poor me* shit, you've gone out of your way to fuck with people . . . me included.'

Rham Jas looked off into the rising darkness as if he were trying to identify landmarks through the trees. 'I don't mean to . . . well, not always.' The swarthy Kirin was not as guarded as usual and looked set for an evening of alcohol. 'Can I tell you something, Kale?' he asked, without looking up from his half-empty bottle of wine.

'Sure,' replied Glenwood. 'Are we bonding now?'

'No, no, we are not. I'm just a little short of company. Of those three friends you mentioned, one is dead, one is stuck in Canarn, and the other is . . . prancing around Ranen somewhere.'

The forger knew Bromvy and Al-Hasim, but he was fairly sure both were still alive. 'Who's dead?' he asked.

'Big, dumb Fjorlander, name of Magnus.'

Glenwood shook his head. 'Never knew him. What did you want to tell me?'

Rham Jas's eyes narrowed and he seemed to be falling into something approaching melancholy. 'I wanted to tell you why I'm doing this,' he said wearily.

'Doing what? Making my life more difficult than it was before?' Glenwood infused more vitriol into the comment than he had intended.

'Fuck you, Kale. This isn't about you . . . or me. Forget I said anything.' Rham Jas was angry now and he huddled up, clutching the wine bottle as a child would a favourite toy. 'Just tell me about Arnon.'

'What do you want to know?' Glenwood shot back, again with needless aggression. 'It's full of clerics and they don't like Kirin.'

'Who's in charge?' the morose assassin asked between gulps of wine.

Glenwood had not been to Ro Arnon for years and was by no means an expert. The church city, known as the City of Black Spires, was traditionally where the three high orders of churchmen made their homes.

'The three lords,' he replied ambiguously. 'One Gold, one Red, one Purple . . . though I'm pretty sure Cardinal Mobius is not currently in residence. That leaves the knight general of the Red, and the Gold cardinal.' He pondered for a moment. 'I think the general is called Malaki Frith. I have no idea who the chief Gold cleric is.'

Rham Jas shuffled his position and sat up on his bedroll. The sun was now just a sliver on the horizon and their campfire's light was taking full effect as the two men sat in a well-hidden forest clearing. Glenwood thought that they'd sight the city the following morning, and he'd already begun forming plans to get them secretly into Ro Arnon and to find a Purple cleric to whom he could betray Rham Jas. Obviously, he'd only confided the first part of his plan to his companion, but he hoped to be well on his way to a sizeable reward by midday.

'The Gold cardinal is called Animustus of Voy,' murmured Rham Jas, not quite getting the pronunciation right. His accent wasn't as strong now that he was not deliberately trying to be misunderstood, but Glenwood was again reminded of how much he'd come to hate the obtuse little bastard.

'Ah, yes,' replied the forger, vaguely remembering the name. 'He ascended after his acquisition work in Ro Canarn as I recall.'

'He plundered all of Lord Bromvy's vaults and stole Duke Hector's family wealth,' reinterpreted the assassin. 'The Gold gain status from theft, it would seem.'

Glenwood snorted. 'Which is so much worse than gaining it through killing people?' he asked with a raised eyebrow.

Rham Jas glared quizzically at his sarcastic companion. 'You know, Kale, I liked you better when you were terrified of me.'

'Those days are gone, my dear Rham Jas,' he responded casually. 'You need me, apparently . . . and, if you plan to sneak into Arnon, you *really* need me.'

Rham Jas sat forward and half-smiled. 'Look me in the eye, Kale,' he said quietly. 'Look me in the eye and tell me that you're not still afraid of me.'

Glenwood tried to maintain his casual demeanour as he, too, leant forward, trying to match Rham Jas for arrogance. He managed it for a moment, before the eyes of the Kirin assassin started to erode his confidence. Rham Jas Rami was not a large man and his style of dress could best be described as common or even shoddy, but something about his movements – the slight, measured twitch of his hands and the way his eyes never seemed to move – made Glenwood involuntarily turn away. 'Okay, I'm still afraid of you,' the forger reluctantly conceded.

'Excellent,' replied Rham Jas, with a wide grin. 'All is right with the world again.'

'Fuck you, Rham Jas,' spat the man of Leith. 'I'm going to sleep. Wake me up when you're less of an arsehole.'

'You'll be an old man, Kale,' replied Rham Jas, with a boyish chuckle.

* * *

The City of Black Spires was well named. Glenwood had not been there for years, but the sight of the various church towers looming over the landscape was every bit as awe-inspiring as he remembered.

All three of the largest cathedrals in Tor Funweir could be found in Ro Arnon: the Stone Cloisters of the Purple, the tallest by far, and surmounted with an ugly-looking black sceptre; the Red High Command, more a barracks than a church, which nevertheless displayed a single high spire bearing a stylized clenched fist at its summit; and Merrin's Cathedral, otherwise known as the Gold Bank, a jewelled spectacle of grandeur, easily identifiable by the massive diamond that shone over the skyline. It was not an easy city in which to be a criminal and, as a result, Glenwood had always avoided it. Slightly more than half of Arnon was given over to the One God in his various forms and, though it was smaller than both Weir and Tiris, it dominated the eastern landscape.

They had risen early and within a few hours had crested a hill and seen their destination. The roads were now full of travellers, churchmen and common folk, and Rham Jas had insisted that they stick to the woods as long as the cover lasted. The last few miles would have to be spent in the open, but Glenwood agreed that the assassin's caution was necessary. Stories of the treatment suffered by the godless Kirin were common, and there was a time when they had been hung from high posts outside the city. The Purple clerics were more bigoted and violent when they were within sight of Ro Arnon, making it well-nigh impossible for Kirin to live in the duchy.

Rham Jas had made no effort to hide his appearance short of keeping his hood up. His weaponry was distinctive, too. The longbow and the katana were rarely used in Tor Funweir and would attract unnecessary attention from men used to seeing longswords and crossbows. 'Can't you stow your weapons? They'll get you killed more surely than your swarthy face,' murmured Glenwood, as they turned from the tree line and made to join the travellers moving towards the purple gate of Ro Arnon.

Rham Jas glanced at the longbow across his back and the katana at his side. Then he frowned and removed his bow. 'I'll have to find another one somewhere,' he grumbled, throwing it into the trees. The katana remained at his side, but he pulled his travelling cloak over the scabbard and did a decent job of hiding the distinctive weapon.

'How long have you had that bow?' asked Glenwood, surprised that the assassin would so casually discard his weapon.

'A few months maybe. My other one got burned in Canarn. Longbows aren't really designed to fire Dokkalfar black wart.' Rham Jas showed no particular attachment to his bow and marched away from the trees without glancing back.

'And the sword?' continued Glenwood, fairly certain that the Kirin had always had the same katana.

'My wife,' said Rham Jas simply. 'And that's the most bonding we're going to do today.'

The man of Leith shook his head and walked after his companion towards Arnon. The Kirin looked less distinctive without his bow, and Glenwood thought they might even get into the city without being arrested, or killed.

An array of Red and Purple churchmen travelled the road, strolling or sitting astride horses, discussing whatever it is that clerics discuss. The watchmen of Arnon, much more formally dressed than those of Ro Tiris, stood on guard with tabards displaying the Grey Roc of Arnon worn proudly over well-made chain mail. There were merchants and common folk, but most of the inhabitants were well dressed. Arnon was not a city for the destitute, and most of those who lived there either owned businesses that catered to the church or were from the lesser noble families allied to the Purple or Gold.

Ro Arnon was the seat of the One God and sat, as a monument to the Stone Giants, across a wide and free-flowing river. The city was built on a natural rocky arch that formed part of the foothills of the Claws, so that Ro Arnon looked as if it had always been a part of the landscape. The three church spires had come into view long before the purple gate or the colossus of Arnon – the huge statue of a Red knight, standing with his sword drawn, under which travellers had to pass in order to enter the city.

Glenwood had always thought the gate security of the church city was lax, considering the wealth and power within. He knew, however, that the resident clerics were enough of a deterrent for most criminals. 'So, we just walk in?' asked Rham Jas with a grin. 'I like it . . . more Ro cities could do with being so relaxed.'

'It's hardly relaxed. They're just confident enough to think that a Kirin assassin would be an idiot to try and kill someone in their city,' replied Glenwood, keeping his back straight and trying to appear as noble as he could.

'Then they clearly underestimate the towering heights of my

idiocy,' replied the Kirin, with a beaming grin that made Glenwood want to kick him in the crotch.

They joined a line of travellers that was sufficiently closely packed for them not to stand out amongst the citizens of the duchy. Rham Jas kept his head down and returned to his role as Glenwood's bound man – a role he played disturbingly well. The forger was not sure what he would do once they were in the city, or whether his friend Mirabel was even still in residence. She was their only real avenue of enquiry into the whereabouts of Lillian the Lady of Death, so he hoped her brothel still catered for the occasional wayward cleric.

Glenwood found himself walking next to a fat Gold cleric, carried on a jewelled litter by four bound men and grunting insults at anyone he thought less important than himself. His main gripe was the state of the road and the rubbish and dust that covered the cobblestones. It was much cleaner than Ro Tiris, but he was obviously happiest when complaining.

Glenwood noticed Rham Jas shoot an annoyed glance at the Gold cleric, before the Kirin subtly tripped up one of the bound men, sending all four servants and their passenger down on to the street. The cleric roared indignantly as he ended up in a bulbous lump of gold and jewels, spreadeagled on top of his servants.

Glenwood, and several dozen others, laughed out loud at the spectacle. Even a few Purple clerics stifled a guilty chuckle. Rham Jas disappeared into the crowd, and the forger was again impressed at his companion's stealth. The first indication that he was still there was when he appeared on the far side of the colossus of Arnon, casually leaning against one of the statue's feet. Despite his deep loathing for him, the man of Leith smiled and, once again, found common ground with Rham Jas Rami.

'Fuck you, Rham Jas,' said the forger with a smile.

The Kirin assassin returned the expression and bowed theatrically, as watchmen stifling their laughter ran to assist the furious Gold cleric. The two of them walked away from the colossus, leaving behind them an unusually jovial scene as they entered the City of Black Spires.

'Where to?' asked Rham Jas, strolling towards the first circle of the church city.

Glenwood took a quick look around to get his bearings. Ro Arnon was arranged in five circles, indicating closeness to the One God, with the Purple cathedral at the centre and the Arnon pits around the outside. The name did not describe any particular poverty or lower class of citizenry, merely that this area was not devoted to the worship of the Stone Giant – and that, if a man required illicit pleasures, that was where they could be found.

'Last time I was here,' said the sardonic man of Leith, suddenly feeling the need for a drink or two, 'there was a lovely little fuck shop called the Feather Bed, run by a dear old bird called Mirabel. If she's still here, she's our best bet for information. You know – how we'd go about finding a Karesian enchantress and getting ourselves killed.'

'Don't you trust me yet, Kale?' replied Rham Jas, grinning under his black hood.

'I wasn't aware that trust was required.' Glenwood pointed to a road that led into a natural depression in the ground. 'That's the way,' he said, motioning for the Kirin to follow. 'They keep the dirty stuff in the pits . . . clerics don't like to admit that they need to drink and whore like the rest of us.'

'Your god favours hypocrisy over pent-up churchmen,' said the Kirin, again showing his disdain for the people of Ro and their god.

'My god?' snapped Glenwood. 'Do I look like I'm kneeling before any altar?'

'No, but it's in your blood . . . you know, being an arrogant warmonger,' said the obtuse assassin, chuckling slightly to maintain the light-hearted mood between them.

'Well, if you give me some of what's in your blood, I'll gladly swap the One for an ability to dodge swords.' Glenwood was only joking, but something in what he said made the assassin become suddenly guarded.

'Leave my blood out of it, you don't want it . . . trust me on that,' Rham Jas said in a whisper.

Glenwood puffed out his cheeks and stopped talking. There were moments when he thought the assassin had not just been put here to make his life difficult. Those moments were generally fleeting and, once they'd gone, Glenwood usually thought about surrendering his companion to a Purple cleric.

'The Lady of Death will likely be close to one of the lords, yes?' asked Rham Jas, with no more humour in his voice.

At least he wasn't grinning. 'Knight General Malaki Frith or Animustus Voy. Probably the two most protected men in the city. Some would say that killing them is impossible,' replied the forger, scratching his neck and trying to remember the way to the Feather Bed.

Rham Jas snorted. 'If they catch me, they kill me . . . and you can go back to Tiris and be a mobster. Let me handle the killing, you handle the information.'

'Yes, sir,' Glenwood replied with a sarcastic salute. 'As long as you don't mind me waiting in the brothel with a cold drink and a warm woman while you go and do your killing.'

'But how will I keep an eye on you if you're not with me?' The grin returned and Glenwood fought the urge to shout *rape*, or something equally alarming.

'Fuck you, Rham Jas.' He didn't care that it wasn't a witty or clever response; he just wanted a moment's peace from the insufferable Kirin. 'Let's just get this done so we can move on to . . . actually, where are we going next?'

'Leith. Your home city,' replied the assassin. 'There's a lovely young enchantress there called Isabel the Seductress. She needs a good bit of killing.'

'There are seven of them, right?' asked Glenwood, as they dropped below street level and entered the less austere part of Ro Arnon. Still, even the taverns and bars had a lick of polish that made them look opulent compared with their counterparts in Tiris and Weir.

'There are five left,' replied Rham Jas. 'I need to kill the others before they kill me or the whole world is fucked – something like that.'

The words were not spoken as a joke and Glenwood frowned. 'Do you ever make sense?' he asked, as the sun disappeared over the walls of Arnon and they entered the shadowy pits.

The Kirin bowed his head and adjusted his hood the better to conceal his swarthy features. 'I make sense if you are me . . . probably not if you are you.'

Glenwood didn't even bother to reply. He noticed a familiar landmark and took a sharp left into a particularly dark section of the pits. The structure of Arnon meant that a good portion of the outer circle was significantly lower than the purple gate and, as a result, saw much less sun than the rest of the church city. Darkness tended to imply the illicit and, even in Ro Arnon, a man looking for debauchery was well catered for. Nevertheless, street crime was minimal and the watchmen that patrolled the area enforced the law of the One with brutality – all of which made the pits the nicest shit-hole Glenwood had ever visited.

Beyond a ratty-looking vegetable stand and opposite a shop that sold cheap steel was the Feather Bed, a building unremarkable except for the ruby-red lips that adorned its sign. Glenwood smiled, glad that the building was still there. He began to concoct a strategy whereby he and Mirabel could make some gold by turning in Rham Jas.

'So, are you going to introduce me to your friend?' asked the Kirin, as they came to a stop in front of the sign.

'I wish I didn't have to,' replied the tired man of Leith, wanting nothing more than to fall into a drunken stupor and forget his life.

Rham Jas grinned at the forger and showed a few teeth, making it one of his wider grins. 'I'm good with women,' he said, smoothing back his greasy black hair and striding towards the entrance.

Glenwood raised his eyebrows and followed, trying to keep his anger in check as he caught the swinging door his companion had flung open. It did, however, occur to him that, if he was going to turn in the Kirin, it would be wiser to do it in Ro Leith, a city he knew well and where his involvement with Rham Jas would be unlikely to get him strung up alongside the assassin.

Inside the Feather Bed was a clean and well-tended bar area, overseen by a rugged doorman. Several attractive young women delivered drinks on silver trays to a mixed clientele. There were clerics, hiding under civilian clothing, and ordinary folk of Arnon, squandering whatever money they had on a night of flesh and sweat. Everyone within was Ro, and Glenwood hoped that the sight of the Kirin might elicit a shout for the watchmen and relieve him of the assassin's company.

'What is your pleasure?' asked a nubile young lady, scantily clad in a see-through nightgown.

Rham Jas motioned for Glenwood to do the talking and made a token effort to hide his face. The lady was the worse for drink and not sufficiently observant to notice a man's race.

'Is Mirabel in tonight, my dear young thing?' asked the man of Leith, with a disarming smile.

'I believe she's entertaining a client,' replied the girl, 'but I'm sure I can service your needs.' She sidled up close to Glenwood and gazed into his eyes. 'You're a handsome devil, sir.'

'Only in Arnon, my dear,' he said with a wink. 'In Tiris, I'm interesting-looking at best.'

Rham Jas subtly elbowed him in the ribs, but didn't say anything for fear his accent might be recognized.

'Perhaps later you can tell me how handsome I am, young lady. For now, I need to speak to Mirabel.' He stroked the girl's face playfully and winked again.

'Kale Glenwood, as I live and breathe,' said a husky voice from further inside the brothel.

Mirabel was a woman in her early forties, but still attractive and with a glint in her eye that marked her as canny and dangerous.

She'd aged well, and the forger smiled as she strode across the entrance hall and flung her arms round his shoulders.

'You're carrying your sword, Kale,' she said, noting the old longsword hanging at his side. 'Pretending to be a noble again, are we?'

'No pretence needed, sweet thing,' he said with a smirk, holding himself upright. 'Can we go and have a little chat?'

'Anything for an old flame, honey,' she said, firmly slapping him on the rear. 'Follow me.'

Glenwood nodded for Rham Jas to follow and the two of them walked casually after Mirabel. The interior of the Feather Bed was garishly decorated with silks and brightly coloured fabrics, and great attention had been paid to making the establishment smell nice, with incense burning throughout.

The mark of a good brothel, in Glenwood's eyes, was that the bedrooms had actual doors, rather than simple cotton hangings, and the sounds of sex were barely audible as they walked along a red-carpeted hallway to a staircase.

'Who's your friend, Kale?' asked Mirabel, gathering the folds of her tightly cut dress in order to ascend the stairs.

'Yes, Kale,' chuckled Rham Jas, 'who's your friend?'

Mirabel half-turned and an interested smile appeared on her face.

'He's nobody,' said the man of Leith, 'a chain around my neck, a Gorlan on my back, a pain in my arse.'

'Well, perhaps you and the pain in your arse would like a drink.' Mirabel reached the top floor of the brothel and opened a heavy wooden door in front of her.

The floor they were on was not for the clientele and no muted sounds of sex could be heard beyond the door. Mirabel was as high-class a whore as Tor Funweir could offer and, like all good madams, she made sure that there was ample space to rest and recuperate within the Feather Bed.

The room they entered was comfortable and more convention-ally decorated than the brothel below. It had expensive-looking leather armchairs and a wide window with an impressive view of the three spires of Arnon. Mirabel demurely took a seat and motioned to an ornate drinks cabinet by the bedroom door.

'Any Darkwald red?' asked Rham Jas, plonking himself into another leather armchair and throwing back his hood.

Mirabel smiled with narrow eyes and the Kirin grinned shrewdly. 'I have Darkwald Reserve, maybe some vintage stuff from Hunter's Cross, my dear Rham Jas Rami.'

Glenwood snorted in amusement, glad that his companion's reputation had spread to the church city. Mirabel was clever and would likely keep abreast of the Wanted posters. He had not seen any depictions of the Kirin's ugly face since he arrived in Arnon, but he could well imagine that the reward would have gone up significantly since Katja was killed in Ro Tiris.

'You specialize in killing those generally considered unkillable,' said Mirabel, drumming her fingernails on the arm of her chair. 'And you have come to Ro Arnon.'

'I need your help, my good lady,' replied Rham Jas, taking a goblet of wine from Glenwood and drinking deeply. 'Young Kale here is by no means an expert on your fair city and he advises me to seek . . . an additional pair of eyes.'

'And why should I wish to assist you?' she replied. 'Our beloved allies do not affect my business one way or the other.'

The Kirin assassin baulked at the euphemism for the Seven Sisters. 'They are not beloved by me,' he said, looking at Mirabel over the top of his goblet. 'I doubt they are truly beloved by many of their new . . . subjects.'

'Enough,' said Mirabel, sipping demurely from a fluted crystal glass. 'I won't endanger my station or fortune by assisting a known assassin.'

Glenwood, who had not taken a seat, coughed. 'There you go, she won't help.' He threw back his drink and smiled. 'Sorry to bother you, Mirabel. We'll be off, then.'

Rham Jas didn't look as if he was about to be off, and Glenwood's glib attempt to get out of the brothel caused Mirabel to raise her eyebrows. 'Sit down, Kale,' she said gently.

'Yes, Kale, sit down,' echoed Rham Jas, with a maddening grin. 'We've had a long walk and your poor legs must need a rest.'

'Fuck you, Rham Jas,' spat Glenwood.

'Do you mind?' said Mirabel, showing mock offence. 'Please watch your language in my establishment.'

'Her name is Lillian the Lady of Death,' said the assassin. 'Where can she be found?' Rham Jas had adopted a businesslike expression and leant forward, allowing his curved katana to show at the side of the leather chair.

'Killing an enchantress is considered impossible. Attempting it with a sword is considered insane.' Mirabel's right hand had fallen casually down to the side of her chair and, from where he stood, Glenwood could see a small crossbow attached to the leather. 'And your capture could be rather financially rewarding.'

Rham Jas showed no sign that he was aware of the weapon as he drained his glass. 'I would think very carefully about using that crossbow, my lady,' he said casually. 'The first bolt wouldn't kill me and I'd get to you before you could reload.'

She frowned and glanced up at Glenwood.

'And he won't help you, he's too scared of me,' said Rham Jas.

'It's true,' replied Glenwood, with a resigned nod of his head.

'Though I am not unsympathetic to your need for money,' said the assassin, his grin returning. 'You will be compensated.'

'By whom?' she asked sharply. 'You? I don't think so . . . from what I've heard, you're a lucky amateur at best.'

Rham Jas said nothing for a moment, letting his eyes do their work. Mirabel blinked and turned away, feeling, as people always did, uncomfortable under the Kirin's gaze.

'What else have you heard?' asked the assassin when the madam had stopped trying to stare him down.

'The Mistress of Pain . . . I assume you've heard of her,' began Mirabel, 'has made it known that you are a danger to Tor Funweir and that any Ro of good conscience has an obligation to do you harm.'

Glenwood smiled at this. 'Since when have you had a good conscience?' he asked, attempting to lighten the mood.

'Since every single churchman in my city started doing whatever these bloody enchantresses say. General Frith has left, on Lillian's orders. He's taken any Red knight that can swing a sword to the Freelands to reinforce the king, while Animustus lets the bitch dip in and out of the Gold Bank as if she were a cardinal herself. I am no naive girl, but I know that it pays to be on the winning side.'

Glenwood locked eyes with his Kirin companion, attempting to detect whether Mirabel had caused real offence and whether violence was imminent. He could see no reaction, but the obtuse assassin rarely displayed his intentions.

The Kirin slowly stood up and took a few small steps towards Mirabel. His face was calm, but guarded. Though his grin was gone, he didn't look as if he would draw his katana.

'Listen to me,' said Rham Jas in a virtual whisper. 'They cannot hide from me . . . they cannot reason with me . . . they cannot enchant me . . .' His grin returned. 'I am their nightmare, as they are yours.'

Glenwood raised his eyebrows and puffed out his cheeks. Try as he might, he couldn't conjure any good reason to doubt the assassin's words. Pragmatic as Mirabel was, she became rapt as the Kirin spoke and something in his demeanour made her simply nod her compliance.

* * *

Ro Arnon was a difficult city to walk around. Once they had left the pits, Glenwood had to make sure that he and Rham Jas kept off the wide boulevards used by the clerics. Luckily, the arrogance of the churchmen meant that the streets they used the most were raised off the ground, with the more common thoroughfares snaking their way beneath. It lent a strange, bi-level effect to the city, which encouraged those not of the One to stick to the narrow, dark and claustrophobic passageways. It was possible, if one wanted to avoid the church's domain entirely, to travel from one side of the city to the other without actually coming face to face with a cleric.

Unfortunately, the location of Lillian the Lady of Death meant that this was not an option for the assassin and his companion. Mirabel had ceased being coy shortly after Rham Jas had stopped grinning. Glenwood was gratified that he wasn't the only person the assassin could manipulate in this fashion. The madam had directed them to the far side of the Gold Bank and they now stood, well below boulevard level, next to a closed sewage pipe that serviced the opulent quarters of the senior Gold clerics. Merrin's Cathedral itself was large enough, but with the numerous palaces that spread away from the central spire in a sprawling spider's web pattern, the aspect of wealth dominated a good quarter of the city.

They had waited until after dark and now they were concealed in shadows beneath a drawbridge that led to the outer sanctum of the Gold cardinal's jewel-encrusted residence. Lord Animustus Voy was not one to let his wealth go unnoticed. Even skulking in the darkness, Glenwood could see solid gold pillars that rose from a few feet above his head to tower over the boulevard, marking the outer wall of the cardinal's apartments.

As he looked up at the towering church building, he could see no feasible way for them to sneak in. If they managed to clamber over the sewer and make their way up to the drawbridge, they'd somehow have to avoid the bound men guarding the entrance to the cardinal's residence. If they chanced a jaunt through the unpleasant-looking sewage tunnels, they were just as likely to emerge in a pool of shit as a cleric's toilet trench.

'Right, my dear assassin,' said Glenwood, surveying walls, sewer and drawbridge, 'even you are going to struggle with this one.'

Rham Jas had been quiet up until this point and was casting a professional eye over the sheer walls that stretched away from them. 'You see that window?' he said quietly, pointing to a barely visible balcony about twenty storeys up from where they stood.

'What, you mean the one that's clearly impossible to get to? Yes, I see it.' Glenwood was not greatly knowledgeable regarding the assassin's tools of the trade, but he thought a sheer climb of such a height would be beyond even Rham Jas Rami.

'I'm assuming that your longsword won't get us into the cardinal's living room, of course,' said the Kirin with a smug grin – one of the more annoying of his arsenal of facial expressions.

'I could be the duke of Leith and they wouldn't let us in there,' replied Glenwood. 'But if you think you're going to clamber up the outside of the cardinal's . . . house, I suppose, then you're mad.'

'There is certainly some evidence to support that theory, Kale,' said Rham Jas, securing his katana to his back and making sure his cloak was tied down.

'You're actually going up there, aren't you?' asked Glenwood incredulously. 'They're gold pillars . . . it's not a fucking rock face, you won't even get a handhold . . . there's nothing to climb.'

'That's why you're staying down here,' replied Rham Jas, as he stepped out into the moonlight and looked intently upwards to the balcony high above. 'You'd get in my way. It's not just the climb, you see, Kale, it's the keeping hidden.'

'You're an idiot . . . and you're going to die.' Glenwood stated this without a smile, attempting to convey as much seriousness as possible. It wasn't that he cared whether the assassin fell to his death or not, but he thought it foolish to throw away his life in such a fashion – especially when he could be turned in for a fortune.

The forger looked up at the drawbridge and saw several Gold clerics standing there. They wore priceless gold breastplates and were some of the few men of the aspect who wore any armour. Most preferred to be carried around on litters so that their gluttonous bellies didn't drag on the ground. Combat was far from the minds of most Gold clerics, but occasionally a violent sadist would ascend to the aspect of wealth and would generally be put to work guarding the cathedrals.

Glenwood and Rham Jas were currently well hidden, with the sewage pipe and drawbridge obscuring their location. However, once beyond the darkness, the Kirin assassin would easily be seen. Flaming braziers flanked the entrance and Rham Jas would have to pass several large globes of firelight.

'Don't go anywhere, Kale,' said Rham Jas, beginning to climb on to the sewerage pipe. 'I won't be long . . . and see if you can get that sewer grate loose, that's our escape route.'

'She could be anywhere in there,' growled Glenwood. 'It's huge . . . what are you going to do? Just wander around asking for an enchantress?'

With great dexterity, the Kirin vaulted upright on to the wide steel pipe and sprang up several feet until he was standing on the base of a gold pillar. 'I'll know where she is when I get in there,' he said quietly. 'Have faith, Kale . . . oh, and if you leave while I'm up there, you know I'll find you.' He directed a grin at his companion.

'Fuck you, Rham Jas.' As he watched the Kirin shin up the featureless gold pillar, Glenwood really did want him to fall and break his head on the street below.

Rham Jas climbed quickly, shuffling skilfully up the pillar until he was just below the drawbridge. It was a climb no normal man would have attempted, let alone successfully completed, and Glenwood was again reminded that Rham Jas Rami was no normal man. Whatever gifts the assassin had, and wherever he had acquired them, he was the toughest bastard the forger from Leith had ever known.

Rham Jas reached a globe of light and dexterously moved round the pillar so that he was climbing up the dark side of the column. Glenwood lost sight of him, and the assassin made no sound as he inched past the Gold clerics guarding the drawbridge and made his way to the balcony.

* * *

Time passed slowly. Glenwood plonked himself down on the dusty cobbles of the street under the drawbridge and waited. He took a cursory look at the rusted iron grating that covered the sewer, but made no particular effort to move it. If, by some amazing twist of fate, Rham Jas actually managed to kill the enchantress and escape, he'd have to remove the grate himself. The forger simply couldn't be bothered.

With nothing to drink and no one for company, Glenwood began to draw. He was far from Tiris and Leith, and becoming increasingly fed up with his situation. Somewhere above him, no doubt skulking in the shadows of the Gold cardinal's halls, was a Kirin assassin who had decided to make Glenwood's life miserable. If he'd stayed in Ro Tiris, he'd be well on the way to establishing his mob by now, recruiting sadistic bodyguards, bribing watchmen and generally having a great time. Instead, he was sitting in a dirty alley, in a dirty part of Arnon, by a dirty sewer grate, waiting for a dirty Kirin to kill a dirty enchantress.

He drew a rough sketch of a voluptuous woman, beckoning outwards with a seductive glint in her eyes. He had no coloured pencils, but imagined she would have blonde hair.

As the minutes turned to hours and the darkness became total, Glenwood felt his eyelids drooping. He was uncomfortable and the cracked paving stones hurt his back, but he began to fall asleep anyway. With the rhythmic sound of dripping water in his ears, he closed his eyes. Sleep did not arrive before a body landed noisily within a few feet of him.

'What the . . .' he spluttered, scrambling to his feet and looking at the bloodied mess that had plummeted from above.

A Gold cleric, his head and chest grotesquely crushed, lay twisted in the dust. He had probably been alive when he fell from the balcony high above, and he was neither armed nor armoured. Whoever he was, the drawbridge guards had obviously seen him and Glenwood had to duck back into the underpass to avoid being spotted by bound men and Gold clerics.

'Rham Jas, you little bastard,' he muttered, preparing to run.

Glancing towards the sewer grate, he heard footsteps running from behind as the guards came to see who had fallen. Glenwood now had little choice but to attempt to enter the sewer and try the assassin's escape route.

With panic beginning to rise, he looked up to see a thickly knotted rope fall down from above and heard several crossbow bolts fired at the balcony. He shielded his eyes from the firelight, but couldn't see clearly what was happening, though a cacophony of shouts came from the guards. He couldn't make out exactly what they said, but the scene had quickly erupted into chaos.

Through the glare, speeding quickly downwards, a figure emerged from the balcony. It seemed that Rham Jas had thrown the man, followed by the rope, followed by himself, in less than ten seconds. The Kirin assassin was wearing gloves of some kind and he slid down the rope at tremendous speed, avoiding crossbow bolts on the way.

Glenwood stood dumbstruck.

'Wake up, Kale, time to go,' called the assassin. 'The sewer . . . get it open.'

Glenwood shook himself and rushed across to the metal grating. The clerics and bound men above were too focused on the assassin to worry about the skulking forger, and he managed to force his longsword in between the rusted hinges and wrench it free. Rham Jas came to an abrupt stop, standing poised on top of the sewer pipe.

'Evening,' he said cheerfully. 'Shall we go?'

Glenwood stuttered as he tried to reply. He ended up simply gesturing wildly at the approaching shadows behind them. The Kirin jumped off the pipe and sheathed his bloodsoaked katana, before grabbing the forger by the shoulder and shoving him into the pipe.

'Close your mouth, Kale, and try not to breathe in,' he said with a grin.

The man of Leith found himself flying forward into a dark and wet pipe that angled sharply downwards.

* * *

Saara the Mistress of Pain fell heavily to the floor. She grasped the sides of her head and wailed liked a wild animal as she felt Lillian die. The pain was excruciating as more men of the One God entered her mind and became her phantom thralls.

'My lady,' cried Kal Varaz from the other side of the room.

Saara had been briefing several of her most trusted wind claws about the deployment of additional hounds. Five hundred thousand more soldiers would arrive in a month or so and she was eager to see them used to maximum effect. The men in front of her had been listening intently to her instructions, but now they stood with anguish on their faces as they saw the enchantress writhing on the floor of the duke's office.

'Get out,' she shrieked in a high-pitched voice.

They didn't hesitate. These were dutiful and loyal men, and deeply in her thrall. Within seconds the door had been closed and the Mistress of Pain was crying and alone on the floor.

She felt the edge of the dark-blood's katana as it severed Lillian's head. She sensed her own mortality for possibly the first time. If he could kill Ameira, Katja and Lillian in the space of three months, he could be at Saara's door sooner than she had thought possible.

The door was opened suddenly and a serving-boy entered. He was perhaps eighteen years of age and likely a bound man of Duke Lyam's. The young man was carrying a mop and bucket and had started cleaning the floor before he noticed the quivering enchantress lying by the desk. With staring eyes, the young Ro servant smiled awkwardly and, leaving his bucket, stepped back to the door.

'No, boy, don't leave,' spluttered Saara. 'Come here.' She couldn't focus well and was not strong enough to enchant the bound man. For the moment, she was just a distressed woman, sprawled across the wooden floor, with tear-filled eyes and sweat on her skin.

'I think I should go,' said the boy, looking terrified and wishing he'd tried to clean another room first. 'I can clean any time.'

She tried to pull herself upright, but ended up merely crawling forward in a predatory pose. 'I won't hurt you,' she growled, baring her teeth and salivating.

'Come here.' The words made the young man stumble back until he was leaning against the door. 'I need your strength.'

Saara pounced at him, letting her basest impulses take control as she latched on to his face and delivered a violent kiss to his mouth. He cried out. Her hands pressed against his temples and she began to draw out his life energy in her aggressive embrace. She growled hungrily as she bit deeply into his lower lip and moaned in pleasure as the young man's blood began to seep from his eyes, nose and ears. The servant's energy slowly rejuvenated her and the Mistress of Pain felt her mind become clear and focused, her new phantom thralls settling into place.

She stood upright, holding the dead body away from her and dropping it to the floor in a pool of spreading blood. A moment later, and Saara walked demurely back to the desk. Her tightly cut black dress was saturated with blood and her hands and face were both red and sticky.

With a deep breath, and not caring to clean herself, the Mistress of Pain sat back in her large leather armchair. Rham Jas had killed Katja and now Lillian and, Saara thought, Isabel the Seductress would be next. The assassin was being methodical in his attempt to thwart the Seven Sisters' plan.

With a snarl, Saara decided to send as many wind claws as she could spare to Ro Leith in an effort to capture the troublesome Kirin.

CHAPTER ELEVEN

FALLON OF LEITH IN THE REALM OF SCARLET

THEY HAD REACHED a cluster of farmsteads late at night and, finding them all deserted, Fallon and his fifty knights had made themselves at home. They were five days' ride from South Warden and deep in the realm of Scarlet. They had not yet met any resistance and the knight captain figured that the common folk of the area had retreated back to the Ranen fortress. Fallon had sent a rider to Ro Hail several days before, and Tristram would send more men after them within a day or two, possibly the reinforcements from Darkwald.

It was still raining and he still hated the Freelands of Ranen. He hated his orders, the Purple clerics who had delivered the orders and, most of all, he hated the prospect of laying siege to South Warden. Their engineers had been ordered to construct trebuchets – tall engines of war able to hurl giant boulders much further than catapults or ballistae. They were used when the knights didn't fancy a protracted siege, and Cardinal Mobius and the king had decided that bombarding the peoples of Wraith and Scarlet was more efficient than keeping the fight clean.

'Rider approaching, sir,' said Sergeant Ohms from the farm's front door.

Fallon puffed out his cheeks and pulled himself up from the armchair where he'd been reclining. It was early morning, and he'd enjoyed the night spent under a wooden roof and the novelty of waking up dry.

'From where?'

'East, sir. Whoever he is, he's riding hard.' Ohms had been on duty for the last few hours and had seen night turn to day across the farms and hamlets of the realm of Scarlet.

Fallon didn't bother to put on his armour.

'Get the men up, but keep them out of sight,' he said.

'Aye, sir,' was the formal response from Ohms.

Fallon sauntered away from the farmhouse. He and his men were nestled between several farmsteads, each small and surrounded by good, black earth. This land was more fertile and cultivated than the Grass Sea or the realm of Wraith, and Fallon found it marginally less objectionable.

Several knights were up and about their duties, scouting out the four points of the compass or preparing breakfast. Ohms quickly roused the others. Most of his unit emerged from haylofts and barns into the cold, wet morning. They took up positions quickly, behind bales of hay and crouched against low walls.

'Theron, Ohms, you're both with me. Quick now,' the captain barked behind him.

His adjutant was fully armoured and flustered as he emerged from the barn where he had been sleeping. Fallon saw that he had hurriedly buckled on his breastplate.

'I'm sure a single rider does not warrant the armour, Theron, but fair enough.'

'I think it best to be prepared, sir.' Theron saluted and straightened his red tabard.

The rider was making directly for their position, though Fallon could not yet make out any distinguishing features. The horse didn't slow down and Fallon drew his sword, holding it casually across his shoulders as a sign of intent. Then he saw a shaved head and sharp, hawk-like features.

'Sir Theron, you can stand down. I know this man,' Fallon murmured to his adjutant, 'though I'd not expected to see him here.'

'Sir?' queried the knight lieutenant.

Fallon sheathed his sword and took a few steps closer to

William of Verellian as he rode towards them. 'He used to be my commander, as I am yours, Theron.'

Verellian pulled on his reins and stopped just in front of Fallon. The knight of the Red looked different, though only two months had passed since they'd become separated in the courtyard of Ro Hail. His right hand was heavily strapped and Fallon vaguely recalled an axe taking off most of his fingers. His clothes were of common design, thickly spun wool and leather, and he carried no weapon.

'I had a feeling you'd be the one they'd send out on patrol,' Verellian said with good humour. 'The worst jobs always go to those with the biggest mouths.'

'You're alive, you lucky bastard.' Fallon smiled. 'How did you manage that?'

Verellian answered with a shrug, as if that was a tale for another time, and began to dismount. 'I saw twenty men hiding, so I assume there are a few more that I missed. I'd guess at fifty in total, yes?'

Fallon nodded. 'Stop showing off. You're talking to a knight captain, don't you know?' A mock expression of superiority accompanied the comment and drew a laugh from Verellian. He jumped to the ground.

'Break cover, boys,' Fallon called over his shoulder.

'Good to see you, Fallon of Leith,' said Verellian quietly.

'And you.'

Theron saluted extravagantly. 'Sir William of Verellian, it is a great honour to meet you. I am Knight Lieutenant Theron of Ro Haran and I have the honour of being Sir Fallon's adjutant.' His words showed deep sincerity. Whatever else he might be, Theron was a true knight of the Red.

'Thank you, sir knight,' replied William, 'though I don't think I deserve such a grand greeting. I was a prisoner of war until five days ago.'

'But you have escaped, Sir William, to join us once again in our war with the barbarians. The One clearly guided your steps.'

216

Verellian narrowed his eyes. 'Clearly.' He stepped closer to Fallon. 'Perhaps we should save the formalities. You and I need to talk.'

'Theron, go and have something to eat,' Fallon said. 'I'll send for you later.' He gestured for Verellian to follow him.

'I'm sorry, sir,' spluttered Theron, 'but shouldn't I be present when you discuss the enemy? I am second in command, am I not?'

Fallon turned sharply and was about to say something clever when William interjected. 'Lieutenant, you have my word that when we discuss the enemy, you will be present. For now, we need to discuss other things.' He frowned slightly. 'And questioning an order is rather foolish, don't you think?'

'Indeed, Sir William,' Theron said, after a moment of indignant silence.

Verellian smiled as the young lieutenant walked away, and Fallon wondered at how the hawk-faced knight of the Red always managed to get men to do what he wanted.

'Is he always like that?' asked William.

'No, he's twice as bad at the moment, he's got two men's cocks to suck instead of just one.' Fallon did not dislike his lieutenant – but he was frustratingly naive. 'Right, you old bastard, what have you been doing for the past two months?' he barked at William. 'I'm the same rank as you now, so I don't need to be polite.'

'You didn't need to be polite before,' replied Verellian. 'You chose to be, out of respect.'

They walked towards the farmhouse. Word had spread quickly among the knights that Sir William of Verellian was alive and a ripple of adoration flowed through the men. Both the senior knights were distinguished, the campaigns in Ro Canarn and the Grass Sea having enhanced their reputations. Fallon would always be known as a killer and would inspire as much fear as respect, but Verellian was known as a shrewd commander and one who put his knights first.

'Are you going to answer me?' Fallon prompted.

'I am,' replied William, 'though I'd prefer it if we were seated.'

Fallon fell back into old habits quickly and shut up, accepting Verellian's decision and stepping into the farmhouse after him.

Once inside, William found the nearest comfortable surface, which happened to be a quilted armchair, and slumped heavily into it. His bones cracked as he stretched out his legs and flexed his back. He was clearly saddle-sore and a layer of dust covered his clothing.

'I can't believe they let you go,' said Fallon, also taking a seat. 'In fact, I'm quite surprised they didn't kill you in the courtyard of Ro Hail.'

'So was I at the time,' replied Verellian. 'They actually tended to my wounds in the end . . . though my sword hand is a bit impaired.' He frowned. 'I can still hold a blade, but anything heavier than a rapier or a short sword and I have no leverage.' Another frown, deeper this time. 'No more longswords for me.'

'Well, if it's any consolation, we're going to be killing a lot of Ranen.' Fallon didn't convey much enthusiasm for the coming massacre.

Verellian sat up. 'The king means to assault South Warden?'

'And Ranen Gar, and any other place where the Free Companies think they can hide. It seems to have become a war of conquest while I wasn't looking,' replied Fallon. 'Mobius has sent for reinforcements to the Darkwald and Arnon.'

William nodded grudgingly and puffed out his cheeks, for a moment seeming like a tired old man. 'They're good people, Fallon. The Ranen, I mean. Not sophisticated, not particularly organized, but good and honourable.' There was a profound sense of regret in his words. 'They don't deserve to be slaughtered.'

'Since when did that matter?' replied Fallon. 'Commander Tristram is convinced that it's all a question of duty to the One.'

'And you believe him? If you can look me in the eye and tell me that this is more than the whim of a king or the design of an enchantress, then I'll accept it.'

William was more bitter than Fallon had ever known him before. 'What happened, sir,' he asked, forgetting that the title was no longer necessary, 'in Ro Hail? This doesn't sound like you.'

The older knight looked around the deserted farmhouse. 'Any food here?' he asked, ignoring Fallon's question.

'Ohms will provide porridge outside. You can have some when we're done.'

'Okay, that's fair. But you won't like the answer.' Verellian was all business now, sitting forward in his chair and adopting a formal tone of voice. 'I've seen some things that knights of the Red are not supposed to see. I've seen women crying over dead brothers, sons and husbands. I've seen men die in pain because we'd killed their only priest. I've seen desperate young warriors, no older than eighteen, trying to fashion serviceable armour from discarded chain and broken plate.' He paused and locked eyes with Fallon. 'This isn't war. It isn't conquest . . . and it certainly isn't honourable. I don't know what it is.' William sounded exhausted.

'Where are you going with this, William? I've been given twenty-four hours' guard duty in the rain for saying less than that. It's dangerous ground.' It was fine to whinge quietly about orders, and Fallon's brand of dry insubordination was generally tolerated, but openly to question the king was dangerous.

'Things are different now,' replied Verellian. 'Red knights generally don't see what I've seen and survive. It changes you.'

Fallon snorted. 'So you saw a few crying Ranen. You've killed hundreds of men and I've never heard you worry about that. You say honour, but what about duty – to me, to the knights, to the One?'

'What *is* duty, Fallon?' William demanded. 'What is duty when your orders are given by a Karesian enchantress?'

Fallon was about to reply aggressively, but his anger evaporated before he spoke. He sat with his mouth open, trying to find some words in response. He considered defending Tristram, or blaming Mobius, but neither sounded right. He began to say that the enchantress who had influenced the king was dead – but there were six more sisters. He closed his mouth and bowed his head.

219

'What does it matter if you're right?' he said in a virtual whisper. 'We're knights of the Red; this is what we do.'

'You're a knight of the Red, my friend. I don't think I can be, not any more.' Verellian spoke as if he had made his decision before today.

'You're the best man I know, but what are you if you are not a knight of the Red?' Fallon did not know how to react.

'I am William of Verellian. I was that before I took my vows and I'll be that when they execute me for turning coat.' Breaking vows was a serious matter. You were a knight of the Red until death. Only the king's younger brother, Alexander Tiris, had ever been allowed to leave the knights.

'Why did you ride west when they released you? You should have found somewhere to hide.' To shout at William for being stupid would be futile. 'Did you think I'd go along with this and just let you go?'

Verellian breathed in deeply. 'I have peace terms from South Warden. I gave my word that, if they released me, I'd deliver them to the king.' The mood between the two men became melancholy. 'I expect to be dead shortly after they tell me the king is too busy to talk to me.'

'I would, you know,' said Fallon. 'Let you go, I mean. If you rode south, you'd make it to Hunter's Cross within a month.'

'I'm the same man, Fallon. I still have honour, and the Ranen deserve to have their words heard.' Verellian was also still a stubborn man, but Fallon couldn't reconcile what he was hearing with the man he thought he knew.

'Well, as a knight captain of the Red, I feel you should deliver those terms to me. Then we can discuss your escape.' He could not pretend that he would detain or harm his former captain. Fallon had already decided to give him the chance to ride south. Whether he would take that chance remained to be seen.

William smiled suddenly and for a moment he was more the man that Fallon remembered. 'Well, Captains Horrock Green Blade and Johan Long Shadow demand that the Ro invaders leave the Freelands of Ranen or be faced with the combined might of the Free Companies.'

Fallon raised an eyebrow, thinking this was a misdirected show of strength that the king would simply ignore. 'And they expect that to meet with something other than laughter?'

'They're serious,' Verellian said grimly, 'and so am I.'

'Has your brain gone soft as well?' grunted Fallon. 'That shit will make the king more likely to kill them, not less.'

William glared at his former adjutant. 'What do you think is waiting for you? South Warden is a shed compared to Tiris . . . Ro Hail is a ruin . . . what does the king want?'

Fallon didn't trust himself to respond quickly.

'Say something, Fallon,' barked Verellian.

'You're a fool,' he replied.

'Anyone who dies for the whim of a king is a fool,' shot back William. 'And you are not a fool.' Each word had been emphasized and now Verellian's teeth were clenched in anger. The two men stood facing each other, only glaring eyes and clenched fists between them. Fallon hated William at that moment – but mostly because he was right.

Knights of the Red lived by a kind of self-deception that enabled them to believe in the absolute rule of the One. It was the duty of a knight to follow his commander's orders and to do the will of king and god. The philosophy was hard to crack and only seasoned knights could see it for what it was – a way of keeping them in line. Fallon and William had seen too much of the world and spilled too much blood to be true believers. They were pragmatic and loyal, but by no means as compliant as a young swordsman like Theron.

Fallon had accepted the hypocrisy and tried not to think too much about it. Now, however, the intervention of the Karesian enchantresses made the cynical knight captain more receptive to Verellian's words.

'Sir Fallon, I'd like to query some of what I just heard,' said Theron, stepping into the farmhouse. 'Your voices carry.'

'Lieutenant Theron, wait outside,' snapped Fallon.

'No need,' said William calmly, stepping towards the idealistic young knight. 'I have peace terms for the king and Captain Fallon would like you to place me under guard until the army arrives.' He turned back to his old adjutant and said, 'Just to make things easier for you.'

'Sir?' queried Theron.

'Just do it,' was the weary response from Fallon.

* * *

Time passed slowly and Fallon's thoughts grew darker and darker. He sat in the abandoned farmhouse, pondering Verellian's words. By mid-afternoon the sun was bright in a cloudless sky and the realm of Scarlet was unusually warm. The ever-present wind reminded him that they were still in Ranen, and it was by no means hot, but at least the rain had stopped. Fallon intended to remain at the farm until reinforcements, and ultimately the bulk of the army, arrived. Once the engineers had assembled their trebuchets and the army was ready for combat they would march on South Warden. William's words would certainly find their way to someone and the old captain's death would likely become just a footnote to the campaign in the Freelands.

'Captain, riders from the west,' shouted Ohms from outside the farmhouse.

Fallon ignored him for a moment, taking as much time as he could before he had to face reality again. Then he exited the house. He had still not put on his armour and, as he joined his unit outside, Knight Captain Fallon of Leith stood out among the many red tabards.

'What do we have, sergeant?' he asked. The question was redundant, however, as dust rising from the west indicated a significant force approaching.

'The banner of Darkwald, sir,' replied the sergeant. 'I'd say a thousand men and engineers. Advance guard.'

The Darkwald yeomanry numbered ten thousand soldiers in all. They were not highly trained but they were notoriously tough. A single purple banner flew in the centre of the approaching column.

Two riders were visible at its head. Brother Jakan rode imperiously under the purple sceptre of nobility. Next to him was Lord Vladimir Corkoson, commander of the yeomanry. He was known as the Lord of Mud, on account of his lesser status among the nobles of Tor Funweir, and had chosen a bunch of grapes against an oak tree as his heraldry. He wore a distinctive moulded-leather breastplate and his white hair was a hereditary touch rather than a sign of age.

'That would be the Lord of Mud, then,' said Ohms, sizing up the lesser noble. 'Leather armour . . . brave man.' The sergeant absently tapped on his steel breastplate.

Jakan was setting a difficult pace for the men on foot to match and the infantry regiments were clearly exhausted.

'Well met, knight captain,' announced the Lord of Mud in a good-humoured way. The two riders trotted on from the rest of the men and approached Fallon. 'Vladimir Corkoson at your service.'

'My lord,' replied Fallon.

'Captain,' said Jakan in a monotone.

'An absolute pleasure as always, brother.'

Jakan and Corkoson dismounted quickly. Of the two commanders, the Lord of Mud was the taller by several inches. He was also slender to the point of being thin and did not look like a true fighting man.

'Do we have somewhere private where we can talk?' asked Jakan.

Vladimir put his hand on the Purple cleric's shoulder. 'And a barrel of something stronger than tea would be welcome.' He turned to Fallon. 'How about it, captain, a few mugs of the good stuff before the bloody work begins?'

'Not for me, my lord,' replied Fallon with a slight smile, 'though, if you're desperate, I'm sure the Ranen that abandoned this place left something behind.'

'Excellent,' said Corkoson with a broad smile. 'You two church-goers can discuss tactics while I drink until I'm at home with the wife.' He strode away, slapping Jakan on the shoulder as he went.

'I like him,' said Sergeant Ohms without cracking a smile.

Jakan glared at the sergeant. 'Silence in the presence of your betters, knight.'

'Go and help the new arrivals get settled,' said Fallon to Ohms. 'Your *betters* will be in the farmhouse.'

Ohms saluted and marched towards the thousand infantrymen of the Darkwald yeomanry. They were now mostly slumped against bales of hay.

'After you,' said Fallon, sweeping his arm in the direction of the farmhouse and smiling at Jakan.

The Purple cleric didn't return the smile and strode away from Fallon, his expensive armour making a considerable noise as he moved.

Theron, who had remained silent during the encounter, stepped next to his captain. 'Sir, would it be impudent of me to say that this Brother Jakan has a rather disagreeable face?'

'And voice,' said Fallon quickly. 'Go and see to the engineers. They shouldn't need any help, but be polite.'

Theron saluted and began to leave. 'And no, it's not impudent at all, the man's an idiot,' agreed Fallon.

A slight smile appeared at the corner of the lieutenant's mouth.

* * *

Fallon appreciated the presence of the Lord of Mud. It meant he didn't have to endure Brother Jakan alone. Corkoson was a good-humoured man in his mid-thirties with a loud voice and a constant need to slap people on the back. His family had been raised by the king due to a perceived need for a lord to command the yeomanry. His father had been a rich wine merchant and that, it seemed, was enough now to make a man noble.

Whatever his claim to lordship, Vladimir Corkoson was known as a moral man who cared for his people and believed that most problems could be solved with a drink. Fallon had often heard it said that, if their soil had been worse and their wine-making less skilled, the Darkwald would have been annexed by Ro Arnon and its people bound into service.

'So, we have five thousand knights and ten thousand infantry. That sounds to me like a force to be reckoned with,' said the Lord of Mud between gulps of mead, a barrel of which had been found in the cellar.

'Trebuchets will be employed and we will reduce their hovels to splinters,' said Jakan with relish.

Fallon and Vladimir were seated. Jakan had remained standing and was pacing up and down. Noise was coming from outside as the siege engines were being assembled. They were five days from South Warden and the trebuchets would be pulled the remaining distance. The bulk of the army would be marching at this very moment, and no amount of inner turmoil felt by Fallon would change what was to happen. They were going to annihilate the Free Companies and continue onwards until the Freelands of Ranen were firmly in the grasp of King Sebastian.

'Captain Fallon, are you listening?' said Jakan, his voice sounding like a high-pitched shriek as it reached the knight's ears.

'No, not really . . . my mind is elsewhere,' replied Fallon. He had not mentioned Verellian and was unsure even how to approach the subject to so blinkered a man as Jakan.

'Well, you should focus quickly, captain. The king and Cardinal Mobius will be here within the week and you will be required to do your duty – which is not to think.' The words were spoken snidely, as if he were trying to provoke Fallon.

Vladimir interjected with a broad smile on his face. 'Easy, brother, we're all friends here and I have the utmost confidence in you both. Are you sure you won't join me in a drink? This mead will certainly soften that prickly attitude, my dear Jakan.' The tone was boisterous and too good-humoured to be taken as an insult even by a man like Brother Jakan. 'Come on, just one slurp. I won't tell anyone.'

Fallon smiled and was again glad of the lord's presence to defuse the tension between Red and Purple.

'There's a man being held in the barn who might like a drink, my lord,' Fallon said to Vladimir. 'He's no longer a knight, so he can pour as much of that shit down his throat as he likes.'

Corkoson, who did not grasp the significance of the comment, smiled broadly. 'Fantastic, let's get him in here. I hate drinking alone.'

Jakan narrowed his eyes and waved down Vladimir's enthusiasm. 'One moment, my lord.' He glared at Fallon. 'Explain yourself, captain.'

The knight stood up and faced Jakan. He used his extra height to look down on the cleric. 'William of Verellian has been released from South Warden and has peace terms for the king.'

'And you tell me this now? You had a duty to inform me of this as soon as I arrived, captain.'

Fallon didn't react to the cleric's anger.

'Have him brought here immediately,' ordered Jakan.

'I told you once before not to give me orders, cleric.' Fallon's response was quiet.

'Please, gentlemen,' interposed Vladimir, 'nothing would be served by us fighting.' He smiled. 'You can't drink, but how about we find some willing peasant girls?'

Fallon tried not to smile, but it was difficult to maintain his anger with Jakan in Corkoson's presence. He turned away from the cleric and said gently, 'We can't whore either, my lord . . . regrettable, I know. All we can do is fight. We can fight and we can moan about duty and honour.'

Jakan snorted. 'You're close to the line, captain. Go and get Verellian. Now.'

Fallon's blood rose sharply and his fists clenched. 'Get your sanctimonious arse out of my face,' he roared. 'If you were a man, I'd call you out and kill you. I'd cut up your piggish face and send it to Mobius as a present.' He punched the cleric's breastplate to punctuate the last word, making the smaller man shrink back.

Jakan stared at the furious knight before him. The cleric was just playing the part of a noble of God, a part he'd been trained to play since he was a boy. When faced with a challenge, he would back down like any other bully.

'I, er . . . don't think we'd accomplish much if you were to kill each other,' said the Lord of Mud, absently taking a swig of mead. 'And I'm fairly sure that Cardinal Mobius would not be thrilled with Brother Jakan's face as a present . . . maybe he'd prefer a vase or something.'

Fallon smirked. He had proved his point and said, this time in a gentler tone of voice, 'I will send Sergeant Ohms to fetch Verellian for you, Brother Jakan. There is, as my Lord Corkoson says, no reason for us to fight.'

* * *

'I was just getting comfortable against that bale of hay,' Verellian joked as Ohms led him into the farmhouse. 'And where did the Darkwald yeomanry come from?' He had a smile on his face. William of Verellian, former knight of the Red, was in strangely good humour.

Jakan had insisted that five men with loaded crossbows surround the doorway.

'I'm afraid I may be responsible for that, Sir William,' said Vladimir, with a grandiose bow. 'I've heard of you.'

'And I of you, my lord,' replied Verellian, 'though I'm surprised to see you so easily pressed into service.'

'Silence, dog,' barked Jakan, his hand on the hilt of his sword. 'You are a vow-breaker and will speak only when spoken to.'

William raised an eyebrow and looked at Fallon. 'I don't think I've met this one,' he said with a more serious expression.

Fallon shrugged and felt strangely conflicted. 'You should probably just keep quiet,' he said to Verellian.

The old knight frowned and nodded his head. He smiled weakly at Fallon. 'I understand, my friend, let us just see what happens.'

'I won't tell you again,' snapped Jakan. 'You have lost any right to speak here.'

Fallon stood and waited, hoping that his minimal faith in the

One would be enough to keep either man from dying. If Jakan pushed the old knight, Fallon was sure a fight would ensue. If Verellian was too disrespectful, the Purple cleric would have no choice but to call him out.

If they were to fight, the outcome would be uncertain. William was the better swordsman, but he'd been captive for several months and would have to use a lighter blade. It was possible to compensate for missing fingers, but only after months or years of training. The more pressing matter was whether or not Fallon could stay neutral if the two men were to fight to the death.

'That's a very disagreeable attitude, cleric,' said Verellian. 'You should consider me a peace envoy from the Ranen . . . or maybe just keep your mouth shut.'

Jakan had a fit of righteous indignation. The man of the Purple stepped closer to William and said, in a veritable shriek, 'I consider you a man who has turned from his duty, a man who has no honour and deserves no respect.' The insufferable man then took the irreversible step of spitting in Verellian's face.

Vladimir Corkoson had moved to intercede, but Fallon held out an arm to stop him. The Lord of Mud was mumbling something about *not needing to be rude*. Fallon knew the situation had proceeded beyond such platitudes.

William wiped the spit from his face, then grabbed Jakan by the throat. The grasp was strong, and the cleric flailed at William's forearm.

'We can talk this out . . . really, we can,' shouted Vladimir.

Jakan directed a solid kick at William's shin, sending him backwards and breaking his grasp. 'A trial by combat it is, Sir Verellian,' snapped Jakan, a look of violent determination on his face. 'I will kill you in sight of the One.'

William smirked.

'Outside, now! One of you, give him a sword.' Jakan marched outside.

'Well, politeness has gone right out of the window in this farmhouse,' said Vladimir, sounding a little drunk.

228

'At least this way it's simple,' William said, with a resigned look on his face. 'A sword is better than a noose.'

'What were we saying earlier about not being fools?' Fallon said, shaking his head.

'Just give me a sword. If you have any respect left, just let the insufferable cunt kill me.' William was no longer smiling as he turned to face his former adjutant. 'Something light, a short sword or a hand-axe. Maybe a shield so he doesn't kill me inside two seconds.'

Vladimir Corkoson carried two short swords, one at each hip. 'I would gladly lend you a weapon, Sir Verellian, but I must ask Captain Fallon whether or not to do so would be . . . in any way offensive or improper.'

'You're okay, Vladimir,' replied Fallon, forgetting to address him by his title. 'You might as well lend him a bottle of mead for all the good it'll do him.'

'Thank you for those words of encouragement,' replied Verellian, with a raised eyebrow. 'Swear to me you will remain a man of honour, my friend . . . and not just a man of the One.'

Fallon was about to respond when William raised a hand and cut him off. 'And don't think of something clever to say, just take the words for what they are.' He turned sharply and followed Brother Jakan out of the farmhouse, absently swinging the short sword as he did so.

'I'm sure there's a story here that I'm not privy to, old boy,' said Vladimir, placing a hand on Fallon's shoulder. 'But I believe Sir Verellian will be killed. Am I right?'

Feeling more cynical, more jaded and more conflicted than usual, Fallon nodded and went to join the others outside.

Ohms and Theron were standing off to the side, talking quietly. A dozen crossbowmen had formed a rough circle in which Verellian and the Purple cleric could fight. The men watching were all used to seeing duels. They were not concerned with the result but saw it as an interesting diversion after a hard day's march.

'For a second there, I thought you'd hit him,' said Ohms as Fallon joined them.

'I didn't, but Verellian couldn't keep his temper. Not that I could have done if a man had spat at me.'

Theron winced. 'Men of honour do not spit at their opponents. They strike them firmly with a glove or a gauntlet.' He was deeply sincere, for all his naivety.

'Your man can't win,' said Ohms quietly. 'By the look of him, he's not held a sword since he lost his fingers.'

Once more, all he could think about was what he would do if faced with his friend's death. Would he be able to remain still and watch Brother Jakan kill William, or would he do something incredibly foolish?

'Step forward, vow-breaker,' snapped Jakan.

The Purple cleric was now wearing a high-crested helmet and held his pristine shield across his chest. He was comfortable with a sword in his hand and appeared considerably more dangerous than he did when blathering on about duty and the One. Fallon still hated him, but he had to concede that the clerics of nobility were skilled warriors as well as irritating fools.

'Will you at least hear the Ranen's terms before you kill me?' asked Verellian, stubbornly sticking to his new ideals.

'I will not. I will kill you and invoke your name as I kill the Ranen of South Warden. I name you turncoat, William of Verellian.'

The old knight of the Red looked at Fallon and smiled, with a kind of gallows humour that did not convey confidence. He then clenched his thumb and remaining two fingers round the hilt of his short sword.

Jakan advanced quickly and showed that he wasn't intending to beat about the bush. His longsword was held high, in practised fashion, and his eyes were narrow and concentrated. 'Time to die, vow-breaker,' he snarled.

Verellian didn't allow himself to get drawn into talk, but levelled his own shield, keeping his sword in close to his chest.

When the attack came, it was from Jakan. The Purple cleric swung powerfully downwards, trying to finish Verellian with one blow. William didn't raise his shield but sprang deftly to the side, directing a fast thrust towards Jakan. The cleric had underestimated his opponent and was forced to back away, wincing at a shallow wound in his side.

'Don't overextend yourself, boy,' said Verellian.

'I will be the hand of the One, dog,' shouted Jakan, advancing again.

His attacks were now more measured. He delivered a series of fast and powerful swings, not extending his arm too far beyond his body, and sending a loud noise of metal on metal around the farmyard as Verellian deflected each blow with his shield. The former Red knight made no attempt to riposte and stayed crouched and braced behind his shield. Each of Jakan's attacks drove Verellian back slightly, but they didn't look like penetrating his defence.

Fallon began to breathe heavily as he watched, echoing the exhaustion he imagined Verellian was feeling. He couldn't see a way for his former captain to win. Even if he could stay away from the cleric's longsword, William would be hard pushed to deliver a telling blow with his small blade.

Jakan maintained his assault and realized that he was the fitter of the two men. With repeated blows, he began to weaken Verellian's grip on his shield. The old knight tried to sidestep, rather than retreat, but he had little opening to mount an attack.

'Hardly fair,' muttered Theron. 'The cleric has little honour.'

'He's got a good sword arm, though,' was the dry response from Ohms.

Verellian looked frustrated more than anything else, evidently wishing he had a fully functioning sword hand with which to kill the Purple cleric outright. Instead, he was rapidly being worn down.

'I can't let him die,' whispered Fallon to himself. 'What would a man of honour do . . .?' He was glad neither Ohms nor Theron had heard him.

Jakan began a complex and powerful series of overhead blows that made the old knight look clumsy. Verellian did his best to deflect them, but Jakan saw the opening when it came. William turned too far in parrying a thrust and left his right side open. The Purple cleric spun round and delivered a deep slash to William's side. The blow was not fatal, but Verellian stumbled and lost his footing on the grass.

Jakan pounced, kicking the former knight in the head. The short sword flew away and William fell over his shield, landing in an undignified heap.

'You are bested, knight,' announced Jakan, kicking away William's shield and leaving the old knight prone on the floor. 'If you beg forgiveness of the One God for betrayal, I will finish you quickly.'

'Just kill me, you Purple cunt,' barked Verellian, holding his wounded side and trying to stop the blood. 'The One has had more than enough of my blood. He doesn't get an apology as well.'

Jakan raised his longsword. Time seemed to stand still as Fallon saw his only true friend prone on the grass. He thought of the battles they had seen and the enemies they had faced. The odds often stacked against them, Fallon and Verellian had bested everyone who had been foolish enough to fight them.

'Stop!' roared Fallon. Everyone looked at him and Jakan paused, his sword still held in the air.

He stood, breathing heavily and gritting his teeth.

'Don't,' whispered Theron. 'They'll kill you.'

Fallon strode forward.

'Captain Fallon, what is the meaning of this?' shouted Jakan.

'You're not killing him today,' said Fallon, holding his sword loosely in his fist. 'Sergeant Ohms,' he shouted behind him, 'put William of Verellian on a horse.'

Ohms obeyed the order without question.

'You two,' the sergeant barked at some nearby knights, 'help me get the man into a saddle. Move your arses.'

Fallon looked up, his eyes dark and aggressive.

'You've approached the line a hundred times, Fallon,' said Jakan, 'but now you've crossed it.'

'Ohms, move faster,' said the knight captain.

'Aye, sir.' The sergeant slung Verellian's arm over his shoulder and hefted the old knight into the saddle. Two other men helped until William was hunched over on the back of the horse.

Theron ordered the knights to arms and they stood protectively behind their captain. The yeomanry did the same behind Jakan, their crossbows held ready.

'Ride south,' he said to Verellian. 'Canarn or Hunter's Cross, I don't care which. Just don't come back to Ranen.'

The old knight was badly hurt, but smiled. 'You are a better man than I, Fallon of Leith. Let me know if you manage to get out of this.'

'I don't think I'd make a good prisoner,' Fallon said, placing a second short sword in Verellian's hand. 'Look after that, or learn to fight left-handed.'

'Captain,' shrieked Jakan, stamping his feet in rage, 'you will be executed for this.'

Fallon slapped the rump of Verellian's horse, sending the man south at speed. Jakan, too enraged to speak, stared at him.

'Subdue the knight captain,' ordered the cleric, almost exploding as the words left his mouth. 'Kill any that stand before him.'

Mumbled complaints from Lord Corkoson did nothing to stop a hundred of the yeomanry from advancing.

'Protect the captain,' shouted Theron. 'We are of the Red and we will stand.' In unison, all of the knights drew their swords.

'Enough,' boomed Fallon, addressing his own men. 'I knew what I was doing.'

'Captain, we can win,' said Theron in a snarl.

'Let them come,' agreed Ohms, banging his sword on his red shield. 'After we kill the first hundred, the rest will shit and run away.'

The knights laughed boisterously in agreement and the yeomanry looked at each other in fear and confusion. They were common folk, simply following the orders of their commander. It wasn't their fault their commander was an idiot.

'No more fighting today,' he said to Jakan. 'I willingly surrender to the justice of the One.'

'Captain,' said Theron, 'we are true to you.'

The knight turned to his adjutant and held out his longsword, hilt first. 'Look after that, Theron,' he said. 'You are a better man than I thought.'

Theron, Ohms and the rest of the unit were angry at having to allow their captain to surrender. Each man glared at Jakan as if he was swearing vengeance.

'Don't take this the wrong way, cleric,' he said to Jakan. 'I still plan to kill you, but honour dictates that I surrender.'

As he was shackled by quivering yeomanry and led away from his men, Knight Captain Fallon of Leith smiled. He had done something that might ultimately bring about his death, but he was happy with what he had done for the first time in months.

EPILOGUE

T HE WINDS THAT blew across the barren plains of Tor Funweir proved a nightmare for a hawk. It was easy to catch the lighter gusts and continue southwards, but Nanon had never been very good at flying. The constant need to make corrections, the strange, chaotic patterns that the wind took you in – he could never feel fully in control of his direction or speed. Real birds must have a high tolerance for frustration.

As the mountains of the Claws appeared on the horizon, he began to descend, gliding towards a small but dense forest nestled in the foothills. He swore loudly, the sound coming out as a shrill caw, as it started to rain. Wet feathers were a burden, especially when about to land. He plunged sluggishly downwards on to a high branch, mostly out of the weather. With an uncomfortable flap, he shook off the worst of the water and looked down to the ground. He was a few miles north of where he needed to be. Maybe four paws would be easier than two wings.

Making sure to stay out of the rain, Nanon hopped off the branch and let out another caw, plummeting to the leaf litter at ground level. Wet, cold and miserable. Stupid birds. With a small surge of energy he took the shape of a brown bear and quickly loped away into the small forest. Bears were easier. They had a sense of solidity and weight that was comforting. The only downside was the smell.

Few men had travelled this path. The Claws were notoriously difficult to traverse. The men of Ro preferred the flatlands and largely left the forests and mountains alone. In the forests, Nanon's people and the Gorlan could live largely undisturbed, and in the mountains, other things lurked.

He ran upwards until the plains were a distant sight below and the higher mountains blocked out the horizon. As a bear, he was safe from most of the local predators. Only the largest Gorlan would dare to attack him, and they were rare at high altitude. He was going to the dark side of the highest mountain to visit an old acquaintance – a very old acquaintance.

After hours of running, a cave appeared through the trees. Taking his bearings from the sky and the mountains, Nanon ran to the cave and stopped. He was beyond the reach of the hardiest explorers and the most adventurous birds. No animals approached the highest peaks. His hackles rose. He felt like prey.

From the open cave echoed a low murmur. It was a repeating throaty gurgle, not the sound of an intelligent creature. The noise had been passed down through generations of Dokkalfar and he recognized it straightaway.

'A long time, knife-ears,' said a resonant voice.

Nanon turned back to his natural form.

'Keep your pet back,' he said.

The gurgle died down and the sound retreated further into the dark cave, hidden behind old magic.

'It hasn't consumed flesh for decades.' The voice was beautiful and would cause pain to lesser beings. Each word had a sharp edge, cutting through the air to reach Nanon's ears. It carried with it a wave of dark magic, flooding out of the innocuous-looking cave.

'It's wet out here. Can I come in?' asked Nanon once he was happy that the pet had disappeared.

'You may.'

He hesitated, composing himself. To cross the illusory barrier of the dark cave entrance would feel like crossing out of reality. It would hurt.

He stepped forward, breaching the barrier that masked the Jekkan ruin from the lands of men. His eyes stung and his head felt heavy. He was powerful enough to withstand the madness that Jekkan magic brought on, but their otherworldly illusions were chaotic and unpredictable.

He stood on black stone, amid massive pillars. The floor gave off a dull glow, illuminating the being standing in front of him. It was tall and slender, its face sharply angled, and its features overly sensual. The eyes were cat-like, wide and hypnotic. It approached him and revealed sharp claws and silken robes.

Nanon's hand shook. He was afraid.

'You look well, knife-ears,' said the Jekkan, its body swaying with each word. 'You would be consumed with honour.'

Nanon tilted his head. 'I told you before that I wouldn't taste good. Stick to eating humans.'

'It is not a punishment. It is the highest compliment I can pay you.' The Jekkan drummed its clawed fingers together in front of its face. 'Why are you here, Nanon of the forest-dwellers? It has been at least two centuries.'

'Closer to three. And I'm here because I need advice,' he replied.

The repeating murmur of the Jekkan's servitor returned. It was slumped in shadow beyond the last visible pillar, its surface a ripple of black bubbles. It covered a large section of floor, flowing like congealed blood. To look too long at a Jekkan servitor was to invite madness.

'Keep your pet away from me,' snapped Nanon. 'We both know I'm afraid, but I'm not weak. Show me the respect I show you.'

The Jekkan preened its luxuriant eyelashes. 'Apologies. I rarely communicate with lesser flesh. Your concept of respect is . . . strange.'

Nanon kept his legs poised. He knew that his sword would be of no use, but running was always an option.

'What advice do you need?' asked the Jekkan. 'If it is in my power to give, I will give. If my forever can caress your now . . .'

'Shub-Nillurath. He has become powerful. How do I stop it?'

The Jekkan became agitated and the servitor moved closer, undulating across the floor and forming grasping tentacles from its rippling mass. Nanon could not take his eyes from the creature or shut out its mocking cry.

'You said you'd help me,' he cried, preparing to run. 'I'm a soldier of the Long War.'

The Jekkan raised its head and the servitor stopped moving. 'You are correct, knife-ears, I did. And you are.'

'The Dead God is a threat to this world.' Nanon was still poised to flee. 'Your ruins will not stay safe for long when the Dark Young spread across this land.'

'We do not fear the Young,' said the Jekkan, waving its clawed fingers in the air. 'They have lived and lost. They will lose again.'

'So, help me,' snapped Nanon, tearing his eyes from the servitor. 'You are of the great race of Jekka. You have seen the world as it is and as it will be. You know what I need to do.'

The black iridescent mass retreated into shadow and the Jekkan's face contorted into a fanged smile. His magic was subtle and Nanon had to concentrate to retain his free will. If he relaxed for one moment, his mind would be lost and he'd be a slave to the Jekkan, twisted and tortured into a fleshy toy.

'The forest halls beyond the world are rebuilt, the maleficent witches bring new worship each day. Soon the Giant's followers will be willing and enchantment will no longer be needed.'

'Jaa made a mistake,' said Nanon. 'He left the thing alive. Now it's strong.'

The Jekkan salivated, licking its lips. 'Forest-dwellers are weak. You never deserved your long lives.'

'Because we didn't follow you?' barked Nanon. 'We had a Giant we loved. We didn't need your god.'

'But you seek my help? My forever? You forgo the old ones, choosing your Giants and their *lands of men*. But still you need my help. Your now is weak and ignorant.'

The Dokkalfar and the Jekkans had never been cordial, even in the long ages before men. Few forest-dwellers could withstand their maddening illusions or defeat their monstrous servitors, but Nanon was difficult to scare and he knew that they possessed great knowledge.

'Must we dance each time we talk?' said the forest-dweller.

'My Giant, your old one . . . these things no longer matter.'

The Jekkan purred, its tongue stroking its huge fangs. 'I like you, knife-ears, you are direct. I must remember that your people do not enjoy the dance of words. You enjoy bluntness . . . and abstinence.'

'So be blunt,' offered Nanon. 'Shub-Nillurath will destroy the lands of men. Tell me how to stop the creature and its witches.'

'This battle of the Long War will cost the humans dearly. A tide of blood in their fledgling ocean. It will cost the forest-dwellers more. A twilight flame, cutting through your trees. In time you may rebuild, but you will never be the same. In the end, the Mistress of Pain will bring down Shub-Nillurath.'

'What?' Nanon blurted out. 'She's his high priestess.'

The Jekkan stepped closer and clawed at the air in front of the forest-dweller. 'You are lost in the moment, knife-ears. Your mind cannot grasp forever. If you are asking about the moment, I can tell you that the dark-blood will fall, and the old-blood is your greatest ally . . . though he will become lost in cracks of beyond.'

Nanon bowed his head. 'You're avoiding the question. I asked how I beat him.'

There was silence but for the maddening trill of the servitor. The creature responded to its master's emotions, but it stayed back, keeping its distance from Nanon.

'Answer me!' shouted the old Tyr.

'You are out of your league,' said the Jekkan. 'You should follow your Giant into oblivion. Light the shadow flame and step into forever.'

'Answer me!' he screamed. 'Use me for your rituals, consume my flesh, but answer me first.'

The servitor reared up, its ropey tentacles stretching forward and its amorphous flesh shifting through different shades of black. Eyes and mouths appeared randomly, forming no pattern or recognizable face, but tearing into Nanon as if they were dead friends.

'Calm yourself, knife-ears. I will answer you.'

239

Nanon panted. He was still ready to run, but anger overrode fear. His head was heavy and his blood felt hot. Every twitch of movement caused burning as the Jekkan magic flooded through his system.

'You cannot defeat Shub-Nillurath. You can only survive. This is what should occupy your mind. Run, hide, wait out this battle of the Long War and be patient.' A sibilant hiss came from the Jekkan's mouth. 'You may wait here if you wish. Spend the coming centuries in beautiful madness.'

The magic softened and the servitor retreated, allowing Nanon a moment of clarity. He couldn't stay much longer.

'Why fight, knife-ears?'

His anger disappeared. His head cleared and suddenly he felt tired. 'I don't know. If I can't win . . . I don't know. Maybe friends . . . or stubbornness.'

'I suspect you knew the answer,' replied the Jekkan.

'No,' he said. 'I feared, but I didn't know. That's why I came here.'

'There are few soldiers of the Long War left. Few old-bloods, few creatures of deep time. No beings stand in the lands of men who can defeat Shub-Nillurath.' The Jekkan relished the words, smacking its lips contentedly.

'So I'll make do with what I've got,' replied Nanon. 'We might surprise you.'

'No!' said the Jekkan. 'You will not.'

He took two steps backwards, towards the cave entrance and the Jekkan barrier. Any longer in the ruin would mean death. Complicated and muddled thoughts filled his head. Pain and madness were an instant away as Nanon threw himself back, through the illusion and on to rain-soaked grass.

BOOK TWO

THE
SHAPE TAKER

The Tale of the One God

THE GIANT SAT in his stone hall beyond the world and wore grey.

The Giant acted with nobility and his followers wore purple, rising above other men to rule.

The Giant acted with aggression and made war upon his enemies and his followers wore red, standing tall and never questioning their duty.

The Giant showed compassion and his followers wore white, healing the sick and valuing peace.

The Giant sought knowledge and his followers wore blue, devoting themselves to learning all they could of the world and beyond.

The Giant became humble and gave to the needy, and his followers wore brown, accepting that they were unworthy.

The Giant sought riches and became greedy, and his followers wore gold, taking all that they could.

At the last, the Giant understood death and his followers wore black.

But the Giant himself remained grey.

PROLOGUE

T HE GIRL WAS born in the Karesian city of Thrakka. Her earliest memories were of high spires, dusty streets and rolling deserts. She remembered anger and hatred, but no love. If the girl had ever known her parents, the memories were lost. The first faces she knew belonged to other street children and criminals, though even they were distant. She recalled no names, just that she was used by unclean men and envied by other girls.

By her fourteenth year, the girl was hard and uncaring. She knew how to hold a knife and where to stick it. She knew how to lie and to whom. She knew how to steal and, most importantly, how not to get caught. She'd seen boys and girls die on the streets of Thrakka, used up by a world that catered only to the very rich. She lived by her wits and resolved to survive. If Karesia used people until they had no more to give, the girl would be a user and not a victim.

She avoided the brothels and harems, preferring to keep her own company as she traversed the underworld of Thrakka. She sacrificed the money and protection offered by the criminal classes, but never sacrificed her freedom. If she was to be used up, it would be on her own terms. A bribe here, a seductive smile there. She was clever and knew when to fight, when to run, and when to manipulate. She lived in the bottom level of an abandoned vizier tower, eating only what she could steal and wearing the clothes of those she'd killed.

Her name was Anasaara Valez and she was destined for more than the streets of Thrakka.

On her eighteenth birthday, a procession arrived in the city. She watched its arrival from her isolated domain, hidden behind moveable rocks. The procession had been long-heralded and two hundred wind claws accompanied the visitors. Rich merchant families and viziers watched from balconies and Karesians of every stripe lined the streets to pay their respects to the matron mother of Oron Kaa. The elderly woman was tall and thin, with harsh features and penetrating eyes. She had with her a procession of young girls, acquired from every Karesian city. The girls had been chosen to form the priesthood of Jaa. They would be tested and tortured until only seven remained. Every family in Thrakka hoped that their daughter would be chosen to join the enchantresses and many threw coins and wealth in front of the procession in an effort to gain the mother's favour.

They walked slowly around the city. At every intersection, the mother stopped and took a deep breath of the air, as if expecting to find something. Each time she passed Anasaara's hovel, the procession stopped for several moments. Nearby, merchants aggressively thrust their daughters forward, hoping that the mother would notice them. After the third circuit of Thrakka, the old woman began to smile. It was a toothy grimace, with no humour.

'Come to me, child,' she said to the air.

Anasaara felt compelled to obey. She removed the loose rocks that hid her dwelling and approached the procession. Hundreds of eyes watched her and the wind claws parted to allow her to come close to the matron mother.

'Do you know who I am?' asked the old woman.

Anasaara said nothing.

'Can you speak?'

Again, the girl was silent.

'You are wilful, girl. But we will break you of that.'

Anasaara looked around her. Angry merchants were returning to their homes, disappointed that their daughters had not been chosen. The girl was not surprised. She knew that she had been chosen long before the procession arrived.

'You will come with us to Oron Kaa,' said the mother. 'Your life is now mine.'

* * *

Everything changed. The girl was pampered and well fed. The journey south was long, but comfortable, and they were transported in litters carried by dozens of muscular slaves. No one spoke about their new life or about the sinister old woman who accompanied them, but each young girl was happy. This changed when they reached Oron Kaa.

The abbey was of stone, rising from the Sunset Coast to touch the clouds. The shimmering deserts of Far Karesia distorted the building, making it writhe in the stifling air. Then the torture began.

The girl remembered the pain and she remembered the questions. Each new day brought new pain and new questions. The matron mother didn't expect answers, but she asked anyway. The girl remained wilful, determined to survive, no matter what. She saw girls skinned alive and thrown into the Scorched Sea to be eaten by sharks. She saw her own skin flayed and healed, flayed and healed. Time and again, she was mutilated and made whole. Each new torture brought more pain and more questions.

'Who are you?'

'What do you fear?'

'What is pain?'

Her body broke a hundred times, but her mind never did. As time passed, the girl realized that she was not ageing. The wind claws who guarded her grew old and died, but the girls remained eighteen. Time was meaningless. All Anasaara felt was pain until it was the only thing she had left.

'Who are you?'

'I am no one.'

'What do you fear?'

'Nothing but Jaa.'

'What is pain?'

The last question was asked a thousand times, but she didn't know the answer. Their faces began to change until all the remaining girls looked the same. They were beautiful, with lush figures and enchanting eyes. Even their voices became similar. The matron mother paid special attention to Anasaara, singling her out from the remaining girls and personally administering her torture. She did not age either, remaining a sharp-faced old woman, as the third generation of their guards died of old age.

She clung to her pain. It became her entire world. Hundreds of years and all she felt was pain, until it no longer hurt.

'Who are you?'

'I am one of the Seven Sisters.'

'What do you fear?'

'Nothing but Jaa.'

'What is pain?'

She paused, no longer doubting the answer. 'Pain is my servant. I am its mistress.'

Her life changed once again. The torture stopped and she was allowed to dress and bathe. She ate food for the first time in centuries and found it gave her no pleasure. She spoke to the other girls and learned their names, but their company was nothing but a distraction. She was their leader and she would remain apart.

As her sisters were tattooed, Anasaara learned of the world. She read books, studied maps and gained wisdom about the lands of men and its gods. The barbarian lands of Rowanoco had formed an order of warrior priests, and the ordered lands of the One were policed by armies of clerics. In contrast, Jaa had invested power in only seven of his followers, gifting each with great power and trusting in quality, not quantity.

When she left Oron Kaa, Anasaara Valez was dead. All that remained was Saara the Mistress of Pain.

PART ONE

CHAPTER ONE

LADY BRONWYN OF CANARN
IN THE CITY OF SOUTH WARDEN

THE REALM OF Scarlet was full of beautiful green pastures and lush forests. The Moon Wood to the north was a magical place where the local farmers prayed to the spirits of earth and rock with which Rowanoco had blessed them. Brytag's Roost to the east was a sacred mountain range where the Ice Giant's raven supposedly perched, watching over the lands of Ranen.

Bronwyn had heard of both places, having been told stories by her father about the groves and glens where the Order of the Hammer heard the voice of their god, but after being in the Freelands for so long she was beginning to take on some of her brother's cynicism. Scarlet Company and their captain, Johan Long Shadow, were tough men and women. They were not inhospitable to the outsiders in their midst, but they still saw Bronwyn as a pampered lady of Ro. She had tried to bond with them, telling stories of her youth in Canarn and trying to display her uncommon knowledge of the peoples of Ranen. Very little of it worked, though, and despite her best efforts Bronwyn still spent most of her time with Al-Hasim, the infuriating Karesian scoundrel, and the survivors of Wraith Company.

They had been in South Warden for several weeks and it was a world away from their previous lodging in the ruins of Ro Hail, or the weeks spent sleeping rough as they fled from the knights of the Red. Bronwyn had been given a room in a tall wooden house overlooking the western stockade. The town, or city as the Ranen liked to call it, was a closely packed circle of wooden halls and cosy homesteads, with a constant smell of smoke and iron from a hundred forges and fireplaces. South Warden was home to a few thousand men, women and children. It was smaller than her home of Ro Canarn, but it easily accommodated the five hundred or so refugees of Wraith Company, and their blue cloaks were now a constant presence alongside the crimson heraldry of South Warden.

'It's early, Bronwyn, go back to sleep.' The voice came from the lump lying next to her and she elbowed him for interrupting her thoughts.

'The Ranen always seem to get up with the dawn,' she replied, pulling the covers tight around her shoulders.

As Bronwyn looked at Al-Hasim, lying next to her, she wandered what her brother would think if he knew she'd given in to his advances. They had begun comforting each other on the journey east. She had adopted a fatalistic attitude to life of late and she felt that taking a highly inappropriate lover was in keeping with her new world view. Brom would likely not appreciate this, and she worried that he'd skewer the Karesian if he ever found out.

'Stone Dog will come knocking on the door when it's time to get up,' mumbled Hasim, his face pressed against the pillow.

She elbowed him again. 'Shut up, I'm thinking.'

'About what?' Hasim murmured, turning over and leaning on his hand. 'How unbelievably attractive I am?' He had a predatory glint in his eye.

Bronwyn didn't smile or give the Karesian any indication that she was in the mood. She then lunged forward and kissed him roughly, biting his lower lip before pulling away.

'Cheeky bitch,' he said. Touching a dot of blood from his lip, he pulled her down to his level, lying flat on the simple wooden bed. 'And it's still too early to be up.'

Bronwyn didn't smile. She dug her nails into his back and pulled him in for another kiss. She was angry and a long way from home, and Al-Hasim knew that his job was to provide a distraction for her. 'Just shut up,' she growled, wrapping her legs round him and sliding further down the bed.

'I'm just a piece of meat to you, my lady,' he said, emphasizing his lyrical Karesian accent and pulling away. 'Do you think Brom knows what a rampant seductress you've become?'

'I don't think he'd care,' she lied. 'He's got forest-dwellers to deal with.'

Hasim grinned and moved down to bite Bronwyn's neck playfully. Then a knock at the door made them both jump.

'Wake up, ladies,' shouted Micah Stone Dog from outside their chamber. 'That Brown cleric from Canarn wants a word.'

Bronwyn didn't let go of Hasim for a moment, letting her thighs grip him tightly before slapping him hard in the face and smiling. 'Calm down, Karesian, we have things to do,' she said in a low whimper, pressing her body against his.

Another knock on the door. 'Get up. You can fuck later. There are a lot of hours in the day, I hear.' Stone Dog's sarcasm and dry humour were in full flow in the mornings. 'Try not to prove everyone right by being a Karesian and a Ro.'

Any kind of sexual mood disappeared instantly. Bronwyn yawned extravagantly and Hasim sat up and rubbed the tiredness from his eyes. The sun was starting to intrude through the shuttered windows and the air was rapidly warming up as they rose swiftly from their bed.

'Who do you think they hate more, the Karesian or the Ro?' Bronwyn asked, pulling on her simple homespun dress.

'I'm not a noble, sweetness,' responded Hasim. 'I'm just exotic. You're a stuck-up Ro.'

'Apparently so,' she said drily, not finding the situation particularly funny.

Stone Dog wearily knocked on the door again. 'There's an assembly first thing and Brother Lanry wants to make sure you don't fuck up if you're asked to speak.'

Bronwyn and Hasim exchanged a concerned look. They'd been told to expect this, but it was still scary news. Captain Horrock of Wraith Company had petitioned to rouse the Free Companies and declare war on the invader knights of the Red. Johan Long Shadow agreed, but the proper way of doing things in Ranen was to allow all sides a chance to speak.

There were dissenting voices, though Horrock was convinced that seeing an army of knights appear over the horizon would silence them. Bronwyn had counselled that William of Verellian, the captive knight of the Red, should be released with peace terms, but most of the Ranen had laughed. It was only the esteem she had gained from Wraith Company that meant her voice had been listened to at all.

* * *

The Ranen assembly of South Warden was a circular stone building in the centre of the town. Bronwyn had seen it every day since they had arrived, but she had not been permitted to enter until now. The assembly was treated with great reverence by all of the Ranen. Even the refugees from Wraith Company knew the significance of Rowanoco's Stone and of the decisions that were made in the assembly. Any Ranen man of good standing was allowed to sit in the cold stone auditorium, and each held a small axe with which he could cast his vote. Father Magnus used to joke that the politics of Ranen were more violent than the wars of Ro and that a decision would never be respected unless at least one man died during their deliberations.

To Bronwyn it was an inconceivable way to run a country. Even Al-Hasim found the Ranen assembly intimidating and, as they walked up the rough dirt track that served as a road, he looked even more nervous than Bronwyn. Stone Dog was apathetic as always, as he walked casually beside them using his vicious-looking locaber axe as a walking stick.

South Warden was built on a natural hill and the central palisade vaguely resembled a wooden fort, with the Ranen assembly the only stone building within the central ring. The family of Long Shadow had purposely built the town to be defensible and every point of the compass had multiple gates and stockades, most of which were not currently manned. Bronwyn was no military tactician, but even she could see that, if Scarlet Company chose to make it so, South Warden would become a nightmare for an invading army.

Brother Lanry was waiting for them outside the inner fortifications, several streets away from the assembly. He had been sent north by Bromvy to tell them of Magnus's death and of the retaking of the city from the Red knights. She liked the old cleric and, aside from Al-Hasim, he was the friendliest face in South Warden.

'A bright and crisp Ranen morning if ever I saw one,' he said cheerfully, as the Ro noblewoman, the Ranen warrior and the Karesian scoundrel approached. 'Horrock said it would rain this morning . . . good to know he's a better warrior than soothsayer.'

'Not by much,' muttered Stone Dog without cracking a smile. 'But I suppose he is old, and his knees are giving up.'

Lanry chuckled guiltily. 'Well, that aside, young Micah, I believe this day bodes well for the cause.'

'And *the cause* is?' asked Bronwyn.

'The cause of good versus evil, my dear lady, right versus wrong,' replied the Brown cleric with a sincere smile. 'I understand that the Ranen fellows will make their decision this morning.'

'And they want to speak to us?' asked Bronwyn, letting her nerves show through in her words.

Micah Stone Dog turned to her. 'You were there, Bronwyn, you saw what happened at Ro Hail. You saw the army of knights, you saw the king's banner, you know what's coming.'

'So why does my word matter?' she replied, trying to worm her way out of having to speak. 'There are hundreds of Wraith Company who were there.'

Al-Hasim, who had remained quiet during their walk to the assembly, said, 'But we're outsiders; it always strengthens a cause when non-Ranen agree . . . unless you're Ro, of course . . . then they tend to ignore you.'

'Not this Ro,' said Stone Dog. 'Her brother wants to ally with the Free Companies. That gives her word some weight.'

Brother Lanry held up his hand, politely asking to interrupt. 'Er, my Lord Bromvy is a good ally to have, young Micah. The lord of Canarn is a nobleman of redoubtable spirit and great honour.'

'I'm sure,' responded Micah with a curl of amusement to his lip. He turned to Bronwyn and Hasim. 'We need to go in . . . if Brother Lanry is quite finished.' He looked questioningly at the Brown cleric.

'Oh, yes, quite finished,' said Lanry. 'Do lead on, young Micah.'

The sarcastic young Ranen was unsure how to react to the cleric. He had spoken to Bronwyn of his reluctance entirely to trust a man of the One God. No matter how often she had told him that Lanry would never harm a soul, Stone Dog was still wary around him.

She knew that Micah had been chosen as the unofficial liaison with Bronwyn and Hasim, and that the other members of Wraith Company were more reluctant to associate with them now that they were in South Warden. The easternmost city of the Freelands had never been under the rule of Ro and had been built long after the occupation. It was a place where the Ranen could be Ranen, where Rowanoco held sway, and Tor Funweir was a world away.

Micah led the way as they walked beyond the inner palisade and approached the assembly. It looked even larger close up, and Bronwyn felt humble in the presence of Rowanoco's Stone. The building was five or six storeys high, with stone galleries rising from a central floor and a large open space in the middle. The seating looked as if it could accommodate several hundred men, though it was currently only half full.

The Ranen that sat in front of them were all silent as Micah led them inside, a low whistle of wind being the only sound as Bronwyn became the first Ro noble to enter the assembly since it had been built a hundred years before. She recognized faces, but many more were unknown and intimidating as she stepped on to Rowanoco's Stone. Captain Horrock Green Blade sat in the middle, his piercing blue eyes regarding her with friendly reassurance. Next to him was Haffen Red Face, Horrock's axe-master and close friend. The warrior of Ro Hail was a boisterous man who had stuck up for Bronwyn on a number of occasions when members of Scarlet Company had questioned her presence in South Warden.

The most intimidating presence in the assembly was Captain Johan Long Shadow, a Ranen with huge shoulders and a tattooed head. The faded, dark blue designs displayed across his scalp were of broken swords and axes, which gave the man an edge of intensity and made Bronwyn decidedly uncomfortable. The captain of Scarlet Company was well into his fifties, but still a respected and astute leader, a man whose word was generally law in South Warden. He sat, on a raised stone chair, facing the assembled men of Ranen and had half the auditorium to himself.

'This assembly welcomes Lady Bronwyn of Canarn,' announced Johan's axe-master, a short and stout man called Mathias Flame Tooth.

A rumble of disapproval flowed through the auditorium and Bronwyn felt exposed for a moment, until Mathias banged the haft of his axe on the stone floor and brought her back to reality.

'Hello,' she said, as demurely as she could. The echo in the assembly turned the word into more of a statement than she had intended.

'You're not supposed to speak yet,' whispered Stone Dog out of the corner of his mouth.

Bronwyn smiled awkwardly and almost said sorry, before Al-Hasim gently grabbed her arm and led her across to the lowest level of seating.

There were a hundred pairs of eyes regarding the lady of Canarn. She observed, rather absently, that very few Ranen men were clean-shaven and that there was a definite smell of sweat in the building.

'Sit there and keep your mouth shut, sweetness,' murmured Al-Hasim, with a cheeky grin. 'Remember, they all have axes.'

Bronwyn glanced around the room and saw that every man held his hand-axe in his fist, as a salute to the newcomers. The only Ranen in South Warden permitted two axes was Johan, and the captain of Scarlet Company let both his weapons remain on the stone floor in front of his chair.

When they were seated, Mathias struck the floor a second time and spoke in a deep, clear voice. 'Never before has a noble of Ro entered this place. I would remind all of the assembled lords that she is here as a guest of Horrock Green Blade and she will be respected as such.'

A few men whispered contrary words to each other and it was evident that Horrock had had to spend many hours arguing before Bronwyn was allowed entrance. She also noted that the captain of Wraith Company no longer had his axe, having already cast it to settle the matter of her attendance.

'My Lord Long Shadow,' continued Mathias, 'we will hear your words.'

Johan did not stand from his seat and did not require any theatrics to be heard. He casually rested a leg across an arm of his stone chair. 'Horrock tells us that the Ro have invaded the Grass Sea,' he said in a throaty rumble. 'An army of Red knights, and the king himself.' A few men growled at this, and Bronwyn sensed great anger among the men of Ranen. 'They have taken Ro Hail and could be here within the month,' Johan continued. 'You all know this . . . and as people of Rowanoco, we cannot let Tiris do whatever he pleases in our land.' Again, the words were spoken with no real volume and Johan Long Shadow revealed himself to be a surprisingly taciturn man. 'Horrock, your turn,' he said dismissively, as if the formality required was a chore.

Mathias Flame Tooth struck the floor again. 'Captain Horrock Green Blade will speak.'

The captain of Wraith Company stood from his seat halfway up the stone auditorium. 'King Tiris has five thousand knights and bound men, minus what we managed to kill in Ro Hail, and we have not the strength to withstand them here.' A slow rumble of disagreement rose from the men of South Warden. Horrock looked down at the stone in front of him, all too aware that he didn't have an axe to cast if things became unpleasant, but he continued anyway. 'Scarlet Company has five thousand fighting men. More if you muster all the clans of the Moon Wood. But that is not enough.' A louder rumble of disagreement arose as men began to bang their axes on the stone in front of them, seeking permission to speak. A few spoke of the Fjorlanders and the age-old presumption that the northern realms of Ranen would save them.

Haffen Red Face, Horrock's axe-master, looked livid with rage as his friend's words were interrupted and he, too, struck stone with his axe. 'Let him speak. The dragon fleet is lost and the high thain dead.'

Mathias Flame Tooth chuckled, letting his substantial stomach wobble as he retorted. 'That's for me to say, Haffen. South Warden has but one axe-master, and he knows his job.' Flame Tooth glanced over his shoulder at Johan, who nodded. The axe-master of South Warden then said, 'Horrock, continue, if you would.'

Bronwyn knew the captain of Wraith Company fairly well. She had seen him fight William of Verellian, she had seen him battle scores of Red knights, and she had seen him inspire his men while standing bloodied and panting on the battlements of Ro Hail. But faced with the Ranen assembly, the tired old axe-man appeared humble and cautious.

'We are not their match for equipment or skill,' he said. 'They have engines of war that could batter half your city to the ground before you got the chance to fight.' More contrary voices arose, louder and more aggressive this time, as several other men stood to shout insults at Horrock, belittling him and claiming that South Warden was a match for any foe, even without the help of Fjorlan. The captain's piercing blue eyes shot around the room and a curl to his lip showed that he was growing angrier. Haffen looked ready to hurl his axe as the assembly was split down the middle, half agreeing with Horrock and half stubbornly refusing to accept that South Warden could not defend itself alone.

'Silence,' roared Mathias Flame Tooth. The axe-master struck the floor twice with the haft of his axe and waited until the assembled Ranen had grown quiet. 'We have heard this before and a man has already died in disagreement. We will hear from the Lady Bronwyn, who has no axe and cannot be killed.'

Bronwyn glanced around the hall and saw the same sets of eyes, but now their blood was up. She looked at Horrock. He smiled weakly and nodded his head at her, with a slight shrug of his shoulders. To the other side, Captain Johan Long Shadow, who had been silent while Horrock spoke, was sitting more upright now and appeared to take an interest as the lady of Canarn stood from her stone seat.

'Greetings, gentlemen,' she said quietly, instantly thinking that was a stupid thing to have said. 'I speak for Canarn and for my brother, Lord Bromvy.' The Ranen were silent, regarding Bronwyn as if she were a curiosity. 'I have seen what Captain Horrock has seen and I agree with his words.'

Instantly the atmosphere changed and she was subjected to a dozen shouted insults about her gender and her race, and how little they cared for her words. Micah Stone Dog and Al-Hasim both stood and glared angrily at those that had insulted her. Stone Dog drew his locaber axe, roaring, 'You're big men when a woman tells you the truth. Come outside and I'll show you how to listen.'

With a deafening strike of his axe, Mathias silenced the assembly. The only sound that remained was a barely audible chuckle from Johan Long Shadow. He had clearly found Stone Dog's challenge amusing and, once Mathias had restored order, he stood from his chair for the first time. He looked larger when standing and his shoulders flexed as he knelt down and picked up one of his throwing-axes from Rowanoco's Stone.

'No man here can cast an axe against the lady,' he said quietly in his deep, throaty voice. 'And another word about her honour or her right to be here and I'll let the little man of Wraith cut a few of you up.' He nodded at Stone Dog in appreciation of his defence of Bronwyn. Micah and Al-Hasim quickly resumed their seats. The auditorium was now the quietest it had been since Bronwyn arrived. She saw the assembled Ranen slowly shrink away from Johan, until only the captain and the lady of Canarn were still standing.

'That's better,' said Johan with another chuckle, this time directed at Mathias, who evidently shared some private joke with his captain. Then he resumed his seat, keeping hold of his axe. 'We can chant oaths at each other or we can deal with the Ro,' he stated. 'It's really that simple.'

The assembly was deathly silent now as everyone present listened to the captain of Scarlet Company. It seemed that no one dared question his words. Bronwyn witnessed a level of respect for Johan that he must have earned over many years of keeping South Warden safe.

'Whether we can match them or not is irrelevant,' he continued. 'I personally think that, in a fair fight, we'd at least bloody their arrogant noses.' A slight ripple of laughter came from certain quarters of the room. 'But the bastards don't fight fair . . . we know this. I would personally like to get Greywood Company down here to show the king that he's not in Ro Tiris any more. If Algenon Teardrop is dead, we have to accept that help won't be coming from Fjorlan.'

Half the room agreed with the sentiment, while the other half stubbornly refused to admit that the men of Scarlet were not enough.

'May I speak?' asked Bronwyn in as loud a voice as she could muster.

Mathias Flame Tooth smiled at her. 'Technically, he's out of order for interrupting you, my lady,' the corpulent axe-master said, nodding at Johan. 'But this lot wouldn't shut up, so things have deviated from protocol.'

Johan smiled knowingly at Bronwyn and resumed his seat, showing a deference that elicited another ripple of disapproval from the assembled men. Horrock and Haffen remained standing and kept their eyes focused on any man who questioned Bronwyn.

She moved away from her seat and came to a halt in front of the assembly, isolated on Rowanoco's Stone. 'My lords, there is much you don't know,' she said simply. 'I admire your confidence and I wish that it were well placed. The king can call for reinforcements from a dozen barracks and a hundred duchies. Loyal nobles and knights of Tor Funweir will flock to his banner, and they will not care about your confidence, or your people, or your way of life.' Her words were now loud enough to echo around the building and to carry over the grumbled complaints of the Ranen. 'You have allies, my friends, and you would be foolish not to call upon them. It's not too late.'

Before anyone could insult her, Mathias Flame Tooth struck the floor heavily with his axe. 'Silence, brothers. Let her continue,' he bellowed.

Bronwyn breathed in deeply several times and composed herself. 'My brother can lend aid, as can Dominic Black Claw and Greywood Company, but time is running out. Your peace terms will be ignored and William of Verellian will likely be killed before your words are even delivered to the king.'

No one shouted at her now, whether for fear of Mathias or because, finally, they were listening. For a moment, she gained confidence to continue. 'This is not a time for stubborn honour or flowery words and oaths of battle. This is a time to defend your land from an aggressor who would see you all as slaves.' The final word was deliberately chosen for its age-old connotation. The idea of a Ranen man being anyone's slave was abhorrent to Rowanoco and his children, and Bronwyn knew the word would not be ignored.

She held her breath and waited for the reaction. When none came, she continued, speaking now to a silent room. 'We have a month. Even if we send for aid now, we will still need to hold South Warden against the king until reinforcements arrive. Much work needs to be done and we cannot afford to be at each other's throats.'

The assembled Ranen began to turn away from Bronwyn and to

look at each other with questioning glances. Horrock and Haffen stood defiantly, lending their silent support to the noblewoman's words. Mathias let the assembly mutter for a moment before calling for silence with a strike of his axe.

Johan stood again. 'I will gladly cast my axe in support of this motion.' He let his grey eyes play over the faces before him. 'The question is whether any of you will cast yours against it.'

Mathias struck the floor again. 'A declaration has been made. Will any man speak against it with axe or words?'

Many of the loudest naysayers hesitated while the assembly looked to them to dictate the tone of further deliberations. If they were to object, Johan would cast his axe, forcing an opponent to cast one in return. The question posed by the captain of Scarlet Company was a fair one. Who was prepared to cast an axe against Long Shadow?

'Time is of the essence, gentlemen,' said Bronwyn without thinking, causing Flame Tooth to direct a chiding glance at her.

'I would speak,' shouted a voice from the left of the auditorium.

Bronwyn looked up and saw a wiry Ranen with blonde hair and cunning eyes. He had not been involved in the previous insults and shouting. Several of her allies, who clearly knew him, exchanged confused glances.

'The assembly will hear the words of Dragneel Dark Crest, axe-master of Brytag's Roost,' announced Mathias.

Bronwyn had not heard of him, but she knew Brytag's Roost to be an ancient and mystical site for the faithful of Rowanoco. The highest peak was supposedly where the Ice Giant's raven perched, watching over the Freelands, and every priest of the Order of the Hammer was expected to climb the mountain at least once during his teenage years.

The World Raven was also the patron god of house Canarn, and Bronwyn had grown up hearing stories of Brytag's love of luck and wisdom. Whether Brytag was actually a god or just an old totem of some kind, she didn't know, but Bromvy had always believed he was literally Rowanoco's pet raven.

'I have never spoken before the assembly,' said Dragneel in a strikingly deep voice. 'I have never felt the need.' He stood up and revealed that he had only one leg. 'But I have seen a third option.'

A curious rumbling flowed through the auditorium and a few men seated near the front jeered at the man, making fun of his being an axe-master of a mountain range rather than a town. However, the one-legged man did not appear angry or insulted, and merely waved his hand to indicate that he wanted silence.

'I can be insulting as well, but I prefer not to be,' said Dragneel. 'I will continue to talk and hope that those with intelligence as well as axes will hear me.' It came across as a subtly barbed insult and several men shut up instantly. 'You talk of staying and fighting. With or without the other Free Companies, I propose retreat.' The words were spoken simply and most of the Ranen did not instantly grasp what he had proposed.

'The raven has no place here,' screamed a man at the front, holding his axe threateningly. 'This is Rowanoco's Stone, not a perch for your bird.'

The man of Brytag's Roost did not react to the insult. He merely sat down and scanned the room with narrow eyes. 'You'll forgive me sitting,' he said. 'My left leg hasn't grown back yet and my right doesn't like having to do all the work.'

A few more jeers and Mathias Flame Tooth struck the stone floor. 'Dragneel, your comments have been noted, but surrendering South Warden is not an option,' said the fat axe-master.

'If Brytag's word is not welcome here, I'll be sure to light a candle for you all when I return to my mountain,' Dragneel replied with a wry smile. 'But stubbornness will get you so far and then it will get you killed . . . remember that.'

* * *

The Ranen had laughed off the counsel of the axe-master of Brytag's Roost, but several hours later it was still playing on Bronwyn's mind. She was not a coward; nor was she indifferent to the indignation of the citizens of South Warden, but something about the way Dragneel had spoken had made her think that he knew something he wasn't prepared to say in front of the assembly.

She waited until the midday sun had begun to disappear and Long Shadow had started ordering his company to prepare the city's defences. Once the men of Scarlet were busy making sure that South Warden's many gates and palisades were reinforced, Bronwyn sneaked away from Lanry and Al-Hasim and found her way back to the Ranen assembly. She was fairly sure that Micah Stone Dog was following her, but the young man of Wraith had not tried to stop her, so she let him creep along behind.

She had been told that Dragneel had a habit of sitting by a small bust of Brytag the World Raven that lay beyond the central fortifications. Most Ranen cities had one, but Rowanoco's raven was only ever of secondary importance to the faithful of the Ice Giant. She could well believe that the axe-master from Brytag's Roost was used to being derided, but his demeanour in the assembly showed that he had intelligence as well as honour.

'Took you long enough,' said Dragneel, as Bronwyn turned a corner and saw the one-legged man lying on his back on the windswept grass.

'You were expecting me?' she asked, making sure to keep her tone formal and commanding.

'I was expecting someone . . . it makes sense that it's you.' The man of Brytag's Roost was smiling and Bronwyn was struck with his youthful appearance. He wore no beard and his blonde hair was braided in a topknot that fell halfway down his back. The hand-axes that adorned his piecemeal leather armour were too small to be used in melee combat and she guessed that Dragneel preferred fighting at a distance. That was probably another reason that he was teased by the axe-men of Ranen.

'You made a certain degree of sense in the assembly,' she said, 'and sense seems to be in short supply around here.'

'They're all going to die,' replied the man of Brytag, letting his smile become a frown and picking absently at the grass. 'But I'm not sure about you . . . the signs aren't clear.'

She sniggered at the axe-master's words. She was not naive and found the prophetic nature of what she was hearing a little trite. 'I'm sure you have access to all sorts of profound omens, Master Dragneel,' she said with a patronizing smile.

'Omens?' was the confused response from the axe-master. 'I'm not a wise woman. I'm using something else; it's called logic.'

Bronwyn was startled by this reply and found herself having to adjust her thinking. She was not used to men using reason to decide things, especially not the passionate and impulsive Ranen.

'You've not met a follower of Brytag before, have you?' he asked with a childlike smile.

'No, I don't believe I have, but I am from Ro Canarn,' replied the confused noblewoman. 'I know of the World Raven.'

Dragneel screwed up his face. 'You don't really . . . but you think you do, so I'll give you the benefit of the doubt.'

She was not used to being spoken to in this manner, and spluttered as she tried to respond. The axe-master grinned and patted the grass next to him.

'Have a seat, my lady. We'll be going on a little journey together soon, so we should probably get to know each other.'

Hesitantly, she lowered herself to the grass of South Warden and regarded Dragneel with suspicious eyes. 'And where will we be going?' she asked.

'The Moon Wood. It will be a long and painful journey.' He grinned. 'Should be fun, yes?'

'And this journey is to be undertaken . . . why?' she asked, hoping to exert at least a modicum of authority over the strange man from Brytag's Roost.

'Perhaps you should ask your friend with the big axe to come and join us, rather than hiding behind that tree.' Dragneel smiled and motioned to where Micah Stone Dog was skulking in a half-hearted attempt to remain out of sight. His curved locaber axe was poking out rather comically from his place of concealment.

'Micah,' said Bronwyn with a wave of her hand, 'we both know you're there. Please come out.'

The young man of Wraith poked his head out from behind the tree and regarded the axe-master with narrow-eyed suspicion. He sauntered over to where they sat.

'Just so you know, axe-master,' said Stone Dog, 'I'm not leaving this woman's side. Horrock asked me to watch out for her and that's what I'm doing.'

'Then you'll be coming with us,' responded Dragneel, with another boyish grin.

'No,' replied Micah with his customary straight face. 'You'll be coming with us.'

Dragneel absently tapped at his wooden crutch and looked the young warrior up and down. 'Do you know how to use that axe, lad?'

Stone Dog didn't show even the slightest expression as he plonked himself down on the grass. 'I chopped down a tree once . . . that good enough?'

'Was it an aggressive tree?' Dragneel didn't move his eyes from Micah. It seemed to Bronwyn that there was no love lost between the two men.

'No,' said Stone Dog, with a shake of his head, 'it was just a tree. Now stop asking stupid questions and answer a few.' He unslung his axe and rested it across his lap. 'Is it true that you're Dominic Black Claw's cousin?'

Bronwyn had heard of Black Claw. He was the captain of Greywood Company and master of Ranen Gar, the great strong-hold of the Free Companies. He was the closest thing the south men of Ranen had to a king and was second only to the high thain of Fjorlan in the respect he commanded.

'No, it's not true,' answered Dragneel. 'I was adopted into his family when I was very young. I'm his brother, sort of, though I haven't seen him since I heard the voice of Brytag.'

Micah turned to Bronwyn. 'Horrock needs us to go north. He can't spare any axe-men to make a decent-sized force, so it's just you, me and this idiot.'

'What about Hasim?' asked the lady of Canarn, suddenly uncomfortable at the prospect of being parted from the roguish Karesian.

'They need him here. He's a tough bastard and tough bastards will be needed when the knights arrive.' Micah was obviously annoyed that he would not be joining the defenders of South Warden, but he was nothing if not dutiful and his loyalty and commitment to his captain were without question.

'The clans of the Moon Wood are our first port of call. The men and women of the crescent are fearsome when angered and we'll need them to hold the knights,' said Dragneel, with a theatrical flourish of his arms.

'I don't like you,' responded Micah with a straight face. 'You're irritating.'

The axe-master of Brytag's Roost pouted, adopting a hurt expression, though Bronwyn couldn't be sure whether it was genuine or not.

'That's why we need you along, young Stone Dog,' said Dragneel with an ever so slightly smug grin. 'I can't irritate our enemies to death.'

'Have you tried?' was the dry response from Micah. 'I think you'd be surprised at just how irritating you are.'

'Please, gentlemen,' interjected Bronwyn. 'This is not a helpful way to begin.' She puffed out her cheeks and addressed Micah. 'So I won't be going back to Canarn any time soon?'

He shook his head. 'No, I'm afraid not. You're a noble, remember. Your word carries weight, and your brother is supposedly our friend.'

Dragneel clapped his hands together excitedly. 'I'm really looking forward to this. It's like a grand adventure into the wilds of Ranen.'

'If you don't shut up, you won't make it out of South Warden,' said Micah stoically. 'This eccentric follower of Brytag act is making me weary.'

'You'd do well to treat the World Raven with more respect, young man,' replied the axe-master. 'He can take away just as easily as he can give.'

Bronwyn frowned in confusion. 'And what does Brytag give, Master Dragneel?'

'Luck, my dear lady. He gives luck,' was the cheeky response.

'A man makes his own luck,' interjected Micah, 'and I don't need a bird to direct my axe.'

'But you need the Moon Clans and Greywood Company to ride south, yes?' The reply from the one-legged man was delivered sharply and Bronwyn detected a serious note in his voice, as if he was trying to exert some kind of authority over Stone Dog.

'Is your bird going to fly us north?' replied Micah. 'If not, shut up.'

Dragneel smiled, recovering his light-hearted demeanour, and turned back to Bronwyn. 'Am I supposed to weather insults all the way to Ranen Gar?'

'Don't get the impression he'll do what I say. He's a man of Wraith. In my experience, they tend to be quite obstinate.' She smiled at Stone Dog, finding herself siding with the young axe-man.

'Very well, as long as I know where I stand,' was the jovial retort from the man of Brytag's Roost.

'So, two horses and a wheelbarrow?' asked Micah with a completely straight face.

CHAPTER TWO

HALLA SUMMER WOLF
IN THE REALM OF URSA

THE AXE-MAIDEN OF Tiergarten was in fair spirits as they trudged past the last inlet of Hammerfall and entered the long, rocky gully that led to the Bear's Mouth. The terrain had become more rugged and uneven over the last week and Falling Cloud had begun to provide a more accurate direction of travel towards Jarvik. They would sight the river fork that marked the southern border of the city within a few days, and all of Halla's company were beginning to prepare themselves for a fight.

The Bear's Mouth was held by Grammah Black Eyes, and he would have a massive advantage over any force attempting to assault it. The mouth was the narrowest point of the gully, with natural shelves snaking their way up the icy walls from the frozen river to the barren plateaus above. There was no reliable way round and Grammah would need only a fraction of a company to hold the gully, where he would be able to hurl axes and roll boulders from positions of cover on to any attackers.

Her company had grown in the last few weeks as more and more common folk of Hammerfall had joined her banner, and a few scattered parties of battle-brothers from the dragon fleet had also found their way inland. Rexel and Oleff had become even more valuable to her as men and women, many of whose homes and villages had been burned, asked what they were going to do and what hope they had left. It was a question she preferred not to answer as they marched slowly but inevitably towards a battle that would see many of them dead.

The force now numbered close to five hundred, though many were too old, too young, or too inexperienced to make useful battle-brothers. The few women were mostly commoners, as confused at the sight of an axe-maiden as were their men folk. She remained the only woman with an axe and she tried to leave her captains to deal with anyone who questioned her leadership.

'Halla,' shouted Oleff from the front of their moving column, 'you need to come and see this.'

'What's the hold-up?' she shouted as Oleff came into view along the narrow pass.

'There's . . . an obstacle in the way,' he said, with a strange uncertainty in his voice.

Wulfrick appeared over Halla's shoulder. 'Well, move it out of the way . . . it's getting cold and we can't camp in this gully.'

Halla had sent Falling Cloud and a few other men ahead to find an area of flat ground, away from the wind, on which to make camp for the night. They were currently spread out in a long line, hugging the icy walls of the gully and doing their best to stay away from the sheer drop to the frozen river below.

'I've tried to get it to move,' replied Oleff, his tone still strange, 'but it doesn't want to.'

Halla shook her head and began to move quickly along the line of men and women towards the front. Every third set of eyes belonged to one of her original company and she received boisterous salutes from many of them. The newcomers had begun to realize that, whatever problem they might have with a woman in command, the more seasoned battle-brothers accepted her word without question.

Wulfrick followed her, adding significantly to Halla's presence as they strode past the company to where Oleff stood. The chain-master stood with several other men, looking towards a·turn in the gully. The column had stopped moving and, as far as Halla could see, the obstacle they were looking at was a person, sitting cross-legged and hunched in the middle of the trail.

'What's going on?' she asked.

Oleff had narrow eyes and his face was screwed up in an expression of confusion and annoyance. 'She was just sitting in the middle of the trail,' he said, 'and she won't move.'

'She?' queried Wulfrick, moving forward to look at the seated figure, whose back was facing them.

Halla joined him and they edged round until they could see an old woman huddled in the snow. She was not in any distress and she wore several layers of thick furs and heavy leather boots. Her hands were clenched tightly shut and appeared to be clutching something. As Halla craned forward to see her better, the woman lifted her head up rapidly and directed her strangely penetrating dark eyes at the axe-maiden.

'They always say the same,' muttered the old woman, in a raspy voice.

Oleff grunted. 'That's all she's said. Woman's lost her mind to be just sitting in the snow like that.'

The old woman unclenched her fist and revealed a palm full of small bones. They were dusty brown and had small stones tied to them, making a dull rattling sound as she shook her palm from side to side. Halla had met wise women who claimed to be able to see the will of Rowanoco in the bones.

'Woman, listen to me,' demanded Halla, kneeling down in front of her. 'If you have wisdom, we would hear you . . . if not, please get out of our road.'

The woman shook the bones and threw them into the snow. She looked at them. 'They always say the same,' she repeated.

Oleff snorted with amusement. 'I've never seen the Order of the Hammer use bones to tell the future. She's mad, kick her out of the way.'

The axe-maiden waved him away and turned back to the old woman. 'What do they say?' she asked.

The response was mumbled. Wulfrick, Oleff and Halla had

to lean in to hear her. 'The Ice Giant can't talk to us any more . . . the blood is almost spent . . . the blood is almost spent . . . but the shades come.'

She babbled the same few sentences over and over until Halla stood up and faced Wulfrick. 'What's she talking about?'

The axe-master shook his head. 'No idea. It sounds doom-laden, though.'

'Hey, woman . . .' snapped Oleff, 'get out of the road.'

'Enough!' said Halla. 'It's as much her road as ours.' She knelt back down in front of the old woman. 'Throw them again,' she said.

The woman gave her another strangely intense stare and nodded. She picked up the ceremonial bones, shook them, and threw them to the ground again. 'They always say the same,' she repeated in a shrill voice.

Halla raised her eyebrows at the bones. They had indeed fallen in precisely the same position as before.

'Now, that's a little eerie,' said Wulfrick to Oleff. 'Algenon used to say that some women could read the future in fish entrails or the pattern of a bird's flight . . . I don't think he ever put much faith in bones, though.'

'Depends who's reading them,' said a loud voice from above.

Halla and her two captains looked up and saw the distinctive features of Rexel Falling Cloud. The axe-master of Hammerfall was standing on the plateau, ten feet above the narrow, icy trail.

'Shouldn't sneak up on a man,' said Oleff. 'Wulfrick could have shit himself.'

'Don't make me push you into the river, piss-stain,' replied Wulfrick, with a boisterous laugh.

Halla shielded her eyes from the glare of the snow. 'What does the ground look like up there?'

Falling Cloud scanned around from his elevated position and puffed out his cheeks. 'Well, there's enough cover up here, but it'll be cramped for five hundred. We'd better start moving everyone up out of the gully.'

'Right,' agreed the axe-maiden. 'And, Rexel . . .'

'My lady?' he responded.

'Do you know this woman?'

He nodded. 'Her name's Anya Coldbane. We used to call her Lullaby . . . something to do with a brew she used to make that sent you to sleep.' He paused and smiled down at the woman. Hearing her name, she looked up and squinted into the light to see who had spoken. 'She was old when my father was a boy,' said Rexel. 'I wouldn't offer any guarantees about her sanity, though.'

Anya frowned and made a series of crotchety, mumbled sounds. 'That's enough cheek from you, Mr Falling Cloud.'

It was the first sign that the woman was even vaguely aware of herself and her surroundings. She retrieved the bones and stood up. Her back made a creaking sound, and at her full height she barely reached Halla's shoulders.

'You know Rexel?'

'Of course,' she barked. 'Silly girl.'

Oleff and Wulfrick stifled a laugh.

Halla crossed her arms. 'What brings you out here . . . old woman?' she asked, angry at being called a girl, silly or otherwise.

Anya stared at her, apparently oblivious to the five hundred Fjorlanders waiting impatiently behind her. 'Where's your father, young lady? I'd like a serious word with him about how you were raised.'

Wulfrick and Oleff stopped laughing. For a moment they looked worried that Halla would take offence at the reference to Aleph Summer Wolf.

'My father is dead . . . as is my mother,' replied Halla. 'If you wish to chide someone, chide me.'

'I knew young Falling Cloud when he was a crying, pink bundle in his mother's arms,' Anya snapped, peering at Halla through beady eyes.

All three looked up at Rexel, who was tapping his feet in embarrassment. 'She was an adviser to Oreck Silver Tongue, back in the days when Ragnar Teardrop was high thain,' said Falling Cloud.

'Well, she's coming with us,' said Halla in resignation. 'We can't leave her sitting in the snow this close to the Bear's Mouth.'

Anya Lullaby scowled at the warriors standing round her. Wulfrick and Oleff towered over the shrivelled old woman, but she didn't seem to care, looking at both the men as if they were naughty children.

'Where are we, young men?' she asked.

They exchanged glances, and Oleff, slightly the older of the two, said to Wulfrick, 'I think she's talking to you.'

'This is the Bear's Mouth, mother,' said the axe-master of Fredericksand. 'The plateaus of Ursa.'

Anya screwed up her face and looked skywards. 'Hmm, I seem to have wandered further than I intended.'

The day was wearing on and Halla knew that the temperature would begin to drop even further within the next few hours. She looked up at Rexel and couldn't immediately see an easy path up to where he stood. 'We can discuss it later, Mistress Lullaby,' she said. 'We need to move everyone up out of the gully and get some fires built.'

With surprising speed, Anya slapped Halla hard in the face. 'You will not address me by that name . . . my tea is very nutritious and good for you.'

Everyone froze. Halla stood, stunned and with the taste of blood on her bottom lip.

'Oh, yeah, she's also a moody old bitch,' said Rexel with a laugh. 'Don't take it personally, Halla.'

'Don't think I won't hit you, Mr Falling Cloud,' snapped Anya, shaking her fist at the axe-master of Hammerfall. 'I'll knock some respect into all of you youngsters.'

'I'm approaching fifty years, you miserable old sow,' growled Oleff. 'Don't think I won't give you a smack either, woman.' The chain-master snorted with annoyance and marched off, back towards the column. 'I'll start to get everyone moving.'

Rexel nodded. 'And I'll organize getting fires built.' He disappeared out of view and on to the plateaus of Ursa above.

Wulfrick remained with Halla and Anya. The huge man of Fredericksand had been more amused than Oleff, and he put a kindly arm round the old woman's shoulders. 'Don't worry, mother, we'll teach them some respect. Now, let's get you out of this weather and in front of a nice warm fire.'

'Yes, thank you, young man,' replied Anya, nuzzling into the embrace of the axe-master.

They made a comical pair as Wulfrick walked her away. Halla touched a spot of blood from her lip. 'Well, at least she didn't call me *one-eye*.'

* * *

The wise women of Fjorlan were an oddity among oddities. Old Father Crowe used to claim that, due to the sheer number of them, they had only a tenuous connection to the Ice Giant and received the will of Rowanoco in portents and vague omens. They stood in sharp contrast to the priests of the Order of the Hammer, who were few in number and powerful in consequence. The old man of Tiergarten thought that when the Ice Giant spread out his power it became less concentrated.

Halla had met a few wise women in her time and had found them to be useful and annoying in equal measure. Whatever else they might be, they were skilled herbalists and were often to be found ministering to the sick and using their concoctions to aid in birth and death. Their obsession with fish entrails and reading the bones was harder to respect. As Wulfrick had said, the old pagan superstitions of Ranen, their earliest beliefs from before the Order of the Hammer, were generally viewed with condescension.

Anya did not seem to care, or even to notice, that most of the Fjorlanders considered her a mad old woman. She stayed close to Wulfrick. She had bonded with him quickly and nestled into his huge presence next to the fire. The rest of Halla's company were seated round campfires, spread out along a low plain. They were a short distance from the gully, with their backs to a small, rugged line of rocks. The accommodation was cramped, but provided adequate cover for all five hundred of them. They were situated well above the frozen river that ran along the bottom of the gully. The plateaus of Ursa were one of the higher points of Fjorlan. Only the mountains of Trollheim and a few peaks of the Deep Cross stood taller. Falling Cloud was a good man to have around in such terrain, because his upbringing, travelling the wilds of Hammerfall and the Wolf Wood, had gained him a mastery of outdoor survival, which had become a lost art among the city- and town-dwelling Fjorlanders.

'How many, do you think?' Wulfrick asked, pulling Halla back to the present.

'What?' she retorted, wrapping her thick cloak around her shoulders and rubbing her hands together next to the fire.

'How many of our new followers will fight?' he asked. 'A few carry axes, but I don't fancy their chances at the Bear's Mouth. We've got the original two hundred, and maybe a hundred more from the estuaries, but what are we going to do with the women and children?'

They had tried not to think too much about the common people who had joined the company. They had been rescued from burning villages or had latched on to the column as it passed their dead livestock and burned crops. Their chances of survival if they stayed in Hammerfall were negligible, but their path through the Bear's Mouth was almost as dangerous.

'If we take the three hundred warriors and clear Grammah Black Eyes and his men, they can follow when it's safe,' she said.

Wulfrick raised an eyebrow and handed her a wooden bowl of steaming stew. Falling Cloud had rustled up something from dried vegetables and Gorlan legs. It tasted horrible, but it was hot and vaguely nutritious.

'I appreciate that we've been driven by passion and the desire for vengeance, but those things won't help when Black Eyes is throwing rocks at us.' Wulfrick was wiser than he often appeared, and Halla occasionally had to remind herself that the axe-master of Fredericksand was no frenzied berserker. 'The Bear's Mouth is like a fortress and we don't have enough men to storm it . . . passion or no passion,' continued Wulfrick, slurping stew from his own bowl.

Halla was thinking. She had not had leisure to formulate a plan, and never having seen the Bear's Mouth, she felt out of her depth. Still, Wulfrick and her captains looked to her with trust and loyalty, and she didn't want to admit that she was at a loss for a strategy. She was also a little afraid. She had become the leader of a mixed company of battle-brothers, women, children and the elderly. She had never expected this when she washed ashore after her encounter with the Krakens of the Fjorlan Sea.

'How many men will Grammah have, do you think?' she asked Wulfrick, stirring her stew with a wooden spoon and trying to identify the roots and vegetables that floated to the top. 'Rulag wouldn't know we survived, so he might not have stationed many men there.' It was a forlorn hope.

Wulfrick spat out a chunk of something that resembled a Gorlan leg bone. 'It's the southern border of Jarvik . . . where else would he put his men?'

'We'll be there in a few days, so I suppose we'll see,' she said. 'Maybe Rexel can get close enough to scout out their numbers.'

Wulfrick raised an eyebrow and nodded, though there was a note of sarcasm in his manner. 'And maybe we won't get killed,' he replied, glancing across the plain to where Rexel sat with Oleff and Heinrich Blood, the novice of the Order of the Hammer.

'Pessimism – that's helpful,' she said with a smile.

'You're a silly little girl,' said Anya through a throaty chuckle. The wise woman had been silent up to this point and appeared to be enjoying Rexel's stew.

Halla did not feel offended this time. Instead, she barely stifled a laugh. She was indeed being a *silly little girl* and she couldn't disagree with the wise woman.

'You've found your sense of humour, my Lady Summer Wolf,' said Wulfrick, genuinely surprised at her reaction.

'Maybe she's right,' Halla responded with a broad grin. 'I have no idea what we should do, where we should go, who we should be looking for . . . none of it. I just know how to swing an axe.'

Wulfrick smiled back and for a moment the atmosphere was as relaxed as it had ever been since the dragon fleet launched from Fredericksand. Time had meant little and Halla was unsure how long they had been moving northwards or how long it was since they had released the king. That realization amused her all the more, and they shared a gallows humour round the campfire as it dawned on Halla that she was really not cut out to be a leader.

'You're better than you think,' said Anya without turning from the fire. 'These men are true to you.' She looked up at Halla with her strangely intense stare. 'Have faith in the Ice Father, young lady.'

The axe-maiden turned slowly to look at the wise woman. Wulfrick was hulking over her, providing cover against the cold wind, and she looked tiny in comparison.

'You know things, Lullaby,' said Halla suspiciously, 'things you shouldn't know.'

Anya moved her hand quickly to slap Halla, but the axe-maiden grabbed her wrist and held the old woman securely.

'Easy,' said Wulfrick protectively. 'She's just a bit prickly, no need to hurt her.'

'She knew what I was thinking,' Halla replied, not looking away from Anya.

The wise woman smiled, an unpleasant sneer that made her wrinkled face crease up even more. 'I did . . . and I do . . . if you want to know how . . . or why,' she said mysteriously. Her eyes narrowed into a mischievous expression. 'You'll take my advice, won't you, Halla Summer Wolf?'

Wulfrick looked at the axe-maiden and his eyes showed that he had become suddenly wary. He backed away from the wise woman. 'Explain yourself, mother.'

'Fear not, axe-master.' Anya seemed dangerously aware all of a sudden. 'I speak only what appears in my head, only what the Ice Father says to me.' She flicked her eyes between Halla and Wulfrick. 'He cannot talk to us any more, so he throws his thoughts out to reach a man, or a woman, of Ranen.' Her face softened now. It took on a warm expression that caused Wulfrick and Halla to relax. 'I hear a little, and you youngsters should listen. I know the way.'

The snow no longer made Halla shiver. She frowned and involuntarily her mind relaxed. The old woman's words had changed from obscure ranting to wise reflection. Suddenly, she was someone to listen to. Across the camp, Heinrich Blood, the young novice, looked towards them with wide eyes. He was still learning to be a priest, but he had demonstrated on numerous occasions that he was deeply devoted to the Ice Giant.

'We know our path, mother,' said Wulfrick, still on guard, but letting his words sound gentle. 'For good or ill, we assault the Bear's Mouth.'

Anya shook her head, but smiled contentedly at Wulfrick's renewed warmth. 'No, no, no. Your path goes beneath, young man.' She stretched out her hands and rubbed them together in front of the fire. 'In the ice caverns you will lose some, but at the Bear's Mouth you will lose all.'

'People don't come back from the ice caverns, mother,' replied Wulfrick.

Halla had never heard of any way beneath the Bear's Mouth. She was leaning in now and listening intently to the wise woman.

'You are almost as silly as the girl, young man,' snapped Anya. She turned back to Halla and smirked mischievously. 'Your path goes beneath. Listen to an old woman who knows more than you can possibly imagine, axe-maiden of Rowanoco.'

Halla maintained eye-contact with the old woman for a moment before looking across the camp and shouting for Rexel Falling Cloud to join them. The axe-master of Hammerfall looked up sharply and made his way over to them. He did not take his eyes off the old woman as he approached. Whatever Heinrich had been saying had put him on guard.

'A cold night,' he said conversationally, sitting down by their fire and warming his hands. 'I'll take ten men on ahead at first light and see what we can find.'

Anya chuckled to herself and nuzzled further into Wulfrick's chest to protect herself against the cold.

'I won't fall for the wise old woman act, Lullaby . . . and don't you even *think* about slapping me,' barked Falling Cloud.

Anya smirked. 'Do not let fear of things you don't understand drive you to foolishness.'

'Keep it to yourself,' said Rexel. Then he turned to Halla and formed his words more respectfully. 'You wanted something, my lady?'

She nodded and waved away the objection Wulfrick was about to make to Falling Cloud's comment. The woman's wisdom aside, it was his way to be suspicious and it was a quality she valued.

'The ice caverns, what do you know about them?' she asked abruptly.

Rexel screwed his face up in thought. 'You mean the spider caverns?'

'Do I?' she asked Anya, who nodded gleefully.

'Shit,' was the simple comment from Rexel. 'Only a madman or a fool would consider that a safer route than the Bear's Mouth.'

'I am neither, young Falling Cloud.' Anya wasn't looking at him and her frail hands were still extended towards the fire. 'You do not have enough warriors to pass the Bear's Mouth. You will all die.' She spoke as if it were the simplest matter in the world.

'Let's not be hasty,' interjected Wulfrick. 'We're hard people to kill.' He spoke with a pride that Falling Cloud clearly shared.

Anya chuckled again. 'You will kill many, and you will die bravely.'

Neither of the men said anything. Instead, both looked at Halla. She was considering her options. Passion alone would not be sufficient to preserve her company against Grammah Black Eyes and an unknown number of warriors. She had women and children, too, to worry about now. If the warriors were killed, they would surely die soon after. But she trusted Falling Cloud's judgement, and she hoped he would have some wise counsel concerning these ice caverns.

'The ice caverns?' she prompted. 'Do you know anything useful about them?'

Rexel nodded and gave a slight frown. 'They're easy to find, if that's what you mean.' He paused and adopted a more serious expression. 'Okay, the ice caverns. They run from Jarvik to . . . I don't know, the sea, probably. They're full of Gorlan, and I mean the big ones that *are* actually dangerous. Trolls don't go down there, that should tell you something.'

They had encountered many nests of ice spiders on their journey north, but Halla had yet to see one of the great beasts that so terrified the common folk of Fjorlan. They were said to emerge with lightning speed from trapdoors and snare men.

'Are they passable?' she asked.

'They are, but I'd prefer a stand-up fight at the Bear's Mouth,' he replied, with a slight twitch of his lip, indicating his eagerness for the fight.

'You have no choice,' cackled Anya, clapping her hands together and bouncing up and down excitedly.

'Shut it, Lullaby,' snapped Falling Cloud.

'Rexel, remember your manners,' Wulfrick growled at him.

'You don't know this old hag. She was half-mad when I was a boy . . .' He stood up defiantly. 'Halla, I will follow you into the ice halls if you bid me to, but tell me you're going on more than this crazed old woman's word.'

Heinrich Blood appeared over Falling Cloud's shoulder, making the axe-master of Hammerfall jump. 'You should listen to her,' said the young novice. 'She might appear mad, but she speaks for the Earth Shaker.'

Anya smiled once more and they all relaxed – even Rexel, whose defiance quickly evaporated. Whatever the old woman might be, Halla was sure she was not their enemy. 'Heinrich,' she asked the young novice, 'do you trust her words?'

He looked at the fire, deep in thought. 'I am not worthy to call myself a priest of the Order of the Hammer – not yet, maybe never – but I can feel the footsteps of the Ice Giants and I have devoted my life to Rowanoco.' He paused and looked at Anya Lullaby with something approaching reverence. 'The blood is almost spent, mother. Samson the Liar is dead, the last old-blood of the Ice Giants has fallen, and the shades come.'

Heinrich had repeated Anya's words, though there were no bones to read – just a glance between the two faithful of Rowanoco.

'Yes,' said Heinrich with conviction. 'I trust her words, and so should you.'

'The ice caverns it is,' said Falling Cloud reluctantly. 'We'd have only ended up massacring a load more Ranen at the Bear's Mouth anyway.'

'Our road hasn't changed,' said Halla. 'We are still bound for Jarvik and a cloud-stone, we're just changing how we get there.'

'And not all dying,' giggled Anya, cuddling up to Wulfrick so that the huge axe-master looked rather uncomfortable.

* * *

Word had spread quickly among the company that their road was to go under the Bear's Mouth rather than through it. Halla heard a variety of responses, from both the battle-brothers and the common folk who travelled with them. Mostly they were pleased they wouldn't be clashing axes with Grammah Black Eyes, but Wulfrick said this was because they didn't truly know what awaited in the ice caverns – not that Halla did either, as she led her company into the dark, forbidding cave that opened before them.

Her captains were at the front of the column, and all except Wulfrick had their weapons drawn. Lullaby stood behind them and they walked forward in a tight group.

They had followed Rexel's directions away from the gully and marched for most of the day until they had found a narrow canyon that dug into the ice plateaus of Ursa. Most of the column, the non-combatants from Hammerfall, waited above on the flat ground while the hardened warriors investigated the cave entrance below. Once the way was clear, Halla would begin to move the column through the ice caverns, hoping that any attack might come at a place where they could defend themselves.

Oleff Hard Head and several others had flaming torches and were taking their first steps into the caverns. Halla and Wulfrick were a step behind and saw a vista of ice open up before them. The cavern appeared as a forest of stalactites hanging down and producing a regular drip of tepid water on to the floor. Irregular paths ran away from them, stretching into the dark caves beyond their globe of light. If there were Gorlan living in these caverns, they were deeper underground. Halla's skin crawled as she imagined a silent attack from the ice spiders.

'Move forward,' she said quietly, holding her battleaxe loosely in her hand.

Oleff took a deep breath and led the first few men into the cave. The firelight spread out and the rest of the column followed slowly. Halla made sure she was close behind Oleff. Wulfrick, who had still not drawn his axe, remained just behind.

Within a few minutes, the first hundred or so battle-brothers had entered the ice caverns and Halla could see their fearful eyes behind her. She had witnessed much bravery and strength among her men since they had escaped the Kraken Sea, but she had not seen fear like this on their faces.

'Stay together. We need to find somewhere where we can camp five hundred people and not get eaten.' Halla tried to sound light-hearted, but she knew that no one felt anything but fear as they advanced further into the ice caverns.

It was a slow process. As soon as the hundreds of non-combatants had entered the cave, their pace slowed to a virtual crawl. The way northwards was relatively easy to navigate at first and Halla found herself walking warily along an undulating road of slippery ice. Either side of them, stalactites descended at irregular heights from the cave roof. As the caverns stretched away from the

Fjorlanders, the column lengthened to pass the narrowest points.

The caves quickly began to all look the same. Within a few hours, it was only Lullaby's unerring sense of direction that kept them heading north, and Oleff's torches that allowed them to see. Halla had placed torch-bearers at regular intervals along the column and looking back through the cave was like watching a slowly moving snake of light crawling through the icy darkness.

Halla had seen no signs of Gorlan. They would pass underneath the Bear's Mouth within a day and then, Falling Cloud assured them, there was an external waterfall that marked the northern boundary of the ice caverns. If they could set a faster pace and sleep for as few hours as possible, Halla hoped they would see the sky in two or three days.

Then, as complaints about tiredness started to ripple through the column, they dropped into a large cavern. Halla called a halt, observing the size of the cave they had entered and the web coating every surface. It was the largest space they had come across since entering the caverns and their first few torches hardly cast any light into the icy expanse.

'What the . . .' said Oleff, as he held up his flaming torch to expose hundreds of web-filled tunnels leading away from them. The mouth of each tunnel was covered with a strange, corrosive-looking fluid and, though she could see no spiders, Halla knew they must be close.

'Did we take a wrong turn?' she asked Anya, who stood in Wulfrick's shadow.

'No, this is the way, young lady, onwards and upwards.' The old woman's words were trembling and croaky.

'We need to keep quiet,' said Falling Cloud, crouching. 'Keep your footsteps as light as possible.'

'Rexel, I'm hardly a waif, you know,' Wulfrick responded. 'I can only stay so quiet.'

They looked at their metal armour and heavy weaponry. Behind them, a hundred battle-brothers whispered anxious words as they followed Halla and her captains into the cavern.

'They sense vibration, and they never make any noise,' whispered Falling Cloud.

'The Ice Father said that many would die,' said Anya intensely. 'But all would die at the Bear's Mouth. Remember that, young lady.'

A grunt of alarm sounded from behind them.

Near the entrance to the cavern, where the column was still entering the vast space, Halla saw the head of one of her men disappear quickly down a thickly webbed side tunnel. Two grotesque, blade-like legs wrapped round the Ranen's head and smothered his cry as a stain of blood sprayed up into the torchlight. The creature's legs were stark white and had a bloated and bulbous quality that made Halla's skin crawl and her mouth turn dry. Other tunnels above and beneath them erupted into movement as more ice spiders reached out and grabbed any man close enough.

Halla hefted her axe and, no longer trying to remain quiet, shouted, 'Move everyone forward, now!'

Wulfrick reared up next to her and, looking ahead, took a sharp intake of breath. 'We need to get the fuck out of here,' he said, with a catch in his voice. 'Look!' The last word was deathly quiet, and Oleff, Rexel, Anya and Halla all peered forward in the direction they had been travelling.

Emerging from a thickly webbed tunnel, which dropped down almost vertically, was a giant, white spider. The Gorlan spread its jagged and bulbous legs on to the cavern floor and shifted its grotesque abdomen upwards. It was coloured a sickly white and looked almost opaque against the ice. The word *spider* seemed inadequate, as a sticky, viscous fluid dripped from two huge fangs and melted the ice beneath the beast.

They froze for a moment in unutterable fear. Not since the Krakens had Halla felt so small when faced with an enemy, and all the battle-brothers clenched their fists around their axes.

The Gorlan was terrifying, but Halla steeled herself and shouted, 'Clear the way,' as she ran at the ice spider, followed by a roaring Wulfrick and other captains.

The beast was clearly blind and the pink orbs of its eyes floated on the sticky surface of its head. Halla had to move slower than she wished to remain standing on the ice, and she almost slid into the massive beast, using her axe as a battering ram.

With a grunt of exertion, the axe-maiden struck the spider between two of its eight eyes, causing the Gorlan to flinch and lash forward with its sticky, gelatinous feelers. One of these was instantly severed by Wulfrick's two-handed axe and Falling Cloud grabbed the other.

'Skewer the fucking thing,' roared Rexel, as Oleff jumped forward and rammed his battleaxe into the creature's abdomen.

Halla pulled back her own weapon and drove it into the spider's head a second time. More of the beast's viscous blood coated her axe and spread on to the ice. The Gorlan made a vile gurgling sound and reared up, baring its fangs.

'Halla,' shouted a voice from behind, 'move to your left.'

She removed her axe and swayed out of the way as Heinrich Blood fired an arrow over her shoulder, which struck the spider between its huge fangs. The creature slumped, gave another hissing gurgle, and flailed its legs. Oleff, Wulfrick and Halla stepped forward as one and drove their weapons deep into the spider's body.

Falling Cloud darted past the dead Gorlan and threw a flaming torch towards their exit. 'The way won't stay clear for long. Get those people moving,' he shouted, crouching down and scanning the cavern ahead.

Halla was breathing heavily and a little stunned. But now she knew that at least the ice spiders of Fjorlan could be killed, and she turned quickly to see how her column was faring.

Dead Gorlan, equally grotesque but much smaller than the first, littered the cavern. Several men were missing, but the rest stood guard over empty tunnels and wounded warriors. A few had been bitten and looked pale and close to death. The deep punctures resembled dagger or arrow wounds. At least two hundred of their best warriors were now in the spider cavern and Halla could see the rest of the column clustered in fear at the entrance.

The cave was silent and no more Gorlan appeared. The dead spiders had all curled up into a misshapen caricature of death and they gave off a stink that made the air near them noxious.

'Come on!' prompted Falling Cloud. 'They'll attack again.'

Halla wiped sweat and Gorlan blood from her face. 'Rexel, Heinrich, take the column forward. Move quickly. Wulfrick, you and Oleff are staying with me.'

She waved at the first few ranks of men and they quickly began to usher the others in. Her battle-brothers stood guard either side of the cavern as the common folk of Hammerfall hurried warily across the web-strewn floor to follow Rexel and Heinrich.

'Anya, go with Falling Cloud.' The old wise woman was huddled up and keeping as far away from the side tunnels as possible.

The column moved slowly and Halla's muscles remained taut as she, Wulfrick and Oleff stood over the largest of the spider tunnels. The wounded men were carried with the others. Rexel and Lullaby had now disappeared with the front of the column which, after a few minutes, cast no more than a shadowy globe of light within the ice caverns. Heinrich had gone shortly afterwards.

When the women and children appeared at the cavern entrance and began to step on the web, Halla held her breath. A white spider leg appeared just as the first child began to cross the cavern and Wulfrick's shouted warning was slightly too late.

'Get back,' he roared, as a Ranen child, no older than ten, was grabbed by a large spider that darted silently out of a wall tunnel.

More large spiders emerged and a clicking sound filled the cavern as they began to swarm.

'Run,' shouted Halla as dozens of Gorlan the size of dogs flooded into the cavern. Others, even larger, came soon afterwards, followed by multitudes of tiny spiders. She bounded over the ice to where the child had been grabbed and kicked two smaller beasts out of the way. Oleff followed, while Wulfrick covered their exit. The non-combatants began to scream with panic.

'She said *run*, you deaf bastards,' repeated Oleff.

The remaining battle-brothers helped the rear of the column

into the cavern and shoved them across the ice towards Wulfrick. The Gorlan grabbed an old woman, then a larger one appeared and snared two axe-men, followed by a young man howling in fear as his entire body was covered with tiny spiders.

Men and women died in pain as the Gorlan tore into their unexpected meal. Halla swung her axe in shallow circles, keeping the blade close to her body as she severed legs and crushed bodies. Wulfrick was roaring at the exit to the cave and his guttural howls echoed around as he killed any spider that tried to cut off their escape.

More men died as the last few ranks encountered a carpet of poisonous Gorlan, and those in front had to fight desperately to reach Wulfrick and get out alive.

'Halla, time to go,' grunted Oleff from her left. 'We're getting overrun.' His words accompanied the last man to enter the cavern. Halla turned to leave and saw Oleff suddenly pinned to the ground by a single large spider. Hard Head shouted in anger as he wrestled with the bulbous, white beast, but he couldn't get any leverage to hit it with his axe. Halla sprang across and kicked it solidly in the eyes, allowing Oleff to stand, just as two huge fangs protruded from the axe-maiden's shoulder.

She gave a sharp and strangled cry. The Gorlan that had bitten her had wrapped its legs round her torso, pulling her backwards.

'No fucking spider kills that lady.' The voice seemed to Halla to come from far away, and all she could feel as she slipped into unconsciousness was a burning pain as the Gorlan venom paralysed her.

* * *

Halla woke in pain and couldn't feel her limbs. She was cold, but she was alive. Her eyes were not focusing well and she had no idea where she was or what the shapes above her might be. She remembered the Gorlan and she remembered the bite. The pain in her chest was a reminder of the creature's fangs and the numbness in her head was a reminder of its venom.

'Wulfrick, her eyes are open,' said an indistinct voice next to her.

Her vision darkened and she felt the towering presence of the axe-master loom over her.

'I can't feel my arms or legs,' she muttered through a raw and scratchy throat. 'And I can't see.'

'You're alive, my Lady Summer Wolf,' was Wulfrick's response. 'Vision is overrated anyway and young Falling Cloud here is eager to act as your arms and legs.'

'It's true,' said Rexel. 'You're not as heavy as I thought.'

'Where are we?' she murmured. 'Are we safe . . . are we clear of the caverns?'

'Can you not see the sky?' asked Falling Cloud, though Halla still couldn't make out his face.

'Give it time,' said Wulfrick, more gently this time. 'Heinrich and Lullaby say you'll be up and shouting at us all in a few days.'

'The spiders . . . how many of us survived?' Halla thought she could still see the bloated white beasts. Their noxious stench would stay with her for a long time to come.

There was no response for a moment and she could sense that Wulfrick and Falling Cloud were communicating something wordlessly above her. Lullaby had told her that many would die in the ice caverns, but she still hoped that the majority of her company had made it out alive.

'A hundred and fifty are still in the spider caverns,' replied Falling Cloud in a quiet and matter-of-fact tone. 'Maybe one or two stragglers will still come out, but most of them are dead.'

'But there's some good news too,' said Wulfrick quickly. 'We're past the Bear's Mouth and will likely sight Jarvik in a day or two.'

CHAPTER THREE

ALAHAN TEARDROP ALGESSON
IN THE CITY OF TIERGARTEN

H E WAS DEEPLY relieved to sight the city of Summer
Wolf. The journey had been hard, cold and even life-
threatening on several occasions. After their encounter
with the troll, Alahan had come to believe that the beasts of
Fjorlan were more active than normal, perhaps sharing the pain
of Rowanoco's land under the yoke of a betrayer.

Timon the Butcher, Alahan's strange companion, had become
no more talkative and refused to be drawn as to how and why
he'd managed to get a hug from one of the Ice Men of Rowanoco.
Even the strange crystals he kept in the pouch at his belt were off
limits, and Alahan had ceased to ask what the pouch contained.

'Will I be welcome in a city of men?' asked the Low Kast berserker as they approached the tall, stone monolith of Tiergarten.
'I don't want to frighten anyone.'

Alahan looked at Timon and smiled. The berserker had once
again bound his huge, misshapen head in leather so that he looked
strange rather than monstrous. 'You'll be fine, friend. I'll slap
anyone that gives you a second glance,' he replied.

'You'd do that for me, friend Alahan?' Timon's mouth was
twisted in an odd caricature of a smile. His eyes showed childish
glee at having found a friend who would stick up for him. Once
again, Alahan was glad he had the berserker as a companion.

'You're my only friend in the world, my dear Timon,' replied the young thain, 'though I might be able to find another one or two in Tiergarten.'

The man of the Low Kast grinned again and lengthened his stride, almost skipping along the snowy path towards the city. The city of Summer Wolf was the oldest in Fjorlan, probably in Ranen and possibly in the entire lands of men. It was made primarily of stone, built into the side of the mountain and constructed with height in mind. The low harbours were smaller than those of Alahan's home city of Fredericksand, but still spread right across three low inlets, though they were currently devoid of any dragon ships.

From the slowly rolling Fjorlan Sea, across a plain of ice and snow, the city followed the natural curve of the rocky cliffs. The thick stone walls had supposedly been built by the first Ranen of Fjorlan. The city grew larger as the cliffs levelled out, with the top stone platform housing the hall of Summer Wolf and the chapel of Rowanoco. Alahan could see the Steps of Kalall, a wide staircase that intersected all the levels and gave access to all areas of Tiergarten, despite the city's vertical design. At the very top was Oreck's Spire, the fortified watchtower that looked out over the seemingly endless southern plains of Summer Wolf.

'It looks like a mountain,' observed Timon. 'Was it built by men?'

'Supposedly,' replied Alahan, 'though my uncle used to say it was put there by the last of the Ice Giants as a gift for the men of Ranen.'

'Varorg is a most generous father.' Timon's response was delivered with deep sincerity.

'Let's hope his generosity extends to helping a displaced high thain,' replied Alahan, playfully making light of his friend's piety.

They were still a good way ahead of Kalag Ursa and the forces sent out by his father, and Alahan hoped there were still enough battle-brothers in Tiergarten to repulse an attack. He wasn't sure how many men were pursuing them, but he knew the men of Jarvik well enough to think they would have sent a significant force after Algenon Teardrop's son – likely enough to assault any place that he might seek refuge.

He didn't know what state the city would be in, whether the loss of the dragon fleet had completely crippled it or whether there remained an axe-master to lead the people. Either way, old Father Brindon Crowe, the priest of the Order of the Hammer, was the best place to start. The old man of Tiergarten had not been with the fleet and he would surely have taken charge and locked down the city when he heard about Rulag the Betrayer's actions.

No one travelled the north–south road that led along the coast. Indeed, Alahan had not seen another man since he was assaulted by Ursa's men almost a month before. The lands of Fjorlan did not lend themselves to easy travel, but it was still surprising that no one should be abroad in the realm of Summer Wolf. If old Father Crowe had called the common folk back to Tiergarten, Alahan was sure that they would prove loyal to the house of Teardrop and not willingly submit to Rulag and his loathsome son.

'They'll have watchers up on the cliff face,' he said to Timon, as they reached the flattest part of the trail that led straight to the northern gates of Tiergarten.

They were now exposed against the white background of Fjorlan and no cover was readily at hand. Alahan had no grand delusions about sneaking up on the city, but he felt slightly foolish marching absently along the road when he knew so many men would be pursuing him.

'Should I signal to them?' asked the Low Kast berserker. 'So they don't think we're hostile.'

'We're not exactly an army. I'm sure they won't be too worried about a frontal assault.' Alahan shielded his eyes from the glare and scanned the cliff face above them. He could not see any people, but if there were any, they would surely be hidden from view.

He slowed his pace, allowing anyone above to see them clearly as they progressed along the low coastline towards the flat plain and the lowest level of Tiergarten. The gates were closed, and ballistae mounted either side of the entrance covered a large area of the snowy plain. If an army were to assault, the people of Tiergarten would have plenty of warning and had ample reason to think they could hold out indefinitely.

Alahan was impressed as the stone city came into clear view. The outer buildings were all of stone and of odd, irregular design. The wooden habitations closer to the middle of each level were Ranen halls of thatch, each crested with the city's heraldry – a howling wolf against a rising sun. The Steps of Kalall were identifiable and Alahan saw tiny figures moving up and down. The city was far from deserted, even if it was locked down and isolated.

'Ho there,' shouted a voice from above the solid wooden gates.

The entranceway was the only part of the lowest level that was not made of stone. The gates were braced with immense steel struts and the wood itself looked thicker than the largest trees.

'Who approaches?' shouted the voice.

'A friend of Tiergarten,' replied Alahan. 'I seek Father Brindon Crowe.'

As the guard spoke quietly to someone behind him, the two companions reached the foot of the gates and came to a halt. 'Who are you? And who's your friend?' The voice was wary, but not hostile.

Alahan craned his neck and spoke quietly to Timon. 'Their reaction to what I'm about to say will tell us whether we have friends here or not,' he said with a wry smile.

'My name is Alahan Teardrop Algesson, high thain of Fjorlan and heir to the hall of Fredericksand.'

There was silence from above and the young Ranen disappeared behind the battlements. Whispered words could be heard from the walls. Alahan heard someone say, 'Go and get Ice Fang, he'll want to see this guy.'

'Wait . . . you below, wait,' said the young voice from above, though the man remained out of view.

'Well, they haven't thrown any axes at us yet,' said Alahan, letting his eyes play over the rugged battlements of the city.

Timon screwed up his face and pouted. 'I don't want an axe thrown at me,' said the berserker. 'They're sharp.'

Alahan laughed. 'Yes, yes, they are . . . they wouldn't be very useful otherwise.'

They waited, while the sound of footsteps came from beyond the wall. Whatever else Alahan had done, he'd clearly caused a bit of alarm within. Whoever Ice Fang might be, he was audibly complaining as he approached the battlements.

'Yeah, Alahan Teardrop is here . . . of course he is,' came a croaky voice from above.

Timon smiled and looked up gleefully as a red-haired man poked his head over the wall. The Ranen was in his mid-forties, though his features were difficult to make out behind his huge, bushy beard. He raised an eyebrow at the two men standing in front of his gate.

'And you are?' he asked.

'Did your man not tell you?' answered Alahan.

The red-haired Ranen called Ice Fang seemed annoyed by this response. 'Don't answer a question with a question . . . it makes you sound like a stupid cunt. Who are you?'

Alahan decided to stop being so guarded. 'I am Alahan Teardrop and I seek friends against Rulag the Betrayer.'

Ice Fang nodded slowly and narrowed his eyes, looking at the young thain. The man had a thick chain wrapped around his chest signifying that he was a chain-master, responsible for the security of the settlement. It was a position of great respect, second only to the axe-master, and marked the man as a leader in Tiergarten.

'And you are?' asked Alahan, attempting to be cheeky and to establish a rapport.

'I am Tricken Ice Fang, chain-master of Tiergarten and loyal battle-brother of Summer Wolf,' he barked, showing some anger at Alahan's cheek. 'I am loyal and I am true to Fjorlan, but I decide who passes this gate, boy.'

Timon frowned, while Alahan resisted the urge to throw out a challenge. 'Careful, Tricken Ice Fang, I am not in the mood to argue with an ally . . .' He paused, his lip twitching at having been called *boy*. 'If you need proof that I'm a man, draw your axe and I'll kill you.'

Ice Fang smiled suddenly and waved behind him. 'Open the gates,' he shouted. 'We have a high thain that needs to get warm.'

* * *

The walk from the lowest level of the city, up the Steps of Kalall, had seemed almost as exhausting as their trek from the realm of Teardrop, but Alahan was glad of the roaring fire in front of him and was looking forward to the mug of mead that was on its way.

They were seated at the end of Aleph Summer Wolf's hall, a single fire-pit warming their backs as Tricken Ice Fang drew two large mugs of mead from one of several barrels off to the side of the large building. It was smaller than the hall in Fredericksand, but not by much, and had similar decorations adorning the wooden walls. Troll skulls and massive war-axes hung on steel hooks, and wooden tables were arranged in two parallel lines down the length of the hall.

Timon was in awe of the city and had stated repeatedly that he hadn't known such places existed in the lands of men. The Low Kast might boast a few impressive halls and the odd large settlement, but there was nothing like Tiergarten. The Butcher expressed surprise that stone could prove such a useful building material and had commented on it being difficult to burn. Alahan had taken this as a joke, though whether it was meant as such he didn't know.

There had been little commotion when they entered the city. Tricken had insisted that there was no need to confuse an already troubled population by announcing that Algenon Teardrop's son was alive. They'd walked briskly up the towering stone steps without stopping at any of the lower levels. In any case, such attention as they did attract was directed towards the monstrous berserker rather than Teardrop's son.

'This hall hasn't seen much drinking of late,' said Tricken Ice Fang, as he delivered two large mugs of mead. 'Since the fleet was lost, most people have stayed indoors. There's an odd atmosphere around.'

'Understandable,' responded Alahan. 'How many battle-brothers do you have left?' The young man of Fredericksand scanned the empty hall and saw no sign that it had been used recently. Currently, there were only the three of them there.

Tricken raised an eyebrow and scratched at his huge red beard. 'You cut straight to the chase . . . why don't we just have a drink for now, my thain?' Alahan found it strange to be addressed by the honorific.

'That's not a thain,' boomed a deep voice from the back of the hall. 'That's a thain's son.'

The speaker was tall and broad, but he walked with a rolling stride that indicated an old leg wound. He had white hair, receding at the temples, and sharp facial features which made his appearance stern. At his side hung an old war-hammer with rough, well-used edges and a worn leather grip.

Old Father Brindon Crowe marched from the end of the hall to stand before Alahan, looking down at him as a teacher might look at a troublesome student. 'You've grown, boy,' he said, with no hint of humour, 'and you carry a man's axe. Does that make you a man?'

Alahan had known Brindon Crowe since he was a boy. His father had sent him to Tiergarten to learn about Rowanoco. Magnus had been wandering Tor Funweir with his friends and had not been able to teach his nephew, so Alahan's study under old Father Crowe had formed a significant period in his young life.

'I've killed with it and defended my life with it,' he replied earnestly. He did not mind this particular man calling him *boy*.

Crowe didn't react to this, but continued, 'And as a man, you can be thain, yes?'

'I can,' was Alahan's simple response.

'You're a fool, boy.' Crowe turned his back on them and strolled over to the mead barrels.

Timon coughed to let Alahan know that he wanted to speak.

The young warrior smiled at his friend. 'If you want to ask if he's always like that . . . yes . . . yes, he is.' He kept his voice low so that Crowe couldn't hear him and felt like a child again.

'Sorry to hear about your uncle,' said Crowe over his shoulder, as he drew a large mug of mead. 'Cloud-stone from South Warden told us what happened in Canarn . . . bad business. It seems Rowanoco's faithful are all being tested . . . Ro Hail, Fredericksand . . . even South Warden is preparing to be annihilated by the Red knights.' He turned and glared at Alahan once more, before continuing. 'Perhaps the appropriate response is to sit in the hall and drink.'

Old Father Crowe heavily took a seat at the end of the bench and let out a groan as something clicked in his back. A weary flinch of pain followed and the priest of the Order of the Hammer threw back a deep gulp of his drink before flexing his back and grunting, 'Nothing to say, boy?'

'I thought reaching here was the important thing.' Alahan had not planned very far ahead and had simply hoped that Tiergarten would have sufficient battle-brothers to hold out against the forces of Ursa. 'As you said, I'm not a thain. Just a thain's son.' He was not trying to be cheeky, but the glare he received in return was withering. He took a comforting sip of his mead.

'How defensible is Tiergarten?' he asked, not looking at the old priest.

Tricken Ice Fang coughed. 'The walls are as defensible as any in Fjorlan. What we lack is men.'

'Maybe two hundred that will stand,' said Father Crowe, draining his mug and standing to get another. 'Two hundred and two, now that a boy and his pet have arrived.'

Timon the Butcher may have been simple, but he knew when he was being insulted. The Low Kast berserker pouted and dropped his head as if he'd been told off. 'I can go, if it's easier,' he said to Alahan.

'Stay where you are, berserker of Varorg,' said Crowe in his booming voice. 'You say you are friends of Tiergarten . . . Well,

Tiergarten needs friends, whoever they are.' He turned to Alahan. 'Good to see you, young Teardrop,' he said, offering his hand.

The young man of Fredericksand was unsure how to react now, but once he saw Tricken wink and nod at him, he took the old priest's hand. Father Brindon Crowe smiled ever so slightly for the first time since he had entered the hall and sat back down with his fresh mug of mead. In a more relaxed tone, he said, 'I feared you'd have been taken when Rulag sacked Fredericksand . . . any word from Ingrid?'

Alahan had been trying not to dwell on his sister and where she might be now. The simple fact was that he didn't know. 'She could be dead, or a captive,' he said quietly. 'She's a cunning one, but I saw her taken away in a net.'

'Don't worry, lad,' said Crowe. 'Rowanoco has a soft spot for precocious children, he'll keep her safe. She's got Algenon's blood, as you have. That makes you both strong.'

'Not strong enough to keep my hall from being taken. That bastard is sitting in my father's chair,' barked Alahan, suddenly allowing months of pent-up frustration to boil over. 'He made a deal with a witch for his honour and now he's proclaiming that Rowanoco values strength above all things.'

'He's wrong,' said the priest, 'and you know that. So do his men probably, but they sold their honour for power and wealth . . . We put a higher price on ours, yes?'

Tricken banged his mug on the wooden table and said loudly, 'The Betrayer won't take Tiergarten. By the time he gets here, we'll have mobilized the realm and every farmer and blacksmith with an axe will be standing on those walls.'

Alahan looked at him with concern. 'Kalag Ursa will be here soon . . . likely within a few weeks.'

'Chasing you?' asked Crowe. 'How many men does the Betrayer's son have?'

'That is another thing I don't know. The lordling had a couple of thousand in Fredericksand. Whether he took all of them after me, I have no idea.' The young thain was tired and his head was beginning to hurt. He was indoors and warm for the first time in months and the prospect of removing his thick hide armour at last was just about keeping him awake.

He rubbed his eyes and saw a worried look pass between Tricken and Crowe.

The priest gulped down some mead and said, 'We can't hold out against that many. We have men, but none of them are battle-brothers. They're brave and they'll die for Tiergarten, but they can't stand against an army. We need time to assemble our defenders.'

'You should have kept running.' Alahan had led the Betrayer's army to the city before its defence was prepared. 'This is the last free realm in Fjorlan . . . my thain.' The chain-master was glaring at him and rubbing his heavily bearded chin.

'Easy, Tricken, that's Teardrop's son you're talking to,' said Crowe, finishing his second mug of mead. 'I have some good news for you, boy.' The priest smiled thinly again. 'Halla Summer Wolf and Wulfrick the Enraged survived the Krakens.'

Alahan sat bolt upright and smiled. To hear that the axe-master of Fredericksand was still alive was the best news he'd heard since he had left his home, and Timon visibly brightened when he heard about Halla.

'The Daughter of the Wolf is alive?' asked the berserker eagerly.

'Have you pledged your fate, berserker?' asked the priest. Clearly, he knew more about the traditions of the Low Kast than did Alahan.

'I have, blessed of Varorg,' Timon responded.

Crowe laughed, by far the most animated he'd been since they'd arrived. 'That's not a title I've heard for a while. Tell me your name, man of the Low Kast,' he said, helping himself to another mug of mead.

The berserker straightened in his chair and towered over the men seated around him. Even Crowe, as he sat back down with his drink, was small in comparison with Alahan's friend.

'I am Timon, called the Butcher, and I have pledged my fate to the family of Summer Wolf.'

Father Crowe leant over slightly and looked at the berserker's belt. Seeing the strange pouch that Timon guarded so closely, he smiled again. 'Ah, you're one of *those* berserkers,' he said mysteriously. 'I hear that your head never stops growing once you start on that stuff.'

Timon looked embarrassed. 'I rarely sniff it any more. Only when I have to,' he said, with what seemed like regret. He glanced at Alahan. A silent look, acknowledging their encounter with the troll, passed between them. Whatever was in the berserker's pouch, it seemed that it made him attractive to the Ice Men of Rowanoco.

'You should get some sleep, Alahan,' said Crowe. 'You've a hall to take back, and another to defend. You need to be well rested.'

* * *

The dreams were more vivid than usual. Alahan had been given a comfortable room with a fur-covered bed, but his mind wandered as soon as his head hit the pillow. He felt the presence of his father. He stood proud and tall and flanked by a guard of Ice Giants, but his face was as sad as usual.

Alahan was expecting the dark woman to appear, but he hadn't expected to see his uncle at this point. Father Magnus Forkbeard of the Order of the Hammer, priest of Rowanoco, was a more powerful presence than usual. He stood behind the wreath of tentacles that emerged from the dark woman's mouth and his appearance made the evil visage seem less disturbing than before. Alahan heard his name called in deep, resonating tones. He did not know who was speaking, but he knew that the Ice Giant was behind the voice. The exemplar of Rowanoco, Alahan Teardrop Algesson, high thain of Fjorlan, woke sharply from his bed.

By the look of the moon, which shone brightly through his window, he had been asleep for less than two hours. The room was simple, but the roaring fireplace and thick fur sheets made a pleasant change from sleeping rough and he felt warm right through his body for the first time in months. He had bathed before he took to bed and the sweat of the road had been scraped from his tired body.

The air was crisp and cold and he dressed quickly, feeling a strange but irresistible pull towards the chapel of Rowanoco. Something had opened at the back of his mind and now he was focused on the Ice Giant and his duty to the Ranen. Whatever he had to do, he knew that first he had to visit Rowanoco's Stone.

Timon had refused his own room and was curled up like a loyal dog on the floor of Alahan's room. Apparently, he was not comfortable when he was treated well, and he had insisted that he stay close to his friend. He was fast asleep and didn't wake as Alahan left the room. He closed the door behind him and looked both ways down the stone corridor. The hall of Tiergarten was quiet and only the sound of the wind accompanied Alahan to the front door. As in Fredericksand, the hall had many levels and numerous bedrooms to cater to the free folk of the city. Most were empty now – a silent testament to the loss of the dragon fleet. Crowe had not told him how many men of Tiergarten had perished when Rulag Ursa turned on Algenon Teardrop, but with only two hundred capable warriors left, the city must have been without several thousand battle-brothers.

Alahan walked into the main hall, warming his hands by the single burning fire-pit. Many wives and children would be without their husbands and fathers. The hall of Summer Wolf would likely remain unused for a long time to come. At least, with Rowanoco's help, the city would remain free and loyal to the family of Teardrop, even if Alahan himself did not yet feel worthy to take his father's place. It was a strange feeling of inadequacy that had really only come over him since he had met old Father Crowe. Before that, he had been too angry and too focused on survival to take in the fact that he was now the high thain of Fjorlan.

'You are more than that,' said a voice in his head.

Alahan dropped to his knees and stifled a cry of pain as he experienced a great pressure on either side of his skull. Whoever had spoken had not done so out loud, but the voice seemed to come from everywhere at once.

'You are expected, exemplar. Rowanoco's Stone awaits you.' The voice was deep and, once the pain subsided, Alahan thought it slightly familiar.

He staggered to his feet and focused on the wooden door that led from the hall to the top level of the city. A few long strides, feeling unsteady on his feet, and he pushed open the doors, making the steel hinges creak. Outside, he barely noticed the biting wind, as the pain in his head reduced to a dull ache. Instinctively, he turned right and saw the low dome that marked the chapel of Rowanoco. As with all chapels to the Ice Giant, it was of stone and built partially into the ground, making the domed building appear subtle in comparison with the massive hall next to it.

Alahan paused and straightened up as much as he could, unwilling to enter the chapel with his hands clamped to the sides of his head. He almost fell backwards as the thick stone door, partially concealed down a set of steps, flung suddenly open. It was not the wind, and all he could think, as the voice ushered him inside, was that it resembled the voice of his uncle, Magnus Forkbeard.

Once out of the cold wind, Alahan leant against the stone passageway and then walked slowly down the steps and into the darkness beyond. There was a globe of light at the foot of the staircase.

'Alahan Teardrop Algesson, high thain of Fjorlan and exemplar of Rowanoco,' boomed the voice from below, 'enter the Stone.'

Even if he had wanted to resist, the young man of Fredericksand was compelled to obey the voice. As he reached the bottom of the stairs and entered the chapel, Alahan was struck dumb. Before him, standing proud and tall over a flaming steel brazier, was a shadowy figure. The form was indistinct, but the outline and misty features were those of his uncle Magnus. The massive war-hammer that hung by his side was Skeld, his uncle's beloved weapon. Yet the shade did not to have a solid physical form and Alahan could see the rock of the chapel through the apparition.

'Welcome, exemplar,' said the shade. There was little or no emotion in the voice and it had none of Magnus's idiosyncrasies. It looked like the former priest of the Order of the Hammer but sounded only vaguely like him.

'What are you?' Alahan spluttered.

'The one I was is caught between worlds, with no body to inhabit and no way to the ice halls beyond the world. I am a memory, nothing more.' Alahan felt the words as much as he heard them, and he winced in pain as the shade spoke.

'You are Magnus?' he asked, not knowing what else to say.

'I am the shade of Magnus, though I do not remember him. The blood is almost spent and I am needed.' The apparition moved round the burning brazier and stood tall in front of Alahan. 'You are the exemplar of Rowanoco. You are the Ice Giant's servant in the Long War. I am here to advise you.'

The man of Fredericksand leant heavily against the stone wall and peered at the shade before him. He had never heard of such things, of men appearing in this way after death. Yet whatever was happening in the chapel of Rowanoco, he knew that the Ice Giant was reaching out to him, stretching a hand from his hall beyond the world to protect the people of Ranen.

'We have high walls, but few men,' said the young man, feeling the need to speak of what was troubling him. 'The forces arrayed against us will become too numerous for this city to hold. The Betrayer did his work well.'

The shade reared up suddenly and its eyes flared with ice-cold anger, making frost appear on the walls and a whistling wind spiral through the chapel.

'It was a witch of Shub-Nillurath,' boomed the shade, making the stone shake and causing Alahan to stumble back against the wall. 'The Forest Giant has awoken and the Long War rages fiercely.'

'I am just a man,' said Alahan, as the icy wind of the shade pelted him with snow and frost. 'I will gladly give my life for Rowanoco, but I need ten thousand men willing to do the same . . .'

The shade stepped back and the temperature quickly returned to normal. The young man's beard was frozen and his hands shook violently, though he stood defiantly upright.

'You are not your father,' said the shade, its words echoing around the stone chamber. 'You think only of men.' These words hurt more than anything else the shadowy presence had uttered, and the young man bowed his head and gritted his teeth.

'My father is dead . . . your brother is dead, whether you remember him or not.' Alahan was not a child any more and he tried to hold his ground against the immense presence of the shade. 'I could never be him, but my name is Teardrop.'

The shade of Magnus stepped back until it was again on the other side of the fire. Its eyes calmed until the shade was once more an apparition of his uncle.

'You will do,' it said simply. 'But you need counsel.'

'I will gladly hear how I am supposed to be victorious.'

'The Ice Giant has many servants, not only men. You should look to the other beasts of the ice.' Alahan now stared deeply into the shade's jewel-like eyes. A wave of sadness flowed through him as he remembered his uncle. Magnus Forkbeard Ragnarson was one of the best men he had ever known, a priest of the Order of the Hammer who had never compromised, never backed down, never abandoned what he knew to be right. Yet the shade was not that man. It spoke with a voice far deeper and more ancient.

'The witches have almost succeeded. Their plans progress faster than ours,' stated the shade. For the first time, there was a note of anger in its voice. 'But we are not helpless. Throughout the lands of men, the faithful still fight. The One has his loyal followers, and so does Jaa . . . the three are not yet defeated and the shades rise.'

The hairs on Alahan's arms began to tingle and a shiver of conviction travelled down his spine, a feeling of deep devotion to the Ice Giant and the lands of Ranen.

'What would you have me do?' he asked, stepping forward.

The shade drew his shadowy hammer and held it ceremoniously in front of his indistinct face. The gesture was more than a show of strength. Alahan's head began to pound once more as he felt a sense of enormity and unknowable time flow from his uncle.

'You will hold Fjorlan . . . you will fight back against the forces of the Forest Giant . . . you will serve Rowanoco until your last breath, exemplar.'

* * *

He did not return to sleep and remained seated on a stone bench on the top level of Tiergarten, weathering the cold wind and gazing down at the Fjorlan Sea. The hall of Summer Wolf was behind him and the chapel of Rowanoco to his left. Alahan could see clear of the city and down to the fields of grain and cattle that marked the southern plains of the realm. In the distant morning haze, he could just about make out the western edge of the Wolf Wood.

The Fjorlan Sea rolled silently away from the coast and he wondered where, in the grey expanse, his father had died. Kalall's Deep was far to the south and the Kraken Sea nestled next to the islands of Samnia, but from the top of Tiergarten the waters all looked the same. Somewhere out there could be the means to avenge Algenon Teardrop. Maybe one day Alahan would feel worthy of his name.

'Are you up early or up late?' asked Father Brindon Crowe from behind him.

The grey morning cast shadows and mist across the stone skyline of Tiergarten. Alahan was surprised that he wasn't the least bit tired. He turned and leant on the back of the stone bench the better to see the approaching priest. 'Something of a spiritual awakening, I suppose,' he replied.

Father Crowe came to a stop in front of the young thain and showed a grim, thin-lipped frown. He was clearly sober and as a result his mood was dark. 'Well, as a priest, I believe I am the perfect person with whom to discuss such things.'

'I need to know something, Brindon,' said Alahan, too distracted to use the proper form of address. 'Something you seem to know.'

'I'll forgive the informality, lad,' replied Crowe, sitting down next to his former student. 'Has this spiritual awakening left you with questions?'

'Just one for now . . . I think the others will come later,' replied the young warrior. 'What is it that Timon snorts? Why do the trolls not attack him?'

Crowe chuckled in amusement and cast his inscrutable eyes over the city of Tiergarten. He showed no further emotion or sign of interest, and he didn't respond right away.

Eventually old Father Crowe said, 'The berserkers of the Low Kast have . . . a certain way of making war. They enter a rage beyond anything you would have seen.'

'I've seen one of your order enter the battle rage of Rowanoco . . . my uncle actually.' The young thain glanced involuntarily towards the chapel of the Ice Giant and remembered the shade of Magnus.

'Those of Varorg make young Forkbeard look like a sniffling little Ro,' responded Crowe. 'They use a crystal found in the deep ice of the Low Kast. When sniffed up the nose it . . . does things to your body.'

'That doesn't answer the question, Father,' prompted Alahan. 'What is it and what does it do to trolls?'

Father Crowe narrowed his eyes and glared down at the young man. 'Why do you want to know?' he asked. 'Timon doesn't want to tell you, so why should I?'

'Because I am the closest thing you have to my father. He's dead and I am alive. Just deal with it . . .' Alahan paused and let his eyes fall to the stone beneath his feet. 'I have . . .' he said, with no remaining fear of his former teacher.

'Very well, my thain, I will answer your question,' replied Crowe, with the barest hint of a smile. 'The Ice Men of Rowanoco produce a crystalline substance. Everything they eat – rocks, trees, men – it all comes out of the trolls as these fine, white crystals.'

Alahan raised an eyebrow. 'Troll piss? They snort troll piss?'

'I don't even know if they have a name for it,' said Crowe, 'but it stinks more than dead Gorlan and has a strange effect on the other denizens of the ice. I've heard stories of trolls joining companies of battle-brothers for months on end, thinking the Low Kast Ranen are a family of Ice Men.'

Alahan found the notion amusing. 'Aren't they embarrassed by this?'

'I don't think they care, lad. I think they use it to drive themselves insane and make their heads crack. Everything else is the will of Varorg.' He coughed and spat phlegm on the ground between his feet. 'You can use this information, but Timon won't thank you for it.'

'If you can think of a better way to defend Tiergarten, I'm listening...' Alahan was determined and if the *other beasts of the ice* could be used to regain Fjorlan, he was sure that Rowanoco would countenance it.

Crowe turned and slapped Alahan hard in the face, making his lip bleed and his cheek sting in sudden pain. 'You're not your father, boy. You're a brave fool ... at best. At worst you're a liability, and I'm not going to pander to you.'

Alahan saw red. Without thinking he reached up and grabbed the old priest by the throat. 'A man slaps me and he gets hurt . . . I don't care if you're a priest, a king or a wise woman. I am a Teardrop and I apologize if my first name is not Algenon.'

Crowe barely reacted to being pinned against the stone bench. The old priest didn't turn his gaze from Alahan, but the thought it betrayed was more of interest than of annoyance. He raised his hand and patted Alahan's wrist to calm the angry young thain.

'Our walls will not be breached easily,' he said, as Alahan released his grip. 'But with so few defenders, we cannot hold out indefinitely.'

'As I said, if you can think of a better way . . .' Alahan didn't like the idea of using Timon to lead a family of trolls to Tiergarten, but with the words of the shade ringing in his ears, he felt that no other option remained.

'If the lordling of Jarvik has a few thousand men and battering rams . . .' Crowe left the sentence unfinished, but his eyes showed his doubt that they could stand against Kalag.

Alahan returned to his seat. He tried to calm his mind and not to take the old priest's words too seriously. Crowe had a well-practised manner, cultivated over many years and designed to make men wither under his caustic demeanour. The young thain had decided that he was no longer going to be cowed by him.

'You're a priest of the Order of the Hammer, Father. You of all people should have faith,' said Alahan with conviction. 'Or at least trust that I do.'

CHAPTER FOUR

RANDALL OF DARKWALD
IN THE FELL

'WE WILL ENDURE,' said Vithar Xaris for the seventy-fifth time since the sun had disappeared over the horizon. 'Your desire to rush our passage south will not change the inevitable.' The Dokkalfar gave Utha the Ghost an exaggerated tilt of the head, and Randall saw his master resist the urge to do something violent.

'You do understand that we're being chased, yes?' asked the cleric, biting his lip in frustration. 'It is a concept that you can accept?'

The Vithar turned his head slowly, but did not make any other movement. His eyes were still and his mouth expressionless. 'I understand more than you can ever know, Utha the Shadow,' replied the forest-dweller.

'Perhaps we should leave it before you manage actually to say something useful,' Randall interjected, pulling Utha away from the conversation and directing a barbed grimace at the obtuse shaman.

The addition of twenty Dokkalfar to their travelling party had not made the journey any easier and Xaris's insistence that they take their time in reaching the Fell had not improved the Black cleric's temper.

They had sighted the edges of the forest several days ago, but the Fell was still distant. They would likely reach some outlying woods in the morning and find themselves safe inside the Dokkalfar settlement within the next few days.

Since leaving Cozz, they had been pursued by a group of Karesian hounds and Pevain's bastards, and it was only the need to stay ahead of their pursuers that had made the Dokkalfar hurry at all.

'They're less than a day behind,' said Utha, as the two of them moved away from the fire to join Tyr Vasir.

'So we'll have to turn and fight at some point tomorrow,' replied Randall. 'I think there's some of Vasir's stew left.' The squire gestured to a small cook-fire and a simmering cauldron.

The Dokkalfar were curt and unemotional. Randall found them difficult companions and his attempts at bonding had been consistently rebuffed. Vasir had not changed, however, and the forest-dweller still preferred the company of the two men in the group rather than his own kind.

'He's a Vithar,' said Vasir as Utha and Randall sat by the cooking pot. 'He isn't used to talking to men . . . most Tyr find them tiresome as well.' He continued to stir the pot and a pleasant smell drifted from the fireplace.

'If I hear *we will endure* once more, I'll go back to my old career as a crusader,' said Utha, clenching and unclenching his fists.

'Please don't say such things,' snapped the Tyr, involuntarily tilting his head in a distinctive Dokkalfar gesture. 'Vithar Xaris is two hundred years old. I'm sure you can forgive him a little vagueness when dealing with the short-lived.'

Utha and his squire exchanged a questioning look.

Randall said, 'You'd think he'd have learned to cook in two hundred years, rather than expect you to do it every night.'

Vasir clearly didn't understand why this was a problem. 'He is a Vithar,' he said, as if that explained everything.

Randall had slowly begun to understand the strange divisions of the Dokkalfar. A Tyr was something akin to a warrior, but the forest-dweller's definition of the word was complicated. A Vithar was the closest thing they had to clerics or priests, but their authority was minimal and, according to Vasir, they functioned mostly as advisers. Randall had heard of other divisions among the forest-dwellers, but they were not comfortable discussing them.

They sat in silence for a moment, with Vasir stirring the rabbit and Gorlan stew, Utha shaking his head and trying to calm down, and Randall wondering how long he had to live. Whatever else happened and wherever they ended up, the young squire had made a number of decisions over the last few months. He knew that he was bound to Utha, likely until his death, and he knew that facing the world with kindness and good intentions might be foolish, but it was all he had left.

He was no longer a young man, experiencing the world through a veneer of naive optimism, but he couldn't quite bring himself to be as cynical and jaded as his master. He smiled, realizing that his function was mostly to provide an optimistic counterpoint to Brother Utha the Ghost.

'They'll hit us before we reach the trees,' said Utha, after Vasir had given him a bowl of stew. 'And I expect we'll be dead shortly afterwards.'

'How likely are your people to emerge from the Fell and rescue us?' asked Randall, smiling at Vasir.

The Dokkalfar did not understand the humour. 'I consider that unlikely, Randall of Darkwald, but a black hawk has been following us for two days.'

Utha wasn't paying much attention and he reclined on his bedroll, gazing off across the southern plains, towards the relative safety of the Fell.

'Well, unless the hawk has a lot of tough friends, I'd say speed is still our best weapon,' said Randall, hoping they could rouse the other Dokkalfar after only a few hours' rest.

They had been travelling on two hours' sleep for almost a week and, each time Vithar Xaris was asked to rouse from his slumber, he'd replied that he *wasn't asleep, but needed further rest*. Whatever the forest-dwellers did instead of sleep was a mystery to Randall, but he sensed that something akin to meditation took place when they stopped at the end of the day.

'The hawk watches us . . . we are not alone.' Vasir looked skywards and tried his best to mimic a human smile.

'I'm glad,' was the dry response from Randall.

Utha lay down flat and rested his head on his arms. The sun was now completely gone and they were well hidden as dark shapes amongst dark shapes, adding an additional texture to the landscape, but not standing out should anyone be watching.

Randall had ceased to feel tired and was functioning on a strangely alert kind of exhaustion that had developed since they'd left Cozz. He'd not complained or pushed for more sleep, but had simply become the rational centre of their bizarre travelling company. He'd helped the Dokkalfar grow accustomed to the scimitars they had acquired, and repeatedly reassured them that they were free now and relatively safe. He didn't know if they appreciated it, or even if they understood. If it were not for the bizarre reverence in which they held Utha the Ghost, the Dokkalfar would probably have proved even more reluctant to travel south. Randall didn't really know what an *old blood of the Shadow Giants* was, but apparently it was quite important to the forest-dwellers. He'd heard them talk about *the one we loved* in wistful terms, and had seen them look at Utha as if he were more than a man.

'Randall,' said the Black cleric, who wasn't yet fully asleep, 'tomorrow, you are allowed to kill anyone who draws a weapon on you. Understood?'

The squire smiled with gallows humour. 'But Vasir says that there is a hawk following us . . . we'll be fine.'

The two men laughed and for a moment things were good. Randall hoped he could stay alive and keep his master alive, too, to see what else fate had in store for them.

As Utha drifted off to sleep, Randall turned to Vasir and smiled. 'I appreciate your staying with us,' he said to their strange companion.

The Dokkalfar sat upright and met Randall's smile. 'I am not overly enamoured with the Fell Walkers, the Dokkalfar of the southern woods.'

Randall frowned. 'Where are you from?' It was strange to realize that he had never asked Vasir anything about himself.

The forest-dweller attempted a smile. 'I was sired beyond the Lands of Silence, near the Drow Deeps.'

'I've not heard of either of those places,' said Randall. 'I assume there aren't many men there?'

'None, as far as I know. I came from a clan of camel herders. It was a simple life, but my path lay elsewhere and I travelled north to Narland. I was captured by Purple clerics in Lob's Wood . . . they were the first men I'd ever seen.'

'Not the ideal introduction to our race, I suppose,' replied Randall, settling down on his bedroll. 'Though I once knew a Purple cleric whom I quite liked.'

'Utha and yourself are far better company. You have balanced out my opinion of men somewhat.' Vasir was beginning to express himself better now when talking to the young squire, but Randall still couldn't tell whether he was joking or not. Either way, the comment made him laugh.

'I should sleep . . . if I don't wake before my master he'll likely chide me for being lazy,' said Randall, feeling surprisingly peaceful, considering the circumstances.

'Sleep well, Randall of Darkwald,' responded the Dokkalfar.

'I'm sure I'll sleep, my friend, but I doubt I'll sleep well,' said Randall.

* * *

The morning light obscured the vista ahead of him, but Randall was sure that he could see the Fell burning in the distance. The Dokkalfar did not react to the sight of their forest on fire, but simply stood on the grassy rise and turned their expressionless faces towards the south.

It was hard to see exactly what was occurring on the southern plains, but the masses of faceless soldiers ranged within a mile of the Fell made him think that someone had declared war on the trees of the Dokkalfar woods. They were armoured in black plate which glinted in the morning sun.

'Hounds,' said Utha, as their small company skulked on the edge of a rise, within sight of the tree line, 'a shit-stack of them.'

They were still distant and he was confident they would not be seen by the armies of Karesia, though to see so many foreign troops in Tor Funweir was strange. The force that had marched on Cozz was a fraction of the army camped, in black spots, on the southern horizon, and the catapults had been used to launch flaming boulders into the Fell rather than to batter down walls. The outer trees were spreading a steady lick of flame amongst the giant oaks that marked the western border of the forest. Many small copses could be seen dotting the landscape, but they were not targeted by the hounds and instead provided their army with cover. Randall could not make out any defenders or Dokkalfar prepared to fight for their trees.

'Why are they attacking the forest?' he asked, taken aback by the sprawling multitudes of men, arrayed across the plains of Weir.

'Maybe they don't like trees,' responded Utha, letting his pale eyes play over the spectacle ahead of them. 'Or maybe they don't like the forest-dwellers.'

They had been told that the Dokkalfar turned into darkwood trees when they died, and they had seen the hounds transporting caged forest-dwellers with them. However, the squire had not imagined that they would attack a forest the size of the Fell in order to procure captives. He didn't know how many Dokkalfar lived in the woods, but the thought of so many more darkwood trees sent a shiver down his spine.

Their non-human companions were arrayed behind them, hidden behind a natural incline of the otherwise flat plain. If they felt anything at the sight of the burning trees, they didn't show it, and their grey faces and black eyes remained as expressionless as ever.

To make matters worse, Tyr Vasir had indicated that their pursuers were fast approaching. With nowhere to hide, they were caught between two different ways to die. Pevain and his men would catch up with them before they reached the trees. Luckily, they were far enough from the hounds that the sound of the impending combat would not be heard. It was a small mercy – in fact, it was barely a mercy at all – but fighting fifty men would be easier than fighting ten thousand.

'The Fell isn't helpless,' said Utha, assessing their situation. 'The deep wood is not a castle or a city . . . it's not Cozz . . . but they won't hold out forever, especially with this *we will endure* horse-shit.'

The black hawk flew overhead and all the Dokkalfar looked skywards. Tyr Vasir joined them at the front. 'We are not alone,' he said.

'Shut up about the hawk,' said Randall. He turned to Utha. 'So, do we stand here or try to fight Pevain in the woods?'

'We can't get to the woods, and those copses of trees are not decent cover,' replied Utha, as a loud cry sounded from above them.

'They are coming,' said Vasir, as the sound of approaching men drifted across the plain.

'How are your lot getting on with those scimitars?' Utha asked Vasir.

'They're heavier than leaf-blades and not as well made, but they'll do.' He still had his two short blades, but the others wielded weapons taken from the hounds. They were twenty-three men and forest-dwellers, and Randall was far from convinced that they could stand for long against fifty warriors.

'I bet I die before you, lad,' said Utha, directing a wry smile at his squire, 'and, if I tell you to run . . . you run.'

Randall returned the smile and drew the sword of Great Claw. His hand did not shake and he was as focused as he'd been for months. He was tired, alert, and determined to stay alive for as long as possible. His arms were taut and he felt stronger than he had ever been. Randall had even begun to think of himself as an average swordsman, rather than a boy with a blade he barely knew how to swing.

'You lot,' Utha shouted at Vithar Xaris and the Dokkalfar. 'Is it too much to ask for you to get on the other side of this rise and draw your weapons?' He spoke with sarcasm but the assembled forest-dwellers merely stood, looking apathetically at the Black cleric.

'Vasir, get them to move,' Randall said quietly to the Tyr warrior.

It was slow, but within five minutes the sound of approaching men had grown louder and the Dokkalfar had assembled behind the grassy rise. They were crouched and were not obviously visible. Utha, Randall and Vasir stood in the path of the approaching mercenaries and hounds, silhouetted against the morning sun, their weapons ready. Randall gripped his old longsword, Utha wielded a sword and a mace, and Vasir held his two leaf-blades low and ready.

'Neither of you fight Pevain,' said Utha in a low growl, 'he's mine.'

'Can I kill one of those blonde twins?' asked Randall, and his master directed a puzzled look at him.

'I see a man before me, my squire,' the Black cleric said, with just a hint of pride in his voice. 'And you can kill any man that draws a weapon on you . . . just not Pevain.'

The black hawk circled overhead and Vasir followed its trajectory north, towards the approaching men. There was no one on horseback, which was probably why they had struggled to catch up, but they could make out Pevain himself and half a dozen others. Karesian hounds were on each side of the advancing group, and they could hear battle cries from the centre.

The mercenary knight had his hair tied back and his groomed beard spoke of a man trying to look more noble than his station allowed. He carried a metal shield, along with his Ranen war-hammer, which he swung over his head, signalling his men to attack.

'The Ghost is mine!' shouted the mercenary.

The hounds drew their scimitars and charged.

'We are not alone,' repeated Vasir, looking at the black hawk. He threw his head back and, in a deep and echoing voice, shouted, 'Tyr Nanon . . . we need your help.'

Utha and Randall looked at him, momentarily turning from the charging hounds. Their eyes flitted quickly upwards. The black hawk began to dive and, still high in the air, transformed into a human-like figure. They gasped as it dropped several items among the approaching hounds, before turning back into a hawk and pulling out of the dive.

Three explosions nearly threw Randall off his feet. Something detonated in the midst of the charging enemies and a dozen hounds were blown to pieces. The remaining men lay in crumpled heaps on the ground, many with missing limbs.

'That's black wart,' said Utha, with an amazed smile. 'We are *not* alone, it would seem.'

A loud cry from above, almost humorous in tone, made them look to the sky again. The hawk was flying in a tight circle above their heads and the Dokkalfar were staring at it with knowing reverence.

The hounds didn't recover from the explosive black wart, though a handful were dragged forward by Pevain and his dozen mercenaries as they took up the charge. With the best part of thirty hounds either killed or incapacitated, the odds had evened out and Randall sensed a change in Utha. The Black cleric was no longer on the defensive, and an expression of violent anticipation had come over his face.

Pevain was a large man and stood out in the middle of the approaching rabble, his eyes focused on Utha. A few of the bastards glanced upwards, terrified that the hawk would strike again.

The hawk came in to land next to Vasir. Once again, the transformation was quick. One moment, a black hawk was standing on the grass, the next, a short-statured Dokkalfar stood by them with a Ro longsword in his hand. The forest-dweller was smaller than others Randall had seen, and he had a much more highly developed human smile than Vasir.

'Hello,' he said cheerfully. 'You're Utha the Shadow . . . pleased to meet you.' The Dokkalfar called Nanon extended his hand enthusiastically to Utha.

'Perhaps we should shake hands later, but thanks for the help,' was the dry response from the albino cleric.

'You're the boss,' replied the newcomer, crouching down, ready for combat.

'Let's kill some mercenaries,' said Randall, with more bluster than he knew he was capable of.

Moments passed in slow motion as the two forces neared each other. With no call for surprise now, Vithar Xaris and the Dokkalfar stood on the grassy rise in full view of their enemies.

Randall saw faces he recognized among the mercenaries. The blonde twins, Parag and Broot, and the man Utha had floored in Cozz. Sir Hallam Pevain stood out as the most dangerous-looking. He was well over six feet tall and his muscled arms flexed as he ran.

Utha took two large strides forward and the two groups clashed, the cleric's mace the first weapon to be swung. Pevain parried the blow with his shield, but was taken aback at Utha's strength. Randall was face to face with Parag and only a last-minute sidestep prevented the mercenary from barrelling into him.

'Time to die, Ghost,' spat Pevain, his war-hammer whistling over Utha's head. He lashed out with his shield, trying to make some forward momentum.

Randall used the reach of his longsword to keep Parag at bay, though he was not used to fighting a man wielding two short swords and was forced to give ground backwards. All around, Dokkalfar fought against men, swinging their scimitars with grace and speed. They lacked strength but used bewildering movements to confuse and disorient the mercenaries. Vasir was as dangerous as ever, staying low to the ground and using his speed to avoid multiple attacks while lashing out with his leaf-blades, causing deep cuts and severing arteries. The real surprise was Tyr Nanon, and Randall had to force his eyes away as the nimble newcomer cut through the mercenaries with his longsword.

Randall received a deep cut on his forearm and lashed out at Parag, grunting with exertion. His blade connected with a short sword and the shock sent the blonde mercenary backwards. The squire followed up quickly and delivered a feint to the man's side that allowed him to kick him in the groin.

Just when he thought he had won, the mercenary's twin brother, Broot, tackled him from the side and forced him to drop his sword as they rolled down the grassy incline. As he fell back, Randall saw Utha take a vicious blow to the chest from Pevain's war-hammer. Utha answered with a powerful thrust, but the cleric was clearly struggling against the mercenary.

'That's my brother, little boy,' grunted Broot, punching Randall in the face and trying to pin him to the ground. He struggled, sensing the rotten breath of the mercenary on his face as Broot punched him again and elbowed him in the ribs. He kicked out, but couldn't get leverage and felt his strength beginning to wane as a third heavy blow struck his jaw.

On either side, Randall saw dead men and forest-dwellers tumbling down the rise, and he could hear roaring from both Pevain and Utha. Then his vision became misty as Broot continued to strike him. It was a fleeting idea of last resort, or perhaps an inkling of his newly acute survival instinct, but Randall managed to draw the small dirk he kept at his belt and drove it into Broot's neck.

Now the pressure on him was relaxed, Randall shook his head and rolled the mercenary on to the ground. Broot stared at the squire with wide eyes as he clutched at his throat in a vain attempt to stop the flow of blood. Randall did not pause before retrieving his longsword. He was dazed, but focused enough to plunge the blade into Broot's chest.

Unsteadily, he made his way back to the top of the grassy rise and was met with a sight of gruesome slaughter. All pretence at duelling had gone and the remaining combatants were hacking at each other, desperately attempting to strike before being struck. The hounds and mercenaries had grown used to fighting the non-humans and the Dokkalfar's lack of physical strength was now all too apparent. Speed would only get you so far against a skilled fighter. Randall breathed heavily and wiped the blood from his eyes. They were losing.

Utha had lost his mace, but was not giving an inch against Sir Pevain as they hammered down on each other. Both were bleeding and the two large warriors had looks of determination on their faces. Utha's arms flexed tightly as he drove his shoulder upwards into Pevain's ribs, using his strength to unbalance the mercenary knight.

Randall couldn't see Vasir, though two dead Dokkalfar lay near to where he had been fighting. Nanon was alive, but in some distress as three hounds surrounded him, and the other forest-dwellers were being whittled down. He turned back to Utha and saw that Pevain had lost his grip on his hammer and received a knee in the face. The Black cleric didn't stand on ceremony and drew his sword across the mercenary's throat. Pevain convulsed and grabbed at the deep cut in his neck, but he was still alive. Utha's urgency to move on to other opponents had allowed the knight to survive.

'Randall, get to the trees,' Utha roared in a dry growl. 'You . . . Nanon,' he directed at the short Dokkalfar, 'fall back.'

Randall was tired, dazed and bleeding, but he grabbed hold of the nearest forest-dweller and turned from the fight. He was joined by others and, in moments, their company was fleeing southwards. Vithar Xaris was running close by. The shaman had lost his right arm below the elbow. He was clenching his teeth and holding the stump across his chest, but he showed no other sign of pain as he ushered his fellows away.

Nanon and Utha covered their escape, as the remaining mercenaries and hounds attempted to swarm over them. Parag was giving the orders now. Nanon had picked up a short sword and whirled his two blades in controlled circles, keeping their enemies from mounting a swift pursuit. Utha was roaring insults and challenges at the top of his voice and brutally throwing aside any man who dared to approach him.

'I am Utha the Ghost,' he roared. 'You'll remember that or you'll die . . . your choice.'

His words became distant. Randall ran unsteadily, weaving a chaotic pattern across the grass, trying to focus on the nearest copse of outlying trees. He could sense the others running with him, but was too dazed to identify their faces. The sounds of combat still rang in his ears as he saw a hazy image of trees appearing before him across the plain.

'Randall, stop,' roared a shaken voice from behind. He reached a tree and swung himself round it.

Looking back, he had expected to see Dokkalfar rushing to join him and the remainder of Pevain's force in pursuit. Instead, he saw two dozen men and Dokkalfar standing, staring in wide-eyed terror beyond where Randall stood. They were no longer fighting and even the wounded stood dumbstruck. A few of the forest-dwellers had dropped to their knees and were muttering indistinct words.

'The priest and the altar, the priest and the altar.' The words echoed from Vithar Xaris and were picked up by the other Dokkalfar.

The tree behind Randall began to move.

Slowly, he looked up. All sound seemed to be drawn from the area, as a dozen or more Dark Young reared up from the ground. The copse of trees had looked to be nothing out of the ordinary, but now he stood amongst them the darkwood trees planted their thickest branches to the ground and their trunks slowly left the earth.

'Run!' roared Nanon.

The mercenaries and hounds fled north, forgetting the urge to kill Utha.

Randall tried to move his legs, but they didn't respond. All he could do was watch as the nearest of the beasts shook earth from its needle-filled maw and tilted its trunk forward. The other trees did the same and, shrugging off their dormant state, the Dark Young scuttled together, using some of their branches as legs and others as reaching tentacles. The texture of their skin was less bark-like than the creature Randall had seen in the oubliette of Ro Tiris and he guessed that they had only recently been birthed from dead Dokkalfar.

Utha had frozen and the forest-dwellers were prostrate on the floor before the beasts, though Tyr Nanon seemed less afraid than the others of his kind.

'Don't move, boy,' Nanon shouted, running towards the Dark Young.

Just as the beasts began to realize that a virtually paralysed man was standing in their midst, Tyr Nanon let out a deep, echoing cry and loped forward on to all-fours. The Dokkalfar had transformed into something else, larger this time. The cry didn't stop, but melded into the roar of a large animal. The creature that had been Nanon was both beautiful and terrifying, with the body of a lion and the head, talons and wings of a giant eagle. Stories would call it a gryphon, but Randall had never believed such a thing could actually exist.

Nanon continued to roar and again took to the sky, flying directly at the Dark Young, flapping his great wings and baring enormous talons on each paw. The beasts flailed in the air as the gryphon pounced, pecking violently at the nearest of them and wrenching it to the ground. Its talons tore into the darkwood tree and the frenzied assault left the Young deprived of tentacles and unable to rear up again. The gryphon sounded a deafening roar and flew out of reach of the other Dark Young.

Randall closed his eyes and was jostled violently by the monsters as they scuttled after Nanon, reaching skywards with their black tentacles and needle-filled maws. After a moment of raw terror, the squire opened his eyes to find himself alone on the grass, with the forest of Dark Young in swift pursuit of the taunting gryphon.

'Get up,' shouted Utha, running to pull Randall to his feet and whisk him away to the south.

Neither of them looked back. They had only the continued sound of Vithar Xaris chanting to tell them that the remaining forest-dwellers were also running to the Fell.

* * *

The forest was dark. The light provided by the minimal remaining daylight was barely enough for Randall to see those clustered around him. Utha had just stopped breathing heavily as he looked back through the trees and listened intently.

The six remaining Dokkalfar, minus Nanon and Vasir, were crouched within the scrub a short distance away. They were silent enough to be hard to make out in the rising darkness. Vithar Xaris had guided them into the deep woods of the Fell, away from the burning forest, the torpid darkwood trees and the hounds.

Tyr Vasir was likely dead, though no one could testify to having seen him fall and Randall maintained a faint hope that his companion would have found a way to escape in the confusion. If he had been wounded and remained on the ground as the mercenaries fled from the Dark Young, he could still be alive.

They waited in silence, with fevered glances and twitchy, agitated eyes. Randall's head was clear now. Though his jaw was aching and his spirit shaken, he was still alive and he had high hopes that he would remain so, at least for the short term.

'Xaris,' Utha whispered over his shoulder. 'Seems we are not going anywhere. Why don't you tell us about your friend . . . the short one that can turn into animals?'

The Dokkalfar shaman tilted his head, seemingly finding the question a fair one. 'He is of the Heart of our people, from the north of your lands of men.'

'And the hawk, and the gryphon?' Utha prompted, speaking of the second animal with incredulity in his voice. 'I flatter myself that I know much of your people, but I did not know that.'

Xaris and the other forest-dwellers exchanged wary glances. Randall sensed that they might not be able to answer, even if they wanted to.

'Tyr Nanon the Shape Taker is old . . . maybe one of the oldest Dokkalfar that yet exists,' said Xaris. 'He has spent much of his forever travelling. He has seen the distant east, where the Jekkan still walk. He has taken counsel with the Volk of the northern ice, and he has flown with the gryphon riders of Imrya.'

Randall didn't understand any of these things. Vithar Xaris had a way of making humans feel like young children and the squire suspected that he did it deliberately. However, he spoke of Nanon with reverence and also confusion, as if the Tyr was just as much of a mystery to him.

'The ability to take the form of beasts is old, old magic . . . rarely practised,' continued Xaris, 'and is often seen as an insult to the one we loved.' He paused, looking at the faces of his fellow forest-dwellers. 'But none of us would think to question Tyr Nanon.'

'Why?' asked Utha. 'What's so special about him?'

'He is descended from the last exemplar of the Shadow Giants and a soldier of the Long War.' There was intense conviction in the shaman's words. 'If Tyr Nanon speaks, you will listen . . . his words travel from further back in time than your species can imagine.'

'Let's not overstate things,' said a voice out of the darkness, causing Utha to jump up and draw his sword.

'Settle, my dear Utha,' said Nanon, stepping out from behind a tree. He had clearly been there a while and it was a surprise that none of them had heard him approach.

'I'd have returned to you sooner, but I had to go and burn the fallen. The last thing we need is more Dark Young.'

Randall stood. 'Did you see Vasir? Is he alive?' he blurted out.

Nanon smiled and pulled the unconscious form of Tyr Vasir from behind the tree. 'He's taken a nasty blow to the head, but he's alive.'

Randall darted over to where his unconscious companion lay sprawled. He had an ugly-looking wound to the left side of his head and black blood was seeping over his skin, but he was otherwise unhurt.

'He'll be okay, lad. We heal quickly, just let him rest,' said Nanon cheerfully, imitating human behaviour more skilfully than the squire would have thought possible.

Vithar Xaris and the other Dokkalfar did not rise, but they looked at the short Tyr with reverence. Randall was surprised that none of them was inclined to help him move Vasir, and was reminded that the forest-dwellers were wary of one another just as much as men.

Utha sheathed his sword and regarded Nanon warily. 'Are you going to explain yourself?' he asked.

'What would you like me to explain?' replied the cheerful forest-dweller. 'I have quite a few catchy explanations up my sleeve. Which would you like first?'

Utha frowned, shaking his head. Randall sensed growing irritation in his master and decided to interject. 'I think he wants to know where you came from, how you knew where we were, and why you helped,' said the squire, hefting Vasir into a more dignified position, seated against a tree.

'Do not question him,' barked Xaris. 'Just thank him.'

Nanon raised his eyebrows in a distinctly human expression of tolerant annoyance. 'Fell Walkers,' he said, as if that explained everything. 'Don't worry, lad, it's what happens to someone who never leaves the tree they were sired under.' He directed his dark eyes towards the shaman. 'Xaris, you're not helping.'

'As you say, most reverend Tyr,' replied the Vithar.

Utha rubbed his eyes and let out a moan of frustration. 'I want a drink,' he said wearily. 'Anything will do.'

Nanon smiled warmly. 'How about some nettle tea?'

'How about you fuck off?' spat the Black cleric.

The Dokkalfar moaned as one at Utha's coarseness, but a raised hand from Nanon silenced them. The old Tyr smiled again and stepped towards Utha.

'Well, you'll get your wish, Utha the Shadow . . . I have to leave for the east fairly quickly.'

'He's just angry,' said Randall, standing up from Vasir and interposing himself between Utha and Nanon. 'He swears when he's angry.'

'You're not my mother, Randall,' barked the Black cleric. 'But thank you.' The last words were genuine and he looked at his squire, grateful that he still had another human for company.

'I took no offence,' said Nanon. 'Coarse language is a curiously human characteristic . . . we have no real equivalent.'

Utha turned away sharply.

'Where are you going?' Randall asked the forest-dweller.

Nanon placed a reassuring hand on the squire's shoulder. 'The dark-blood needs me,' he said cryptically.

'The what?' replied Randall.

'Among men, he's known as Rham Jas Rami.'

Randall snarled in anger. The Kirin assassin had killed Brother Torian.

'Without the dark-blood we are lost,' said Nanon. 'You have your duties and I have mine.' He then turned his attention to the Dokkalfar. 'Vithar Xaris, take the Shadow and his squire to the Fell Walk and guard them. I'll meet you there when I've rescued Rham Jas Rami Dark Blood.'

CHAPTER FIVE

KALE GLENWOOD
IN THE CITY OF RO LEITH

THE SIX HILLS of Leith were much as Glenwood remembered them and the air of his home was the freshest he'd felt for many years. Tiris smelt of sweat and money, Arnon of arrogance and greed, but Leith felt welcoming.

There were no walls round the city and no guard towers or stockade to police the comings and goings of the duchy's people. The farmers and landowners who worked on the land to the south, across the fertile plains of Leith, took a relaxed attitude to security and a sense of shared need and community spirit had been fostered over the years. The people of Leith were proud of their duchy and proud of their city. Not having a large church presence or a massive army, they relied on their love of nature and a sense of living within the seasons to maintain their identity. Even a man like Glenwood, who had long since left his home, felt a strange sense of completeness at seeing the six hills again.

'Where is your family from?' asked Rham Jas, evidently enjoying the warmer weather in the south of Tor Funweir. 'Is there a Glenwood manor somewhere nearby?'

The Kirin assassin had been in relatively good spirits as they had made their way south from Arnon through the foothills of the Claws. The lands through which they'd been travelling were sparse and unpopulated, with few people to avoid and plentiful game to hunt. Glenwood had made sure that they had hugged the mountains and stayed as far away from the Wastes of Jekka as possible, and the journey had been strangely relaxing.

'The last ward of the glen was only a distant relative,' replied Glenwood. 'I doubt they'd have kept my father's house . . . it was falling apart when I left.'

Rham Jas had removed his cloak and now wore only a sleeveless black waistcoat, with his other belongings stowed in a pack over his shoulder. The sun had been a constant companion for the last couple of weeks and, though the weather was crisp with the onset of winter, it was still considerably warmer than Tiris or Arnon.

'Shame,' said the Kirin with a good-natured smile. 'I would have liked to meet your family.'

Glenwood raised his eyebrows. 'Another time maybe.'

They reached the first hill of Leith just after midday and he was glad that nothing had changed. Atop the hill, and in chaotic patterns all around its base, were small, cosy homesteads, well spaced and separated by gardens and flower beds.

Glenwood took a deep breath of the clean air. Leith was far from being an idyllic city, but the criminals were a decidedly rare breed who seldom killed people. Wandering the cobbled streets that weaved their way through the hills, even Rham Jas was affected by the city's tranquillity. It was unlike the other great cities of Tor Funweir, its isolation having kept it free of clerical interference.

'Have a look over there,' said Rham Jas.

Security around the fifth hill was suspiciously high. At the base, where there were tree-lined paths and quaint wooden buildings, could also be seen patrols of city watchmen and strangely armoured Karesians. The four sets of steps that led from the road up the sides of the hill were all guarded and, though people were being allowed through, they were all being searched.

'Who are the Karesians?' asked Glenwood. 'I've never seen that armour before, or those wavy knives.'

'They're wind claws,' replied Rham Jas, deep in thought, 'the faithful of Jaa.'

Glenwood had never had occasion to visit the fifth hill when he had lived in Leith and it intimidated him. The Lady Annabel was known as a benevolent duchess, but she still felt the need to have an ornate residence out of step with the rest of her city. Known simply as her *house*, the building was in fact a palace, with spires and arched windows lending a fairytale appearance to the hill.

The knight marshal's office and Annabel's house perched side by side on a level section of ground with their foundations built deep into the hill. Around the two large buildings were manor houses and chapels. Glenwood chuckled to himself at this reminder that, though he might play at being a noble, and might even have a claim to nobility, he was just as much of a scumbag as Rham Jas.

'That spiky building,' said Rham Jas, pointing to Annabel's house, 'that's where the duchess lives?'

'Yup . . . nice, isn't it?' replied Glenwood, with a smirk.

The assassin scanned the steps that led to the top of the hill. 'Tricky,' he said, after a few moments.

'Are you joking?' replied Glenwood incredulously. 'I saw you climb up a sheer gold column in Arnon. This should be a breeze.'

'What I wouldn't give for a sheer gold column to climb up here.' Rham Jas wasn't grinning and his eyes flicked from side to side, betraying the complicated thought processes going on in his head. 'Those wind claws make things awkward,' he said.

'Scared?' asked Glenwood with a smug chuckle.

The Kirin assassin puffed out his cheeks wearily. 'Every second of every day, but that's not the point here. The point is why were there no wind claws in Tiris or Arnon? As far as I know the Mistress of Pain doesn't have a particular favourite among her sisters, so why is this one protected? It's not like Leith is the jewel of Tor Funweir or anything.'

'I'm sure you have a theory,' said Glenwood, with half an eye on a nearby tavern.

'Still in the early planning stages, my dear Kale,' replied Rham Jas. 'However, the most likely reason is that they are here for us . . . or, more accurately, me.'

'Can we go and have a drink and forget about killing people for an hour or two?' asked the man of Leith. 'The bitch will still be up there later.'

Rham Jas considered it, without moving his eyes from the wind claws guarding the bottom of the fifth hill.

'Okay, a drink seems appropriate.' His grin returned. 'Will they have Darkwald red?'

Glenwood screwed up his face in a show of mock offence. 'This is Leith, my dear Rham Jas. Drinking Darkwald red around here will get you arrested . . . have you not heard of the grape wars?'

The assassin shook his head and, for once, looked confused.

'The Corkoson family, the nobles that make the wine you're so fond of, refuse to ship their product down here. Apparently, there was a falling out over some of the grapes used in the Sixth Hill Reserve. Wine-making is a very serious business in Ro Leith.'

Rham Jas shrugged and began to stroll towards the tavern's welcoming embrace.

* * *

The presence of a Kirin bothered the locals very little as the two companions settled down in a corner of the quiet tavern and ordered a bottle of the Reserve. The barman was a jovial fellow in late middle age, who commented on not having seen a Kirin for a while and what a nice treat it was to encounter another one. Rham Jas was taken aback at this reaction, usually having to keep his face hidden while travelling in Tor Funweir, but he relaxed quickly enough as the bottle of fruity, full-bodied wine went down.

'You're a better travelling companion when you're not constantly worrying about things,' said the Kirin, as a second bottle of red wine appeared on their table. 'Doesn't it feel better just to let life take you along on a wave of chance and uncertainty?'

'I certainly prefer sitting in a tavern to skulking around dark back alleys,' replied Glenwood, pouring out two large goblets.

The assassin shrugged. 'It's a part of the job, I'm afraid.'

'Your job,' corrected Glenwood. 'To me, it's like I'm doing time in a bizarre walking prison, with you as the warden.'

Rham Jas laughed. 'I, er, I suppose I appreciate your help,' he said awkwardly.

Glenwood burst out laughing and banged his hand on the table. 'Fuck you, Rham Jas,' he said with a broad smile. 'I bet it hurt to say that.'

The Kirin shrank into his chair. Out of habit, he scanned the tavern to see if Glenwood's outburst had attracted any attention.

'Making friends is not counted among my skills,' he said.

'No shit. You're one of the most unlikeable men I've ever met . . . but at least you're sincere about being a bastard.' The forger glanced around the tavern. Aside from a few quizzical looks, he was gratified that most people were minding their own business. 'And you shouldn't worry too much about the common folk knowing who you are around here. As far as I remember, Lady Annabel is not known for following royal decrees and I doubt any Wanted posters would have made it this far south yet.'

Rham Jas grinned again and reclined further into his wooden chair. 'It's the wind claws I'm worried about,' he said. 'Saara is not an idiot and she could have figured out that this would be our next destination. Tiris, Arnon . . . Leith is the logical next stop.'

Glenwood knew little about the faithful of Jaa, aside from their legendary brutality, and was concerned at his companion's reaction.

'What's so special about wind claws?' he asked.

'Depends on your point of view,' replied the assassin. 'Al-Hasim's father was a wind claw – the greatest among them, apparently – and he was one of the nastiest men I ever met.'

'Does that make them any worse than Purple clerics?' Glenwood thought that the churchmen of nobility were as unpleasant as men could get.

'There's a line that the Purple won't cross. Whether they're misguided or not, they believe in the nobility of their god. The wind claws take the word of Jaa literally, which means they enjoy causing fear. If they're here guarding Isabel the Seductress, I may have to be creative.'

'I acknowledge that this may be a stupid question,' began Glenwood, 'but are their names chosen solely to sound scary, or can we expect some kind of . . . I don't know . . . seduction?'

'Not sure,' replied the assassin. 'I certainly didn't see any spiders with the Mistress of Spiders.' He bit his lower lip in thought. 'Though the last time I saw the Lady of Death, she was pretty dead.'

Both men burst out laughing, and for a moment Glenwood didn't hate Rham Jas quite so much. He even momentarily forgot about the need to turn him in. Strangely, the man of Leith would have had no compunction about turning in his companion to the clerics or watchmen, but it would feel strange if he had to betray him to these wind claws. Whatever else Kale Glenwood might be, he was still a Ro, and instinctively he disliked the Karesian presence in Ro Leith.

A movement caught his eye and Rham Jas suddenly became wary. On the far side of the tavern, two men had emerged from behind the bar and taken seats near the door. They were dressed well and were making an effort to appear relaxed, though something about the way the other patrons were regarding them made the man of Leith think they were not regulars in the establishment. Also, they had not come in through the tavern entrance.

'You see them?' he asked in a low voice.

Rham Jas nodded and placed his wine goblet further on to the table, allowing him to see the two men in its reflective surface without turning round.

'I do,' he replied. 'They're both armed and making an effort to appear unarmed . . . that, my dear Kale, is what we in the trade call *suspicious*.'

Glenwood was facing the men and took a sip of wine, surreptitiously sizing them up. Both men wore hard-wearing leather boots of military design and, although their clothing was common, it did not sit entirely comfortably on their shoulders.

Both were Ro and their weapons were hidden under long travelling cloaks – cloaks that were clean and showed no signs of recent use.

'Are they clerics?' he asked in a whisper.

'One is,' replied Rham Jas, returning to his ice-cool professional manner. 'The other is a watchman . . . maybe a sergeant, by the look of his hands.'

Glenwood frowned. 'His hands? How can you tell that?'

'Sword play is not kind on the hands, Kale. A cleric wears gloves or gauntlets, a luxury not afforded to common men. This man has scarred hands, which means he's been doing whatever it is he does for a while, hence, a sergeant.'

The forger nodded, reluctantly impressed by his companion's abilities. He tried to appear relaxed as he smiled and poured each of them another glass of wine. As he placed the bottle back on the table, the tavern door opened and three more men walked in.

'I've been stupid,' said Rham Jas with a grunt, watching the new arrivals in his wine goblet. 'Of course she'd have people in the town.' He chanced a look over his shoulder to the back of the tavern, trying to spot additional exits. 'Someone must have reported seeing a Kirin.'

The three men sat at the table opposite the cleric and the sergeant, making sure that both sides of the main door were covered. None showed any overt sign that they were there for Rham Jas, but even Glenwood could tell that these were not common folk looking for a drink. The tavern's other patrons were utterly oblivious – twenty or so people, sipping drinks and commenting on the weather, quite unaware that violence was likely to erupt in short order.

One of the newcomers was a Karesian, though his hood was covering half his face. The other two had scarred hands like the sergeant, though less pronouncedly so, and Glenwood thought they must be watchmen.

'I make that three watchmen, a cleric and a Karesian,' he said out of the side of his mouth.

'There'll be more outside,' replied Rham Jas, still not turning to look directly at the men who had entered. 'At both exits, most likely.'

Glenwood gulped and looked down to reassure himself that he still had his sword. Any chance of getting out of this situation with a reward was rapidly disappearing.

'Do you have a plan?' he asked.

Rham Jas had his hand inside his cloak, resting on the hilt of his katana, but otherwise looked calm. 'We can't fight them in here,' he said, his eyes flicking around the tavern.

'What do you mean *we*?'

'My dear Kale,' said the assassin, his grin returning, 'you are at best an accessory, at worst an accomplice. If I were you, I'd draw your sword when I draw mine and run when I run.'

Glenwood shook his head in resignation and rubbed the sweat from his eyes. 'Can you beat five men?' He suspected that the answer was no, but held out a slight hope that the assassin's gifts would stretch that far.

'We're in a crowded tavern. This presents certain logistical issues. Outside . . . I don't know, maybe. But we still need a way to escape.' He raised his eyebrows cheekily. 'Let's just hope the men outside don't have crossbows.'

'That is not reassuring,' grumbled Glenwood.

Just as Rham Jas was tensing his body in preparation for some kind of – no doubt impressive – combat manoeuvre, the Karesian stood up from his table and approached them. They looked up at the man and he greeted them with a suspicious smile. He motioned to an empty chair next to Glenwood.

'May I join you?' His accent was thick, indicating that he had not been in Tor Funweir very long.

'By all means,' replied the Kirin conversationally, still keeping half an eye on the others in the burnished surface of his wine goblet.

'You are Rham Jas Rami?' asked the Karesian as he sat down.

Glenwood noticed two wave-bladed knives sheathed across his chest and guessed that the man was a wind claw.

'No, I'm King Sebastian Tiris, you idiot,' was the barbed

response from the assassin. The comment was not delivered quietly, and now the other four men stood up and approached their table.

'I'll ask again,' said the wind claw. 'And your answer will determine how you are treated.'

Rham Jas grinned broadly at the Karesian and scanned around the tavern, more blatantly this time. The four men stood behind him, allowing their hidden weapons to be seen. The cleric – possibly Black, possibly Purple – was a tall man in his early forties, casually holding a longsword across his shoulders, whilst the three watchmen each had heavy maces.

Glenwood craned his neck upwards to see out of the tavern window. His breathing quickened as he saw a squad of watchmen with levelled crossbows, and several more wind claws, standing outside the main door.

'What's your name, wind claw?' asked the assassin, his hand still resting on his sword.

'I am called Kal Varaz and I am the right hand of Saara the Mistress of Pain.' The words were spoken proudly and there was a glint of mania in the Karesian's eyes.

Rham Jas chuckled and the wind claw looked offended. The assassin then took a deep drink of his wine. 'Well, if you ever make it back to Weir, tell the bitch that I'm going to kill her.' He threw his goblet directly into the Karesian's face.

Kal Varaz grabbed at his nose and fell backwards. Rham Jas sprang away from the table, causing two watchmen behind him to stumble on to the floor in an ungainly heap. The Kirin rolled to his feet, his katana whistling free of its scabbard.

The common folk in the tavern remained silent and watched with startled looks as the lightning-fast Kirin struck out. His katana sheared down into the head of a watchman and his right foot kicked the cleric solidly between the legs.

'Now's the time to drew that sword, Kale,' said Rham Jas breathlessly, as Kal Varaz pulled himself to his feet.

The two remaining watchmen attacked at once, using their maces with strength rather than skill, aiming at the Kirin's head.

Rham Jas ducked under the clumsy attacks and sliced one man across the chest before doing another forward roll to end up by the door.

Two of the watchmen were dead and the cleric was rolling around on the ground clutching his groin. Kal Varaz recovered quickly, but his nose had been broken by the goblet and, as he drew his two knives, he swayed unsteadily.

Glenwood drew his longsword and moved towards Rham Jas, while the remaining watchman tried to mount some kind of counter-attack. The man of Leith had not used his sword in a fight for many years and was dangerously out of practice. Rham Jas moved to engage Kal Varaz and Glenwood found himself facing the watchman.

He parried the first blow, but the shock that travelled up his arm nearly made him buckle. He parried the second blow more by luck than skill. As he saw Rham Jas kick Kal Varaz in the face, Glenwood felt his back touch the wood of the tavern door.

'Guards!' shouted the wind claw, spitting out blood. 'To me!'

Outside the tavern, the other watchmen and Karesians began to move forward.

Glenwood spun round, letting the watchman's mace strike the door. Remembering some of his lessons, he thrust hard at the man's side. The fountain of blood was a surprisingly pleasing sight as his blade bit deeply into the exposed midriff.

Before he could celebrate winning his duel, the door was kicked open and a heavy crossbow poked into the tavern. To his right, Rham Jas was keeping out of the way of Kal Varaz's knives and delivering a series of swift but shallow cuts around his chest and stomach. The crossbowman quickly took in the scene, moving his aim from Glenwood to the Kirin. Without really thinking, Glenwood shoved the man aside and caused the bolt to fire wild.

Then the remaining men rushed into the tavern. He darted backwards and vaulted over the bar to take cover behind the wooden counter, while Rham Jas disengaged and attempted to do the same. The man of Leith had been close to the bar, but the Kirin was quickly surrounded.

Crossbows were poor weapons against a man as fast as Rham Jas, but two bolts hit him nonetheless. The assassin winced as his thigh and shoulder were pierced, but he didn't appear to be hampered. He killed another watchman with an elegant thrust and spun round, delivering an impressive roundhouse kick to the head of a wind claw. Glenwood considered running out of the back of the tavern, but a quick look told him that another ten men were approaching and he'd likely find himself as isolated as the Kirin.

Kal Varaz stood back, allowing his men to surround Rham Jas. Tough as he might be, the assassin clearly could not best twenty men in tight quarters. The Kirin was crouched, keeping his katana loose in his hands, but with nowhere to move, he couldn't rely on his agility. Instead, he concentrated on defending himself. Glenwood looked on amazed as he parried, blocked, dodged and sidestepped, seeming almost to predict thrusts before they came and to avoid blows that would have killed any normal man.

The patrons had now mostly fled to a corner of the common room and were huddled behind upturned tables. The barman was crouched not far from Glenwood, holding a club protectively in front of his cash box as if this were a robbery of some kind. Glenwood poked his head round the bar and saw armoured men enter from all sides. They wore the green tabard of Leith over chain mail, and took up positions to cut off any chance of escape. Strangely, they paid no particular attention to the sweating forger behind the bar. The hatch to the tavern's wine store was just next to him and he was essentially unobserved.

'He's just a man . . . subdue him,' shouted Kal Varaz, as Rham Jas deliberately fell to the floor and whirled round, slicing through three men's legs, just below the knee. There was an instant when it looked as if the assassin might possibly escape, but then the cleric stood up. Glenwood didn't know who he was or why he was fighting alongside the wind claws, but as the pain of being kicked in the balls began to fade, he shoved two watchmen out of the way and attacked Rham Jas. It was now apparent that he was of the Black aspect, his eyes burning with malevolent fury.

'Elihas, we need him alive,' ordered Kal Varaz, as the cleric swung downwards at the Kirin.

Rham Jas raised his katana and parried the blow, but received a solid kick to the chest an instant later and another crossbow bolt in the back as he fell into a broken table. Then the watchmen were on him, kicking, punching and venting their frustration.

As he edged towards the hatch and silently exited the tavern, Glenwood was sure that Rham Jas was still alive. How long he would remain so was open to debate.

* * *

Glenwood couldn't get drunk, no matter how much alcohol he poured down his neck. He had wanted to be free of Rham Jas and he had wanted the annoying Kirin to suffer in some way, but his stomach was knotted and he couldn't get the assassin's bloodied face out of his mind.

He'd cleaned the blood from his sword in a fountain and wandered aimlessly around the fifth hill of Leith for several hours. None of the men that had come after Rham Jas had cared about the forger. The wind claw, Kal Varaz, had not spared more than a cursory look round the tavern before hauling the unconscious assassin away. Glenwood had watched him from the back of the establishment after having pulled himself out of the wine cellar.

He had tried to calm down, but even now, as he sat on a grassy verge with a bottle of Sixth Hill Reserve, he was a little dazed. It was getting dark and he had nowhere to stay and no idea of what to do. The fact that he'd chosen to get drunk within sight of the fourth hill, where the dungeons of Leith could be found, was testament to his confusion.

The fourth hill was one of the smallest, and the large stone structure that perched on top of it was probably the ugliest building in Ro Leith. It had been designed by a particularly militant knight marshal who had been attempting to replicate the look of a Red church barracks. He had succeeded admirably and the building was a squat, castellated lump, which contained hundreds of gaol cells.

Glenwood had casually wandered round the hill several times and had already identified the cell where Rham Jas had been taken, and the feeding trough that led to it. There was little he could do with this information but, on some level, he felt that by watching the dull light that emanated from the assassin's cell he would be empathizing with his companion's plight. In reality, this was horse-shit and all he wanted was to feel composed enough to return to Ro Tiris.

As he drained the last of his bottle of wine and settled back against a tree, Glenwood thought that the Kirin's twitchiness might be rubbing off on him. He had identified a dozen wind claws patrolling the base of the fourth hill and had noticed a slight blind spot in their guard pattern. If a man was so inclined, he could wait until one was out of sight and the other had not yet emerged, and simply walk past to reach the feeding troughs. Further to this, as the faithful of Jaa seemed only to be worried about the road, and not the troughs behind them, it was likely that a man could remain unobserved once past the perimeter.

The man of Leith smiled to himself and looked at the empty bottle in his hand. He was well aware that a slight dulling of his senses from alcohol was likely responsible for the sharpening of his criminal instincts and that, were he to enact his unwise plan, he would probably need another bottle first. Unfortunately, he didn't have one, and the forger silently chided himself for even considering so foolish a plan, rather than thanking his luck and leaving Ro Leith as quickly as possible.

The wind claws continued their patrol. As one of the warriors disappeared round the base on the fourth hill, Glenwood began counting down from ten. Without really thinking about it, he stood and ambled slowly away from the grassy verge and towards the street.

'Eight, seven,' he whispered to himself, stepping into the dark cobbled street.

'Six, five,' he continued, making his way off the road and towards the stone walls of the dungeon.

'Four, three,' he muttered, hoping his timing would be accurate and the shadows sufficient to conceal him.

'Two, one, zero.' Just as he said the last word to himself he reached the top of the feeding trough. He hugged the stone wall that extended from the outside wall of the dungeon and separated the various troughs. The sound of armoured feet began to rise again and he saw a second wind claw approach from the other direction and continue his patrol. A mixture of fear and elation flooded over the slightly drunk criminal. The faithful of Jaa would continue their patrol, oblivious to the fact that Glenwood was skulking in the darkness at the top of the sloped feeding trough.

At the bottom of the incline were solid steel bars and a dull glow of firelight. The troughs were an anachronism from the days when food had been thrown down to the prisoners. The knight marshal who had built the dungeon had done so with meticulous attention to detail, and with numerous unnecessary touches. It also had a large overhang above, from which, in ages past, criminals would have been hanged. These days, those judged worthy of death were given a slightly more dignified end.

There were voices coming from below, though he couldn't make out individual words and would have to climb further down in order to find out what was transpiring inside the Kirin's cell. With the taste of wine still on his lips, the forger slowly inched down the gradual incline. There was no light, except what came from below and he was well hidden beneath the overhang.

He stumbled several times, but used the sides of the trough to steady himself. Crouching down, he took up position to the side of the barred window. Rham Jas was hanging in the centre of the stone prison cell, his hands chained to the ceiling and his feet shackled to the floor. Next to him, in a corner of the room, was a chair with leather and metal restraints. Some kind of torture device, the like of which was not commonly used in Tor Funweir, Glenwood thought. A flaming brazier was positioned next to the chair and a well-tempered knife protruded upwards through the flames.

His wounds had disappeared completely, though his grin was gone too, and he wore only a small piece of cloth covering his groin area. The one scar remaining was on his left shoulder and looked to be from an old crossbow wound. He was muscled but wiry, and he looked pathetic hanging helplessly in the stone room. There were two people with him, keeping their distance as they spoke.

One was the Black cleric. He was now armoured in black plate and wore his longsword in a simple scabbard. The churchman of death had a haunted look in his eyes, though he exhibited none of the telltale euphoria that marked those under the sway of enchantment. Next to him, though, and wearing a figure-hugging red dress, was Isabel the Seductress. Glenwood had never seen her before, but her appearance was similar enough to Katja that she had to be one of the Seven Sisters. Her facial tattoo depicted an elaborate and beautifully designed coiled snake, though its beauty was somewhat diminished by the look of anger on the woman's face.

The criminal turned away from the barred window, remembering the assassin's advice to not look too long at one of the sisters.

'You will answer her question, Kirin,' said the Black cleric in a monotone rumble. 'Or you will suffer more pain than you can endure.'

There was a pained chuckle from Rham Jas. 'Why don't you get the bitch to enchant me? Oh, that's right, she can't.'

A silvery laugh emanated from the enchantress. Glenwood shook his head, desperately trying to remember that she was as malevolent as she was beautiful.

'My dear Rham Jas,' said Isabel, 'you do not know true suffering . . . not yet.'

There was silence for a moment. The assassin glared at the enchantress. She was clearly not used to this, as other men would never attempt to stare her down for fear of her entering their minds.

'I have nothing to say to you, bitch,' said the assassin, spitting on the floor. 'Just kill me, if you can.'

Another lyrical peal of laughter and Isabel stepped in closer.

'My lady,' said the Black cleric, 'be wary, he is a slippery foe.'

'I do not fear him,' she replied, running a single finger down the Kirin's chest. 'As he does not fear me.'

Her manner was deeply sensual – in keeping, Glenwood thought, with her title of Seductress.

'You will bend to my will, dark-blood, whether it takes an hour, a day or a year. You will become my devoted servant, with no mind of your own. You will think only of my pleasure . . . I will call you my pet.' She bit her lower lip and Glenwood felt a heat rise in his body. 'Now, I will ask again, where is the old-blood?'

Rham Jas narrowed his eyes and snarled at the enchantress. 'Fuck you!'

The cleric stepped forward and struck the Kirin across the jaw with a gauntleted fist, causing blood to spray from the side of his mouth.

'Hit me again, you fucking coward,' growled Rham Jas. 'Do it . . . hit me as hard as you can . . . the answer will be the same – fuck you.'

The Kirin's stubbornness was spectacular, but surely even the famous Rham Jas Rami would break under torture. Glenwood didn't know who the *old-blood* was, or why the enchantress referred to Rham Jas as *dark-blood*, but he was increasingly of the opinion that the Kirin assassin was the toughest man he'd ever known.

The Black cleric drew his sword and rested it against the prisoner's neck. 'I *can* kill you, you know,' he said in a dispassionate voice. 'It would be easy . . . just a slow cut across the neck and we could leave you here to bleed.'

Rham Jas grinned at the bulky cleric. 'Your name is Elihas, yes?'

The churchman nodded. 'I am Brother Elihas of Du Ban, Black cleric of the One God,' he replied formally.

'So tell me, Brother Elihas, have you officially converted to worship of the Dead God, or are you just on loan?' His grin was defiant.

'Silence,' roared Isabel, displaying her first real sign of agitation.

'Why?' retorted the assassin. 'What will you do to me if I refuse?'

Elihas struck him again, harder this time, causing the Kirin to spit out a globule of blood. 'Ouch,' he said out of the corner of his mouth.

'Where is Utha the Ghost?' shrieked the enchantress.

'Fuck you!' replied Rham Jas.

Brother Elihas drew back his foot and kicked the assassin squarely in the groin. The blow winded the Kirin and caused him to writhe uncomfortably in his hanging position, gritting his teeth in pain.

'Well, I won't be servicing your mother later,' he barked through a pained laugh.

Another kick to the groin and Rham Jas howled in pain.

'Harder, you fucking woman,' he shouted, though his eyes were now watering and a trickle of blood was running down his leg.

Just as Elihas drew his leg back a third time, Isabel stepped forward and placed a gently restraining hand on his armoured shoulder. 'Enough, my dear Elihas,' she said in a girlish voice.

The trickle of blood had stopped quickly and she narrowed her eyes. 'Do all the wounds you receive heal so swiftly?' she asked.

'Stab me in the face and we'll find out,' was the barbed response from the prisoner.

She chuckled and glanced over her shoulder to the chair in the corner of the cell. 'Do you know what *inching* is, my dear Rham Jas?'

The assassin clearly did know what it was, even if Glenwood did not, but he showed no particular fear of the word.

'I saw a man inched in Kessia,' replied the Kirin. 'Before I got kicked out for shooting one of your sisters in the face.'

'You've killed four of my sisters, dark-blood.' Isabel allowed a predatory curl to appear at the corner of her mouth, again revealing that she was not quite as calm as she wished to appear.

'True,' replied Rham Jas casually. 'One of them was a long time ago . . . Actually, now I think about it, I've killed two separate people called Lillian the Lady of Death. The name seems so apt.'

Isabel didn't change her expression as she slapped the Kirin in the face. It was not a heavy blow, and caused little damage, but it made Glenwood smile. Rham Jas could extract a reaction from the most controlled of people.

'Elihas, please transfer the prisoner to the chair,' said Isabel, a look of imperious mania in her eyes.

The Black cleric released the chain holding Rham Jas to the ceiling. His hands were still shackled and Elihas pulled on the chain to keep him subdued as he locked the leg-irons to the shackles. The assassin fell forward and let out a groan of pain as he struck the stone floor. In a moment, he was bent double with no room to move. He was then dragged across the floor and dumped in the large metal chair. His arms and legs were placed in leather and steel restraints, securely fastened to the chair. His head was wrenched back and held with a tight leather band, forcing him to sit upright.

'This is the most comfy I've been for hours,' said Rham Jas, trying to flex his neck and ease the soreness of being hung in chains.

Isabel walked round him, drumming her elegant fingers demurely on her chest. 'We found your daughter, you know?' she said quietly, causing the assassin instantly to become alert.

'Young Keisha was a pleasure slave in Rikara. She'd been servicing a pestilent merchant prince when my sister bought her.' The enchantress breathed in deeply and closed her eyes. There was pleasure on her face and she moved side to side in a sensual dance.

Rham Jas clenched his fists and tensed against his restraints. For the first time, Glenwood saw real doubt in the assassin's face, as if the news of his daughter was one of the few things that he feared. As he skulked at the bottom of the feeding trough and listened intently, the forger found himself surprised to hear that Rham Jas had children.

'She's alive?' asked the Kirin, without further bravado.

'She is . . . and she will remain so, as long as you behave,' replied Isabel, opening her eyes again and smiling with intense pleasure. 'We can be . . . excellent allies.' Walking round to stand in front of the assassin, she ran a seductive finger along his bare shoulders and down his chest. 'Perhaps you will even enjoy being my . . . ally.'

'I have enough friends,' replied Rham Jas.

'But only one daughter,' retorted Isabel. 'Do not let her die as you did your son. I saw Zeldantor at the end, you know.'

The Kirin bowed his head as best he could within his restraints and tears appeared in his eyes. His normal bravado was gone, replaced by the anguish of a father confronted with news of his child's death. He clenched and unclenched his fists, trying to remain calm. Glenwood thought the assassin would crack soon. It was emotion, rather than pain, that achieved the best results.

'Zeldantor and Keisha would understand,' said the Kirin, closing his eyes.

Isabel laughed once more, a beautiful sound that cut deeply into Glenwood's mind, causing him to turn away for a moment to gather his thoughts.

'Do you know, Rham Jas, in Kessia a skilled incher can command a great salary. The trick is to cut an inch, and only an inch.'

The forger turned back and saw Elihas take the red-hot knife from the brazier next to the chair. It was designed to hold the knife up into the flames so as to heat it evenly. The Black cleric had to reach under the flame to remove the blade from its sconce.

'I've only done this once,' said the cleric coldly.

'I'm going to kill you both,' replied the assassin, keeping his eyes closed and his teeth clenched.

The smoking knife was placed against his fingertips. Rham Jas howled in agony as an inch was removed from his left hand with a smooth, sawing cut. He'd lost the ends of three fingers, but Glenwood guessed that the procedure would not stop after the first inch.

'Do you think they will grow back?' asked Isabel, clapping her hands together excitedly as the Kirin struggled against his restraints. 'I'm sure you've not had the leisure to test your healing abilities.'

Rham Jas was shaking and his whole body tensed. Elihas of Du Ban cut a second inch from his fingers, levelling out the first cut and causing the tips to fall to the floor in a small pool of blood. The heat of the blade was not sufficient fully to seal the wounds and smouldering flesh clung to the knife.

'This is certainly better than my first attempt,' said Elihas, displaying no particular emotion.

'You are doing so very well,' said Isabel, in a sinister chuckle. 'Now, the third inch is when most people crack.'

Elihas placed his hand firmly on the assassin's wrist. Rham Jas closed his eyes. The blade was drawn across the back of his fingers and took the third inch, but this time he did not cry out. Instead, he shook violently as sweat poured down his torso.

'That one didn't even hurt,' he said, opening his bloodshot eyes.

Elihas placed the knife back in the fire, with the blade protruding up through the burning coals, and turned to the enchantress.

'Perhaps we should let the Kirin sit for a while . . . see if he can heal back his missing fingers.' He did not say it with any relish.

'An excellent idea,' replied Isabel, with a flutter of her eyelashes. The two of them regarded the shaking prisoner. Both tried to make eye-contact but Rham Jas stubbornly refused to meet their gaze, and then they left the cell.

Glenwood sat at the bottom of the feeding trough, to the side of the barred window and, as he leant back heavily against the stone, he felt as if he were about to vomit. The mania of the enchantress, the indifference of the cleric, to say nothing of the smell of seared human flesh – his stomach twisted into knots and he had to exert all his willpower not to be violently sick.

Through the barred window, he could see Rham Jas, the man

he had thought he hated more than anyone else in the world. But having heard of his children and seen him tortured in such a fashion, he began to doubt his hatred.

Rham Jas shook and sweat ran over his near-naked body. Without knowing that he was being watched, the assassin wept uncontrollably.

'I'm sorry, Keisha . . . I'm so sorry,' he sobbed to himself.

CHAPTER SIX

FALLON OF LEITH
IN THE REALM OF SCARLET

THE TENT WAS kept on the eastern edge of the camp. Since the arrival of Tristram, Mobius and the king, Fallon had not been permitted to leave his makeshift prison and had only three bound men for company.

Brother Jakan had been most insistent that the captive be executed at the earliest opportunity. However, Commander Tristram had not listened to the whingeing idiot and had decided to deal with Fallon once South Warden was secured. The crime of blasphemy had been levelled at him. That was code for having pissed off a Purple cleric. There were plenty of witnesses and little chance he'd escape execution, even with his men supporting him and Tristram's reluctance to see him executed. Theron and Ohms had been loyal to their captain and insisted that Jakan had goaded him, though Mobius had quickly dismissed this and sided with his fellow cleric.

Fallon had been moved with the army towards South Warden. He'd been placed on a horse and closely guarded by a squad of bound men as the lumbering force of armoured men made their way through the realm of Scarlet. Once the Moon Woods had come into sight, Tristram had ordered the Darkwald yeomanry to take up a picketed position across the grassy plain, while the engineers constructed trebuchets and the knights readied themselves for a siege.

Fallon knew all this from his knowledge of combat tactics, rather than from anyone talking to him. His men had been forbidden from contacting him and he had only soldiers' gossip and his intuition to tell him what was occurring.

He'd been stripped of his armour and sat, with his hands shackled behind his back, looking through the billowing tent entrance at the sprawling military camp outside. Ten thousand yeomanry and five thousand knights. It was a force to rival any that the lands of men could muster and one of the largest armies of which Fallon had ever been a part. He'd even heard rumours that the Red cardinal, Knight General Malaki Frith, was on his way from Arnon. If this proved true, King Sebastian was gathering the bulk of his army, leaving only the local garrisons to police Tor Funweir. The ranks of watchmen and the army of Ro Haran would not be coming, but they were inadequate to face the hounds of Karesia, who were apparently swarming across the lands of Ro.

Strangely, Fallon had not wavered in his conviction since he had been arrested. If anything, he was even more concerned with his personal honour now. It was as if taking the first step – as Jakan had said, *crossing the line* – had made continued insubordination easier. He had stubbornly decided that he was not going to continue killing men who had not wronged him. The Ranen were simple people and did not deserve the death that was coming to them. For Fallon, to be given an order was no longer enough, and he didn't care if his honour got him killed.

The tent flap was pushed inwards and Knight Commander Tristram marched in with angry eyes and gritted teeth. He waved away the bound men. 'Go and have some food. I need to speak with this fool.' They saluted and left, making sure Fallon's restraints were securely fastened before they did so.

Tristram sat opposite the Red knight and leant forward, resting his chin on his fist. 'How can one man cause so many problems without actually having killed anyone?' he asked. 'Most people I execute at least have the good sense to have done something violent. All you did was stop a turncoat from dying.'

'I disagreed with a Purple cleric; is that so bad?' asked Fallon, but not in any great hurry to talk his way out of execution. 'I've killed thousands of men, but you arrest me when I save someone's life . . . Doesn't that seem a little stupid to you?'

'What happened to you? Verellian was a good man, but he's not worth dying for.' Tristram had been told exactly what had happened before and after the duel and had dismissed any talk of honour as naive and foolish. 'So he had a spiritual awakening in Ro Hail . . . any way you paint it, the man betrayed his oath. By letting him escape, you aided a vow-breaker.'

'So execute me,' said Fallon defiantly.

'You know I can't,' barked the commander. 'If I kill Sir Fallon of Leith, how do you think the other knights will take it? They're angry at being so far from home anyway and most of them respect you . . . as they respected Verellian.'

'A month ago you told me that Mobius could have me killed if he wanted. What's changed?' Fallon gathered that certain things had occurred since he had left Hail. He'd heard whispered talk of the king falling into madness.

Tristram looked at the grass under his feet and frowned. 'I just want to get this campaign done and take these men home.'

'And the Ranen?' asked Fallon.

'If bombarding them with big rocks means we can get out of the Freelands sooner, then that's what I'll do.' He reached behind him and parted the tent flap, indicating that Fallon look off to the left. 'Twenty trebuchets, ready and sighted,' said the knight commander. 'We start the bombardment when the sun goes down and, hopefully within a few weeks, we can fuck off back to Tor Funweir . . . maybe leaving some of the yeomanry as an occupying force.'

Fallon raised an eyebrow and shifted his shoulders to sit more comfortably with shackled hands. 'You honestly believe that?' he asked. 'That this will end with South Warden?'

'It's not your place to ask these questions, captain,' snapped Tristram. 'You are a knight of the Red.'

Fallon bowed his head and breathed in deeply. He had said the same thing to William of Verellian. Just as his old commander had, the young knight knew the answer. 'Not any more . . . I don't think I can be,' he said quietly.

Knight Commander Tristram stood and glared at his subordinate. He opened his mouth several times, as if he had something to say, but only after a few moments of thought did he speak. 'You're going to hang, Captain Fallon. When South Warden is secure, I will have no choice but to string you up.' He didn't wait for a response, just banged his fist against his breastplate in salute and left the tent.

Fallon watched him leave and, as the commander disappeared into the sea of red banners, the trebuchets once again came into view. He wasn't sure which concerned him more, his impending execution or the upcoming assault on South Warden.

He felt for Lord Vladimir Corkoson and the Darkwald yeomanry, men who had been pressed into service and who likely cared even less for their orders than Fallon. He liked the Lord of Mud and hoped that he'd keep his mouth shut, carry out his orders, and return to the Darkwald with only a few men lost. At least the knights of the Red had the luxury of blind obedience to fall back on, a gift not enjoyed by the commoners of the yeomanry.

Fallon had never liked the idea of men being bound to fight when their lord commanded it. Those bound to the Red were normally violent idiots who liked to play at war and to bully others, whereas the yeomanry of Darkwald and Hunter's Cross were common men, forced to serve for fear of having their homes annexed by the crown and their way of life destroyed. At least, as occasional soldiers, they could return home to their vineyards and farms and forget about Tor Funweir until they were called upon next time.

He wished he could change things. He wished that Tristram would see reason and that the brave men outside would not be forced to kill an enemy that had done them no wrong. It was his only wish and, as he tried to get comfortable in his canvas prison, he did not feel like praying to the One. Not any more.

Fallon didn't often dream. Verellian used to say that, once a man had killed more than a hundred enemies, his brain would stop letting them escape into his dreams. It was a theory to which the man from Leith had never given much thought. He had become pragmatic over the years to the point where the vagueness of dreams and omens was just a long-forgotten indulgence. However, as he stole a few hours' sleep before the bombardment of South Warden began, Fallon fell into a deep and contemplative slumber that forced him into the world of dreams.

He was back in Ro Arnon, treading the dusty training grounds of the Red cathedral and looking at the rusted black sceptre of nobility that dominated the skyline. He was not alone, though the other knights around him were faceless and did not acknowledge the dreamer. It was a warm day – early afternoon, by the sun – and Fallon was wearing his full dress uniform. His red cloak was clean, his helm had its entire plume intact, and his armour was spotless.

He strode up to the statue that dominated the grounds, a Red knight facing a Purple cleric. He remembered it well. He looked at the two stone figures, each gripping the other's forearm in a warrior's salute, and felt strangely hollow.

The plinth displayed the inscription, *where war and nobility meet, honour will be found*. This had been the original motto of the Purple clerics back in the days when being noble was more important than being *a* noble. Fallon had not seen a man of the Purple with the slightest hint of true nobility, much less honour, for many years.

'Why did you not pray?' said a voice, coming from far away. The accent was Ro, but the echoing tones conveyed a depth of intent that made Fallon toss and turn in his sleep. 'Your end is near, surely you turn to God in these moments?'

The dream changed and the training ground fell away until the knight captain was standing on grass. He looked around and saw an army of Red knights before him and the forward battlements of

South Warden at his back. He was no longer dressed as a knight and the sword in his hand was not his own.

He could feel that the speaker was still present.

'Prayer just makes me bitter. Good men die, foolish men prosper . . . and the One has no place here.'

At these words the ground shook and the army of knights charged. Fallon did not feel in any danger, but he could sense that whoever had spoken was angry. He watched the multitude of red tabards plunge across the grass towards him, but did not flinch until, at the last moment, they froze in place. Before him, arrayed across the plains of Scarlet, were thousands of knights, each one as still as a statue, with rage in their faces.

'Tell me, knight,' said the voice, 'do you know why the Purple clerics were formed?'

Each word made Fallon's head throb.

'The nobles of the One,' he responded, wincing. 'The highest order of cleric . . . those who would be lords over all others.'

'No!' roared the speaker, making Fallon drop to his knees and cry out in pain. 'That is what men have made them.'

The dreamscape shifted again and he found himself in Ro Canarn. The city had just fallen and the inner keep was full of knights and bound men. William of Verellian was escorting Magnus Forkbeard up to the great hall to see the execution of Duke Hector. Fallon couldn't see himself, but he knew that he'd be there somewhere, probably complaining at the mercenaries' treatment of the captive population.

'What do you want from me?' he asked skywards, looking at the crossed longsword banner that hung above Canarn. 'I'm just a man.'

'You are a knight of the Red,' replied the speaker.

He couldn't argue or even respond and his head began to burn with the enormity of the voice speaking to him.

'You follow those of nobility *and* honour. The Purple clerics were intended to have both.'

'Who are you?' The words spluttered out and the knight saw

354

a distant vision of a cleric, standing in plate armour and wearing a tabard of nobility.

'I am the shade of Brother Torian of Arnon,' replied the speaker, 'and you are the exemplar of the One.'

* * *

When he awoke, his mouth was dry and he had a headache. He didn't feel the slightest bit rested and the dream stayed with him in more vivid detail than he would have thought possible. He knew the name he'd heard, but he had not seen Brother Torian since his youth in Ro Arnon and only vaguely remembered the cleric's face. They had never spoken, and Fallon did not know what had become of Torian.

It was coming on night-time now and, as Fallon pondered his dream, he felt even more content with his decision to save Verellian and defy Jakan. He had been allowed to sit at the entrance to his tent and watch the spectacle outside. As soon as the sun went down, the trebuchets had begun their bombardment and now, with the coming of darkness, they had been hurling boulders at South Warden for three hours. The army was in high spirits, with few duties to attend to other than watching the engineers annihilate the wooden stockade of the city. There was much good-natured banter from the Darkwald yeomanry, who were expecting a quick victory.

He had seen Vladimir Corkoson march back and forth across the lines and had, on a few occasions, tried to attract the Lord of Mud's attention. Of all those present, Fallon felt that the lesser noble of the Darkwald would be the best person to talk to about his dream. Without Verellian to confide in, the newly faithful knight found himself seeking additional counsel. It had only been a dream, but Fallon couldn't shake the feeling that something had changed. He knew that he was the exemplar of the One, but he did not yet know what that meant – only that it meant everything, and that his honour was the only armour he needed.

He turned back to the city of Scarlet Company and observed that the Ranen had built South Warden well. It contained gates and killing grounds designed to snare an invading army. From this distance, Fallon could not make out any of the city's defenders, but he guessed that they would not have been prepared for the range of the Ro siege equipment and had chosen to stay under cover, hoping for a chance to meet their attackers face to face.

Scarlet Company had a reputation as fearsome warriors and, given the chance to swing their axes, they would surely cause a dent in the king's army. Unfortunately, following the strategy of Cardinal Mobius, the army of Ro was not offering the Ranen a target to aim at or an enemy to fight. They had catapults mounted on the western defences, but the Ranen heavy weaponry did not have the range to reach the army massed on the plains of Scarlet. They simply had to wait out the bombardment.

Fallon's unit was nowhere to be seen and he guessed that they were stationed at the far end of the lines to keep them away from their captain. Though he had gained a new respect for Theron, he doubted that his loyalty would stretch to a rescue. The bond between knights was strong and they would remain his men until the end, an end that was rapidly approaching. If he did manage to escape, he felt that his knights should not have their reputations tarnished by assisting him – not that escape seemed possible, and he wondered why the shade of Torian should have appeared to him now, when he was of little use to the One God.

More rocks were hurled and Fallon's attention was drawn back to reality. He could hear the distant sound of screaming and saw jubilant knights chanting death to the Ranen. Across the plains, the trebuchets had breached the outer walls and killed a number of warriors within. Purple clerics were shouting boisterous prayers, and Mobius himself stood on a raised dais facing the front. The cardinal was slightly manic as he led his clerics in raucous prayer. The king was nowhere to be seen, but his bodyguard, Cleoth Montague, was standing next to Mobius, joining in the prayers. Fallon felt uncomfortable listening to the nobles of the One, their words tinged with the same hollowness he had sensed in his dream.

His head began to throb again and the presence of Brother Torian entered his mind. He was not asleep, and the shade's face came from all around him, but very much in the real world. 'Am I supposed just to watch this?' asked the Red knight, without taking his eyes from the Purple clerics.

'You are supposed to act as your honour dictates,' replied Torian's shade. 'You are not alone and it is not your destiny to die in a tent.'

An ironic smile appeared on Fallon's face. 'You can't be a Purple cleric, you made me laugh,' he said.

'I am the memory of a Purple cleric, and you are the first churchman of the One to glimpse a long-forgotten truth, that nobility without honour is meaningless.'

'Tell that to him,' replied Fallon, nodding towards Mobius.

'The cardinal's will is not his own. He follows another.' Torian's shade spoke with anger and a deep sense of regret.

'The Seven Sisters,' said the knight in a growl.

'This army does not march under the banner of the One,' replied the shade. 'It unknowingly follows another god, a Forest Giant of pleasure and blood.'

'And I'm a man in a tent with no sword,' said Fallon drily, gazing out at fifteen thousand armed men. 'Maybe I'll just bide my time. I might sneak up on them unawares.'

Knight Commander Tristram was not joining in the boisterous praying but stood with his senior staff just outside his command pavilion, directing the bombardment of key points of the Ranen defences. The outer gates had gone and splintered wood was strewn across the first killing ground. The trebuchets were now concentrating their fire on the second gate.

The distant screaming had grown louder. Men wailed in pain and anguish, moving dead and broken bodies from the shattered gates. Several of the Ranen catapults fired hopelessly on to the plains of Scarlet in a gesture of pure frustration. A series of concentrated volleys directed at the second gate left the city of South Warden looking dangerously exposed. The two wooden palisades were now in a splintered heap, leaving a wide avenue undefended. Men moved across the empty space. Shields were raised and an attempt was made to plug the gap with hastily moved carts and wooden beams.

The men of Scarlet were distant, but the Red knights still jeered at them, shouting oaths of death across the dark plains of Ranen. Torches moved along lines of knights, creating a striking background to the army as it began to sense victory. After a few moments the bombardment stopped and the breach in South Warden's defences was, to Fallon's eyes, wide enough for a frontal assault.

A horn was blown from the centre of the lines and Fallon turned sharply to see King Sebastian Tiris emerge from his tent. The knights stopped shouting. Cleoth Montague and a unit of king's guardsmen escorted the monarch to the raised platform occupied by Cardinal Mobius.

Vladimir Corkoson was now close to Fallon's tent and the Lord of Mud looked both concerned and angry at what he was witnessing. Whatever orders Brother Jakan had given the yeomanry, they were not well received. The common folk of Darkwald had been instructed by their Purple cleric commander to form up in ordered ranks before the raised dais and behind the line of trebuchets. They were ordered beyond the knights, and Fallon experienced a sinking feeling as he recognized the telltale build up for a frontal assault.

'My knights . . . my yeomanry,' shouted the king in a cracked and manic voice.

The Purple clerics banged their fists on their steel breastplates and loudly saluted their king. The knights of the Red were less enthusiastic and Fallon again heard whispered words concerning the monarch's state of mind.

The shade of Torian appeared next to him. Bathed in dull firelight was a fully armoured cleric, resplendent in the regalia of nobility. The shade shone brighter than the other Purple clerics, but was unseen by all but Fallon.

'Should I just go and kill him?' asked Fallon, only half-intending it as a joke.

'That would accomplish little beyond your death, exemplar.' The reply echoed with an intensity that again made Fallon wince in pain. 'You must wait.'

'I'm getting impatient and, without a sword, I'm of little use to you . . . or the One.' He was growing angry. The spectacle of arrogant rhetoric and bloodlust going on before him was about to cost a lot of men their lives, both Ro and Ranen.

The king stepped to the front of the dais and, flanked by Mobius and Tristram, drew a highly ornamental longsword. 'This night, we take back our land from these peasants and lesser men.'

He gestured to Brother Jakan, who was standing off to the side with Vladimir Corkoson. The Purple cleric was staring with righteous fervour as King Sebastian called him forward. He was wearing full dress armour and the purple sceptre on his tabard had been replaced since his duel with Verellian.

'Your forces will have the honour of striking the first blow at the enemy, Brother Jakan,' the king announced in a virtual shriek. 'The breach lies before you . . . let the men of Darkwald take the first blood of the battle.'

'It shall be done, my king,' responded Brother Jakan. 'We will kill these peasants and lesser men in your name.'

'. . . and in the name of the One.' The king's eyes were wide and bloodshot.

The Darkwald yeomanry comprised ten thousand men, divided into companies of five hundred. They carried spears and maces, with the occasional crossbow or sword. Their armour was chain mail and of inferior quality compared with the breastplates of the knights. It was strange that they were being sent into the breach, and stranger still that only four companies were being committed to the first assault.

The two thousand soldiers shook with nerves as Brother Jakan ordered them to stand to attention in front of the rest of the army. The Lord of Mud was highly agitated and Fallon could see him angrily insisting that he be allowed to speak to Commander Tristram. His complaints were rebuffed and Corkoson could only stand by as his captains were ordered forward.

'There are some very clever military minds out there,' Fallon said to Torian's shade. 'So why are they letting an idiot child like Sebastian Tiris decide the strategy?'

'You presume they have a choice,' was the shade's unhelpful response.

'Two thousand auxiliaries have no chance at that breach. They need a slow advance to take the ground inch by inch, not a frontal assault.'

Fallon noted that Jakan was not intending to lead the four companies of yeomanry into South Warden. The cleric of nobility now sat astride a horse and was delivering empty words of encouragement to his new command – ill-chosen rhetoric about their service to the One God and their responsibility to Tor Funweir.

Through the press of knights, yeomen and clerics, Fallon caught sight of Knight Lieutenant Theron. He was at the rear of the column, on guard duty. He and Sergeant Ohms were standing casually in front of a small tent that housed a number of yeomen who had been caught drinking or sleeping on duty. Fallon's unit looked bored and decidedly unimpressed at having been given such a mundane duty.

'At least Theron won't have to watch the men of Darkwald get slaughtered,' said the imprisoned knight, mostly to himself.

'This night will contain much slaughter, exemplar,' replied Torian's shade, 'and you will have to watch.'

He began to respond, but a horn blew from the centre of the column and the four companies of yeomanry advanced. They moved quickly, crossing the plains of Scarlet as fast as they could to avoid any possible assault from South Warden's catapults. The companies were disorganized and spearmen mingled with crossbowmen and standard bearers in no kind of recognizable formation. As they came into range of the Ranen catapults, several volleys caught the massed ranks of yeomanry and men fell before they had reached the outer walls. The sound of the advance grew indistinct as they moved beyond the first shattered gate and were into the narrow breach.

A moment of relative silence, then roars of defiance erupted from the Ranen. The defenders rushed from positions of cover and attacked the yeomanry from three sides at once. It was a brutal but effective strategy, which forced the common men of Darkwald into a bottleneck where they could be hacked to pieces by the axes of Scarlet Company. In moments, the shattered companies began to fall back. It was not an easy retreat and most simply ran into their own advancing men. They met a swift end as the Ranen continued their flanking attacks, cutting a path through the disorganized yeomanry and boxing them in.

'Pull them back,' shouted Vladimir Corkoson, his face livid with rage. He gestured wildly at Brother Jakan and jostled the Purple clerics around him to get closer to the command dais.

'Silence, my lord,' replied Cardinal Mobius, raising a hand and dismissing the Lord of Mud. He turned manic eyes back towards the walls of South Warden. 'They will die in sight of the One.'

'Fuck the One,' roared Vladimir. 'Those are my men, I won't see them slaughtered like this.' His words were not well chosen and a dozen Purple clerics surrounded him with drawn swords.

Fallon turned back to the city, where he could make out a handful of yeomanry limping away from the breach. The Ranen did not harry their retreat but melted away into their places of concealment.

'Lord Corkoson, your blasphemy will not be tolerated,' screamed Cardinal Mobius, his face eerily like that of the king. 'My clerics, detain the Lord of Mud.'

Vladimir thought about resisting, but he was not a warrior and, faced with a guard of Purple churchmen, the lord of Darkwald had no choice but to submit. The yeomanry showed their displeasure as Vladimir's sword was removed and his hands shackled, but a few stern words from Brother Jakan silenced them. The commanders exchanged looks with their lord, but Vladimir waved them down.

'Stay your hand, exemplar . . . it is not yet your moment,' said Torian's shade.

'They'll kill him for that,' replied Fallon.

'Your allies assemble,' was the cryptic response from the shade.

Vladimir was relieved of his armour and dragged towards the dais. Cardinal Mobius and the king looked down arrogantly at the lesser noble. Cleoth Montague drew his longsword and stepped on to the grass. With a grunt, he kicked Corkoson in the leg so that he dropped to his knees.

'You kneel before your betters,' shouted the king's bodyguard.

'My betters?' asked Vladimir incredulously. 'My betters have just caused the death of hundreds of my men . . . what am I meant to do?' He was evidently in pain, rubbing his leg.

As the retreating column of yeomanry made it back to their lines, the king ordered Cleoth to deliver a beating to the Lord of Mud. The Purple cleric struck him around the head and chest with the hilt of his longsword and seemed to be enjoying it more with each blow. Any member of the yeomanry that moved to intercede was prevented by an armed cleric.

'I will not hear defiance from one of my own lords,' shrieked the king. 'This is my land. I will take it from any man who thinks to defy me.' His manner was that of a petulant child.

Corkoson was bloodied now and lay face-down on the grass. Cleoth Montague had ceased beating him and returned to stand next to the king on the raised dais, while the Lord of Mud was pulled upright by other clerics.

'Would anyone else defy me?' shouted King Sebastian, a look of wild insanity in his eyes. 'I will raze your homes and massacre your people if you raise one hand to stop my righteous campaign. I am the king!' The words were directed at the Darkwald yeomanry. They were far from home and, with no lord to speak for them, were at the mercy of the deranged monarch. If they were to resist or to refuse Jakan's orders, they would surely be executed without the benefit of a trial – or would return home to find the Darkwald a smoking ruin.

362

Knight Commander Tristram, who had been at the far end of the lines, directing the bombardment, now approached the dais with several knight captains. The other Red knights followed his path towards the Lord of Mud with anticipation on their faces.

'Step aside,' Tristram said to the clerics surrounding Vladimir.

'What is the meaning of this, my knight?' demanded King Sebastian.

'I am your humble servant as always, your grace, but Lord Corkoson should be imprisoned to await sentencing.' Tristram approached the monarch and said, loud enough for all to hear, 'His trial and execution should take place once the city is secure and all men can see the justice of the One . . . and your wisdom in executing him for blasphemy.'

Tristram was being very clever.

Sebastian Tiris considered his words, placing a hand on the knight's shoulder. 'Of course, my knight, your counsel is wise as always. Brother Cleoth Montague, take the Lord of Mud to a holding tent to await our justice.'

'Please allow me, my king,' said Tristram.

The knight commander directed men to pick up Vladimir and carry him away from the dais. 'Put him with Fallon, they'll have ample time to lament each other's lack of honour and wisdom.' Through the massed warriors, Fallon thought he detected a shallow nod from his former commander.

'Show's over, lads,' shouted Tristram to the assembled knights and yeomanry.

The remainder of the four companies now melted back into the army and medical attention was given to the wounded, many of whom had lost limbs and hastily discarded their weaponry as they ran from the defenders. The rest of the common folk looked fearful, but Fallon could sense no imminent threat of rebellion among their ranks. The king's words clearly still rang in their ears.

A knight of the Red threw Vladimir down at the tent entrance, where he was picked up by one of the bound men and brought within.

'At least give him some water and a cloth to clean himself up,' said Fallon. 'He's a mess.'

'Should have kept his mouth shut, then, shouldn't he?' was the guard's caustic response.

Torian's shade had disappeared. The apparition had been strikingly real and the captive knight felt it strange that he had not for one moment questioned the shade's words. He had trusted Torian and, as he moved across to help Vladimir into a seated position, Fallon found himself at peace with his honour.

'You'll be okay,' he said reassuringly.

'Really?' the other wheezed. 'Because it feels like the bastard broke a few things that I like to keep intact . . . my nose, my jaw . . . my ears. How has he managed to make my ears hurt?'

'He smacked you in the side of the head with his sword hilt, your ears will ring for a while.' Fallon had received most kinds of wounds himself and knew that the beating Vladimir had suffered would not leave any permanent damage other than a few ugly-looking scars.

'That royal cunt is going to kill all my men, isn't he?' asked Vladimir, wincing in pain.

Fallon considered the question. 'I don't know. It depends how long the Ranen can hold out and whether Tristram can employ proper strategic thinking. The problem is Jakan. The man's an idiot. He couldn't organize a frontal assault on your cock.'

Vladimir spat out blood and tested a few of his loosened teeth. 'I hurt,' he said wearily. 'Don't suppose there's anything to drink around here?'

'Unless you can get drunk on righteous horse-shit, I think you're out of luck,' replied Fallon.

The Lord of Mud chuckled. 'Don't make me laugh, Sir Fallon, it hurts.' He pulled himself up some more and looked out of the tent flap. 'They're forming up for another assault, aren't they?'

'Looks like,' replied the former knight of the Red, 'and don't call me *sir*.'

'Ah, yes, that's right, we are two traitors together . . . at least you can drink now . . . thank the One and all that.'

Even as a battered and bruised prisoner of the king, Vladimir took a philosophical view of the world which Fallon found refreshing. Unfortunately, ironic humour would neither save the lives of his men nor keep his own neck from being stretched at the end of a rope once South Warden was taken.

'What do we do?' asked Vladimir.

Fallon leant forwards and tried his best to smile. 'We wait,' he said quietly. 'I'm afraid that's the best I've got.'

Vladimir scanned the lines of Darkwald yeomanry. Another four companies had formed up and again Brother Jakan was delivering a rhetorical speech about duty to the house of Tiris and the honour of dying for the One.

'Do I have any options that won't get me summarily executed?' asked Vladimir. 'It's probably best that you tell me now before I get so drunk I try to piss on the king.'

'You can wait . . . like me,' replied Fallon.

'Has anyone ever told you that you're rather poor company when you're charged with blasphemy,' said the lesser noble.

'It's hard to fathom how to react when you've turned your back on the only thing you've ever known,' replied the man of Leith. 'I suppose I respond by being laconic and miserable.'

'It suits you,' replied the Lord of Mud. 'But if it's all the same to you, I'll respond by getting drunk.' He looked round the tent and turned up his nose. 'There must be some alcohol in this camp, somewhere . . . You,' he barked at one of the men standing guard, 'get me some booze.'

The bound man didn't know how to react. He frowned and looked at the man standing beside him. 'I don't think we're allowed –'

'I'd get him some booze if I were you,' interjected Fallon. 'He's still a noble, and he clearly needs a drink.'

'And this is Sir Fallon of Leith,' said Vladimir. 'Apparently, he's a tough bastard . . . could probably fillet you two with his fingernail.'

The guards exchanged glances.

'Booze,' shouted the Lord of Mud. 'Now!'

The sudden note of command in Vladimir's voice made them move to do as they were told. The first man scanned round the supply wagons and walked over to a crate of bottles, whilst his fellow had spied a barrel by the entrance to a pavilion.

'Is that a magic power of some kind?' asked Fallon. 'Or just an innate ability to get a drink whenever you need it?'

'They're idiots. Easily swayed when they hear someone order them around.' Vladimir frowned, touching the parts of his body that had borne the brunt of Cleoth Montague's assault. The wiry noble was obviously not used to being in pain and his jaw and neck were badly swollen.

'I'd like to make some kind of bold statement of allegiance, my friend, but all I can think to say is that I want to go home,' said Vladimir, flexing his neck and emitting a deep-throated cough.

'I feel further away from home than I ever have,' replied Fallon wearily. He had made an effort of late to appear calm and collected, even while his world was falling apart. Now, as a prisoner accused of blasphemy, Fallon simply felt tired.

'You're from Leith, yes?' asked Vladimir.

'I've not been back there for a long time, but yes, originally . . .' He disliked remembering his home and had long ago decided that it was easier to think of himself as belonging to the Red church. 'I just remember trees . . . lots of trees.'

'I went there once,' said the Lord of Mud, 'to visit some winery or other. They wanted to know why the soil in the Darkwald makes the best wine and offered a cartload of coin for the secret.' He smiled. 'I'm not sure they understood when I said it was all about luck.'

Fallon narrowed his eyes. 'Your wine made you a lord . . . that's a claim to nobility few men can boast of.'

'Your sword arm made you a knight. Is that any different? Either way it's luck . . . or an accident of birth if you prefer.'

Vladimir craned his neck and beckoned one of the bound

men back to the tent. The man carried two bottles of mead and hesitantly passed them through the tent flap.

The Lord of Mud pulled out the cork with his teeth and offered the bottle to Fallon. 'Your first drink in . . . how long?'

He took the bottle. 'There was a night in Arnon, maybe four years ago, just after Verellian was made captain. We sneaked out of the barracks and got drunk in a yard behind a brothel.' Fallon smiled, remembering the incident. 'It was the most rebellious I ever saw him.' He licked his lips and took a deep swig of mead. 'Nice,' he said, passing the bottle back.

'It'll do,' replied Vladimir, taking his own drink.

A horn sounded from outside and the captives looked out on to the darkened plains of Scarlet. The Darkwald yeomanry had moved beyond the rest of the army and formed up. They moved reluctantly, pushed forward by Brother Jakan and stumbling over their weapons.

'So, what do we do?' asked the Lord of Mud.

Fallon rubbed his eyes and his head began to hurt. Torian's shade was not present and the tired knight thought he must simply have a headache. After all that had happened since he first came to the Freelands of Ranen, all he wanted to do was sleep.

'We're an army of two . . . for now, we watch,' he replied.

PART TWO

CHAPTER SEVEN

BROTHER LANRY OF CANARN
IN THE CITY OF SOUTH WARDEN

A BROWN CLERIC of poverty was not supposed to see this. Standing with Al-Hasim, beyond the third gate of South Warden, he could see an entire army of his countrymen laying siege to the city he'd done his best to protect.

Now that Lady Bronwyn had departed, travelling north with Micah Stone Dog and Dragneel Dark Crest, he was the only Ro left. He tried hard to ignore the sideways glances and thinly disguised glares of the men and women of Scarlet Company. Their distaste at his presence was easy to understand. He wished he could simply wander out to the clerics and Red knights and make them understand there was a better way, a more peaceful way, a way that did not conflict with his own well-defined set of morals.

The first wave of attackers, sent in disorganized fashion after the second gate had been destroyed by trebuchets, had been repulsed quickly by the tough warriors of Scarlet and Wraith. Brother Lanry recognized the banner of Darkwald and guessed that King Sebastian was prepared to throw away his auxiliary forces to secure a quick victory.

'Why don't the knights attack?' asked the Karesian scoundrel standing next to him.

Al-Hasim had been a friend of Lord Bromvy and Lanry had been advised to trust him. The Karesian had not joined the defenders at first, staying out of sight with the bulk of their forces while Johan Long Shadow committed only those necessary to repulse the assault.

'Because they're not expendable, I suppose,' replied Lanry. 'Think of the yeomanry as a way to soften us up before the elite warriors attack.'

Al-Hasim shook his head in disapproval. 'So, the common folk do the bulk of the dying? Your king has a strange way of making war. The Ro tell anyone who'll listen about their amazing military skill but, when it comes to battle, they throw boulders at us and send in untrained militia.'

Both men looked down at the killing ground exposed between the first and second walls of the city. The grass was stained red and hundreds of Darkwald yeomanry lay dead amongst the splintered wood of South Warden. It had taken a relatively small force of Free Company men to repulse them and, after filtering them into a small channel, the Ro auxiliaries had had little chance of survival.

'Charging that breach is suicide,' said Al-Hasim.

Lanry tried his best to smile as he smoothed back his grey hair. 'Those men are with the One now. They can get a drink and a warm bed in the stone halls beyond the world. Their earthly bodies are spent and they can rest.'

The Karesian raised an eyebrow. Lanry felt out of place. He was a cleric of the One God and his pious summary of events did not sit well with his companions.

'Well,' said Al-Hasim wearily, 'I'm sure they'll re-form and come again. Trained or not, there are a lot of them.'

Lanry poked his head over the wooden palisade and looked out over the plains of Scarlet. Little could be seen beyond the huge military camp spread out across the horizon. It was a sea of soldiers, torches and trebuchets which could be glimpsed through the darkness.

'Why do they attack at night?' he asked.

'A soldier's prerogative,' answered Al-Hasim. 'They attack at night because they think that's the time the enemy would least like them to attack.'

'They're probably right,' replied Lanry. 'I could certainly do with being tucked up in bed.'

Hasim laughed and patted the cleric on the shoulder in comradely fashion. 'Spirits up, my dear Lanry. You should have seen Ro Hail, it was much worse than this . . . at least we have a decent wall to hide behind here.' The Karesian pointed to the third gate, a reinforced structure, thicker and more solid than the outer two. 'As long as that thing holds, they won't commit to a full assault.'

Lanry scanned behind him to the inner mount of South Warden with the Ranen assembly at its centre. The majority of Free Company men had fallen back to this most fortified area of the city, while the women and children were safely out of sight within Rowanoco's Stone.

'Here they come again,' shouted a voice from below. 'Hasim, get your arse down here.' The speaker was Captain Horrock Green Blade of Wraith Company. He stood, axe in hand, to the side of the killing ground.

Al-Hasim smiled thinly at Lanry and drew his scimitar. 'Don't go anywhere, brother,' he said, with as much cheer as he could muster.

'Don't . . . get killed . . . or something equally foolish,' spluttered out Lanry.

Hasim jogged down the wooden steps to join a large group of warriors.

They had not moved the dead bodies from the previous assault. The Ranen clearly planned to catch anyone that entered South Warden in a flanking meat-grinder as before. When the first assault came, none of the yeomanry made it to the second shattered gate before being chewed up by Ranen defenders. Lanry had to turn away from the efficiency of the Free Companies. They were men committed to die for their land and their people, and that lent them a ferocity which showed in every swing of an axe and every severed limb. In contrast, the Darkwald yeomanry were just common men, thrown away in pursuit of a doubtful military goal.

The yeomanry had been reluctant to make their second frontal assault on the breach. Purple clerics were giving the orders. One in particular was verbally whipping his troops forwards and, though less committed than before, at least two thousand men had begun to cross the ground. They carried long spears and crossbows and wore low-quality chain mail and pot helmets. Several men at the front wielded two-handed swords, but they looked ungainly. Perhaps the large weapons had been thrust into their hands with little ceremony or training.

Below him, flanking the sides of the breach and waiting in ambush, were the men of Ranen. On one side stood Captain Horrock, Al-Hasim, Haffen Red Face and the men of Wraith Company. On the other, Mathias Flame Tooth, the corpulent axe-master of South Warden, led the men of Scarlet, while Johan Long Shadow stood in plain sight with a small group of his toughest warriors. The plan was simple, to draw the attackers into the killing ground and trap them between three forces of defenders. As Hasim had said, so long as the third gate remained intact, the Ro would be unlikely to break the defence and would be forced to engage in a protracted siege. This would play into the hands of the Free Companies and give Bronwyn and Dragneel time to rouse the clans of the Moon Wood.

Horns sounded from the army of Ro and the ranks of yeomanry picked up speed as they came into range of South Warden's catapults. As before, several volleys thudded into the mass of troops.

Long Shadow stood out below, his tattooed head contrasting sharply with the wild and matted hair of his fellows. He stepped forward, a lone man facing the oncoming yeomanry, and shouted, 'This is our ground . . . our land . . . our city. These men want to take it . . . they want what is ours. Show them no mercy, for their masters wish nothing for us but a cage.'

The men of Ranen gripped their axes and prepared to get bloody once more in defence of their home. Lanry frowned and again felt a deep well of conflict within him. He believed what the king was doing was wrong, and what the Ranen were doing was right, but he had never questioned the vows he had taken as a boy or the direction his life had followed. Now he was in a city besieged by his countrymen. Despite what Lord Bromvy might believe, it was not simply a matter of right and wrong.

He was certain that, if the city should fall, he would be treated better than the Ranen. They would not think to kill a Brown cleric. In fact, the Purple traditionally ignored the aspect of poverty and would probably regard Lanry as a wayward brother in need of re-education. There was a part of him that resented this. He knew, too, that were he a younger man, he'd find a quarter-staff from somewhere and join the defenders. But he was an old man and he remained behind the third gate, watching from above.

Behind him, the Ranen assembly and the chapel to Rowanoco provided the last lines of defence, the ultimate fall-back position should the third wall be overwhelmed. He had heard it said that the defences of South Warden would allow men to fight and retreat, fight and retreat, until they had their backs to Rowanoco's Stone. Lanry hoped it wouldn't come to that.

Half-hearted shouts rose from the advancing column as they reached the outer walls. The Ranen held their ground, waiting for the yeomanry to enter as far into the breach as possible before springing their ambush. The yeomanry had to slow down to pick their way among the splintered wood and dead bodies. Their lines narrowed as they were funnelled into the breach. Many of them had caught sight of Long Shadow, who was making no effort to remain hidden. He did not move to meet them, but simply stood in front of the last gate and beckoned them on with predatory eyes. Either side of him, the Ranen waited for their opportunity to destroy the invaders.

Horrock Green Blade was an impressive figure, standing at the head of his men with a hand raised to hold them back until the optimum moment. Next to him, Al-Hasim looked out of place. The Karesian was calm and measured, crouching low and weaving tight patterns in the air with his scimitar. He was not a fighter who relied on strength, but Lanry suspected he would prove more dangerous than many of the men of Ranen.

The dead bodies from the previous assault made the ground treacherous as the yeomanry began to charge Long Shadow and his men. Several stumbled and were slowed to walking speed, allowing the Ranen to mark their targets well.

'Cut them down,' roared Long Shadow, once the bulk of the yeomanry had funnelled into the breach.

The Free Company men were suddenly visible and their cries of defiance were deafening as all three forces advanced. Horrock's men attacked first, using the shock of the impact to drive the first few ranks of Ro on to the waiting axes of Mathias Flame Tooth and his men. Johan Long Shadow rushed forward and split a man in two with a great swing of his axe. The yeomanry quickly dissolved into a rabble, trapped between the three forces of axe-men. They had the advantage of numbers but they were no match for the Ranen's skill and ferocity.

The scene was grim as the meat-grinder did its work. The rear ranks of yeomanry tried to force their way forward but succeeded only in pushing their fellows further on to the waiting axes of South Warden. In moments, dozens lay dead or mutilated.

Horrock and Long Shadow led their forces in a triangular formation, driving the body of the yeomanry towards Mathias and his men. Al-Hasim and Haffen were on the left flank, where there was no duelling, only a brutal hacking apart of men who had nowhere to run and no hope of defending themselves.

'Let them retreat,' shouted Lanry, well aware that his words would not carry over the sounds of combat. A few scattered men of Ro had indeed managed to squeeze through the press of bodies and run in panicked groups out of the killing ground, but the majority were simply being cut to pieces.

Lanry was forced to turn away again as he felt the nausea rise from his stomach. The Darkwald yeomanry had little interest in South Warden, but the king had forced them into a position where the men of Ranen had no choice but to cut them down.

'Hold your ground,' shouted Johan Long Shadow, as the defenders met in the middle. 'Do not pursue them.' Most of the slaughter was now over. Barely a few hundred yeomanry had made it out of the breach. The Ranen cheered raucously.

Lanry did not join in the cheering and a tear appeared in his eye.

* * *

The night lasted forever. Lanry was frequently called upon to rush down from the wooden palisade and attend to wounds. The yeomanry were ordered to storm the breach a total of four times. Each time they were repulsed, a handful of Ranen met their ends, and the breach became more and more clogged with the dead.

Al-Hasim, who had taken no rest since the first assault, was slumped down next to a wall with sweat running down his face and a superficial wound to the left side of his chest.

'How long till dawn, brother?' he asked the cleric.

'An hour, maybe two . . . you need rest, my dear boy,' replied Lanry, kneeling down to inspect the wound. 'I saw that last fight and you could barely stand and lift that . . . weapon, sword . . . thing.'

The Karesian scoundrel smiled wearily. 'It's a scimitar. I stole it from Horrock's collection in Ro Hail. I never liked longswords or axes – too heavy for prolonged fighting.'

Haffen Red Face, the axe-master of Ro Hail, was nearby, pouring an entire bucket of water over his head. 'Can you not swing a blade, brother? We could use another pair of hands down here.'

'Some men are built for fighting and some are not. I have the luxury of years and the curse of squeamishness. I am too old and far too weak of stomach to kill anyone, I'm afraid.'

'I suppose you are a Ro,' he said, as if that explained everything.

Haffen slumped down next to Al-Hasim. Both warriors were exhausted and Lanry doubted whether they could remain effective for much longer. The defenders of South Warden were vastly outnumbered and the king's willingness to throw away the Darkwald yeomanry in futile assaults was beginning to take its toll. Horrock Green Blade estimated that, if they could hold the breach until sunrise, they would be able to rest and meet the next day's attacks with fresh arms and clear heads. However, the tactics of the Ro had given them no time to recuperate and, unlike the attackers, every one of the Ranen was needed for each defence. They had no reserves or reinforcements, and Lanry was all too aware that the king had not yet ordered his knights or clerics to attack.

'We've got two hundred dead and almost that many wounded beyond fighting,' said Haffen between deep gulps of water. 'I reckon we can stand for one more assault, and then . . .'

'And then what? You all die? That doesn't sound like a strategy,' remarked the cleric.

'Well, maybe we could buy the king a present and hope he forgives us for killing all his men,' said Al-Hasim with a wry smile.

'They're not really his men, they're just common folk.' Lanry was uncomfortable with fighting in general, but to see men thrown away so freely was disturbing in the extreme. 'They're just auxiliaries, they have no choice.'

'What do you want us to do?' asked Haffen. 'Try diplomacy?'

'I've just never seen so many men wasted so badly,' replied the Brown cleric.

The breach had been cleared of the fallen and funeral pyres had been built. The dead had been moved in plain sight. The Ranen bodies were taken beyond the third gate and arranged on separate pyres next to the assembly. Words would eventually be spoken over them to speed their passage to the ice halls beyond the world.

The defenders were in surprisingly good spirits and gallows humour was the order of the day. They had spent the hours of darkness fighting, killing and watching their friends and family die, and yet, as the Darkwald yeomanry formed up for yet another assault, the men of South Warden remained boisterous and defiant, telling off-colour jokes and boldly declaring how drunk they would get once the city was safe.

Lanry was less optimistic. He returned to his position beyond the third gate and prepared for another spectacle of slaughter to be played out before his eyes. Horrock was leaning on his axe and looked particularly weary as a horn was sounded across the plains of Scarlet. The massed forces of Darkwald were approaching once more. They moved more slowly this time and Lanry gasped at their numbers. The previous assaults had been carried out by several companies of yeomanry, while the others remained in camp. This time they had left no one in reserve, and several dozen Purple clerics were also riding behind the common folk, pushing them forward.

'They're committing everyone, lads,' shouted Johan Long Shadow, moving down to join his men. 'That's the best part of six thousand men.'

It was a desperate gambit on the part of the king and his clerics, and it looked as if it would be their last attack of the night. Even with the narrow breach and the Ranen meat-grinder, the difference in numbers was overwhelming. The Ranen had been whittled down throughout the night and, although they had lost far fewer men than the Ro, their losses had more of an impact. Even more worryingly, in the distance, just as the first shards of blue appeared on the horizon, the trebuchets were being moved up. The giant engines of war had been silent since the breach had been opened. They rumbled across the grassy plain, manoeuvred into position by teams of engineers, with carts behind them full of large stones.

The Free Company men had noticed the trebuchets. Mathias Flame Tooth, axe-master of South Warden, stood before his men and motioned them to form up on the right of the breach. 'They won't shell us with their own men in here . . . nothing's changed, lads. We still fight, we still kill, and we still defend this ground,' he shouted.

Lanry glanced behind him at the central mount of South Warden and saw clustered women and children peering out from the Ranen assembly. It was central and solidly built, making it the logical place of refuge for those who could not fight. However, as the trebuchets inched ever closer behind the advancing yeomanry, Rowanoco's Stone looked dangerously isolated.

Below him, the defenders were forming up in their flanking positions. The approaching army of Ro had spearmen at the front, with crossbows positioned between them. The Purple clerics giving the orders were keeping them in tightly organized ranks and the advance had a much more determined feel than the previous assaults.

'Hold your ground, lads,' said Long Shadow. The captain of Scarlet Company was no longer standing in plain sight. Instead he'd pulled his force to the right and now stood next to his axe-master and opposite Captain Horrock. 'This is it. We hold this one last time, and then we can get drunk.' The words were loud, but Lanry could detect concern in Long Shadow's voice, as if he doubted what he was saying.

Hasim, the most pragmatic of the defenders, glanced up at Lanry and shrugged, as if to say *we're in trouble*.

The column reached the outer walls and stopped, not pushing into the narrow breach as before. The spearmen levelled their weapons and held the ground firmly as hundreds of crossbows were levelled across the killing ground. The defenders were all behind cover and did not present a target for the yeomanry, but the measured nature of this final assault had thrown the Ranen off their strategy.

'Men of Ranen,' shouted a cleric from the rear of the column. 'I am Brother Jakan of the Purple, commander of the Darkwald yeomanry. I order you to surrender South Warden to your king.'

The defenders looked at each other for a moment before a laugh erupted from Mathias Flame Tooth. The barrel-chested axe-master of South Warden was a good-humoured man at the best of times, but clearly he found the offer of surrender, after so much death, highly amusing. The laugh rippled through the rest of the Free Company men.

'There will be no mercy shown if you do not lay down your axes,' shrieked Brother Jakan. 'This is no longer your land.'

'Come here and say that,' growled Long Shadow, resisting the urge to break cover and run at the attackers.

The rumbling sound of the trebuchets ceased and Lanry saw that the engineers had begun loading them with large boulders. They were closer now, though still out of range of South Warden's catapults. Lanry had a sinking feeling. It looked as if the slingshots would be firing right over the third gate rather than into the existing breach.

'I am the servant of the One God,' proclaimed Brother Jakan, 'and this is your last chance to surrender.'

Long Shadow took a step forward and, though still out of sight, stood within a few feet of the first line of spearmen.

'I will not surrender. My men will not surrender,' he said in a controlled shout. 'Our mothers, our wives, our children, none of them will surrender.' His voice grew emotional and the defenders were carried along with the passion of his words. 'We will die on this ground, defending *our* land and *our* people, but we will not surrender!' His voice cracked and there was a tear in his hard, grey eyes.

There was silence for a moment.

'So be it,' replied Jakan. He waved his hand theatrically and the Ro trebuchets sprang into life.

The massive counterweights, hanging between upright wooden beams, were released. Each swing-arm described a wide arc above the machine, dragging with it a long slingshot and flinging a huge boulder high into the twilight sky.

A strangled cry of *no* echoed from Scarlet Company as rocks smashed into the Ranen assembly and caused fissures to appear in Rowanoco's Stone.

Lanry stood aghast. Those that huddled within the stone building tried to avoid the falling masonry and flee the crumbling structure, but more boulders followed. By the time the first volley had ceased, the sounds of dying women and children echoed from the centre of South Warden. The men holding the inner wall rushed up the raised ground to assist the wounded, but many were hit by pieces of the outer stone wall. The sacred building was gradually collapsing to the ground.

Glancing back at the breach, Lanry observed astonished faces and indescribable rage amongst the Ranen. Some of the men were wrestling with battle fervour. Johan Long Shadow shook with righteous anger. The men of Darkwald didn't react; nor did Brother Jakan. They simply held their ground at the entrance, keeping their spears levelled and crossbows ready. Then a guttural roar erupted from several men of Scarlet as the battle rage of Rowanoco took over.

'Hold your ground,' shouted Mathias Flame Tooth. The axe-master of South Warden tried to hold them back, but to no avail, as half a dozen men went berserk and charged the line of Ro spears.

'Don't die like this,' roared Horrock, trying to wrestle a frenzied Haffen Red Face to the ground. Other men of both companies began frothing at the mouth as they saw wives, sons and daughters trying to pull their crushed and bloodied bodies from the wreck of the assembly.

The scene grew chaotic. More and more of the defenders succumbed to unthinking rage. They ran from their defensive positions and into the breach to be cut down by a blanket of crossbow bolts or skewered on the end of long spears. Lanry saw a man of Wraith impaled on a spear and scarcely seeming to notice. He pushed forward, driving the wooden haft through his body until he hung limply within a few inches of the spearman.

'Hold,' shouted Al-Hasim, one of the few men not possessed by battle fervour. Several others shouted *hold*, including Horrock, Mathias and Lanry, who was waving his arms and trying to attract Al-Hasim's attention. The Brown cleric could think of nothing but getting these men to fall back. Then his eyes were drawn to the shaking form of Johan Long Shadow.

With a deafening roar the captain of Scarlet Company reared up. His eyes had gone black and his teeth were gritted in an animal expression. All pretence at defending the breach was gone as the leader of South Warden entered the battle rage of Rowanoco and charged the line of spears. With no further need to restrain their men, Mathias and Horrock ceased trying to hold the breach and let their warriors fly into a berserk rage and join their captain in an out and out attack.

Long Shadow wrenched a spear from a man's grasp and threw him roughly into another one of the yeomanry, before splitting a man in two with his axe and trying to push forward into the bulk of the attackers. He received crossbow bolts in his leg, shoulder and neck, but none slowed him down.

The men of Ro were stunned by the suicidal ferocity of the Free Company men, but they were still vastly the greater force. A few men brutally hacked apart by rage-infused berserkers did not make much of a dent in the attacking army.

The battle had changed completely. The Ranen no longer attempted to hold the breach and the Ro no longer attempted to storm it. All the yeomanry had to do was hold their spears level and rapidly reload their crossbows as more and more defenders fell. Horrock, Mathias and Al-Hasim were still thinking clearly, but they had little choice but to join the others in attacking the yeomanry.

'Kill them all,' ordered Brother Jakan from the rear. 'Show no mercy, for you shall receive none.' The Purple cleric drew his longsword and ordered the other twenty or so clerics of nobility to do the same. Lanry followed their movements as they made their way through the yeomanry to the front line.

Al-Hasim darted forward through the killing ground, avoiding two crossbows and trying to reach Long Shadow, who was completely surrounded. Haffen Red Face was swinging his axe in wild but powerful arcs, killing and maiming men as he drew further and further away from the rest of Wraith Company. Horrock was trying to reach his friend, but had his hands full with massed spearmen keeping him at bay. Lanry could no longer see how these brave men could survive.

Haffen was the first to die. Lanry gasped as the axe-master of Ro Hail received a crossbow bolt at short range to the left side of his chest. Once he was off-balance, the Ro surrounding him attacked from all sides, stabbing in short thrusts with knives and short swords until a powerful spear thrust pierced his stomach.

'Haffen!' roared Horrock with anguish in his voice as he saw his friend die. Other members of Wraith Company cried out in despair at the sight of the warrior sprawled on the ground, in a motionless and bloodied heap.

Al-Hasim had glanced back to see Red Face fall and had almost lost his head to a spearman. With no time for grief, he continued his attempt to rescue Long Shadow, who was now far in front of the other defenders and staying alive through sheer force of will. Hasim ducked under a spear and sliced a man across the throat. He dived forward, barrelling two Ro to the floor and skewering another as he stood up. The Karesian was faster than the Ranen and was not hampered by uncontrollable rage. He reached Long Shadow and stood back to back with the captain of Scarlet Company.

'We need to get the fuck out of here,' he shouted over the sounds of combat.

'Death first,' was the growled response from Johan.

'Forward,' commanded Jakan from somewhere within the mass of soldiers.

The defenders of South Warden were isolated now into small pockets of resistance. Even if they did manage to fall back, there would no longer be enough of them to hold the breach. Haffen was dead, Long Shadow was surrounded, and the Darkwald yeomanry were levelling their spears and pushing towards the third gate, flooding round the sides of the Ranen and claiming the ground.

Several hundred Ranen had died within minutes and now Lanry saw the Purple clerics reach the front of the lines. As ferocious as the Ranen were, they were no match for the skilful nobles of the One. Mathias Flame Tooth and Horrock Green Blade moved to intercept them, but the outcome did not seem in doubt. Neither of the Ranen warriors was enraged as they coldly tried to hold the third gate, with only a handful of men to support them.

Brother Jakan led the clerics and he didn't hesitate for a second as he engaged Horrock, starting with a powerful combination of overhead blows that forced the exhausted captain backwards. Flame Tooth tackled a second cleric to the ground, but was quickly swarmed by yeomanry and relieved of his axe. The axe-master of South Warden shouted insults at the men who grabbed him, but Lanry lost sight of the barrel-chested warrior amidst the kicks and punches of the swarming men of Darkwald.

Horrock was outmatched and, despite the conviction in his eyes, was too weak and tired to put up much of a fight against Jakan. The Purple cleric delivered a feint to the captain's side that allowed him to follow up with a blow from his shield, dazing Horrock. Then Jakan delivered a powerful cut that sliced open the Ranen's stomach and sent him flying back to land in a bloody heap against the third gate of South Warden. He was alive, but had no fight left in him and looked skywards, panting heavily.

Back at the front, Lanry saw Long Shadow and Al-Hasim still fighting a lone battle. Johan had three crossbow bolts protruding from his body, but even the one through the side of his neck seemed not to register on his face.

'Surrender!' shouted Lanry in a quivering voice. 'There'll be another day, another fight . . . don't die here.'

If he heard the words, Al-Hasim showed no sign of recognition as he took a heavy mace blow to the back and a crossbow bolt thudded into his chest. Long Shadow wrapped an arm round the staggering Karesian and tried his best to keep the enemies at bay, but he was a lone figure now among the enemy soldiers.

Brother Jakan and his clerics killed the few remaining Ranen guarding the third gate. Then he turned to issue a command to his men. 'Stand to, I want him alive.'

The men surrounding Long Shadow and Hasim backed off and encircled the two men. The yeomanry lowered their spears and took aim with crossbows, but did not attack. Johan was no longer enraged and his black eyes had turned back to grey. He stood protectively over the unconscious body of Al-Hasim and made no effort to attack. The pain from his wounded neck seemed suddenly to register and he grasped at the protruding shaft.

With the battle over, all Lanry could hear was the muted groans of dying men. He was breathing heavily. From his position on the third wall, he could hear the gate below being battered down by the thousands of yeomanry, who then flooded into the undefended city. A horn was blown from the rear of the column to signal to the king that South Warden was taken.

Brother Jakan sheathed his sword and stepped over to where Long Shadow and the dying Karesian stood. They were penned in, with no chance of escape. Lanry had lost sight of Mathias Flame Tooth, but couldn't imagine that the axe-master had survived.

'Throw down your axe,' said Jakan in an imperious voice. 'You are beaten.'

Johan Long Shadow, captain of Scarlet Company, made sure that Al-Hasim was placed carefully on the bloody ground before he stood to face the Purple cleric. He winced in pain, but otherwise remained stoic, as he reached up and grasped the shaft of the bolt in his neck. With a defiant growl, and maintaining eye-contact with Jakan, the Ranen warrior pulled the bolt free, causing a sudden rush of blood to flow down his battered leather armour. To Lanry's eyes, the wound was obviously fatal and the captain's rage had been the only thing keeping him alive.

'Death first,' he muttered, charging at the Purple cleric with his axe held high.

The captain of Scarlet Company did not reach his target. He was peppered with a dozen more crossbow bolts almost before he had moved and lay dead a moment later, his tattooed head a symbol of bloody defiance at the feet of Brother Jakan.

Al-Hasim and Horrock were not moving either, as the few survivors were relieved of their weaponry and placed under close guard. The third gate had been battered down and Ro filled the centre of South Warden. The rest of the army was advancing now and the Brown cleric suddenly felt faint. He saw yeomanry quickly ascend the nearby stairs and run towards where he stood with crossbows held high.

Holding up his hands to indicate that he was not armed, he said through chattering teeth, 'I am Brother Lanry of Canarn . . . and I surrender.'

* * *

As the sun rose high over the plains of Scarlet, Brother Lanry found himself shackled in a Ranen house converted into a Ro prison. He did not know what had happened to Horrock or Al-Hasim, though the whispered opinion was that the captain of Wraith Company would die from his wounds before nightfall. Several thousand citizens of South Warden had been dragged from their homes and corralled on the central mount of the city to await whatever justice the king had in mind, while the rest of his army made themselves at home.

Lanry had been placed with a disgraced former knight of the Red and an unconscious nobleman who had apparently drunk himself insensible while the battle was raging. The knight's name was Fallon of Leith. The cleric of poverty had heard tales of his martial prowess and vaguely recalled that he was part of the force that had taken Ro Canarn. What he had done to have his tabard removed and his arms bound with steel was a mystery.

When the awkward silence between the two men had reached its height, and the lord of Darkwald had started snoring, Lanry decided to speak. 'Er . . . what was your crime, sir knight?' he asked, unable to think of anything better to say.

Sir Fallon smiled thinly, but the strange intensity did not leave his eyes. 'I prevented a man from dying,' he replied cryptically. 'And don't call me sir.'

'Well, as a fellow man of the One, I wish you luck with your trial,' said Lanry, and suddenly his mind felt as exhausted as his body.

'You should sleep, brother,' said the disgraced knight. 'A voice in my head tells me that you're my ally . . . and we have a lot to do.'

The Brown cleric smiled politely, but he had no idea what Fallon meant.

* * *

Al-Hasim was hurt. Again. He had a crossbow bolt in the right side of his chest, a few ribs broken by a mace, and a deep gash down his neck. Luckily, his piecemeal leather armour had taken enough of the sting out of the bolt that the head stuck only a little way into his flesh. It still hurt, but he was fairly sure the wound wasn't too serious. The cut down his neck looked and felt worse, but the blood had stopped flowing quickly and he had not passed out or felt the need to offer his final words to Jaa.

He had played dead when the Darkwald yeomanry had begun to assemble the bodies of the fallen defenders of South Warden. Now, with the killing ground mostly cleared and the day drawing on, he lay under a pile of bodies. It was not the first time he'd pretended to be dead in order to get out of a tricky situation.

Haffen Red Face was dead, Johan Long Shadow was dead, and Mathias Flame Tooth was dead. The only slight ray of sunshine was that Captain Horrock Green Blade, the redoubtable leader of Wraith Company, was still alive. The green-eyed axe-man of Ro Hail had been hauled away by knights and his wounds tended to. Al-Hasim reckoned that, as the most senior Ranen still alive, the king would want to use him as an example. The rest of the citizens of South Warden had not been so lucky. There had been large-scale executions. Any man who had raised an axe was swiftly strung up. Most died quickly with their necks broken, but some had hung for several minutes as the air was slowly strangled out of their chests.

The common folk of the realm of Scarlet were not the kind of people to submit readily to occupation. Most had tried to defend their homes and families from the men of Ro. Old men had clubbed at knights with rusted family heirlooms and women, clutching their children to their breasts and refusing to be dragged from their homes, had spat in the faces of bound men. It had not been a pleasant sight.

After a few hours, most had surrendered rather than continue their futile resistance. Thousands of common men, women and children of South Warden were corralled into fenced-off areas of the inner city, under the guard of knights and bound men. The yeomanry were less keen to pillage the city and brutalize the population. Hasim had heard whisper that their commander, a noble of Darkwald called the Lord of Mud, had been arrested by the Purple clerics on some trumped-up charge of disloyalty. It was clearly only fear of Brother Jakan that was keeping the yeomanry in line.

He shifted position and shoved a limp man's arm out of the way the better to see what was going on. A cart next to him contained a dozen dead Ranen, hacked to pieces or riddled with crossbow bolts, and the stench of death was vile. Many had already been burned, but it now seemed that the majority of bodies would be incinerated the following morning, when the men of Darkwald had had a chance to rest.

The Karesian rogue had seen combat in Canarn, Hail and now South Warden. He had broken any number of his personal rules about not getting involved in battles and deep down, in the pit of his stomach, he was amazed he was still alive. Quite how he had ended up on the receiving end of the king's advance into the Freelands was a question he couldn't really answer. One moment he'd been enjoying the hospitality of Fredericksand as a guest of Algenon Teardrop, the next he'd been skulking around Ro Canarn trying to avoid capture. He'd stood on the battlements of Ro Hail as Wraith Company repulsed the advance of the Red knights, and he'd stood next to Johan Long Shadow as South Warden was battered into submission.

'What the . . . am I doing here?' he asked himself, as a drop of blood fell on to his face from a dead body lying across him.

He'd not seen Brother Lanry since the last attack and he hoped the Brown cleric was being treated as the non-combatant he was. If the Purple clerics who commanded the army had any semblance of honour, they'd allow Lanry to return to Ro Canarn and tell

Bromvy what had happened – but he very much doubted that they would.

Hasim began to shuffle his way to the edge of the pile of dead. No one was on guard around the low funeral pyres. Now the yeomanry had fallen back to their tents to rest, the centre of South Warden was like a ghost town. He had not removed the crossbow bolt from his chest, for fear of causing the wound to worsen, and his movements were jerky and uncomfortable as a result. He did not even try to stand as he made his escape, preferring instead simply to crawl away and pull himself into a deep toilet trench that ran alongside the central ground of the city, and then make his way towards the outer walls.

'What does a man have to do to get killed,' he muttered through gritted teeth.

CHAPTER EIGHT

DALIAN THIEF TAKER
IN THE CITY OF RO LEITH

THERE WAS LITTLE greenery in Karesia aside from palm
trees, cacti and the occasional garden, and Dalian found
the city of Leith strange in comparison. The wilds of Tor
Funweir were full of forests, but their cities were built of stone
with little greenery. He liked the duchy of Leith, with its wide,
tree-lined roads and pleasant, smiling people.

The journey south had been straightforward and those he
followed had made no effort to cover their tracks. Rham Jas Rami
was no more than a few hours ahead of him and, as he entered
Ro Leith, he was optimistic that Jaa would guide his search for
the Kirin assassin. Leith was home to all manner of native and
exotic birds. Around the second hill fluttered a variety of brightly
coloured wings and the birdsong was a pleasant accompaniment
to Dalian's arrival in the city. He had made his way past the third
hill and found a seat outside a tavern from where he could watch
the comings and goings, and he had picked up the talk on the
street that a Kirin criminal had been apprehended in a tavern
nearby, though the locals were confused as to why half a dozen
watchmen had been killed during the arrest. Whoever he was, it
had taken more than twenty men to subdue him. This had made
Dalian sure that Rham Jas Rami had been captured less than
four hours before.

Leith had little need for a well-guarded gaol. The building
was large and ugly and more reminiscent of a Red church than

a town gaol. The wind claws that patrolled the perimeter were a new addition. As a black hawk flew down and perched on a nearby tree, Dalian saw a man emerge from the darkness between the feeding troughs. He was a little drunk and, by the look of his pale, clammy face, the old Karesian guessed that he'd been sick in the recent past.

'Another drink, sir?' asked a Ro serving-boy.

The presence of a Karesian did not concern the people of Leith, though Dalian had made a particular effort to appear old and unthreatening. He'd discarded his hound armour and wore a simple brown robe. Tor Funweir was more cosmopolitan in the south and, after bypassing Arnon, he had experienced little problem regarding his race.

'Yes,' he replied, 'another glass of this excellent wine would be delightful.'

The servant smiled and moved back inside the tavern. A moment later he returned with a bottle of Sixth Hill Reserve and poured Dalian a large measure.

'Your first time in Leith, my lord?' he asked, clearly accustomed to dealing with visitors.

'Indeed,' replied the Thief Taker. 'I must say that I find your city most relaxing.'

'We get a fair few Karesians, my lord. I think they like the trees and woods.'

'Tell me, young man, what is all this I hear about a Kirin criminal?' he asked.

The servant turned excitedly. Evidently, the altercation earlier in the evening had been one of the more interesting things to happen recently. 'It was the bloodiest thing ever,' he replied, with the wide eyes of an eager child. 'The Kirin killed twenty men with his curved sword. There were body parts and blood everywhere. My dad said he was an assassin or something.'

'Did you hear his name by any chance?' asked the old Karesian conversationally.

'It was a strange Kirin name. Rami, or something.'

'Thank you, lad,' said Dalian, throwing a silver piece towards the boy, who caught it and ran back into the tavern.

'Well, lord,' he said addressing Jaa, 'it seems we have a prison-break to plan. Any advice you can give me would be gratefully received.'

Turning back towards the dungeon, the drunken man stood partially concealed in shadow, waiting for a gap in the guards' patrol pattern before he emerged on to the street. There was an old longsword at the man's side. A caw from the hawk that had landed nearby alerted the drunkard to the wind claws' presence and prevented him from being seen. Once the way was clear, the hawk cawed again and the figure moved swiftly across the street.

Dalian surmised that the enchantress in Ro Leith would want to keep the assassin alive for as long as possible, prolonging the man's suffering for weeks on end if she were able. This meant that time would be on the Thief Taker's side. If the drunken man was the criminal from Tiris he'd been told about, and if he knew where the assassin was being held, Dalian thought they might have a chance of rescuing Rham Jas Rami before the enchantress had finishing amusing herself.

'I could do with some guidance, lord,' said Dalian to the air. 'Or maybe a company of hardened warriors.'

The drunkard was now lounging back on the grass and shaking his head. Dalian was not impressed. In Kessia, the title of mobster was one of respect. They were community figures who came from old families and dedicated themselves to keeping crime within certain honourable bounds. This man, apart from being a Ro, was slovenly and too far gone with drink to be of much use to anyone.

'I'd rather rely on help that can stand upright without vomiting, lord.' He spoke with an ironic smile.

The black hawk circled once more, and the forger waved it dismissively away and revealed a second bottle of wine. 'Yes, that's sensible,' muttered Dalian ironically. 'Drink more, drown your sorrows, leave Rham Jas to die.'

The hawk landed on the grass next to the forger. It fluttered its large wings a few times, hopping up and down. When he rolled over on the grass and turned his back to the agitated bird, it stopped making a noise and took to the air again. The Thief Taker followed the bird's flight as it circled the drunken forger. After a few moments, its circle widened to encompass the tavern and the hawk gradually came closer to the ground until it disappeared into a small copse of trees.

'I like birds, lord, really I do,' said Dalian, 'but they have certain disadvantages when it comes to wielding weapons effectively.' He took a long drink of wine and reclined back in his chair. It was a pleasant evening and he enjoyed sitting outside under the darkening sky, at peace for a few moments after the rigours of recent weeks. The razing of Cozz had not been an enjoyable thing to witness and as the Thief Taker had travelled south his thoughts had been dark and morbid. He did not flinch at death, or even wholesale destruction, but the things he'd seen in the merchant enclave had stayed with him.

A sound from the undergrowth nearby shook Dalian out of his reverie. The sound was made by a man stuck in the brambles, complaining about the sharp thorns.

'It's not polite to skulk in shadows, friend,' said Dalian.

'No, no, it is not,' replied a strange voice. 'Give me a second to disentangle myself and I'll skulk in the moonlight.'

The Thief Taker narrowed his eyes at the speaker's bizarrely lyrical accent. 'Who are you?' he asked.

'One second . . .' The speaker loosed a short torrent of curses at the brambles. 'Nanon . . . you can call me Nanon.'

Dalian watched a thin, robed figure step from the bush and lean casually against a tree. His features were hidden, partially by the darkness, partially by his hooded cloak, but he was armed and his movements were fluid and graceful.

'Maybe I should have asked *what are you*, friend,' said Dalian, facing the stranger.

'I would show you, but folks around here might not be as worldly as you,' the figure replied.

Dalian could not place the accent, though he was certain that the speaker was neither Ro nor Karesian. He checked that none of the tavern's other patrons was paying any attention. The terrace was mostly empty, with the other drinkers sitting inside, leaving Dalian to enjoy the evening air with just three more men for company.

'Are you a risen man?' asked the Karesian, using his minimal knowledge of the forest-dwellers to make an educated guess.

A hollow chuckle emanated from the shadowy figure and the Thief Taker reckoned his guess had been correct.

'Some of your people would call me that. I prefer Nanon, if it's all the same to you,' said the forest-dweller, stepping far enough out of the shadows to render his face visible.

Dalian had seen them before, but this one was shorter than those he'd encountered. The skin was still a flawless grey, the eyes slightly angled and the ears leaf-shaped. His longsword was of Ro design and looked out of place at the side of the slender non-human. The strangest thing, however, was the broad smile he wore.

'You'll forgive me not joining you at the table,' said the risen man. 'I work better in the shadows of men than at their side. Your cities are difficult places.'

Dalian frowned. 'It's not my city. I'm from a long way south of here.'

'You're still a man, Dalian, devotee of Jaa,' responded Nanon, taking a step back into the shadows. 'Your mind works the same . . . broadly speaking.'

'You are beginning to irritate me, grey-skin,' Dalian snarled. He disliked the idea of his name being known by a strange creature in the shadows of Ro Leith.

'Settle down, Karesian man,' said Nanon. 'I'm not your enemy and I sometimes blurt things out when I meet a new person. Sorry.'

Dalian placed his wine glass on the table and stood up. He casually straightened his robes and looked around. After a slight stretch to alleviate a stiff neck, he strolled towards Nanon. The forest-dweller quickly became visible as the Thief Taker joined him in the darkness.

He locked eyes with the non-human and began to stare him down. The forest-dweller carried on smiling and showed only the slightest blink of awkwardness at the Karesian's glare. After a few moments, Dalian darted forward and grabbed the risen man by the throat, shoving him hard against the tree. His grip was strong and Nanon gasped for breath, surprised by the sudden flash of violence.

'I don't play games, grey-skin,' said Dalian in a deathly quiet voice. 'Neither should you.' He tightened his grip. 'Tell me how you know my name, or I'll kill you.'

Dalian surmised the strange creature was built for speed rather than strength and would be easy to subdue. The wind claw narrowed his eyes and drew his scimitar, placing it across the forest-dweller's throat.

'Well,' began Nanon, showing little alarm at being held by his throat against a tree, 'it's a little difficult to explain.' He craned his neck as best he could and looked towards the unconscious forger from Tiris. 'I know his name too.'

Dalian snarled. 'Three seconds and I take more blood than you can spare, grey-skin . . . one . . .'

'Hm, perhaps you should calm down,' said Nanon, still not showing any fear.

'Two,' continued the Thief Taker.

'This is really not a productive way to spend our time, Karesian man,' said the forest-dweller.

'Three,' concluded Dalian and started to push his weight forward against the creature's throat.

Nanon winked. The gesture looked bizarre on his grey features and was well practised rather than natural. Just as Dalian's scimitar was about to bite into his skin, the forest-dweller raised his elbow with lightning speed and shoved away the Karesian's forearm. He gripped the man's wrist and twisted it with surprising strength. Dalian grunted in pain, involuntarily dropping his weapon as he was spun round and pinned to the tree.

'You're very good at fighting, Karesian man,' said the forest-dweller, 'but I can kill you with a wink. It seems that it is necessary to establish this before you'll calm down.'

'Release me,' barked Dalian.

'You don't sound calm yet,' responded the grey-skin. 'I really was trying to avoid this. My choice was between a drunken Ro and a hot-tempered Karesian . . . which would you have chosen?'

'It's hard to be calm when your arm is twisted behind your back,' Dalian said drily. 'Release me, now.'

The forest-dweller loosened his grasp on Dalian's arm and stepped back a few paces, allowing him to turn from the tree. He slowly retrieved his scimitar, placing it back at his side.

'What do you want, grey-skin?'

'I want to rescue Rham Jas Rami, as you do,' replied Nanon, smiling broadly.

* * *

Saara the Mistress of Pain cradled the cloud-stone gently in her hands and wondered why, of all the races of men, the Ranen had discovered such an unusually useful item. The Ro and the Karesians had no device or craft that enabled long-distance communication.

She could see the smiling face of her sister, Isabel the Seductress. 'I have inched him up to the knuckles, beloved sister, and we have left him to squirm in pain.'

The Mistress of Pain clapped her hands together excitedly. 'I think it's worth experimenting to see how extensive his healing abilities are.' She was gratified and relieved that Rham Jas Rami was no longer a threat.

'The Black cleric has proven most useful, dear Saara, he obeys orders without question.' Elihas of Du Ban's motives were unclear, but Saara suspected he was more than simply a traitor to the One God.

'The Kirin apostate has just arrived in Ro Weir and we are

making sure that she is . . . well looked after,' said Saara with evident relish.

'Excellent news,' responded Isabel. 'The dark-blood knows that Keisha is ours now. He actually seemed upset at the news.'

'For all his faults, Rham Jas is a dutiful father and it's the best way of keeping him in line. I'll keep his daughter safe for as long as he cooperates.' Saara felt elated at their victory. It was strange to admit that she had actually been afraid of the dark-blood, but now she realized how foolish she had been.

'Are you well, sister?' asked Isabel, concerned at Saara's manner.

'I am . . . I am,' replied the Mistress of Pain. 'I found myself worried for a moment . . . just a moment. The assassin has killed three of our number and I am relieved.'

'Fear not, beloved Saara,' said Isabel. 'The father of pleasure and blood protects the worthy.' She looked down. 'I hate to say such a thing, but it seems likely that Ameira, Katja and Lillian were unworthy.'

Saara nodded reluctantly. 'I will pray to the Dead God that their replacements are built of stronger stuff, my dear sister.'

'Have you spoken to the matron mother?' asked Isabel.

'I have not spoken to the old witch since I was a girl,' replied Saara, shivering slightly at the memory of her own harsh treatment at the abbey. 'She knows her job.'

'Take some rest, beloved sister,' said Isabel with a pout. 'You look exhausted.'

'I can rest later,' she replied. 'What news of the old-blood?'

Isabel considered the question. 'The assassin insists that he has not allied with the Ghost, and Elihas is convinced that Utha the Ghost would never work with a Kirin.'

'Hm, let us hope that Sir Pevain turns up at some point. He's disappeared for now.' The last she had heard, the mercenary knight had left Cozz with a small force of hounds and headed south after Utha.

'What do you wish me to do with the dark-blood?' asked Isabel.

'Leave him for half an hour and then continue the inching.

Once he's lost an arm, leave him overnight to see if he heals.' The Mistress of Pain was sorry that she would not be able to witness the torture first-hand.

* * *

Dalian had relaxed slowly, allowing Nanon to apologize a few times before he conceded that he needed the strange creature's help.

The cries of pain from the assassin's cell had stopped now and he guessed that Rham Jas must have been inched up to his elbow. The Thief Taker had administered hundreds of inchings in his life and had relished every one. To hear that one of the Seven Sisters was using Jaa's punishment offended Dalian greatly.

It was rapidly approaching midnight and the dungeon of Ro Leith was dark and quiet, though the wind claws continued their regular patrol.

'So,' muttered Nanon, 'we have an impenetrable dungeon and a small army of wind claws?'

Dalian was leaning against a tree, holding a bottle of Ro wine. They were within sight of the feeding trough that led to the assassin's cell. The drunken forger from Tiris was nearby, but the man had begun snoring an hour ago and would likely prove useless.

'Do you drink?' he asked Nanon. 'To drink seems the appropriate reaction to an impossible problem.'

The forest-dweller leant forward. 'No, I don't drink,' he replied. 'You're a traitor to these wind claws, yes?'

The Thief Taker raised his eyebrows. 'They believe me to be an enemy of Karesia,' he replied. 'The Seven Sisters have twisted the wind claws into their personal guard. They probably want me almost as much as they wanted the assassin.'

'There are too many to fight,' said Nanon, 'and they all know who you are, so stealth is a little redundant. Hm . . .' The forest-dweller craned forward and turned his head to one side. He seemed to be listening for something, though his face was expressionless. 'Do you hear that?' he asked quietly.

Dalian took a moment to listen, but heard nothing. 'I hear birds, the wind, and the forger snoring, nothing more.'

Nanon pushed back his hood and tucked his black hair behind his ears. Their elongated shape suggested a keener sense of hearing than that of men, and the forest-dweller could obviously make out something that concerned him.

'What do you hear, grey-skin?' asked Dalian.

'I hear grunts of pain, from the cell.'

'He has plenty of reason to be in pain. It's not so unusual.' The Thief Taker had only ever seen a handful of men inched up to the elbow. Most gave in or died well before that.

'But he'd been quiet,' said the forest-dweller. 'Rham Jas can take pain and he's been on his own for at least an hour. He's up to something.'

'You said that he's strapped to an inching chair. And he only has one arm,' responded Dalian. 'He can't be up to much.'

'He's a dark-blood,' said Nanon, as if that explained everything. 'I honestly don't think the maleficent witches know what they're dealing with.'

Dalian was too proud to admit that he had no idea what Nanon was talking about. The Thief Taker wanted to rescue the assassin so that he could kill the Mistress of Pain, but he was beginning to realize that he was not the only one who wanted Rham Jas to escape, and his reason might not even be the most pressing.

Nanon winced, as if he was feeling the Kirin's pain. 'He's doing something to himself.' Another wince, worse this time. 'Rham Jas, what are you doing?'

'Grey-skin,' demanded Dalian, 'what are you hearing?'

Nanon turned away from the feeding trough. 'He was waiting for them to inch him up to his elbow,' he said, as if reading the Kirin's thoughts, 'so that he can squeeze the stump out of his restraints.'

'He's in an inching chair, the stump of his left hand won't do him any good.' He was tough, but the idea that he could free himself from the chair was wishful thinking.

'Come with me,' said the forest-dweller.

Dalian joined him. 'Where are we going?' he asked.

Nanon didn't answer. He merely smiled and pulled his hood back over his head, obscuring the non-human features that might get him arrested or killed. With his hands tucked inside his robe, the forest-dweller left the shadows and walked to the road that ran round the third hill of Leith.

Dalian checked the patrol pattern of the wind claws as he joined Nanon. 'If we're going to his cell, we'll need to . . .' He was about to warn him to wait until there was a gap in the guards' movements, but the forest-dweller had stepped into the road and walked directly towards the feeding trough.

'Sorry, lord,' said Dalian. 'I have little choice but to consider this creature an ally.' He stepped off the grassy bank and followed behind Nanon. The forest-dweller had timed his walk perfectly and they briskly slipped into the shadows opposite.

'Very slick, grey-skin,' said Dalian, crouching down next to the stone walls of the trough.

'Thank you, Karesian man,' said Nanon cheerfully.

Rham Jas was panting heavily and emitting low snarls. The trough sloped away to the small barred window below street level. There was a flickering light coming through the window and Dalian guessed there was a brazier in the cell, with a red-hot inching knife thrust up through the coals. He followed Nanon down the stone incline, as quietly as possible and chancing glances behind to check the wind claws had not seen them. The sounds of exertion grew louder as they reached the barred window and crouched down on either side of the trough.

Within was the assassin, naked and bleeding, with gritted teeth and his body covered in sweat . He was still in the metal inching chair, though the bloodied stump of his left arm was now free. Rham Jas had deliberately dislocated his shoulder in order to wriggle out of the restraint. His face was a mask of agony, but Dalian detected anger as well. He had half his forearm still intact, but his hand and wrist were in a small bloody pile on the floor.

The Kirin looked much as Dalian remembered him, though it was strange actually to see him after so many weeks in pursuit. He was tantalizingly close, but the Thief Taker was realistic enough to know that simply getting out of the chair would not be sufficient. The Kirin was a mess and he still had leg restraints and steel bars between him and freedom, not to mention the guards that would no doubt be patrolling within the dungeon.

'Rham Jas,' whispered Nanon through the bars.

The Kirin's head was held back tightly by a leather restraint, but he heard the voice and turned to the window. He was panting heavily and clenching his remaining fist against the arm of the chair.

'It's Nanon.' The forest-dweller was unemotional, but his fingers moved rapidly against the bars and displayed great agitation.

'I don't need help,' growled Rham Jas. His voice sounded like rocks grating together and he spat the words through quivering lips.

The assassin then twisted his mid-section and slammed the bloodied stump of his left arm into the flaming brazier at his side. The knife pierced his forearm and emerged through the flesh pointing upwards. An agonized roar came from the Kirin's mouth. Then he used all his remaining strength to wrench the knife out of the fire, twisting his forearm and using it as leverage. The smell of burning flesh filled Dalian's nostrils as Rham Jas pulled the knife from the brazier, arming himself in the most painful way imaginable.

The assassin threw his head back, bracing himself against his restraints and grunting rapidly. He moved the stump of his arm up to the headrest of the inching chair and used the protruding blade to cut the leather restraint. The pain showed clearly on his face and Dalian could barely conceive of the strength of mind and body Rham Jas was displaying.

'He's going to bleed to death,' said the wind claw.

'Just watch,' responded Nanon impassively.

The Kirin flexed his neck and shrugged off the newly cut restraints. He freed his other arm with the knife held in his bloodied stump and bit his lip hard to keep himself from screaming out in pain. Then Dalian gasped as he saw the wound begin to heal. The assassin had caused considerable additional damage in the process of acquiring the knife, but the jagged cut mark along his forearm was now disappearing.

Once his hand was free, Rham Jas removed the knife from the stump and bent over, panting heavily. He gripped his forearm as the flesh quickly knitted together over the wound.

'How can he do that?' the wind claw asked, incredulous at the assassin's healing ability.

'He's a dark-blood,' replied Nanon. 'I'll explain when we get him out of there.' The forest-dweller looked down at the bars and assessed their strength. 'Hm, you might want to turn away, Karesian man. I'm about to do something you won't like.'

Dalian kept his eyes firmly on Nanon.

'Suit yourself,' said the forest-dweller.

At first, the Thief Taker wasn't sure what he was seeing. Before he'd had time to guess what Nanon was about to do, a large, thick-bodied snake appeared where the forest-dweller had been. Dalian gasped and leapt backwards as the green and black reptile began to wrap its large coils round the prison bars.

'I will fear nothing but Jaa,' he muttered.

The snake turned towards him and tilted its head, its forked tongue flicking at the air and its thick body tightening round the steel bars. Dalian locked eyes with the snake and saw that, though the forest-dweller had changed his shape, his eyes were still the same. The Thief Taker knew nothing of substance about the risen men and was overawed by Nanon's strange, magical abilities.

'The Kirin is free,' shouted a voice from within, drawing Dalian's eyes away from the snake and back to the cell.

Through the barred cell door, a few feet from where Rham Jas was cutting his leg restraints, a watchman stood. The man of Ro looked nauseous but was professional enough to try and raise the alarm. He shouted repeatedly down the corridor to alert the other guards.

The snake saw this too and began to constrict the bars, tightening its huge body and causing the mortar to crack. Rham Jas finished freeing himself and, as the watchman fumbled with the keys to the cell door, sprang to his feet and let out a tortured scream. His severed arm and dislocated shoulder left him with a grotesque, misshapen appearance, but he managed to barge the metal inching chair towards the door and brace it under the heavy steel handle. He straightened and, with an audible snap, pushed his shoulder back into its socket. Struggling to remain conscious, he shuffled towards the barred window.

'Get men to the outside trough,' shouted a Karesian voice from within the dungeon.

Dalian drew his scimitar and, getting as close to the snake as he dared, jammed the blade into the crumbling stone. Nanon continued to constrict and the bars were now buckling together as an opening began to appear. With Dalian's help, two of the steel bars were wrenched out of the stone, and the snake bent the others to a point where they could easily be twisted aside.

Rham Jas was dragging his feet heavily across the cell and using his remaining strength to stay upright. As he moved, his eyes began to roll back and, before he had reached the window, the assassin fell forwards. He had used up every ounce of fortitude he possessed and would need to be helped out of the cell.

Dalian didn't hesitate. He ducked down and swung through the window, landing deftly on the stone floor next to the unconscious Kirin. Opposite him, wind claws were trying to gain entrance. Rham Jas had blocked the door well and the Karesians would need time to bash through the metal inching chair. He pulled the wiry assassin upright. Rham Jas was well muscled, with little fat, and his taut body was covered in sweat and dried blood. Nanon had resumed his normal form and was braced against the side of the trough, reaching down to the assassin.

'Pass him up,' he said. 'We need to move quickly.'

Dalian wrapped his arms round the Kirin's waist and lifted him into the air. 'There will be guards on the street in a minute or two,' he grunted, as Nanon grasped the assassin's remaining hand and pulled him up into the feeding trough.

'We need some horses,' replied the forest-dweller.

'Why don't you just turn into one?' said Dalian, leaping up after Rham Jas and grabbing the lip of the window.

'It's the Thief Taker,' shouted a wind claw from the cell door. 'Jaa demands his death.' Dalian was seized with the urge to return and kill the insolent traitor, but wisdom overrode his anger and he hauled himself out of the window.

'Karesian man, hurry up,' snapped Nanon. The Thief Taker emerged at the bottom of the feeding trough to find his companion dragging the Kirin up the bare stone.

'We can't escape the city,' said Dalian, helping to haul the unconscious assassin out on to the grass that encircled the hill. The road was still dark and no wind claws were immediately visible, but he knew they would be running towards them with murderous intent. Also, lurking somewhere within the dungeon, was Isabel the Seductress. She would never allow the Kirin to escape if it were within her power to prevent it. Dalian felt a shiver travel up his spine at the prospect of matching his strength against the witch's.

Nanon slung Rham Jas over his shoulder, taking the weight with ease. 'You kill anyone that tries to stop us. I'll find some horses,' he said, darting into the street.

Two wind claws were approaching from the dungeon. On the grassy bank opposite, the forger from Tiris was awake now and looking incredulously at the unconscious Kirin.

'Horses at the back of the tavern.' Dalian pointed towards the terrace where he'd been sitting earlier. 'Be swift, grey-skin.'

'Grab the forger before we leave,' shot back Nanon.

'Do we need him? He can barely sit upright.' He saw little value in taking the Ro criminal with them.

'Just grab him,' said the forest-dweller, with authority in his voice.

Nanon hefted the assassin into a stable position and sprinted towards the light. The two wind claws saw the running figure and shouted words of alarm. Sounds of armoured feet came from around the base of the dungeon.

Once in the middle of the street, Dalian paused. Several wind claws and watchmen were converging on his position. He let the forest-dweller get ahead of him, amazed at the speed Nanon could maintain with an unconscious body over his shoulder.

'Kill the Thief Taker,' barked a voice from his left.

It was gratifying that these men considered him the more pressing fugitive, that they were more concerned about killing him than recapturing the assassin. That would likely change as soon as Isabel the Seductress appeared to redirect her troops, but for now Dalian proved an excellent distraction.

'Kill me if you can, boys,' he challenged, standing brazenly in the middle of the road. 'Jaa demands it.'

The first two wind claws were upon him simultaneously and both attacked from high up. It was a simple manoeuvre to duck out of the way and kill one of them with a blind-side cut to the neck. He kicked the second man in the groin and followed up with a powerful thrust through his visor, sending blood over the cobbles. Two watchmen loaded crossbows and took aim. Dalian ducked back into the feeding trough and heard the bolts thud into stone. With a glance round the corner, he rushed the men of Leith. One tried to parry with his crossbow, while the other fumbled to load a fresh bolt into his weapon. Dalian severed the first man's head and ran the second man through, shearing his chain-mail armour with a high-pitched grating sound.

'This is too easy, lord,' he said to Jaa. 'A challenge would be welcome.'

More watchmen appeared, rushing from both directions, but they were uncoordinated and were merely responding to the loud alarm bell that was ringing an insistent peal from the dungeon.

'You, Glenwood,' he barked at the forger. 'I'm on your side . . . some help would be nice.'

'Who the fuck are you?' demanded the criminal, rubbing his eyes and nervously grasping his longsword.

'I am Dalian Thief Taker, greatest of the wind claws. Get your cowardly arse over here and stand.' Dalian emphasized the point by engaging three watchmen. He sidestepped a clumsy downward attack and sliced the man at the knee, severing his leg. He then whirled round to open the second man's stomach and barrel the third to the ground. They weren't used to fighting a killer of Dalian's skill, but he knew that he couldn't maintain this level of exertion for long. His muscles were beginning to ache and sweat rolled down his face.

'Glenwood, here. Now,' repeated the Thief Taker, with a sharp intake of breath.

'How do you know my name?' shouted the forger.

'We talk later . . . we fight now.'

Glenwood was approaching hesitantly. He had drawn his sword but was clearly reluctant to use it. Something about his grip made the old Karesian think the forger was no skilled swordsman.

'Cover my back,' grunted Dalian, feeling exhaustion in his tired old limbs.

'Er, from the five watchmen? You must be joking,' responded Glenwood. Wind claws and watchmen ran towards them, with a bulky Black cleric behind them.

'Forget the old man, find that Kirin,' shouted the churchman.

Summoning his remaining strength, Dalian grabbed Glenwood. 'Time to go.'

They ran across the street, towards the shadows that flanked the tavern. A few steps behind them ran a dozen watchmen and the Black cleric. Dalian kept hold of Glenwood's arm as he headed for the rear of the dark building. The forger was of no particular help, confining himself to shouting at the Thief Taker to hurry up. The sound of horses was audible ahead of them as the two men darted through the undergrowth, emerging into the stables at the rear of the tavern.

'You should probably be leaving now,' said Nanon from astride a horse. The forest-dweller was still smiling as he pulled Rham Jas across the pommel and threw a set of reins to Dalian. 'You and

Glenwood, take this horse . . . I'll catch you up.' Nanon swung out of the saddle and patted Dalian on the back.

'They're two steps behind us, grey-skin,' said the Karesian. 'Come with us.'

Nanon shook his head. 'I need to collect something first. Ride south until you see the Fell. I'll meet you there at the tree line. Go now.'

Glenwood had already pulled himself into the saddle of the first horse. The forger looked at the unconscious, mostly naked, body of the Kirin assassin with amazement and looked nauseous. Shouted words came from the front of the tavern and Dalian realized there was no time to argue. He maintained eye-contact with the forest-dweller and quickly stowed his weapons.

'Keep your head down, grey-skin,' he said, mounting the horse. He turned to the forger. 'Ride fast!'

Dalian didn't look back. The wind claws shouted after him, and they would surely mount some kind of pursuit, but the two men and the unconscious assassin would have a good head start. Travelling south, riding in an erratic pattern round the hills of Leith, Dalian broke his horse into a dead run and tried to slow his own breathing. For now, they were safe and clear.

* * *

Dalian awoke to the sound of screaming. Rham Jas had regained consciousness shortly after they'd left the city and, aside from requesting some clothing, had done little except weep and stare at the stump of his left arm. Glenwood had not been much more talkative, though the forger from Tiris had at least contributed when it came to making a fire and standing on watch. They were travelling through the grassy scrublands in the foothills of the Claws and were several days from Leith.

The screaming was from the Kirin. Dalian rubbed sleep from his eyes and glanced across the burning embers of their nightly fire to see Rham Jas grunting in pain and holding his left forearm.

'I will need to get some sleep, you know,' muttered Dalian,

sitting up from his position against a tree. 'And the screaming is not conducive to restful slumber.'

Rham Jas turned to look at him and held up the stump. 'It's growing back.'

Dalian blinked the better to see in the darkness, and gasped. The bloodied stump was slowly extending. As Dalian watched, the flesh was flowing over the charred skin and slowly knitting itself back into some semblance of an arm. Disturbingly, the arm looked somewhat bark-like for a moment, before it took on the swarthy skin tone common to Kirin men.

'Fuck me,' said Glenwood from the other side of the fire. The forger had obviously fallen asleep, despite being on watch, and now he looked at his companion with disbelieving eyes. 'What are you, Rham Jas?'

The Kirin didn't answer and let out a wail of pain as his wrist began to take form. He was grasping the forearm so tightly that his fingers were turning the new flesh red and his eyes were bloodshot.

'I'd try to relax and let it happen,' offered Dalian, unable to think of any sensible advice. 'Perhaps pray for an end to your pain. Jaa wouldn't listen to a godless Kirin, but the One is more . . . provincial in his outlook.'

Rham Jas glared at the old wind claw and was about to retort when another wave of pain took him and his hand began to reappear.

'F u c k . . .' he said, spluttering out the expletive and elongating each letter. 'This really hurts.'

Glenwood leant in closer, transfixed by what was taking place in front of his eyes. 'It's growing back,' he said, as if he couldn't believe it. 'Your arm is actually growing back . . . That's . . . really strange.'

Rham Jas wriggled and convulsed uncomfortably on the grass as his fingers began to appear. Each digit was black and strangely textured for a moment, before turning into a red-raw version of a normal human finger. When his hand was fully formed, he tried to flex it and doubled over in pain again, wailing like a trapped animal.

'How is this even possible?' asked Glenwood, half to the Kirin, half to Dalian.

'I've seen enough of the world to know that I haven't yet seen everything,' responded the wind claw. 'But the simple answer is, I don't know.'

Rham Jas was breathing heavily and trying to get his newly healed limb to move. He acted as if a bad cramp had gripped his limb and every slight movement caused him agonizing pain.

'So, does this mean he can't die?' asked Glenwood, amazed that he should be asking the question. 'You're a religious man, you should have some kind of divine insight into this, Karesian.'

Dalian frowned at the forger and was reminded that the common folk of Tor Funweir had a very different relationship with the Gods than he was used to. 'My name is Dalian. Please address me as such,' he said sternly. 'And I have no insight, divine or otherwise, to give you.'

'And that risen man, Nanon or whatever he's called?' continued the forger.

'I don't think he knew the extent of the assassin's healing abilities either,' replied the Thief Taker.

'My name is Rham Jas. Please address me as such,' mocked the Kirin when he had stopped wailing in pain. He had an exhausted smile on his face, as if he had just awoken from an uncomfortable sleep. Smoothing back his greasy black hair, he panted with a degree of relief. 'I'm not sure I can convey quite how happy I am to be a whole man again.' There was a broad grin on his face and he looked much more like the jovial assassin that Dalian remembered.

'I share your happiness. You wouldn't be able to kill Saara the Mistress of Pain with only one arm,' said the Thief Taker, thus reminding the two men of why he had been pursuing them in the first place.

'When you're happy, you should smile,' said Rham Jas cheekily.

'Silence, boy,' barked Dalian. 'Do not mock a man who has recently saved your life.'

Rham Jas hung his head and replied, in the manner of a scolded child, 'I'm sorry, Dalian.'

'That's better. It's good to know that spending time with my son has not completely robbed you of your manners.' Dalian needed the assassin, but he wasn't prepared to tolerate rudeness from the younger man.

'Yes, Dalian,' said Rham Jas, with a shallow nod of his head.

Glenwood looked confused. 'Is there something I should know about you two?' he asked with a wry sneer. 'Are you ex-lovers or something?'

The assassin winced, trying to convey just how unwise it was to insult the greatest of the wind claws. 'Sorry, Dalian,' he offered. 'He doesn't know who you are.'

'I am far too old to beat a young man of the One God simply for rudeness . . . though your clerics have a lot to answer for if they allow you to address your betters in such a disrespectful way.' His dark eyes cut into Glenwood.

A sound from the darkness alerted all three of them and Dalian quickly stood up.

'Their god is . . . changeable, compared to yours,' said Nanon, stepping into the firelight.

The forest-dweller was smiling and was evidently none the worse for having stayed behind in Leith. How he had caught up with them so quickly was anyone's guess, but Dalian couldn't discount the possibility that the strange creature had merely taken another shape that allowed swift pursuit.

'How's the arm, Kirin man?' he asked Rham Jas.

The assassin returned the smile and wiggled his new fingers. 'All better . . . bizarre as it may sound,' he replied.

'You're a dark-blood, so it can't be totally unexpected,' said the forest-dweller, retrieving a curved scabbard from his hip 'You'll probably want this back.' Nanon threw the sheathed katana across the small camp to land in Rham Jas's lap. 'I had to go back for it. After all, it was a present from your wife.'

CHAPTER NINE

ALAHAN TEARDROP ALGESSON IN THE CITY OF TIERGARTEN

H E SLEPT FITFULLY, waking each hour or so in a clammy sweat to soaking bed sheets and total darkness. Each time the dreams forced him from sleep he hoped that morning would come, and each time he was disappointed. The hall of Tiergarten was kept warm by fire-pits and flaming braziers that dotted the stone corridors, but the warrior needed peace as well as warmth for a restful sleep, and he felt he would know little peace until Timon the Butcher returned.

Tricken Ice Fang, the chain-master, estimated that the lordling Kalag Ursa and his battle-brothers would reach Tiergarten in a day at the most, leaving little room for error in Alahan's plan for their defence. There were still tough and loyal men, and no few axe-maidens, ready to die on the walls of their city, but he wanted to achieve more than a glorious last stand.

As he dreamt, the voice of Magnus's shade echoed through his mind. 'You are troubled, exemplar,' said the shade, a strange and seamless melding of his uncle and something else.

'I worry that there are many unknowns,' replied Alahan, uncertain whether he was asleep or awake. 'I worry that Tiergarten will fall.' He paused and thought about Timon and the task he'd been set. 'And I worry that I've sent my friend to his death.'

He felt the enormity of the shade's presence step into his consciousness, and a strange, light-headed sensation suggested the apparition was thinking on Alahan's words.

'Death is the only thing of which you can be sure,' was the cryptic reply.

'That isn't enough,' said the stubborn young warrior. 'I don't accept that we all have to die . . . not here, not now, not while I'm still alive and can swing an axe.'

'And your allies?' asked the shade.

Alahan had grown more accustomed to the strange presence in his mind, but his head still throbbed whenever he beheld the incorporeal image of his uncle.

'I have few,' he responded.

'You have more than you know, exemplar.' The words were spoken knowingly and were slightly barbed, as if the shade had inherited some of Magnus's impatience. 'The Ice Father can no longer commune directly with his followers, but their stubborn refusal to lie down and die has brought you loyal and hardened battle-brothers . . . and sisters. Even now they try to contact you.'

'Unless they're hiding somewhere in Tiergarten, they're of little use to me.' The comment was glib and Alahan regretted it as soon as the words had formed.

In a show of annoyance, the shade stood tall in the young thain's mind. 'Think not only of the instant, exemplar . . . you are a soldier of the Long War,' boomed Magnus.

'What do you want from me?' replied Alahan. 'I have no army and no hall. I'm an errant thain at best.'

'You are the exemplar of Rowanoco,' roared the shade, causing pain to erupt in Alahan's mind.

He awoke sharply. The thick, bear-skin blanket was wet with sweat and he was panting rapidly. A quick look at the outer window showed the barest glimmer of blue cresting the horizon. He had spoken with the shade of Magnus a number of times over the past few weeks and each time the exchange had left him with more questions than answers. All that was clear was that the Ice Giant had lost the ability to contact his followers directly and was roaring his instructions from somewhere in his halls beyond the world. Rowanoco's anger had been sufficient to prevent Father

Magnus Forkbeard leaving the lands of men entirely, and he now functioned as a sort of interpreter, trapped between worlds, passing on advice to the exemplar.

The empty space on the floor where Timon had slept made Alahan feel the weight of what he had asked his friend to do. That the berserker of Varorg had not questioned the plan, but had acted with absolute trust, made him feel worse, as if he had manipulated the simple man of the Low Kast into a course that could mean his death. He'd had no other option, but he would greatly regret Timon's death.

Dressing quickly in his moulded leather armour and heavy wolf-skin cloak, he retrieved his weaponry and stepped into the cold and empty corridors of Aleph Summer Wolf's hall. He placed his two hand-axes on his belt and slung his battleaxe across his back, instantly feeling better for being armed and armoured.

There were no guards in the corridors and the large stone building was cavernous and empty. The walls were bare, without tapestries or trophies of war. The winding passageways functioned as living quarters for the city's lords and Alahan wondered whose bedroom he had borrowed. As he made his way to the great hall, he felt a tingle at the back of his mind and stopped walking. He had come to accept the pain that accompanied talking to the shade, but this sensation was different, softer somehow, and he turned sharply. He headed towards Oreck's Spire, the tower that contained the cloud-stone of Tiergarten.

He passed no one on his way and had only the sound of his armour and the whistling wind for company. Beyond the master suite, used by the city's thain, was a winding stone staircase that led directly upwards. As he stood at its foot, he was greeted with a biting chill that travelled sharply downwards and reminded him that winter in Fjorlan was as harsh as a grumpy troll. The realm of Summer Wolf was considered the least inhospitable part of Fjorlan and it contained more farms and livestock than the other realms put together, but even here the winds were unforgiving.

Pulling his cloak tight around his shoulders and placing his hands across his chest, Alahan began to walk up the steep stone steps. They circled round a central stone column that rose from the back of the hall. The spire itself was not visible from the rest of the city and was accessible only to the thain of Tiergarten and his axe-masters.

The wind continued to bite as he ascended Oreck's Spire and the temperature dropped even further once he had emerged at the top. The platform was circular, protected against the wind by nothing more than low walls and arches, which left the top completely exposed. In the middle of the small space was a plinth upon which sat the cloud-stone of Summer Wolf, and an ever-burning torch provided the only warmth and light.

A figure huddled next to the torch surprised him. A pipe protruded from the hood that covered the figure's face. Whoever it was, was small and frail, with gnarled hands shivering against the cold as they touched a small taper to the bowl of the pipe.

'Greetings, young man,' said a female voice from under the grey hood. 'I am Runa Grim, cloud-mistress of Tiergarten. How may I help you?' The old woman raised her head to reveal sparkling blue eyes and a face that couldn't be much less than a hundred years old.

'Cloud-mistress?' queried Alahan. 'I thought all of your order were dead and gone.'

Runa chuckled and took a deep puff of her pipe. 'We will be when I am gone. I'm the last.'

'There hasn't been a cloud-mistress in Fredericksand for fifty years or more . . .' He had heard stories of old women tasked with interpreting the visions received through cloud-stones, but had not expected to find one residing in Tiergarten. 'Well, mother Grim, I am Alahan Teardrop Algesson and I need to use the stone.'

'A thain, no less?' said the frail old woman, her blue eyes scanning his face. 'That explains the visions.'

'The visions . . .?' he began, stepping closer to the torch.

'A one-eyed maiden and an enraged axe-man seek your counsel.

They are far away and desire to speak to you for very different reasons. Step closer to the stone, Alahan Teardrop,' she said with a smile.

He turned away from her and approached the cloud-stone of Tiergarten. It was milky white in colour and the size of a man's head. Its surface shifted and pulsated in the manner of waves crashing against rocks. Deep within it, Alahan glimpsed far-off places and people, some dead, some not yet born, and he sensed that the stone was one of the oldest in all of Ranen. As he peered into its white depths, he saw faces come into clearer focus and the unmistakable skyline of Jarvik, the city of Ursa.

The cloud-stone whirled and spiralled, pulling Alahan further and further into it, until he could make out a specific face. Bearded and battle-worn, he saw the comforting face of Wulfrick, axe-master of Fredericksand.

'Alahan!' exclaimed the huge warrior. 'You're alive . . . Rowan-oco gets a drink for that.'

Alahan felt a tingle of joy flow down his spine and he smiled warmly at Wulfrick. 'Please tell me you have an army, my friend . . . we're a bit short of men here.'

The axe-master raised his eyebrows and frowned. 'Not an army, but five hundred tough men and women who are still loyal.'

'How did you get to Jarvik? Have you taken the city?' Alahan had a hundred questions and something about the presence of Wulfrick made him babble like a young boy.

'Settle down, we're safe for now,' replied the huge warrior, talking from the other side of Fjorlan. 'A few of us sneaked into the chapel and borrowed Rulag Ursa's cloud-stone. There aren't too many of his men here, but he appointed a new thain of Hammerfall and he's being a pain in the arse.'

Alahan leant back. Suddenly he felt better. It was a slight feeling, but enough to infuse the young thain with sufficient conviction to maintain hope.

'I'm not sure I can convey how glad I am to see you, Master Wulfrick.'

'It's mutual, lad . . . we're a long way from you, but we're up for a fight,' replied the axe-master. 'Halla plans to take on Grammah Black Eyes and then march on Tiergarten.'

Alahan frowned and moved closer to the stone the better to see his old friend.

'Aleph's daughter . . . she's alive?' he asked, surprised that Wulfrick would follow a woman into battle.

The axe-master suddenly became defensive. 'She's our captain. She's saved a lot of Ranen lives, lad. I'd listen to her if I were you.' He smiled again. 'If she ever gets out of bed, the lazy bitch. One little Gorlan bite and she's on her back for weeks.'

'Tell her that her father's hall is warmer than mine,' he said, relieved to have allies, no matter who they were.

'Between you and me, Alahan, she's not entirely on your side. Your father killed hers . . . that kind of scar doesn't go away overnight.' The axe-master was wise and Alahan found that it helped just to hear his voice.

'I can live with that. As long as Halla hates Rulag more than me,' he replied, feeling suddenly wide awake.

'You can at least be sure of that,' said Wulfrick. 'We've seen what that bastard and his men have done to Hammerfall.' He continued, 'Are you safe in Tiergarten? I'm not going through all this to find you dead when we get there.'

Alahan nodded, again feeling like a small child. 'As safe as can be expected. Kalag and a bunch of his battle-brothers tracked me out of Fredericksand. Unless they're complete idiots, they should be on our doorstep in a day or two.'

'Is Brindon still there?' Wulfrick leant back from the cloud-stone to reveal three other people clustered round him, listening to the thain's words.

'I think he wishes I was my father, but yes, he's still here,' responded Alahan.

'He's a prickly old sod. Don't let him get to you . . . tell him I won't be pleased if he doesn't lend you all the assistance he can.' Wulfrick squared his shoulders and adopted a more protective demeanour, reminding the young thain that men with honour still existed in Fjorlan.

'I'll tell him, but he'll probably slap me again.' Alahan glanced over Wulfrick's shoulder. 'Who are they?' he asked.

'Rexel Falling Cloud, Oleff Hard Head . . .' He paused and gestured to the third figure, a hunched-up old woman with a crazed look on her face. 'And this is Anya . . . she's cleverer than she looks.'

'When Halla recovers, tell her that I'm grateful for all she's done . . . keeping you alive to become my axe-master. There must be thousands of men in the halls of the Wolf Wood . . . make sure they know that I'm still alive and fighting.'

Wulfrick nodded. 'By the time we reach you, we should have an army that can at least give Rulag the Betrayer something to think about.'

A moment of silence followed as the two warriors exchanged silent oaths of kinship. Alahan was glad to see that Wulfrick's companions looked equally sure of their allegiance and, though he worried what he would say to Halla, at least he knew that he was no longer alone.

'Just stay alive, Teardrop,' said the axe-master of Fredericksand.

'I certainly intend to . . . I have a plan. Even if it doesn't work, it should scare the piss out of Kalag.'

The axe-master narrowed his eyes, but didn't press the issue. The image became indistinct and his grizzled face began to disappear.

'The cloud-stone will not let you talk any more today,' said Runa Grim from the other side of the spire.

'The thing has a mind of its own?' queried Alahan.

'No . . . but it has a will not of its own.'

* * *

History does not recall a time when the Ice Men of Rowanoco were not a presence in Fjorlan. Alguin Larson, first thain of Fredericksand, wrote about them five hundred years ago and his book *Memories from a Hall* has remained the definitive text on the trolls of the northern ice.

Alahan was no scholar, but like all Ranen children he'd grown up hearing stories of the Ice Men and the danger they posed to anyone and anything that lived in Fjorlan. He had always respected and feared them, as he had been told to do, but had given them little thought before his encounter on the ice when Timon the Butcher had revealed a strange kinship with the beasts. They were not monsters, like the ice Gorlan or the Krakens, but rather a remnant of a simpler time when the Ice Giant's followers were more numerous and widespread than men. If they worshipped Rowanoco, or even if they had a concept of the Gods, was unknown. Even old Father Crowe spoke about them in hushed terms, as if no one could truly understand them.

What was known was recorded in scattered stories from a hundred settlements that had weathered their attacks and a thousand battle-brothers who had encountered the Ice Men. They were dangerous in a way that the south men of Ro and Karesia could not possibly understand. They treated rocks, trees, beasts, men and steel as food. Cross in the extreme, it was only their habitual keening that rendered them a manageable hazard.

Even cities were not immune from their attacks. Several famous stories told of families of trolls getting lost far from Trollheim and attacking Fredericksand in search of food. The last such incident had happened a hundred years before and involved six trolls, the deaths of a hundred battle-brothers and the destruction of dozens of houses. The encounter had ended when the defenders of the city shot flaming ballista bolts among them, provoking a confused stampede away from Fredericksand. Records of Ice Men actually having been killed were extremely rare and, without exception, it was trickery that had been successful rather than brute strength.

To use them in the way Alahan planned had never been attempted. Brindon Crowe repeatedly reminded him that it was inviting disaster. He had only Timon's word that they would not assault the city, and only their bond with the Low Kast berserker to ensure they would attack Kalag and his men. If Timon really could direct the trolls, a stampede would break the lines of any army, no matter how big, and the forces of Ursa would surely be routed. However, there were many *maybes* and *what ifs* in the plan and, if Timon did not return in timely fashion, Tiergarten would be sacked.

Alahan had met with Tricken Ice Fang and several of his men as soon as they awoke and now they all stood at the top of the Steps of Kalall surveying the city beneath them. Old Father Crowe was seated on a stone bench with his ever-present mug of mead and a deeply sceptical look on his weathered face. The priest had said little while Alahan and Tricken planned the defence, confining himself to snorting in derision whenever someone said *maybe* or *hopefully*.

'We've put men on the two bluffs overlooking the pass,' said Tricken, pointing to the narrow path that led along the coast towards Tiergarten. 'We'll have at least some warning when they arrive.'

'Is there any point in blocking the pass?' asked Alahan, wondering if a landslide or some such would buy them time.

Another of Tricken's men, a barrel-chested old warrior called Earem Spider Killer, stepped forward. 'Those cliffs wouldn't shift if Rowanoco himself threw his hammer. You'd have an easier time causing a landslide at the bottom of the Kraken sea.'

'So, once they enter the pass, we'll have . . . how long?' he asked.

Tricken scratched at his bushy red beard. 'An hour or two. I suppose it depends how many men they have.'

Alahan looked down the stairs of Tiergarten. Arrayed across the stone, tentatively emerging from their houses, were several hundred men and women, holding weapons of various kinds. Some were family heirlooms, not used for centuries, others had been hastily forged in the past few weeks, but all were held in uncertain, shaking hands. The battle-brothers and sisters of Tiergarten were not an army. He surveyed their faces and was deeply sorry at having to ask them to fight. If they'd been seasoned warriors, they'd have been with the dragon fleet and would now be dead. As it was, they were farmers and craftsmen who had never imagined they would have to defend their city from other Ranen.

Stepping forward to stand at the edge of the highest level, Alahan considered what words would inspire the citizens of Tiergarten and whether anything he could say would make their situation appear less hopeless. Telling them that a family of trolls was coming to their rescue would likely be met with laughter. Confessing that his strategy relied on a Low Kast berserker who wouldn't fight seemed equally unwise. As he muddled these things through in his head, he chuckled to himself at the absurdity of it.

'Something funny?' asked Tricken.

'Something . . . everything,' was the vague response. 'It's probably not the time for inspiring words, is it?'

Brindon Crowe emitted a throaty laugh from behind him, before loudly taking a swig of mead. 'You'd need to be an inspiring person to offer inspiring words,' he said, wiping the residue of the honey liquor from his mouth.

'Why don't you shut up?' replied Alahan, not turning to see the priest's reaction. 'You're not helping.'

'I'm not here to help, lad. Think of me as your doubting adviser.' The priest was on to his fourth mug of the morning and didn't look as if he were about to slow down.

'Well, if you could doubt quietly, I'd appreciate it,' responded Alahan, turning back to Tricken and Spider Killer.

He pointed to the narrow pass that ran along the Fjorlan coast and served as the north–south road through the realm of Summer Wolf. 'Once Kalag gets his men within sight of the city, they'll charge . . .' He swept his hand across the flat, icy plain between Tiergarten and the low gullies of the deserted harbour. 'We can pick off a few of them with catapults and ballistae, but they'll get to the gate in a few minutes.'

'They won't have ladders,' said Spider Killer, 'and with burning pitch thrown down at them, they might just run their treacherous arses away.'

'Not likely,' supplied Tricken. 'Tiergarten isn't hidden. They'll at least have battering rams . . . in fact, that's probably why they're not here yet. Finding trees to cut down takes time around here.' He stepped forward to stand next to Alahan. 'Where's your friend going to come from?'

'The northern gullies,' he replied. 'The trolls won't get close to the sea, so they'll avoid the men of Ursa unless Timon can lead them on to the plain.'

'Optimism or stupidity, I can't decide which,' interjected old Father Crowe.

Alahan turned to the priest. 'Go and have another mug of mead,' he said, attempting to keep his temper in check.

Father Crowe said nothing further and confined himself to grunting with disapproval. Alahan was about to move towards the top of the Steps of Kalall and address the populace of Tiergarten, when he was interrupted by a single flaming arrow, fired from the cliff tops that flanked the north–south road.

'Tricken, does that mean they're coming?' he asked.

The chain-master peered across the icy plains, his eyes following the trajectory of the arrow. Before he could answer the question, another arrow was fired from the adjacent cliff, and then another from the low harbour, causing the citizens of Tiergarten to stop their hasty preparations and look skywards.

'Three arrows,' said Tricken. 'That means they all saw them at once.' He screwed up his bearded face. 'That means there are a lot of men out there.'

'How many?' pressed Alahan.

Ice Fang considered the question as more arrows were fired from the lookouts. 'A few thousand at least . . . probably enough to sack Tiergarten.'

'They're not here to sack the city,' interjected Father Crowe. 'They're here for him.' He pointed at Alahan and stood up from his bench. 'Rulag and that poisonous son of his know that they can never truly claim the hall of Fredericksand until he's dead.'

Tricken puffed out his chest and gripped the chain wrapped

around his torso. The mark of office gave him comfort and he stated boldly, 'They'll have to get through gates, men and . . . and me, before they take the son of Teardrop.'

'Strong words, my friend,' responded Alahan, 'and I thank you for them.' He placed a brotherly hand on Tricken's shoulder and saw the concern just discernible through the chain-master's bushy red beard.

'I'll trade strong words for a few hundred battle-brothers,' replied Ice Fang.

'Spider Killer . . . get to the ballistae. Mark your targets well,' ordered Alahan.

'Aye, lad,' said Earem. 'And the trolls?'

'They'd have fired a lot more arrows if they'd spied Ice Men,' offered Tricken. 'I think we're on our own for now.'

'See you in the ice halls, lads,' said old Father Brindon Crowe, draining his mug.

* * *

Alahan stood on the second level of Tiergarten, to the side of the Steps of Kalall and within sight of the city gates. Tricken's men had carried great wooden struts to the outer wall and braced them against the solid wood of the gates, while Spider Killer had lit burning braziers along the battlements, intending to light his ballista bolts before firing them.

Crowe had joined the young thain. Since the enemy had been sighted, the old priest had made no further insulting or unhelpful comments, though his continued presence was more intimidating than reassuring. Several hundred of the common men and women of the realm were arrayed across the lower two levels of the city. They huddled in close groups, around small fires and protectively in front of their houses. He had counted no more than a hundred seasoned battle-brothers, and many of those were approaching old age or had missing limbs. The uncomfortable fact was that any man still in Tiergarten would have been too old or incapacitated to join the dragon fleet, meaning that the city's defenders were cast-offs, farmers and the infirm. There was also no small number of children, young boys and girls, eagerly holding axes too big and heavy for them.

Alahan breathed in deeply as he considered the forces at his disposal. They had thick walls and ample conviction that their cause was just, but those would not be sufficient to hold back a determined force intent on taking the city.

'Look yonder,' said Crowe, pointing across the ice.

Scanning the white horizon, he saw a mass of dark figures emerge on to the plain in front of Tiergarten. The lordling Kalag and his men had passed the docks and were now spread out across the north–south road, moving towards the outer walls. They were in organized ranks, with giant battering rams and mobile ballistae.

Suddenly, old Father Brindon Crowe shouted, 'This is the realm of Summer Wolf.' His words carried and every citizen of Tiergarten turned their eyes to look at him. 'This city has stood for thousands of years and it will not fall to the men of a betrayer and a child killer.' He raised his hammer above his head and gestured at the approaching forces. 'We will drink in the ice halls before we feel fear.'

His cry was taken up by Tricken Ice Fang and the men guarding the forward battlements. In moments, every man and woman of Tiergarten was chanting, 'We will drink in the ice halls . . . we will drink in the ice halls.'

Alahan felt goosebumps rise up on his arms. 'Honourable words, Father, and I thank you for them,' he said with conviction.

'They weren't for you, lad,' replied the priest. 'They were for the men and women about to die for you.'

'I never wanted this.'

'And yet it is happening, whether you wanted it or not,' replied Crowe, with a stern look in his dark eyes. 'And now is not the time to feel sorry for yourself, boy.'

Involuntarily, he gritted his teeth at being called *boy* once again, but he said nothing. Reacting to the old man's insults would not help the gates to hold.

As the ranks of Kalag's men came closer, he estimated the force arrayed against them as close to five thousand battle-brothers. Not all would be seasoned warriors, but they were sufficiently organized to make Alahan suspect that most were. In the centre of the army, flanked by rolling ballistae and crews of men carrying battering rams, was a platform, recently constructed from tree trunks. The men either side set the platform down just out of range of Tiergarten's own ballistae, and the army paused in tight formation.

'What are they waiting for?' he wondered, mostly to himself.

'Kalag's going to call you out, I suspect,' replied Crowe. 'Finish you quickly in front of his men and yours.'

Alahan pondered this. The thing he and Tiergarten needed most was time. If a duel against the lordling would buy Timon sufficient time to arrive with his *friends*, it might be worth doing.

'He'll expect you to say no, but honour dictates he make the offer,' said Father Crowe. 'I'll bet you a mug of mead he's got a priest with him. Killing you personally would be the only way to make his claim to lordship legitimate in the eyes of Rowanoco's faithful.'

'Why would a priest of the Order of the Hammer follow that troll cunt?' spat Alahan.

Crowe looked at him as if it were a stupid question. 'Even betrayers need the Ice Giant, lad . . . your family isn't squeaky clean either. Algenon killed my thain out of hand to secure the rescue of his brother, remember.'

Alahan lamented what had happened to Aleph Summer Wolf. His father's action in killing the thain of Tiergarten might yet determine the fate of many.

A horn sounded from the platform in the middle of the icy plain and several men climbed to the platform to stand before the city.

'I am Kalag Ursa,' roared Rulag's son, 'thain of Jarvik and rightful heir to the hall of Fredericksand, son of the Lord Bear Tamer. I demand that the son of Teardrop show himself and be judged before the Ice Giant . . . I offer him single combat.'

The lordling was a large man, slightly older than Alahan, and possessed the bright green eyes of all the lords of Ursa. He carried a battleaxe and wore heavy furs over chain armour. His thick brown beard was unkempt, though his fluid movements and stern voice spoke of a man who knew what he was doing. He would be a dangerous opponent.

'You have no right to demand anything here,' shouted Tricken Ice Fang from the forward battlements. 'This is not Jarvik or Fredericksand. This is Tiergarten. If you want something, you ask politely.'

Kalag was obviously annoyed at the chain-master's words, but a thin man standing on the platform whispered something quietly in his ear and calmed him down.

'That's Father Grey Claw,' supplied Brindon Crowe, 'Rulag's confessor . . . be wary of him, lad.'

'If he's a priest, surely he can be trusted,' said Alahan, instantly realizing how naive he sounded.

'In the same way that I can be trusted,' replied Crowe. 'Those in the Order of the Hammer are not saints, boy. We can be trusted to speak the word of Rowanoco, but that word is often not gentle.'

'I wish no harm to the people of Tiergarten,' boomed Kalag. 'None of you need die today, but I mean to kill Teardrop and any man that stands in my way.'

Alahan closed his eyes and gathered his thoughts. If he fought Kalag and won, the men of Ursa would surely sack the city. If he fought and lost, he'd have abandoned Fjorlan to its fate and betrayed the memory of his father.

'I can't win this, can I?' he asked Crowe.

The priest shook his head. 'Not really, no . . . either way Fjorlan is fucked.' A twisted smile appeared on the old man's face. 'There is still one thing in your favour, though. He doesn't expect you actually to go down there and fight him.'

'Because only a fool would do so,' replied Alahan. 'If I kill him, his men will kill me and annihilate the city.'

'But you wouldn't be trying to kill him, lad, you'd be trying to buy time for your berserker friend to return with reinforcements.' Crowe could at least be trusted to advise what was best for Tiergarten. 'Our gates are strong, but those battering rams will need less than an hour to smash through them and then . . . well, we won't hold out for long once they're inside the walls.'

Alahan looked skywards and wished for the presence of his uncle's shade to guide him. For now at least, the Magnus had left him to make his own decisions. With a deep breath, he unslung his two-handed axe and strode down the Steps of Kalall towards the gates of Tiergarten. One step behind him was Father Brindon Crowe. It was apparent that the old priest intended to accompany him.

'Thains shouldn't die alone, lad,' was all Brindon said, as he hefted his war-hammer and fell in beside the young thain.

The men and women of Tiergarten watched with wide-eyed astonishment as the two men walked towards the gates in answer to the lordling's challenge.

'Tricken,' said the priest, 'keep those ballistae trained on the platform. At the first sign of treachery, light the bastards up.'

'Aye, Father,' replied the chain-master, clearly uncomfortable at what he was witnessing.

Alahan waved at the guards to indicate that the reinforced wooden struts be removed. They paused for a second in evident confusion before doing so.

Beyond the gates, the vista was one of armoured men standing on a stark white ground and poised for combat. Most wore chain mail and carried glaives, though no few hammers and axes were also present. Kalag's army had units of skirmishers, carrying throwing axes, and half a dozen sled crews stationed off to the side, trying to keep their dogs quiet.

Alahan and Crowe stood in the gateway for a moment to give the warriors of Ursa a chance to have a good look at them. Most of the battle-brothers were silent now, surprised that the young thain was answering Kalag's challenge. A few more recognized the priest and exchanged whispered words about Crowe's fearsome reputation.

'You want to fight me?' challenged Alahan, locking eyes with Kalag Ursa for the first time.

The lordling seemed unsure, but quickly regained his composure and drew his own axe. At his shoulder, Father Grey Claw was glaring at Crowe and hefting his own hammer. The two men of Rowanoco would not fight, but Alahan knew that they would ensure the duel remained fair.

'Hasten to your death, boy,' said Kalag, jumping down from the platform.

Another deep breath and Alahan began to walk away from the wooden gates. Crowe followed and the gates of Tiergarten were closed, leaving the two men facing each other on the plain. They walked slowly and Tricken Ice Fang was able to lower the trajectory of his ballistae to cover the two men.

To the north, tall cliffs framed the sea and towered over the coast road. To the south, the arable plains of Summer Wolf stretched as far as the eye could see. Alahan felt small and insignificant, a dot on the featureless white plain, with nothing but a bitter old priest and an army of enemies for company.

The battle-brothers of Ursa did not advance, remaining in loose ranks behind their lord. Once Alahan was within axe-throwing range he stopped and turned to old Father Crowe. 'If you happen to see my sister, please tell her . . . that I tried, but I'm not our father.'

'Don't worry about buying time, lad . . . don't worry about your hall, your followers or even Fjorlan . . . just kill him,' responded the old priest. Emotion showed in his eyes for perhaps the first time since Alahan had arrived in Tiergarten.

The young warrior tried to smile, but the expression got lost around his eyes. Instead, he turned to Kalag and stepped forward. The lordling of Jarvik was carrying a well-used battleaxe and he held it skilfully, showing he was an experienced fighter.

'Your father was a treacherous troll cunt,' said Alahan, spitting on the snowy ground. 'He killed my father and now I'm going to kill you.'

Kalag advanced until the two men were face to face. The lordling had an army at his back and Alahan had the city at his. Both knew that the duel meant more than just life or death.

'That axe got a name?' asked Kalag, gesturing to Alahan's weapon.

'Not yet,' was the growled response.

'Not ever,' retorted the lordling, launching an overhead strike at Alahan's head.

The blow was easily avoided, but Kalag followed up with a series of wide, arcing attacks, trying to finish him quickly. He grunted with exertion at each attack and Alahan had to give ground backwards to avoid being split in two.

Kalag was strong and each attack would be sufficient to kill if it struck home. He tested Alahan's defence, continuing the series of powerful downward swings of his axe. The young thain didn't parry or raise his weapon at first, preferring to stay out of reach and look for an opening. When no obvious line of attack appeared, Alahan decided to test Kalag's speed instead.

He spun round, avoiding a thrust and tensing his arms for a horizontal swing. Alahan's axe split several links of Kalag's chain mail and caused the man of Ursa to back off, but no blood was visible.

'You're quick, boy,' said Kalag, surveying the slight damage to his armour.

Alahan growled at the insult and attacked again. He took a leaping stride to the left and swung his axe in a controlled arc at Kalag's mid-section. The lordling parried and jumped back, only to be met with another axe swing. Alahan didn't let up and pressed on with the attack. Kalag roared with frustration as his opponent darted from side to side, relying on his superior speed.

Alahan tuned out their surroundings, keeping his breathing even and preserving his energy as he began to realize that he was the superior fighter. Kalag was well trained and strong, but he was not used to fighting a man who wasn't scared of him.

'I'll eat your fucking entrails,' spat Kalag, overextending his arm in an upward swing.

Alahan avoided the attack and sent a powerful kick against the haft of Kalag's axe, unbalancing the lordling. A second kick to his chest, and the man of Ursa had lost his footing and fallen backwards, albeit with a firm grip on his weapon. Alahan pounced, driving his knee into Kalag's stomach and pressing his axe haft across the man's throat. His opponent raised his own weapon and the two men engaged in a desperate wrestling match as Alahan fought to break his opponent's neck. The two axe handles made a dull, hollow sound as they grated against each other. Kalag gritted his teeth with exertion, while Alahan used his extra leverage to press down with all his body weight.

They locked eyes. The lords of Jarvik were all cursed with bright green pupils – a punishment for a past act of dishonour – and Alahan thought he detected fear behind the anger in the pools of shimmering green. Kalag's arms were beginning to shake and his resistance to falter. Alahan flexed his shoulders and, with a sudden knee to his opponent's groin, the high thain of Fjorlan drove his axe haft into Kalag's throat.

The lordling's eyes widened and he lost his grip on his axe. His hands flailed around Alahan's shoulders, trying to squirm free, but the strength quickly left his body as the young warrior on top of him began to crush his neck.

'Alahan!' shouted Father Crowe in warning, just as a burning pain erupted in the young thain's side.

He released the pressure on Kalag's neck and looked down to see where a throwing-axe had struck him, causing an ugly wound and a gush of blood. His strength waned and his head swam, though he saw Brindon Crowe dart forward to crouch protectively over him.

'Dishonourable bastards,' shouted the priest at the man of Ursa who had thrown the axe.

Kalag tried to sit upright and say something, but the wound to his neck wouldn't allow the words to form. Alahan fell forward on to the snow and saw the lordling of Ursa turn red as he struggled to speak through his crushed windpipe.

Father Grey Claw raised his hammer. 'Kill them both,' he ordered.

The battle-brothers of Ursa hefted their weapons and Alahan smiled thinly, realizing he was about to die.

'Tricken,' shouted Crowe towards Tiergarten, and half a dozen ballistae filled the air with their massive projectiles. Ice Fang had sighted his weapons well and the bolts thudded into the massed army on either side of the two men.

Then the keening started, coming from all directions at once. Alahan's vision was growing cloudy. All he could make out was the tall figure of Brindon Crowe, crouching over him, but the panicked faces of the men of Ursa were indistinct as they looked around, trying to see where the low, rumbling sound was coming from.

'Kill them,' spluttered Kalag, clutching his neck in pain.

More keening, louder and angrier, and Alahan cried out, turning to look towards the northern ice fields of Summer Wolf. He blinked rapidly, trying to shut out the pain in his side and focus on the shimmering figures that were emerging from the snowy glare. The battle-brothers of Ursa had backed off and no words of Father Grey Claw or Kalag could make them move.

A loud, hollow bell sounded from Tiergarten.

'Ice Men . . . from the north,' screamed a man of Ursa.

Dotted across the northern landscape, a dozen distinctive shapes loped forward. Alahan smiled, barely able to move, but he could make out the lumbering figure of Timon the Butcher across the plain.

The enormous trolls moved slowly, keening loudly at every step. None of them appeared to notice the army of men at first. Kalag's battle-brothers were silent and still now, all too aware that they had nowhere to run, nor any chance of repelling so many Ice Men of Rowanoco. The keening echoed around the plain, bouncing off rocks and walls. Some men began to run towards the Fjorlan Sea; others ran towards Tiergarten. But most were rooted to the spot with fear as the trolls spied a huge meal and ran forward.

They were gigantic, well over fifteen feet tall, and each beast's shoulders were as wide as the city gates of Tiergarten. They were dusty white in colour and a few had distinctive grey or black stripes in their dense fur. Their claws were bared and scythe-like, extending in front of their muscular bodies and reaching out as they charged. Once again, Alahan thought their appearance would be comical, if they weren't so dangerous.

'Stay still,' barked Crowe, hunkering close to the ground and pulling the dying thain close to him.

Timon, who stood at the front of the charging trolls, let out a deafening roar and sprinted forward with his strange allies.

Then the two forces clashed. Trolls barrelled into five men at a time, biting off chunks of flesh. There was little physical resistance from the line of warriors as the monsters simply batted fully armoured men aside. Within seconds, the army had degenerated into a chaotic mass of men, screaming with fear and trying to get clear of the charging Ice Men. Alahan began to laugh weakly.

If they had had any chance of halting the charge, it disappeared as soon as Father Grey Claw was picked up like a child's toy and had his legs bitten off by a hungry troll. Other men tried to raise glaives or axes and found that the Ice Men cared nothing for wounds as they feasted on panicked men. Each troll was a match for a hundred warriors, and the small pockets of men that tried to fight back were quickly overwhelmed. Their weapons could barely penetrate the hide of the trolls, and even their heavy, two-handed axes barely caused them to flinch. A few of the trolls decided to use dead bodies as weapons and clubbed men to death with their fellows. Other beasts simply stationed themselves on the ice and grabbed at any man that came close enough, biting off heads and limbs, then waiting for the next man.

Timon the Butcher reached Alahan. 'Friend Alahan, you are hurt,' said the berserker.

'I can heal him,' replied Crowe, looking around the plain in amazement, just as shocked as Alahan that the plan had worked. 'Are we safe here?'

Timon nodded enthusiastically, stroking the dying thain's head. 'They won't attack my friends . . . let's go back to the city.'

Alahan fell into Timon's embrace and locked eyes with Kalag Ursa once more. The lordling of Jarvik was sitting up now, still clutching at his throat. His deep green eyes were bloodshot and showed fear. Alahan maintained eye-contact as a troll bent down and scooped up Rulag's son. The treacherous man of Ursa didn't cry out as the Ice Man bit him in two. It casually threw away his legs and waist, then crushed his head in its enormous jaws, leaving a red smear on the snowy ground.

'We should leave now,' said Timon, 'before the Ice Men run out of things to eat.'

* * *

Alahan didn't remember leaving the plains of Summer Wolf or being carried back to Tiergarten. He had a vague recollection of feeling unusually cold as he was held in Timon's arms, and a disturbing view of his own blood flowing over his twisted and split armour.

There was a part of him that was ready to die, that would even welcome it – a part of him that was tired of trying to live up to his father, and failing. But old Father Brindon Crowe and the shade of Magnus had other ideas for him. He was shocked back into consciousness by the heavy-handed healing skills of the old priest, and found himself lying on a long trestle table in the great hall of Summer Wolf. Timon stood nearby, as did the chain-master, Tricken Ice Fang, and their looks were both incredulous and happy.

'You're alive, friend Alahan,' exclaimed Timon, smiling grotesquely and slapping Brindon Crowe on the shoulder with gusto.

'Easy, lad, you're stronger than you think,' grumbled the priest, rubbing his shoulder and looking incredibly weary. 'If you want to hit someone, hit Alahan.'

'I'd rather he didn't,' said the young man, sitting up and feeling sore all over. 'Did we win?'

Tricken and Crowe exchanged glances and a thin smile passed between them.

'I'm not sure I'd say we *won* as such . . . but Tiergarten is no longer threatened,' Tricken replied. 'Last I saw of those bastards from Ursa – well, the ones that didn't get eaten – they were running towards the sea.'

It was generally known that water was the one thing the Ice Men of Rowanoco did not consume.

'And the trolls?' he asked, causing both the men of Tiergarten to look at Timon the Butcher.

'I, er, I marked the city gates as my territory. They won't cross the threshold,' said Timon, looking embarrassed.

'He pissed at the gates,' translated Tricken, finding the situation extremely funny.

Alahan tried to laugh, but ended up coughing instead and grabbed at his side in pain. The wound was healing, but Brindon Crowe had not been especially gentle and the young thain could still feel where the throwing-axe had embedded itself in his side.

'So, all we have to worry about is an angry father who might want to know who tore his son in half.' Alahan imagined that Rulag Ursa would find out about Kalag's defeat in a matter of weeks. What he would do with that information was, for the present at least, a mystery.

'Halla is still alive, Alahan,' said Old Father Crowe. 'We're not alone. She's a long way east, but she's a tough bitch and we can count on her.'

'And Wulfrick is with her,' added the man of Fredericksand, smiling as he mentioned the huge axe-master. 'They have men and they have even more reason than us for hating Rulag.'

CHAPTER TEN

TYR NANON IN THE FELL WALK

THE AUDITORIUM WAS quiet and had been so for almost an hour. Around the edges of the massive tree stood several hundred Fell Walkers, looking up at the assembled Vithar shamans and exchanging puzzled glances at the presence of so many men.

Like all Dokkalfar settlements, the Fell Walk was built below the forest, using the bases of great trees as the foundations for their homes while the leaf litter above disguised the presence of the forest-dwellers. The Walk was built in a natural depression in the ground. The ceiling, built by old craft from a tapestry of knotted brambles and wooden branches, was high above the actual forest floor.

Nanon was of the Heart and found the austerity and lack of humour of the Fell Walkers strange. Their settlement was a sombre place, where the song of the Dokkalfar was mournful and the people miserable. He accepted that they had ample reason to feel they had been given a hard lot in life, but really they needed to cheer up. They behaved like an oppressed population, feeling sorry for themselves and refusing to accept that men had a place in their woods. It was only on the insistence of Nanon that Rham Jas, Utha and the others had been allowed to remain in the first place.

Vithar Xaris, more confident now that he was back amongst his own people, had called for an hour of meditation, and the Dokkalfar who sat around the auditorium all had their heads bowed in silent contemplation. Nanon did not know many of these forest-dwellers and found himself more comfortable sitting next to the men.

Rham Jas Rami Dark Blood was more respectful of the Fell Walkers and their peculiarities than the other men. Utha the Shadow had, on more than one occasion, been told to shut up. Also, he had had to be physically restrained from attacking the Kirin assassin as soon as he'd seen him. The others, Dalian Thief Taker, Kale Glenwood and Randall of Darkwald, had been too overwhelmed to say much at all. They confined themselves to sitting and staring with wide-eyed wonder at the spectacle of the Fell Walk.

Nanon sat next to Utha and opposite Rham Jas, who had been kept away from the old-blood for his own safety. They were confined to a small section of the auditorium, guarded by serious-looking Tyr warriors. Both Utha and his squire continued to glare at the Kirin assassin, and Nanon understood that Rham Jas had killed a close friend of theirs in the recent past. The dark-blood didn't seem to care, and had directed a series of maddening grins at the two men sitting opposite him.

The wind claw, Dalian Thief Taker, was taking things in his stride. Nanon had found that he liked the implacable man from Karesia and agreed with his insistence that Saara the Mistress of Pain should be their first priority. Whether the Vithar accepted it or not, having a devout servant of the Fire Giant on their side could not but help their cause. The Thief Taker himself was pragmatic enough to accept the strange situation in which he found himself as a part of the larger task he had been set by Jaa.

The one slight anomaly was Kale Glenwood. He was the only man present who was not directly involved and had found himself in the Fell more or less by accident. He was not a priest or an old-blood and had, as far as Nanon could tell, no faith at all. As the Dokkalfar meditated, the criminal sat awkwardly next to Rham Jas, trying not to make eye-contact with the forest-dwellers and keeping a hand on his longsword for comfort.

'How long will this silence last?' asked Utha.

'As long as they think necessary . . . could be a few days,' replied Nanon. 'The Fell Walkers aren't known for being quick to decide things.'

The old-blood nodded. 'Yes, I've been on the receiving end of Xaris's *we will endure* horse-shit a few times.'

Utha was growing impatient. Nanon surmised that it was only the calming presence of his squire that was stopping the albino cleric from shouting at the assembled Dokkalfar.

'Just relax,' said Randall. 'At least no one is trying to kill us.'

'Not yet,' replied Nanon. 'It's only a matter of time before the hounds and those Dark Young reach the Fell Walk.'

'So what the fuck are they waiting for?' Utha said, louder than he'd intended, causing several of the Tyr to glare at him.

'Problem?' Utha barked at the nearby forest-dwellers.

'You will be silent!' replied Tyr Ecthel, the larger of the two Dokkalfar on guard. 'You are not permitted to speak here.'

Utha looked as if he was about to object until Randall put a hand on his shoulder. 'Just leave it,' said the squire. 'They don't understand us any more than we understand them.'

'You have wisdom beyond your years, Randall the squire,' said Nanon, with a smile. 'Whatever else happens, it's your job to keep this man alive.' He pointed to the old-blood.

It was clear, even to Nanon, that the bond between master and squire was a largely unspoken trust built on shared experiences. He valued the little people as much as he did the great, and he was too wise to assume that Randall would not have a role yet to play in the Long War.

Across the wooden auditorium, Rham Jas yawned loudly, causing several of the forest-dwellers to look at him.

'And when can I kill that fucking Kirin?' barked Utha.

Nanon tilted his head and made a few puzzled noises. 'Do you know who . . . what he is?'

'Other than an assassin, no,' replied the albino cleric. 'He killed my friend.'

'He's what we call a dark-blood. A man with certain . . .

advantages.' Nanon was not deliberately trying to be obtuse, but he was not sure how Utha would react to the knowledge that Rham Jas was infused with the power of the Dark Young. 'He's our only hope of killing the maleficent witches. If you choose to kill him, we'll need to find another dark-blood.'

Nanon could sense great unease among all the men present, none more so than Utha the Shadow. The Dokkalfar couldn't be relied on to put them at their ease, no matter how much they were needed.

'I'm getting impatient,' said Utha.

'Yup, me too,' replied Nanon cheerfully. 'How about we play a game?'

'A game?' queried the old-blood, raising an eyebrow. 'Like, Spot the Happy Dokkalfar?'

'I was thinking more along the lines of word association . . . I say a word and you say the first word that comes into your head.' Nanon grinned with childlike glee, certain that Utha found him utterly confusing.

'You're strange, my grey-skinned friend,' replied the cleric.

'You are not the first man to remark on that.' Nanon turned to Randall and said, 'How about you, Randall the squire, want to play a game?'

'Er, I'd rather just wait, if that's okay,' replied the young man.

'Suit yourself.' Nanon was trying to be jovial, but there was a limit to the flippancy he could sustain.

With no one to play a game with, he sat back on the wooden terrace and joined the others waiting for Vithar Xaris to speak.

Across the way, sat on wooden chairs of twisted design, were a dozen Vithar. Each had their heads bowed and their eyes closed, sitting in silent meditation. Nanon knew they found him frustrating, but impossible to ignore. The old Tyr hoped that his reputation and age would be enough to force the stolid Fell Walkers into something approaching swift action.

'Wait here,' he said to Utha and Randall. 'I need to speak with Rham Jas.' The name elicited an angry growl from both men.

Nanon stood quietly and made his way down the terraces of wooden seating that framed the auditorium. Once on the flat ground in the centre, he paused for a moment to take in the spectacle. The auditorium was raised from the forest floor and hung between two great tree trunks, with thick branches weaving around solid pillars and providing support. The Heart, far to the north, used vines and moving platforms to traverse the trees, whereas the Fell Walk consisted of beautifully constructed staircases and ornate arches, linking together the open spaces between the trees. It was impressive, even to an old Tyr like Nanon, and he empathized with the men and the awe they must be feeling. It had no comparison in the lands of men, where the spires of Ro Tiris and the cathedrals of Ro Arnon were clumsily built and ugly in comparison.

Nanon was largely ignored by the Dokkalfar as he walked across the open space. A few Tyr nodded in acknowledgement and a few more looked at him with something approaching reverent fear, but he was not impeded as he made his way up the opposite line of seating to where the other men sat.

Rham Jas was between Dalian Thief Taker and Kale Glenwood. The Karesian refused to be cowed by the strange spectacle before him, and the lowly criminal tried not to stare at things he did not understand. Nanon directed his warmest and most reassuring smile at the three men and sat down in front of them.

'Hello there, pointy ears,' said Rham Jas, offering his hand to his old friend.

'I hope this isn't boring you, Kirin man,' replied the Dokkalfar, shaking his hand enthusiastically, before offering the same greeting to Dalian and Glenwood.

'I won't, if you don't mind,' replied the Karesian, maintaining his ice-cold demeanour.

Nanon smiled and thought again that he liked the wind claw. The forger from Leith did shake the forest-dweller's hand, but seemed to do so without really thinking about it.

'Don't worry, Ro man,' he said to Glenwood. 'Strange things broaden the mind . . . you'll get the hang of it.'

'What?' he replied, a look of abject confusion on his face.

Rham Jas put a reassuring hand on his companion's shoulder. 'Just ignore him, Kale, you'll never get used to it. You're better off just accepting it.'

'Can I get drunk?' asked the Ro.

Rham Jas shook his head. The Kirin had frequently lamented the fact that the Dokkalfar did not understand alcohol.

'They have tea,' said the assassin. 'It's not the same, but we could pretend.'

Dalian Thief Taker, less fond of small talk than Rham Jas, leant forward and interjected. 'I am becoming tired of this waiting,' he said seriously. 'We are wasting time. We have agreed that this man . . .' he gestured at the assassin, 'needs to be taken to Ro Weir so he can kill Saara the Mistress of Pain.'

'I *am* still here, Dalian,' said Rham Jas quietly, offended at being referred to as *this man*.

'Quiet, boy,' spat the Karesian, and the Kirin shrank under the glare of the older man.

'Sorry, Dalian,' replied Rham Jas, like a scolded child.

The Thief Taker turned back to Nanon. 'What are they waiting for? Their forest is being destroyed by hounds.'

Nanon smiled in as human a fashion as he could manage. 'They're meditating on the presence of the Shadow – him.' He gestured towards Utha, who was sitting quietly, oblivious to the effect he was having on the forest-dwellers. 'He's even more important than the Kirin man here.'

Dalian let his dark eyes play over Nanon's face and the forest-dweller felt awkward, realizing he'd spent little time with the faithful of Jaa during the course of his long life. They seemed to live constantly in fear, trying to achieve the kind of divine terror that the Fire Giant demanded.

'I don't care about the old-blood,' replied Dalian. 'I care about Karesia and Jaa . . . and I care about killing the Mistress of Pain.'

Nanon met the wind claw's stare and tilted his head, confused by Dalian's evident need to appear intimidating all the time.

'Everyone here reveres Jaa almost as much as you. He gave us the gift of immolation that we would never again birth the Dark Young.' They were sincere words, and the Thief Taker appreciated that fact.

'But you are not Jaa's people,' replied the wind claw.

Nanon stared at the obstinate man of Karesia, endeavouring to identify some common ground between them. The old Tyr knew that he would need more time in his company truly to understand Dalian. What he *did* know was that all five of the humans were important – some more so than others, but all had a role in the Long War. Even the near-catatonic forger from Leith had a purpose, though Nanon did not yet know what it was.

Behind him, the assembled Dokkalfar began to stand, signalling that their long meditation was coming to an end. Nanon held a finger up to his lips to indicate to the humans that they should remain quiet. Across the auditorium, Utha and Randall were eagerly awaiting the Vithar's words. Rham Jas and his two companions were more laid-back, and Dalian and Glenwood took their cue from the blasé Kirin.

Vithar Xaris was the first to speak, though he was not the oldest, or the wisest, shaman present. Sitting behind him was Vithar Loth, a Dokkalfar almost as old as Nanon, who was also known as the Tree Father. He claimed to have planted the first shrub of the Fell Walk. It probably wasn't true, but few of the forest-dwellers would deign to question the old shaman.

Xaris took a step away from his wooden throne and spoke in a deep and commanding voice. 'We welcome the children of men to the Fell Walk . . . we ask that they respect our forever as we respect their now.' He thrust out his chin and raised himself up to his full height. The Vithar was over seven feet tall and more slender than any man. 'We sit in the presence of the one we loved and in the embrace of the shadows provided for us.' His words were formal and dry.

Vithar Xaris spoke slowly, and his long, drawn-out sentences echoed around the auditorium. He droned on about the maleficent witches, though he lacked any practical knowledge concerning them. He spoke of the need to challenge the Dead God, but his words carried no conviction. By the time he addressed the old-blood in their midst, Nanon was becoming annoyed. He rarely felt the emotion and found it deeply uncomfortable now.

'The Shadow,' he said, motioning towards Utha, 'is our greatest weapon and he should be protected in the Fell for as long as possible . . . he will endure as we will endure.' Another long pause and Xaris resumed his seat. 'We will now meditate on how to answer the coming threat.'

The Dokkalfar all bowed their heads and followed the Vithar's instructions. Nanon puffed out his cheeks in frustration and the men turned towards him with questioning looks.

'I'm a patient man, Nanon,' said Rham Jas in a whisper, 'but this is getting dangerous.'

The old Tyr couldn't disagree and a glance at Utha told him that the old-blood thought the same. Reluctantly, Nanon stood up and prepared to interrupt the meditation.

'What are you doing?' asked Rham Jas, aware of how rude Nanon's intervention would seem.

'I don't want to pin my life on *we will endure*,' replied the Dokkalfar, cheerfully slapping the Kirin on the shoulder. 'I'm going to offend some of my people.'

When he stood up he had been uncomfortably reminded how short he was compared with the other forest-dwellers. He was over six feet tall, taller than all of the humans except for Dalian, but slight for a Tyr. The guards standing before the humans were all well over seven feet in height, and several significantly more, and they towered over Nanon. They grasped their heavy leaf swords in ceremonial position.

Taking a few strides down the stepped seating, Nanon coughed in mimicry of the human method of attracting people's attention. As one, the seated Dokkalfar slowly tilted their heads at the interruption.

'Nanon, you may not speak yet,' said Vithar Loth, the Tree Father, in a gravelly croak of a voice.

'I wasn't asking for permission,' replied Nanon. He nudged his way past the guards and stepped into the centre of the auditorium. 'I will speak.'

Vithar Xaris looked offended, but he was stopped from speaking by a raised hand from Loth. The Tree Father peered at Nanon through narrow, black eyes. His head was not tilted and he appeared to be assessing the short Tyr standing in front of him. Nanon could not sense the Vithar's thoughts and he knew that the restriction was mutual. They were the oldest two beings in the Fell Walk and they would have to rely on words alone. Their usual gifts of perception and premonition would not work on each other.

'When did we last meet, Shape Taker?' asked Loth. 'And how is your mate?'

Nanon stepped to the front, feeling only slightly naked under the gaze of so many tilted heads and black eyes. 'I haven't seen Jasn in many years. I hope she is well,' he replied, silently pleased that he'd remembered her name a few months ago. 'And I believe we met three . . . or maybe four hundred years ago.'

The humans whispered incredulously as Nanon revealed his age to be much greater than they had believed possible. Rham Jas merely smiled. Nanon winked at him across the auditorium.

'And now you are a soldier of the Long War,' continued the old Vithar, leaning forward to observe Nanon's human clothing and Ro longsword. 'In the lands of men . . . Have you abandoned your forever so easily?'

Nanon chuckled and glanced around. A hundred Dokkalfar appeared to agree with Loth's barbed comment.

'You're an old fool,' he said cheerfully, causing dozens of other Tyr to grasp their leaf swords and stand more upright. 'And if we sit here and meditate, we'll be meditating on our own deaths in a few days.' He stopped smiling and thrust out his chest, reminding them who he was.

'Wake up!' he shouted. 'You've been asleep too long.' He turned away from the seated Vithar and addressed the other forest-dwellers. There were a hundred Tyr, and many more Dokkalfar watched from below.

'We will *not* endure . . . not like this . . . we will die, and from our bodies will grow new Dark Young. Our forests will burn and the Dead God will rise.'

'Silence, Tyr Nanon,' ordered Vithar Xaris.

'Make me,' replied the old Tyr, growing suddenly very angry. 'Rham Jas, come here.' He gestured to the seated Kirin who, a little awkwardly, got up and made his way to the centre.

'Excuse me,' he said, looking up into the implacable face of an eight-foot Tyr warrior.

Nanon grabbed the Kirin by the shoulder and pulled him to stand at his side in the middle of the open space. 'This is Rham Jas Rami Dark Blood. He can kill the maleficent witches.' Nanon then gestured to the muscular albino sitting to his left. 'Utha, here please.'

The old-blood was less compliant than the dark-blood and glanced across at his young squire before slowly standing up. Utha had not taken his eyes off the Kirin assassin.

Utha the Shadow didn't need to ask anyone to move. They all got out of his way without comment, and he sauntered over warily to where Nanon and Rham Jas were standing.

'Make it quick or Randall and I are going to find somewhere else to sleep this evening,' said Utha. 'And I'll break that Kirin's neck before I go.'

'*Me*? What have *I* done?' asked Rham Jas, with an exaggerated look of innocence on his face.

'Enough!' interrupted Nanon, through gritted teeth. 'This is Utha the Shadow, last old-blood of the Shadow Giants.' He paused. 'You might not like me and you might want your safe little world to endure . . . but these two men are soldiers of the Long War and we are wasting their time.'

'We will endure,' stated Vithar Loth, placing his hand on his chest and ceremonially bowing his head. 'And meditate on the ones we loved.'

'Then I defy you,' said Nanon. 'I go to fight the invaders . . . I go to fight the Dark Young . . . Maybe I'll kill some of them before they kill me, maybe I won't.' He gave Rham Jas and Utha a weak smile, before adding more quietly, 'But I won't endure any longer. I will wait one hour so that anyone who wishes to join me can make themselves known.' With a snarl, Nanon turned from the Vithar shamans and strode from the auditorium.

* * *

Nanon was not human and it took him time to calm down. When Dokkalfar became genuinely angry it was with a stubborn and persistent anger that refused to abate until its object had been eliminated or reconciled. As neither had yet occurred, he chose simply to sit on a high tree branch and wait.

The hour he had given his people was a kind of ultimatum to which the forest-dwellers were not accustomed. Even those Tyr who wished to accompany him found the concept of a time limit a strange one.

Beneath him, down a winding wooden staircase, several dozen Dokkalfar warriors stood in impassive silence. Each had leaf blades and black wart strapped to their wooden scale armour. All of them were young, and they had all agreed that meditation was merely going to see their people killed and their forests destroyed. This had calmed Nanon somewhat, but he still scowled whenever a new recruit came to him asking to join the fight.

Rham Jas and the other humans had been confined to a high balcony. Much to Utha's annoyance, they had not been allowed to leave. Nanon had no intention of permitting them to join him in repulsing the hounds and the Dark Young. The old-blood and the dark-blood were far too valuable to be thrown away defending the Fell. When he led his host west, Utha would go south and Rham Jas north. With luck, that would reduce the risk that they would have to kill each other. Dalian was going to return to Ro

Weir and lay the groundwork for the assassination of Saara the Mistress of Pain. Randall and Glenwood were to accompany Utha and Rham Jas, respectively.

'Why is this entire place built vertically?' asked Rham Jas, suddenly appearing from above. 'Would it kill you to have flat ground?'

'It's not my settlement,' Nanon replied. 'I have no idea why the Fell Walkers do what they do.'

The Kirin assassin plonked himself down on a thick tree branch next to Nanon and handed him a steaming mug of nettle tea. The old forest-dweller smiled thinly and took the mug, raising it to his nose and inhaling the refreshing scent.

'You still in a mood?' asked Rham Jas.

Nanon nodded, exhaling wearily. 'I'm too old for this stuff. Occasionally it would be nice just to sit and meditate. But I have responsibilities.'

'Don't we all . . .' was the solemn response from the dark-blood. 'Me, you, Utha, Dalian . . . rest isn't exactly on the cards for any of us, is it?' Nanon sensed that the Kirin was seeking some kind of reassurance.

'I can't give you what you want, Kirin man. I can't tell you it'll all be okay.'

He bowed his head and closed his eyes for a moment, allowing his mind to feel the assassin's anxiety. There were lingering doubts in Rham Jas's mind, mostly centred around his daughter. He was also dwelling on his friends, Bromvy and Al-Hasim. His concern for their well-being helped the Kirin keep himself grounded while he was immersed in so much that he didn't understand.

'I wish I knew what was going to happen, Rham Jas, but I don't . . . the future is a murky cup of over-brewed tea.'

'Profound . . . very profound,' replied the dark-blood. 'Useless, but profound.'

'At least you have a path to follow, Kirin man,' said Nanon, attempting a smile. 'And at least you accept what you are. Utha is more conflicted.'

'Not about me, he's not,' replied Rham Jas.

'If you'd known what he was, would you still have killed his friend?' asked Nanon, already knowing the answer.

'Yup, though I'd maybe have apologized afterwards. It's not Utha's fault that the Purple are all cunts.' Rham Jas's face broadened into a wide grin. Nanon was reminded how much he valued the friendship of this strange Kirin man.

'Utha the Shadow . . .' The Dokkalfar spoke the name with confusion, as if even he didn't believe the old-blood was still alive. 'He has the most difficult path of all.'

Rham Jas frowned. 'Why, where's he going?'

Nanon smiled and took a deep and refreshing drink of tea. 'You wouldn't believe me if I told you. *He* certainly wouldn't. Which is why I haven't told him. I think someone . . . or something . . . else is going to be his guide.'

The Kirin shook his head. 'Can't you ever give a straight answer?' he asked.

'I can. I just choose not to,' replied the Tyr. 'The problem I have is that Utha doesn't know me and has little reason to trust me. At least with you I have a degree of trust.'

'I trust you, you know that. I got my katana and my left hand back because of you.' His words were heartfelt. 'So where is the Ghost headed?'

Nanon turned to face his friend and raised his eyebrows, emphasizing the importance of what he was about to say. 'He's the last old-blood, the last man who can reach the halls beyond the world. He's going to Oron Kaa, in Far Karesia.'

'What's in Oron Kaa?' asked the Kirin.

'An abbey, of sorts,' replied Nanon. 'It's where the maleficent witches are trained. It's also where the last Fire Giant ascended . . . there's a staircase . . . and a labyrinth . . . and a guardian . . . it's very complicated.'

Rham Jas screwed up his face, trying to make sense of what he was being told. Nanon could sense his confusion and was uncomfortably reminded how difficult it would be to explain all this to Utha himself. The concept of the halls beyond the world was difficult enough for humans to grasp, but the idea of actually going there would drive many a man to madness. Nanon hoped that because Utha was not a normal man, he would be able to understand what had to be done – even if he did not fully comprehend the journey.

'He'll understand when he gets there,' Nanon said, mostly to himself. 'And his squire should keep him sane on the journey.'

'That's a lot of responsibility for a young lad whose hand shakes when he holds a sword,' retorted Rham Jas.

'I saw him fight a bunch of mercenaries with no shaking at all. He has a stronger heart than you or I, Kirin man.' Nanon was fond of Randall. The young squire had a clarity of mind that permitted little doubt to intrude. He was also utterly devoted to his master, and that would count for much.

'Enough about the Ghost and his boy,' said Rham Jas, shaking his head. 'What about me and Kale . . . and Dalian?'

Nanon found himself falling uncomfortably into the role of wise old mentor. He was not a leader, just an old Dokkalfar who knew more than he wanted to. 'You've never needed my permission or advice, Kirin man,' he said drily. 'Kale stays with you, Dalian goes to Ro Weir . . . you'll need him when you go after the Mistress of Pain. She's more dangerous than all the others put together.'

The assassin grinned, more like himself than he had been since Nanon rescued him from Leith. He glanced down at the fingers on his left hand. 'And you go to your death against ten thousand hounds and a load of Dark Young?'

'I'm not that easy to kill, my friend,' Nanon replied, confident that his destiny was not to die defending the Fell. He remembered something else and cast his mind back to Lord Bromvy Black Guard, waiting in Ro Canarn, far to the north. 'And keep an eye out for the Red Prince,' he said cryptically. 'I think he's important . . . certainly to Bromvy and Tor Funweir.'

Rham Jas burst out laughing, causing the assembled Tyr below to look up at him and tilt their heads. 'You are the most obtuse bastard I've ever met . . . and I flatter myself that I know a lot about being obtuse.' The Kirin struck Nanon on the shoulder in a manly fashion.

'I have never fully understood why you humans have to strike each other to show affection. Shaking hands I understand, but hitting me?' The forest-dweller glanced down. 'It's okay,' he said. 'He wasn't actually attacking me.' The waiting Tyr resumed their quiet contemplation. Rham Jas carried on chuckling to himself and made no comment regarding the Red Prince, whoever he might be.

From below, Nanon heard gasps from the Tyr. Making his way through the press was a giant Dokkalfar warrior with a longbow slung across his back. He had not been present in the auditorium and Nanon did not recognize him. As he made his way upwards, Nanon felt the forest-dweller's name. He was Tyr Dyus, called the Daylight Sky by the other Dokkalfar, and Nanon sensed a great wellspring of age and power within the huge warrior.

'An honour to meet you, Daylight Sky,' said Nanon, with a wary smile.

Dyus removed his bow and sat cross-legged on the top step, just below Nanon, and bowed his head respectfully. 'The honour is mine, Shape Taker,' he said, with reverence. 'I have two gifts for you . . . the first.' He passed his longbow to a confused-looking Rham Jas. 'She is called Sky Reader and will serve you well, dark-blood.'

The Kirin looked at his friend and shrugged. 'Er, thank you . . . looks like a good bow.'

'It is better than any longbow made by men,' replied Daylight Sky, without a hint of arrogance. 'Its arrows fly straight and true.'

'And the second gift?' asked Nanon.

'The second gift is my life, Shape Taker . . . I pledge it to you, to the Long War and to those we loved.' The words carried a deep sense of sadness and conviction, and in a great show of trust between warriors he allowed Nanon to feel this.

With a smile, Nanon gathered himself and leapt from the branch, landing before the assembled Tyr. There were close to forty Dokkalfar who had pledged to assist him in defending the Fell. With the coming of Tyr Dyus, he felt ready to begin.

'Greetings,' he said cheerfully. 'My name is Tyr Nanon. I am called the Shape Taker of the Heart, and I go to fight . . .' He looked down at the dark faces of the Tyr before him, identifying Tyr Ecthel, Tyr Vasir and many others whose names he did not yet know. 'We are outnumbered and many of us may die,' he continued, 'but I promise each of you that I will lead from the front and ask nothing from you that I will not undertake myself.' He paused, glancing up at the Kirin. 'We are forty against ten thousand . . . to say nothing of the Dark Young, but we know this ground, we know these trees and we can deal death from cover, never giving the invaders a target . . .' Another smile, broader this time, and Nanon concluded, 'Make no mistake, we *can* win.'

* * *

The forests of the Fell had an atmosphere all of their own. Nanon closed his eyes every few miles to allow himself to feel the texture, smell and vibrations of the woods. The ground was uneven, dotted with tree trunks and lined with deceptively sharp brambles that made it difficult to travel quickly. There were no straight lines and visibility was limited unless you found higher ground or climbed a tree.

They were spread out in a long line, sweeping through the Fell in the direction of the hounds and their Dark Young. It was strange to Nanon that they should be actively seeking out those monstrous entities. He wasn't sure why he was immune to the fear of the darkwood trees, but he knew that he could slowly transfer his courage to the Dokkalfar who travelled with him and eventually they would be able to resist the insidious terror.

'We're close, aren't we?' asked Tyr Dyus from the tree above.

Daylight Sky was a valuable presence within the host, second only to Nanon in power and skill.

'We are,' replied Nanon. 'The hounds will be under the influence of drugs and enchantments. They won't be afraid of the Dark Young. We'll meet the Karesians first.'

Either side of him, the line of Tyr stretched into the sombre forest. Each Dokkalfar carried sacks of black wart and high-poundage short bows, designed to kill at close range. Most wore heavy leaf blades on each hip, though a few carried two-handed leaf swords, and Nanon himself still had the longsword he had acquired in Ro Canarn.

He held up his hand to signal that the line should advance. In silence, the forty forest-dwellers moved through the dense undergrowth. A few crouched in the low branches of trees, acting as spotters and scouts, staying a little way ahead of the host.

'Shape Taker,' whispered Dyus after ten minutes, 'Humans ahead . . . scouts, maybe fifty.'

Nanon raised his hand again and motioned for the host to halt and take cover. In an instant the forest-dwellers had melted into the undergrowth. The old Tyr inched forward, keeping his longsword low to the ground. As they waited, the noise of complaining voices carried through the trees to their sensitive ears. Nanon saw shapes, clustered together and hacking at vines and branches with their scimitars, trying to penetrate the dense forest. They made no effort to remain quiet and were spread out in disorganized patches of black metal across the old Tyr's field of vision. They wore plate armour, with no individuality or character, and their helmets were closed and expressionless.

Nanon smiled as the Karesians blundered through the Dokkalfar woods. They were ignorant children who had not yet grown out of their barbaric beginnings. Not that they were any worse than the Ro, but Nanon always found the intractability of Jaa's followers more difficult to understand. These men and women were criminals, sentenced to die in the hounds. Maybe they would be lucky to be killed by him rather than by some disease or drug overdose.

When all the hounds were within view, Nanon stepped out from behind a tree and raised his hand. The soldiers of Karesia saw him and were momentarily stunned as the short forest-dweller smiled at them and let his hand drop.

Arrows shot through the undergrowth, whistling on low trajectories past tree trunks and bramble bushes to lodge into the bodies of the hounds. The high-poundage bows breached their armour easily and half of the invaders had died before they'd had a chance to cry out.

'Kill them!' shrieked a man, fumbling to draw his scimitar.

An arrow whistled through the trees as Tyr Dyus shot the speaker in the throat. The Dokkalfar reloaded quickly and a second volley cut into the scouting force. The handful that remained were cut down from above as a dozen forest-dwellers jumped from low branches and despatched them efficiently with their leaf blades.

'All men are dead, Shape Taker,' announced Dyus from a tree, nimbly reloading his short bow while balancing on a narrow branch.

'Marvellous,' replied Nanon with a human-like smile. 'Let's move on, shall we?'

The Dokkalfar increased their pace. Nanon estimated that they would reach the hound lines within the hour. Where the Dark Young lurked was a mystery. Maybe the beasts would be out on the plains of Leith rather than rampaging through the Fell.

'Shape Taker, signs of fire ahead,' said Tyr Dyus after a further hour's advance.

Nanon ordered a halt and the host hunkered low to the ground in readiness. Ahead, a slowly rolling bank of smoke approached them. A few burning embers carried with the smoke and Nanon felt a great sense of pain at the loss of so many trees. Either side of him, the Dokkalfar displayed expressions of anger and loss.

'Hold for a moment,' whispered Nanon, closing his eyes and breathing in deeply, trying to project serenity into his fellow forest-dwellers. He wanted them focused to enact a swift revenge.

Then a deafening sound reached his ears and a tree trunk flew towards him through the smoke. He ducked just in time and the trunk thudded into the undergrowth behind him.

'Dark Young!' roared Tyr Dyus from the trees, just as a tentacle lashed towards the line of Dokkalfar. Nanon's host jumped back and took cover behind trees as the beast emerged from the smoke. It was newly birthed and its surface was a shimmering black, not yet having developed the bark-like appearance of the older Dark Young. Two of its tentacles were planted solidly on the charred ground, pushing it upwards in a grotesque ripple of movement. Its other limbs flailed in the air, uprooting tree stumps and pulling it forwards.

The Dokkalfar were panting heavily and trying to resist the desire to flee from the madness-inducing beast. Nanon was unaffected and seized the opportunity to take a good look at the Dark Young. The beast seemed not to have noticed the concealed forest-dwellers and its gummy roar seemed to be a natural sound rather than a particular cry of war. He could see no eyes, but the feelers that undulated from its maw were reaching into the air and giving the creature a sense of its surroundings.

'Okay, so you can't see,' Nanon muttered, reaching for his short bow and a black-wart arrow from the quiver on his back.

He stood up quickly and took aim. He was no more than ten feet from the Dark Young. A glance either side of him told him that the other forest-dwellers were wrestling with their fear and struggling to nock arrows to their short bows. One or two were beginning to mouth the words *the priest and the altar*, though they were doing so quietly.

'Hey!' Nanon shouted at the tentacled monstrosity in front of him. 'This is our ground. You are not welcome.'

The Dark Young reared up at the words and pulled itself towards Nanon. The Dokkalfar turned to him. Though they all hesitated, it was clear that their leader's courage was beginning to infuse them.

Nanon grinned at the advancing beast and released his bow-string, sending an explosive arrow into the creature's maw. Tyr Dyus and Tyr Vasir also fired black wart. A deafening and shrill cry rose from the beast, and as it flailed in the air a series of explosions tore it apart. It did not die straightaway and the high-pitched wail continued until it stopped moving. At that moment, a shrivelled darkwood tree with a blasted trunk took root in the ground.

'Not my priest and not my altar,' said Nanon defiantly.

'That's one down,' muttered Daylight Sky from above, his eyes fixed on the darkwood tree.

'There could be a hundred of them,' Nanon replied, with a tilt of his head. 'But they die just like anything else.' He then addressed the assembled Dokkalfar. 'You see . . .' he stated in a loud, clear voice. 'They can die . . . they can die and they *will* die . . . Fire was our gift from Jaa and with fire we will vanquish them.'

He knew that the longer the host spent with him, the more resistant they would become to the disquieting effects of the Dark Young. 'We will hold this tree line and make them come to us,' he announced, motioning along the last stand of trees before the burnt-out area ahead of them. 'Each and every patrol they send into the Fell will die like the first. They won't reach the Walk and they will capture no more of our people.'

It was a gamble, and Nanon knew it. They couldn't fight the hounds and the Dark Young on the plains of Leith, and if they stayed in the forest, they risked being bombarded with more fiery projectiles. The gamble was that the Seven Sisters would want the Dokkalfar captured rather than dead, so sooner or later they would need to launch a ground assault rather than just deforesting the Fell.

CHAPTER ELEVEN

UTHA THE GHOST IN THE FELL

A S HE RECLINED in the Dokkalfar hammock, he dreamt. He dreamt he was flying over mountains and through clouds. He dreamt that the land beneath was a dot, a tapestry of colour and texture, just out of reach, elusive and half-remembered. He felt more than man. He entered the high shadows cast by towering peaks and rumbling cloud formations, only to emerge from other shadows, some distant, some close, but all his to manipulate.

He felt the peace of isolation. Or was it just euphoria at the enormity of what he was seeing? Either way, wind caressed his fingertips and ruffled his stark white hair. He was no longer just a man, no longer merely a cleric of a god or the servant of a church. He was beyond it, beyond them, and he breathed in deeply and felt that he had taken the first step on a longer path.

'Enjoy the peace, old-blood,' said a hollow voice out of the darkness.

He was not startled. He felt that nothing could harm him as he dived in and out of the shadows. He paused in his flight and addressed the speaker, whose voice seemed to have come from the base of an enormous mountain.

'Who speaks?' he asked.

'In this place I have neither name nor form, old-blood,' the reply echoed through the clouds. 'I am a memory, a remnant, an echo.'

Utha allowed himself to glide down towards the mountain. It was a single peak, rising from an endless craggy plain and topped with snow. With complete command of the shadows around him, he manoeuvred through dark clouds to emerge at the mountain's base. With the tingling in his fingers abating, Utha felt rock beneath his bare feet and saw a gothic structure of rock – perhaps natural, perhaps crafted – rising in front of him. It resembled a primitive altar, a raised platform, framed by two scything rock protrusions and dug slightly into the mountain. No figure was visible as Utha approached.

He observed that he was not wearing armour or carrying a weapon, but he did not feel in danger or unprepared. He wore just his brown robe, with his feet bare, and his limbs were exposed to the wind as the fabric rolled and fluttered in the breeze.

'I am Utha of Arnon,' he said with a bow of his head. 'And this is my dream.'

'Is it?' came the hollow reply.

Now that he was closer, the old-blood could identify a strange quality to the voice. The words were somehow sharp, as if the speaker was not used to the speech of men and had to concentrate in order to be understood.

'If you won't tell me *who* you are, will you at least tell me *what* you are?' Utha asked, stepping towards the jagged altar.

'I am nothing . . . and less than nothing . . . and more than nothing.' The speaker emitted a strange, chirruping sound between each word.

Utha smiled at the cryptic response. 'Were I awake I would likely say something caustic and clever,' he responded.

'Were you awake you would be able to see me, old-blood . . . but, in the halls beyond the world, I am as formless as the Giants that dwell here.'

Utha paused and took a step back. Looking around him, he suddenly experienced a majestic vista. This was not the land of men; nor was it anywhere a man could travel in his dreams. His blood had taken control of his mind and he had fallen effortlessly into the lands beyond the world.

Above him, stretching into the void of deep time, were the halls of the Giants. His mind could not interpret what his eyes were seeing, but he knew that countless gods, demi-gods, urges, spirits and other things he could not name dwelt within view. Palaces, caves, spires, as numerous as grains of sand on a beach, flowed together in an undulating mass of divinity, each stranger and more enormous than the last – gods with no names and no followers, urges that fed off desire and pain, spirits of natural forces, and everything in between. Halls of rock, water, air, fire, shadow and death, bizarre and unknowable, they unfolded before him, and Utha the Shadow knew that he was not afraid. Instead, he felt a deep sadness and a rising anger.

The vista before him was tied to the lands he remembered, of which the lands of men were only a tiny part, but as he looked, Utha could sense that the ties had been severed. The Giants could no longer influence their followers and each shouted blindly into the void in the hope that someone would hear. The voices were beyond his comprehension, but he knew that each carried the ages of deep time within it. Some called to men, but most of them screamed at things for which Utha had no name.

'You have brought me here? Why?' he asked the alien presence.

'I have done nothing. I merely followed as you slept. Think of me as a guide.' The voice was utterly inhuman and Utha's skin began to crawl. 'When you awake, old-blood, you will know your task,' stated the speaker. 'And you will seek me out.'

He breathed in the crisp air and allowed his mind to settle. Whatever the being was, Utha was sure it meant him no harm. He was also sure that it was close, perhaps even waiting somewhere in the Dokkalfar woods, waiting for an old-blood to address, to guide, and perhaps to teach. He had been told that he was the last old-blood and that he had a responsibility to the lands of men and to the Gods.

He had never truly believed this. In his cynicism, he had merely sought sanctuary and to remove himself from his fellow men.

Now, as he began to wake, Utha of Arnon, Black cleric of the One God, knew who he was and who he was not. He was no longer a cleric and his path was no longer the path of the One.

Nor was it a path that any other man could take. He was the only man capable of reaching the halls beyond the world.

The last hazy image of his dream was of a stairway, a labyrinth and a guardian. They were all shrouded in mist and Utha could not make out their actual lines or forms. Instead, he felt a powerful pull towards them.

* * *

'Bad dreams?' asked Randall, from the adjacent hammock.

'Strange, certainly,' Utha replied, turning to smile at his squire. '*Bad* doesn't seem to apply . . . neither does *good*.'

Randall sat up and rubbed his eyes. He had expressed his concern that they should be waiting in the Fell Walk while the Dokkalfar went to war, and Utha was proud of his squire's desire to assist in the defence of the settlement. It was only Nanon's insistence that they remain behind that had made him submit to sleep instead of combat.

'How long did I sleep?' he asked his squire.

'Two hours maybe . . . you were restless, though,' replied Randall. 'I made a bet with a passing forest-dweller that you'd fall out of that stupid hammock thing.'

Utha yawned. 'You lost,' he responded, with little humour.

'Don't take it out on me . . . just because you didn't sleep well.' Randall was smiling and Utha was grateful for the young man's presence.

'Any word from Nanon or Vasir?'

The squire shook his head and rubbed his eyes again. 'They have probably reached the hounds by now, but no one's said anything. These Dokkalfar are difficult to talk to, though, so I doubt they'd tell us if they'd had word.'

'Well, I suppose it doesn't matter,' said the old-blood. 'We'll be leaving soon anyway.'

Randall raised an eyebrow. 'And where are we going, master?'

Utha smiled. He knew that his squire trusted him, but he didn't feel like burdening the young man with talk of dreams, disembodied voices and strange floating halls beyond the world.

'For now, there's someone, or something, we need to speak to.'

'And after that?' pressed Randall.

'A sea voyage, my dear boy. Followed by a long trek south.'

How he knew this was a mystery. Suffice to say, he had woken up with a clear path in his troubled mind. There was a stairway, a labyrinth and a guardian. That this was their path, he didn't doubt.

'Er, that's not what I expected to hear,' replied the young man of Darkwald. 'I couldn't tell you what I *did* expect to hear . . . but it wasn't that.'

'Come on, we've got things to do.' He scanned the nearby hammocks. 'Is that Kirin still around here someplace?' Utha had not yet lost his desire to pummel Rham Jas to death for the murder of Torian.

'They left an hour or so ago. The Kirin and that forger from Tiris. I think they're going to Ro Haran. The Karesian man, Dalian, is going back to Ro Weir.' Randall had clearly been paying attention to the comings and goings of the other men present in the Fell. Utha felt glad that they had all departed.

'Just thee and me, then,' said Utha, with a broad and friendly smile.

They clambered down from their hammocks, pausing only to retrieve their weapons from a convenient knot in the tree. The Dokkalfar settlement had not been designed with men in mind, and they were forced to negotiate several sheer drops and tentatively supported walkways on their way to the forest floor.

Most of the forest-dwellers were inside their wooden huts and places of contemplation – meditating, no doubt, on Tyr Nanon's chances of survival. Utha didn't fancy the odds of a few dozen Dokkalfar against thousands of hounds and Dark Young, but something about the strange little shape-taker gave him confidence.

'Do you think he's limited to things with wings?' asked Randall, seeming to sense his master's thoughts. 'Gryphons and hawks and things?'

'I've no idea. The first I knew of this shape-taking business was when he dropped a load of black wart on Pevain's men.' Utha had not heard of forest-dwellers doing such things and had no idea of its limitations.

'You never know,' said Randall somewhat mischievously, 'maybe he can turn into a Stone Giant or something and smash the Dark Young to bits.'

Utha laughed, slapping his squire on the back in comradely fashion. 'While I remember, young Randall, we need to step up your lessons. You've developed a few bad habits with that sword of yours.' Utha pointed to the sword of Great Claw which Randall had buckled around his waist as they wandered through the Fell Walk.

The young man looked slightly hurt. 'I'm still alive, master . . . I think I did quite well against the mercenaries.'

'*Quite well* is what lucky swordsmen do, lad. You need to rely on skill, not luck.' Utha had been tutoring him most days since they had left Voy, but their journey had taken a frenetic turn over the past few weeks and the lessons had become less regular.

'Can we expect to be doing a lot of fighting?' asked the squire.

'Probably . . . maybe . . . who knows? It's better to be prepared, don't you think?' Utha pointed to a break in the tree line on the eastern side of the settlement. 'That's where we're headed,' he said, following the insistent pull at the back of his mind.

'Where exactly are we going, master?' asked the squire.

'Just trust me,' responded Utha, not feeling inclined to explain.

Randall snorted with amusement. 'Lead on, master . . . a nice walk in the woods would be pleasant.'

The old-blood gently cuffed his squire across the back of the head. 'Stop being cheeky, boy.'

'Whatever you say, master,' was his even cheekier response.

'You know what, Randall? I think I liked you more when you were meek and afraid of your shadow.'

'I'll do my best to return to that . . . if it pleases you, master.'

Randall really only called Utha *master* when he was being

cheeky. There had been a gradual transition from genuine respect to unspoken teasing, and the old-blood found that he valued the young man of Darkwald more and more each day.

'Just shut up,' barked Utha, holding a finger across his mouth to indicate that he didn't want any clever retort this time.

They walked down a shallow incline that led away from the bulk of the settlement until they could once again see the sky. Having spent the entirety of the previous day hidden in the woods, it was strange to emerge only to find themselves under another canopy of trees. It was lighter and airier than the Fell Walk, but the forest was still dense and had a primeval quality. There were no paths and the two men of Ro had to pick their way through the undergrowth, as Utha followed the direction he had sensed in his dream.

The incline became steeper and they had to use nearby shrubs and overhanging branches to steady themselves as they travelled down into a deep hollow in the forest floor. The air was stagnant and the light minimal. They edged down the side of the hollow to a craggy rock formation, nestled in the greenery at the bottom.

'Is it me, or is this place ever so slightly sinister?' asked Randall, following closely behind his master.

'I'm not sure any men have ever been down here before, my boy . . . the forest doesn't seem to like us.'

Utha was wary. Before them, a series of low cave entrances plunged into the rock face.

'Watch your step, lad,' he said, as Randall half-stumbled, half-jumped down the last few feet.

Utha cast his eyes over the caves. The same shiver he'd felt in his dream travelled up his spine. Ahead of them, partially concealed within the overgrowth, was a single large cave entrance with a thick layer of dense web across the opening.

'Would now be a good time to tell you that I'm a little . . . funny . . . around spiders,' said Randall, clearly in distress.

'Funny?' queried Utha. 'What, you like to tell them jokes?'

'Er, no . . . I'm terrified of the bastards,' replied the young squire, beads of sweat rolling down his face and his hand involuntarily going to his sword.

Utha chuckled at his admission. 'I don't think we're in any danger here,' he said, placing a reassuring hand on Randall's shoulder.

Just as the atmosphere relaxed, a hand-sized Gorlan scuttled down a nearby tree and darted into a cave. Randall jumped back and turned almost as white as his albino master.

'It's only a small one, my boy . . . easy to squash if it comes too close.' He interposed himself between Randall and the spider.

'Fear is a strange thing,' replied the squire. 'I know they're not all dangerous. It's just something about the way they move and never make any noise.'

Utha smiled again and gently removed Randall's hand from the sword of Great Claw. 'I don't think you'll be needing that.'

'Makes me feel better to know it's there,' he responded, visibly shaken.

The old-blood's skin began to crawl again as a rumbling sound came from the large cave in front of them. Utha turned sharply, making sure that Randall was behind him. Then he took a step towards the cave.

'I am Utha of Arnon . . . you called me here.'

He didn't need to look behind him to know that his squire was shaking with fear – which he began to share as a voice came from the cave. 'I know who you are, old-blood.'

It was similar to the voice he'd heard in his dream, but more organic. Behind the words, he could sense an unpleasant grating noise that did not seem to emanate from human mouth parts.

From the cave entrance, obscured slightly, the two men saw eyes appear. Both gasped at the number of eyes and the size of the creature they must belong to. A clicking sound accompanied its movements and Utha involuntarily took a step backwards.

'Do not fear me, old-blood,' said the voice, spitting and gurgling out each word.

'Reveal yourself,' said Utha, his hand going to his sword.

'I wish you hadn't said that,' was the quivering retort from Randall.

From within the dark cave, a single spider leg emerged at around head height. It was thick, segmented and covered in dark brown hairs. Utha and Randall backed off and brandished their swords defensively, standing close together. The enormous leg rose slowly and, in one sinuous movement, swept aside the web that covered the cave entrance.

For a moment, Utha did not know what he was looking at. The darkness cast a many-layered reflection across the shimmering black chitin, and until the beast actually moved, the old-blood thought it little more than a shadow. The eyes appeared first – strange orbs of reflective blacks and greys, floating on the hairy surface of the Gorlan's head. Its feelers were thickly haired and twitched rapidly from side to side as the creature inched forward into the light. The fangs beneath were curved and reminiscent of vicious daggers, though they were tucked behind the feelers and not poised for a strike.

It took a few seconds for the spider fully to emerge from the cave. Its legs were clutched closely around its bulbous black abdomen, making it difficult to estimate the creature's full size, but Utha didn't doubt that the Gorlan was as large as four horses.

'I want to run away,' Randall blurted out, his hands shaking and his voice high-pitched.

When the Gorlan spoke, it used its feelers to generate the sounds, clicking them together against its fangs to mimic human speech. 'There is no need to run, human.'

Utha didn't take his eyes from the beast as he pushed his squire further behind him. 'Just back off slowly,' he told Randall, brandishing his sword defensively.

The Gorlan flexed its legs and lowered its huge body, stretching out to double its previous width. 'You are not in danger,' said the spider, speaking in a manner utterly alien to Utha's ears. 'I have recently fed.'

'Why is the Gorlan talking?' asked Randall in near panic. 'How can it talk? It's a spider.'

Utha had no answer. He had travelled far in the lands of men, but had never heard stories or legends of such things. The creature before them was by far the biggest of its species he had ever seen, but to hear the beast speak was almost too much to believe. If it hadn't been for his dream, the old-blood would probably have already attacked it. Somehow, he knew that the creature was not his enemy.

'You may call me Ryuthula,' said the creature.

'A name, it's got a name,' quivered Randall.

'If you have a need to speak . . . speak,' said Utha, doing his best to remain calm as the monstrous Gorlan flexed its legs again. 'I spoke to you as I slept.'

'You did not,' replied the Gorlan called Ryuthula. 'Though I will one day speak to you . . . from the halls beyond the world.'

Utha did not understand. The voice from his dream had called itself a *memory*. The old-blood was beginning to feel small and ignorant under the weight of things he did not know.

'Well, you're not there yet,' said Utha, without lowering his sword. 'So speak.'

The Gorlan hunched up again as if it were trying to lessen its terrifying appearance. 'You have a journey ahead of you, old-blood,' said Ryuthula, 'to the lands of silence far to the south.'

'I'm just a man,' replied Utha. 'I can't even comprehend what is expected of me.'

'You are *not* just a man, old-blood, as your name suggests.'

Utha retched involuntarily at the sight of the spider's gummy, ooze-filled mouth.

'Do I disturb you?' it asked.

'Yes, yes, you do,' interjected Randall, his eyes wide and fixed on the beast before him.

'I think the question was directed at me,' said Utha, trying to remain between Ryuthula and the terrified squire.

'Yeah, sorry . . . I'll shut up.' The young man of Darkwald was rooted to the spot with fear.

'It takes a lot to make me afraid,' responded Utha. 'You're unknowable . . . but I don't fear you.'

Ryuthula flexed, its eyes glinting as a ray of dusky sunlight filtered down through the canopy. 'You must not fear me, for I am to be your guide,' it said, making a grotesque squelching sound as it did so.

Utha's irritation at things he couldn't understand began to get the better of him. 'I don't need a spider as a guide. A map might be useful, maybe a local who knows where Oron Kaa is, but a spider? I don't think so.'

'Don't make it angry,' said Randall, hunkering down behind his master.

'I'm sick of being told what I am and what I'm supposed to do,' replied Utha. 'What if I see my *own* future and it involves a tavern and a woman?'

The Gorlan pawed at the grass with its front two legs and bared its fangs in a threat display, causing Utha to raise his sword and shove Randall back.

'Just try it, spider,' he said, unafraid.

Ryuthula twisted its body forwards until its bulbous black abdomen was sticking up in the air and its fangs were displayed. It was a sight that would make most men run for the hills or fall down in catatonic fear, but Utha the Ghost was not most men, and he took a step forwards.

'You put those fangs away or I'll start cutting off your legs,' he growled.

Randall was panting rapidly and staring up at the spider as it towered over them. Utha had no idea how easy would it be to kill the thing . . . .

After a moment of silence, Ryuthula retracted its fangs and lowered itself back down to the ground, gathering in its legs.

'I apologize, old-blood,' said the beast, 'but I cannot always control myself when I am angry.'

'When *you're* angry?' retorted the old-blood. 'What have *you* got to be angry about?'

'You were dismissive of my help. That makes me angry.' The Gorlan was low to the ground again and appeared less threatening. 'To look upon you is difficult for those of my kind.'

Utha almost laughed. 'You're the huge spider . . . I must be positively lovely to look at in comparison.'

'You misunderstand me, old-blood. I am a Gorlan mother, not a spider as you insist on calling me. My kind has revered the Shadow Giants for longer than your race has existed, for longer than the Dokkalfar have existed. We called them the *ones we loved* long before the trees of the Fell became tall and strong.' Ryuthula backed away and coughed out a globule of milky, viscous liquid. 'Apologies, it can be difficult for me to maintain the speech of men.'

Utha lowered his sword. 'I had no idea the Gorlan had gods,' he said, genuinely interested by the revelation.

'Not the Gorlan you mean,' responded Ryuthula. 'Not the spiders of the lands of men. They are to us as you are to the Giants you revere.'

'How old are you, Gorlan mother?' he asked.

'I have no conception of the time of men. Your years are meaningless to the world and to those of us that dwell through the long ages of deep time. Your species are a cough, a blink in the tapestry of forever.'

Utha was no longer certain that his earlier outburst had been wise.

'I say that it is difficult for me to look upon you, for you wear the visage of the Shadow Giants, the pale skin and pink eyes of those we loved.'

Utha raised an eyebrow and tried to appear respectful. 'The Shadow Giants were albino?'

Ryuthula almost reared up again, but quickly regained its composure. 'No, they were not, but they had pale skin and pink eyes. All those with the blood of Giants have some kind of deformity. A stain of deep time, if you prefer. Yours is better than most; I have seen old-bloods with tentacles for arms and lamprey beaks for heads.'

Utha baulked at the description of his albinism as a stain, but refused to be insulted by the beast's manner of speech. 'Which Giants had tentacles?'

'Water Giants. Formless beasts that long ago left their halls,' replied the Gorlan mother. 'You may meet them if you follow my guidance and if you travel far enough.'

'What if we don't want to meet horrible things?' blurted out Randall, still cowering behind his master. 'Perhaps, I don't know, a few months' rest and recuperation first?'

'Randall, just shut up,' murmured Utha, trying to concentrate on what he was hearing.

'Will your servant be accompanying us?' asked the Gorlan.

Utha raised his chin. 'He's my squire and my friend, but he's no servant. Not of mine and not of yours.'

Randall glanced up at his master in acknowledgement of the words.

'He goes where I go,' said Utha.

'That may prove difficult when we reach the labyrinth,' responded Ryuthula, cryptically referring to part of Utha's dream. The old-blood had seen a stairway, a labyrinth and a guardian, but the images had been vague and made little sense to him.

'You can lead us to this labyrinth?' he asked.

'I can and I will,' replied the Gorlan mother.

Utha pursed his lips, wondering how a huge spider could accompany them to Karesia. Ryuthula had likely lived in the Fell for centuries and would be unaccustomed to travelling the lands of men.

'How are you going to do that?' he asked, deciding simply to be blunt. 'You wouldn't exactly fit in my pocket.'

He had no idea whether Ryuthula found the comment amusing, but the Gorlan mother did back away and hunch up even more. 'If it makes things easier . . .' it began, slowly shrinking in size.

Utha and his squire gasped. The beast flowed and contorted, its hair disappearing and its legs melding together into a grotesque amalgam of man and Gorlan. A few moments later, a naked woman crouched where Ryuthula had been. 'You may call me Ruth,' said the woman. 'I will need some clothing.'

The two men stared at each other for several seconds, neither knowing what to say, nor even if words were appropriate.

The woman that had been Ryuthula stood up, seemingly oblivious to her nakedness. She was dark-haired and her eyes were black. Her form conveyed nothing of her arachnid nature. Her body was slim, with few curves, though she was attractive enough. Utha shook his head, breathing in deeply. 'Another shape-taker,' he muttered under his breath.

'Master, it's a woman,' said Randall from behind him. 'It was a big spider . . . and now it's a woman . . . I may need to sit down for a minute.'

'I'm not a shape-taker, old-blood.' She attempted a smile, but it had a strange, angular quality that sent a shiver down Utha's spine.

'And my name isn't *old-blood*,' replied the albino. 'If we're expected to tolerate you for more than a few hours, you'd better get used to our names. I'm Utha and this is Randall.'

'Master,' the squire asked quietly, 'where are we going?'

It was a fair question and one that, without Utha's strange dream, would have been more than a little difficult to answer. He turned away from Ruth and placed a hand on his squire's shoulder.

'We're going to Far Karesia. There's a stairway, a labyrinth and a guardian.' He tried to smile. 'And after that, the halls beyond the world.'

Randall frowned. The young man of Darkwald had followed his master without question, never asking anything for himself. At that moment, Utha wished more than anything that he could just allow Randall to have a normal, happy life.

'Okay,' said the squire. 'I may need to take up heavy drinking before we leave, though.'

EPILOGUE

RHAM JAS DISLIKED horses. He'd ridden many in his life and he still hated the big, smelly beasts and the stupid sounds they constantly made.

It was just growing dark across the northern plains of Leith and he had been riding half-asleep in a daze for several hours. The Kirin assassin looked at his left hand and flexed his fingers. Glenwood, the sullen presence slumped over his own horse behind, had frequently quipped that the assassin was impossible to kill. Rham Jas frowned as he realized he had no idea what it would take to kill him. Now that he knew his daughter was still alive, he found himself more worried about his own survival than he had been for many years.

He had been shot with crossbow bolts, struck with swords, scimitars and no few axes and knives. He had never needed to seek healing and he bore no scars except from the wound in his shoulder. Rham Jas wondered if he could be killed. He wondered what it would take to end his wretched life and rob the world of the only man capable of killing the Seven Sisters.

He genuinely tried to care about the lands of men, but the jaded assassin found he only really cared about his daughter. If Keisha was alive, he would move mountains, shake the earth and kill a thousand men to see her safe. Rham Jas scowled at the sky as he vowed to see his daughter at least once more before his life was ended.

'Are we going back to Leith?' asked Kale, in a wearier voice than Rham Jas would have thought possible.

'Not yet,' he replied, feeling disinclined to talk.

'So . . . Ro Haran?' Glenwood drawled each word. He couldn't speak clearly and the words merely fell out of his exhausted mouth.

'The Red Prince,' said the assassin cryptically. 'He's got an enchantress called Shilpa the Shadow of Lies who needs killing.'

'Who's the Red Prince?' Kale sounded as if he were about to fall from his horse.

'When Nanon mentioned him, it rang a bell. Bromvy calls Alexander Tiris the Red Prince. He used to be a Red knight and he is the king's brother – hence he's red and hence he's a prince.'

'I've heard of him,' muttered Kale. 'Duke of Haran, used to be a general or something.'

'I neither know nor care,' responded Rham Jas. 'But I trust Nanon when he says that the Red Prince is important. If I kill Shilpa, it will free up Xander Tiris.'

Glenwood snorted to show his annoyance. Rham Jas had grown used to the miserable man of Leith and had even found himself liking his companion, but he would still have felt more comfortable with Bromvy or Al-Hasim for company.

'Do you only think about killing?' asked the criminal. 'Hasn't there been enough of that? That Nanon bloke is probably being eaten by a monster at this very moment.'

Rham Jas didn't respond. He kept his eyes turned up to the darkening sky and tried to tune out the criminal's voice. He didn't doubt that Nanon was in danger, but he was difficult to kill. The old grey-skin had been fighting for longer than any man and he was still alive.

As for the Black cleric, the Kirin hoped that Utha had found some kind of peace. Rham Jas didn't know the name of the Purple cleric who had been Utha's friend, and he didn't really care. All clerics of nobility were deserving of death on some level, but Utha had never been the Kirin's enemy and he was slightly annoyed that the albino old-blood should hate him so.

The blue tinge on the horizon was just disappearing and Rham Jas began to think about finding a place to camp. He was tired, both mentally and physically, but didn't feel like sleeping. His mind was still racing and he felt a few more hours of riding would probably be a good idea.

The Dokkalfar war-bow across his back was heavier than the longbows he was used to, but it was comforting to have a ranged weapon again. His katana had not been sharpened for several weeks. He knew that his wife would soon come back from the dead and chastize him for not looking after her gift.

'Are you ignoring me?' asked Glenwood, with irritation in his voice. 'I'm not just your fucking servant . . . not any more.'

'What are you now, Kale?' countered Rham Jas, wishing to be left alone with his thoughts.

'Well, apparently, I'm helping you save Tor Funweir.'

Glenwood had said very little since they had reached the Fell, though the forger was a clever man and had clearly been listening to everything the Dokkalfar had said.

'I don't give a fuck about Tor Fun-fucking-weir,' snapped Rham Jas. 'I'm not doing this for the Ro, or the Karesians, or the Ranen . . .'

'So, your daughter then?' replied Glenwood, and the Kirin pulled back on his reins to face his companion.

'Mention my daughter again, Kale, and I'll hurt you.' Rham Jas felt irrational anger at the comment and was a moment away from punching him.

'Is it Keisha?' Glenwood retorted quickly.

The Kirin didn't pause before he stood high in the horse's stirrups and launched himself at him. He collided heavily with the startled forger and rammed his fist into his face. Both men tumbled to the ground and Rham Jas had the wind knocked out of him, unable to get a good hold on his companion.

'Fuck you, Rham Jas,' barked Glenwood, through a bloodied mouth.

The forger rolled over and kicked the assassin squarely in the chest, sending him backwards across the grass. Then he jumped on top of Rham Jas and tried to return the punch. He was clumsy and uncoordinated compared with the Kirin and his arm was easily deflected. The assassin then grabbed him by the throat and turned him over roughly, pinning him to the ground until all Glenwood could do was grab at the restraining arm in an attempt to free himself.

Rham Jas's anger disippated quickly. He realized it wasn't his companion he was angry with. He'd probably not admit it, but the Kirin was angry with himself – for getting Zeldantor killed, for getting Keisha sold into slavery, for leaving Bromvy in Ro Canarn, for just about everything he had ever done. He had given little to the world beyond death and sarcasm, and for once in his life he felt worthless.

He released Glenwood and stood up. 'I don't want to hurt you, Kale,' he said quietly, 'but please don't talk about Keisha.'

The forger clutched at his neck and rubbed the red marks left by the assassin. He didn't stand up but shuffled backwards, apparently in fear of his deceptively strong companion.

'I don't hate you any more, Rham Jas,' said Glenwood, taking the assassin by surprise. 'You dragged me out of Tiris, you forced me to help you kill a bunch of enchantresses, you made me a wanted criminal . . . but you did it for Keisha and I can understand that.'

Rham Jas looked at the ground and felt like more of an arsehole than usual. After a moment of self-pity, he offered his hand to his companion and hefted him back to his feet.

'I'll help you, Rham Jas,' said Glenwood, 'but not just because you're unkillable and a dark-blood or whatever . . . but because I think you might actually need the help.' He smiled. 'If you ask me to help, I'll help.'

'If I ask you?' said Rham Jas, taken aback at the forger's words.

'Admit you need the help . . . admit that you can't do this alone.' Glenwood was still smiling, but the assassin knew he was deadly serious.

'You want me to . . .' stuttered out Rham Jas.

'Yes. Yes, I do,' replied the man of Leith, with a nod. 'You're stronger than me, you're faster than me.' The smile disappeared and Glenwood narrowed his eyes. 'And yes, you're much tougher than me.' He stepped closer and Rham Jas realized that the forger was no longer afraid of him. 'But you're not cleverer than me,' he concluded.

Rham Jas thought about punching his companion again. He thought of a variety of clever things to say. He even considered ignoring him, but he confined himself to saying, 'Fuck you, Kale.'

* * *

Saara the Mistress of Pain stood at the top of the lighthouse of Weir, looking out to sea. The dead wind claw lying in a pool of his own blood at her feet had done little to alleviate the pain in her head, and she was beginning to think she would have to consume the life force of many more men before the week was done. She had killed lovers, servants, guards and wind claws – each lending her their essence to strengthen the faithful of Shub-Nillurath.

Saara was becoming impatient. Instead of waiting in the duke's residence for additional forces to arrive from Karesia, she had been standing at the top of the lighthouse for several hours. Her fingers were drumming on her leg and her feet shifted anxiously.

'Where are you, sister?' she said to the wind, addressing Sasha the Illusionist. Saara's sister was accompanying a few hundred thousand additional hounds, with the captive daughter of Rham Jas Rami.

A snarl escaped her lips as she thought of the dark-blood's escape from Ro Leith. She knew Isabel had not been to blame and that the Kirin assassin had had help. By all accounts, a risen man and Dalian Thief Taker had broken him out in a brash assault on the dungeon. The uncomfortable conclusion was that Saara's enemies were not as helpless as she had hoped.

Dalian was still alive and had somehow made it to the lands of Ro. The forest-dwellers were acting with an urgency that was deeply out of character. The only consolation was that her scheme for conquering the Freelands of Ranen was progressing smoothly.

'I will not fail you, master,' she said to the Forest Giant of pleasure and blood, who she would serve with her last breath and with every ounce of her being.

BESTIARY

COMPANION WRITINGS ON BEASTS
BOTH FABULOUS & FEARSOME

THE TROLLS OF FJORLAN, THE ICE MEN OF ROWANOCO

History does not record a time when the Ice Men did not prowl the wastes of Fjorlan. A constant hazard to common folk and warrior alike, the trolls are relentless eating machines; never replete, they consume rocks, trees, flesh and bone. A saying amongst the Order of the Hammer suggests that the only things they don't eat are snow and ice, and that this is out of reverence for their father, the Ice Giant himself.

Stories from my youth speak of great ballistae, mounted on carts, used to fire thick wooden arrows in defence of settlements. The trolls were confused by bells attached to the arrows and would often wander off rather than attack. Worryingly, there are few records of men killing the Ice Men, and those that do exist speak of wily battle-brothers stampeding them off high cliffs.

In quiet moments, with only a man of the Hammer for company, I wonder if the Ice Men have more of a claim on this land than us.

FROM 'MEMORIES FROM A HALL' BY ALGUIN TEARDROP LARSSON,
FIRST THAIN OF FREDERICKSAND

THE GORLAN SPIDERS

Of the beasts that crawl, swim and fly, none are as varied and unpredictable as the great spiders of Nar Gorlan. The northern men of

Tor Funweir speak of hunting spiders, the size of large dogs, which carry virulent poisons and view men as just another kind of prey. Even the icy wastes of Fjorlan have trapdoor Gorlan, called ice spiders, which assail travellers and drain the body fluids from them.

However, none of these northerners know of the true eight-legged terror that exists in the world. These are great spiders, known in Karesia as Gorlan Mothers, which can – and indeed do – speak. Not actually evil, they nonetheless possess a keen intelligence and a loathing for all things with two legs.

Beyond the Gloom Gates is a land of web and poison, a land of fang and silence and a land where man should not venture.

FROM 'FAR KARESIA: A LAND OF TERROR'
BY MARAZON VEKERIAN, LESSER VIZIER OF RIKARA

ITHQAS AND AQAS, THE BLIND AND MINDLESS KRAKENS OF THE FJORLAN SEA

It troubles me to write of the Kraken straits, for we have not had an attack for some years now and to do so would be like tempting fate. But I am the lore-master of Kalall's Deep and it must fall to me.

There are remnants of the Giant age abroad in our world and, to the eyes of this old man, they should be left alone. Not only for the sake of safety, but to remind us all that old stories are more terrifying when drawn into reality.

But I digress. The Giants of the ocean were formless, if legend is to be believed, and travelled with the endless and chaotic waters wherever tide and wind took them.

As a cough in Deep Time, they rose up against the Ice Giants and were vanquished. The greatest of the number – near-gods themselves – had the honour of being felled by the great ice hammer of the Earth Shaker and were sent down to gnaw on rocks and fish at the bottom of the endless seas. The Blind Idiot Gods they were called when men still thought to name such things. But as ages passed and men forgot, they simply became the

Krakens, very real and more than enough when seen to drive the bravest man to his knees in terror.

FROM 'THE CHRONICLES OF THE SEAS', VOL. IV,
BY FATHER WESSEL ICE FANG, LORE-MASTER OF KALALL'S DEEP

THE DARK YOUNG

And it shall be as a priest when awake and it shall be as an altar when torpid, and it shall consume and terrify, and it shall follow none save its father, the Black God of the Forest with a Thousand Young. The priest and the altar. The priest and the altar.

FROM 'AR KRAL DESH JEK' (AUTHOR UNKNOWN)

THE DOKKALFAR

The forest-dwellers of the lands of men are many things. To the Ro, arrogant in their superiority, they are risen men – painted as undead monsters and hunted by crusaders of the Black church. To the Ranen, fascinated by youthful tales of monsters, they are otherworldly and terrifying, a remnant of the Giant age. To the Karesians, proud and inflexible, they are an enemy to be vanquished – warriors with stealth and blade.

But to the Kirin, to those of us who live alongside them, they are beautiful and ancient, deserving of respect and loyalty.

The song of the Dokkalfar travels a great distance in the wild forests of Oslan and more than one Kirin youth has spent hours sitting against a tree merely listening to the mournful songs of their neighbours.

They were here before us and will remain long after we have destroyed ourselves.

FROM 'SIGHTS AND SOUNDS OF OSLAN' BY VHAM DUSANI,
KIRIN SCHOLAR

The Great Race of Ancient Jekka

To the east, beyond the plains of Leith, is the ruined land. Men have come to call it the Wastes of Jekka or the Cannibal Lands, for those tribes that dwell there are fond of human flesh.

However, those of us who study such things have discovered disturbing knowledge that paints these beings as more than simple beasts.

In the chronicles of Deep Time – in whatever form they yet exist – this cleric has discovered several references to the Great Race, references that do not speak of cannibalism but of chaos and empires to rival man, built on the bones of vanquished enemies and maintained through sacrifice and bizarre sexual rituals. They were proud, arrogant and utterly amoral, believing completely in their most immediate whims and nothing more.

Whatever the Great Race of Jekka might once have been, they are now a shadow and a myth, bearing no resemblance to the fanged hunters infrequently encountered by man.

FROM 'A TREATISE ON THE UNKNOWN', BY
YACOB OF LEITH, BLUE CLERIC OF THE ONE GOD

The Jekkan Servitors

The war did not last long. The Great Race of Jekka had no desire for the forests. At length we fought them back to their mountains and threw down their altars.

But their pets had to be defeated. As the masters fled, their servitors covered their retreat. They were terrible, amorphous things of no fixed form, shaping their flesh as their masters ordered.

Fire did not burn them, arrows did not pierce them, blades did not cut them. Only the touch of cold caused them to flee. The mightiest Tyr wielded swords of deep ice and the wisest Vithar conjured snow and freezing winds.

The servitors were defeated, though it cost many lives. In the long ages that followed, whispers remained of the terrifying beasts, that they skulked in Jekkan ruins or guarded long-forgotten lore, but they were never again seen by Dokkalfar.

FROM 'THE EDDA', AUTHOR UNKNOWN BUT ATTRIBUTED TO THE SKY RIDERS OF THE DROW DEEPS

CHARACTER LISTING

The People of Ro

The house of Canarn – descended from Lord Bullvy of Canarn
Hector of Canarn – duke of Ro Canarn – *deceased*
Bromvy (Brom) Black Guard of Canarn – disgraced lord of Ro Canarn, soldier of the Long War, son of Duke Hector
Bronwyn of Canarn – daughter of Duke Hector, twin sister to Bromvy
Haake of Canarn – Duke Hector's household guard

The house of Tiris – descended from High King Dashell Tiris
Sebastian Tiris – scion of the house of Tiris and king of Tor Funweir
Lady Alexandra – wife of King Sebastian
Alexander Tiris – the Red Prince, duke of Ro Haran, the king's brother
Archibald Tiris – regent of Ro Tiris, cousin to King Sebastian
Bartholomew Tiris – the king's father – *deceased*
Christophe Tiris – son to King Sebastian, prince of Tor Funweir – *deceased*

Clerics of the One God
Mobius of the Falls of Arnon – cardinal of the Purple
Brother Rashbone of Chase – Purple cleric, adjutant to Cardinal Mobius
Severen of Voy – cardinal of the Purple
Brother Jakan of Tiris – Purple cleric of the sword, protector to King Sebastian Tiris
Brother Cleon Montague – Purple cleric, bodyguard to King Sebastian Tiris
Brother Torian of Arnon – Purple cleric of the quest – *deceased*

Animustus of Voy – Gold cleric

Brother Lanry – Brown cleric, confessor to Duke Hector

Brother Elihas of Du Ban – Black cleric, working with the Seven Sisters

Brother Utha the Ghost – Black cleric and last old-blood of the Shadow Giants

Brother Roderick of the Falls of Arnon – Black cleric

Brother Hobson of Voy – White cleric

Knights and nobles

Mortimer Rillion – knight commander of the Red army – *deceased*

Nathan of Du Ban – knight captain of the Red, adjutant to Knight Commander Rillion – *deceased*

Wesson of Haran – knight marshal of Cozz

Rashabald of Haran – executioner and knight of the Red – *deceased*

William of Verellian – former knight captain of the Red

Fallon of Leith – knight captain of the Red and the army's finest swordsman

Taufel of Arnon – knight captain of the Red, adjutant to Knight Commander Tristram

Theron of Haran – knight lieutenant of the Red, adjutant to Knight Lieutenant Fallon

Tristram of Hunter's Cross – knight commander of the Red

Ohms of the Bridge – knight sergeant of the Red

Vladimir Corkoson – the Lord of Mud, commander of the Darkwald yeomanry

Dimitri Savostin – major of the Darkwald yeomanry

Hallam Pevain – mercenary knight

Castus of Weir – bound man and gaoler – *deceased*

Leon Great Claw – a knight, first master to Randall of Darkwald – *deceased*

Lyam of Weir – duke of Ro Weir

Common folk
Auker of Canarn – guardsman of Ro Canarn
Bracha – old knight sergeant
Broot of Weir – a mercenary of Hallam Pevain
Callis – sergeant in the Red army
Clement of Chase – watch sergeant of Ro Tiris
Elyot of the Tor – watchman of Ro Tiris
Fulton of Canarn – tavern keeper
Kale Glenwood (formerly Glen Ward) – forger, resident in
   Ro Tiris, companion to Rham Jas Rami
Lorkesh – guardsman
Lux – watch sergeant of Ro Tiris
Lyssa – child in the Brown chapel
Mirabel of Arnon – brothel owner in Ro Arnon
Mott – a bandit
Parag of Weir – a mercenary of Hallam Pevain
Randall of Darkwald – squire to, in succession, Sir Leon Great
   Claw, Brother Torian of Arnon, and Brother Utha the Ghost
Robin of Tiris – watchman of Ro Tiris
Rodgar – child in the Brown chapel
Tobin of Cozz – blacksmith and fixer

THE PEOPLE OF ROWANOCO

The Ranen of Fjorlan
*The high lords of Fjorlan have, since the first, sought to keep
their names alive through their children. Those of minor houses
are afforded no such honour and many deliberately strike their
father's name due to dishonourable actions.*

*The house of Teardrop – named for Alguin Teardrop, the first
high thain of Fjorlan.*
Ragnar Teardrop Larsson – father to Magnus Forkbeard
   Ragnarsson and Algenon Teardrop Ragnarsson – *deceased*

Magnus Forkbeard Ragnarsson – younger brother to Algenon
Teardrop Ragnarsson, priest of the Order of the Hammer,
friend to Lord Bromvy – *deceased*

Algenon Teardrop Ragnarsson – high thain of Ranen, elder
brother to Magnus Forkbeard Ragnarsson – *deceased*

Ingrid Teardrop Algedottir – daughter to Algenon Teardrop
Ragnarsson

Alahan Teardrop Algesson – son to Algenon Teardrop
Ragnarsson, heir to the hall of Fredericksand

Oleff Hard Head – chain-master of Fredericksand

Wulfrick the Enraged – axe-master of Fredericksand

Thorfin Axe Hailer – lore-master of Fredericksand

Samson the Liar – old-blood of the Ice Giants

*The house of Summer Wolf – an ancient and respected house,
named for Kalall Summer Wolf*

Aleph Summer Wolf Kallsson – thain of Tiergarten – *deceased*

Halla Summer Wolf Alephsdottir – daughter to Aleph Summer
Wolf, axe-maiden

Borrin Iron Beard – axe-master of Tiergarten – *deceased*

Tricken Ice Fang – chain-master of Tiergarten

Earem Spider Killer – warrior of Tiergarten

Rhuna Grim – cloud-mistress of Tiergarten

Father Brindon Crowe – priest of the Order of the Hammer

Heinrich Blood – novice of the Order of the Hammer

*The house of Hammerfall – home of the cloud-men and the
Wolf Wood*

Grammah Black Eyes – new thain of Hammerfall

Rexel Falling Cloud – axe-master, survivor of the dragon fleet

Moniac Dawn Cloud – axe-master

Anya Coldbane (Lullaby) – wise woman of Rowanoco

The berserkers of Varorg
Timon the Butcher – berserker of Varorg
Rorg the Defiler – berserker chieftain

The house of Ursa – a new house with no honourable lineage,
they name as they see fit
Rulag Ursa Bear Tamer – the Betrayer, sits in the high thain's
    hall. Previously thain of Jarvik and father to Kalag Ursa
Kalag Ursa Rulagsson – lordling of Jarvik
Jalek Blood – axe-master of Jarvik
Father Oryk Grey Claw – priest of the Order of the Hammer

The Ranen of The South Lands

The Free Companies are common folk who earn their names of
honour and have never sought nobility or family names.

Wraith Company – protectors of the Grass Sea
Horrock Green Blade – captain of Wraith Company,
    commander of Ro Hail
Haffen Red Face – axe-master of Ro Hail
Freya Cold Eyes – wise-woman of Ro Hail
Micah Stone Dog – young axe-man of Ro Hail
Darron Moon Eye – priest – *deceased*

Scarlet Company – protectors of South Warden
Johan Long Shadow – captain of the Scarlet Company
Mathias Flame Tooth – axe-master of South Warden
Dragneel Dark Crest – priest of Brytag the World Raven

The People of Karesia

The Seven Sisters – enchantresses, formerly of Jaa, now of Shub-Nillurath

Saara the Mistress of Pain – leader of the Seven Sisters, bears no mark
Ameira the Lady of Spiders – marked with the sign of a spider's web – *deceased*
Katja the Hand of Despair – marked with the sign of a howling wolf
Sasha the Illusionist – marked with the sign of a flowering rose
Lillian the Lady of Death – marked with the sign of a hand
Shilpa the Shadow of Lies – marked with the sign of birds in flight
Isabel the Seductress – marked with the sign of a coiled snake

The wind claws – men who give their life to Jaa
Dalian Thief Taker – greatest of the wind claws
Larix the Traveller – *deceased*
Kal Varaz – servant of the Seven Sisters
Kamran Kainen – servant of the Seven Sisters

The hounds – criminals serving as the Karesian army
Izra Sabal – whip-mistress of the hounds
Turve Ramhe – whip-master of the hounds

Common folk
Al-Hasim, prince of the wastes – exile and thief, friend to the house of Canarn
Emaniz Kabrizzi – book-dealer of Ro Weir
Jenner of Rikara – Karesian smuggler, brother to Kohli
Kasimir Roux – adjutant to whip-mistress Izra Sabal
Kohli of Rikara – Karesian smuggler, brother to Jenner
Voon of Rikara – exemplar of Jaa, missing somewhere in Karesia

The Godless

Kirin – a mongrel race, neither Ro nor Karesian

Rham Jas Rami – assassin, dark-blood and friend to Bromvy Black Guard of Canarn

Zeldantor – son to Rham Jas Rami, slave to Saara the Mistress of Pain – *deceased*

Keisha of Oslan – dark-blood and daughter to Rham Jas Rami

The Dokkalfar – an ancient race of non-human forest-dwellers

Tyr Dyus the Daylight Sky – warrior and Fell Walker

Tyr Nanon the Shape Taker – warrior of the Heart and soldier of the Long War

Tyr Rafn – warrior of the Heart – *deceased*

Tyr Sigurd – warrior of the Heart

Tyr Vasir – warrior of the Drow Deeps

Vithar Joror – shaman of the Heart

Vithar Jofn – shaman of the Heart

Vithar Loth the Tree Father – shaman and Fell Walker

Vithar Xaris – shaman of Narland

Mysterious others

Ryuthula – Gorlan mother

Torian's shade – apparition and servant of the One God

Magnus's shade – apparition and servant of Rowanoco

ACKNOWLEDGEMENTS

Is the second book cursed? Is it the 'difficult second book'? Do writers struggle to replicate the good points of their debut? If I've managed to avoid these things, I have the following people to thank: Simon Hall, Kathleen Kitsell, Marcus Holland, Benjamin Hesford, Scott Illniki, Carrie Hall, Martin Cubberley, Tony Carew, Karl Wustrau, Mark Allen, Paolo Trepiccione, Terry and Cathy Smith, Becci Sharpe, Mathilda Imlah, Diane Banks.

ALL THAT WAS DEAD WILL RISE.
ALL THAT NOW LIVES WILL FALL...

PREVIEW

THE
RED
PRINCE

'MARTIN MEETS LOVECRAFT' SCIFI NOW

A.J. SMITH

The Tale of the Old Bloods

A s the Giants became fewer and mortal creatures became more numerous, before ages had names and time was still in its infancy, the blood was still strong.

The weak beings of this age took the blood gladly and mortal mated with Giant until mighty creatures rose to rule the rock, tree, earth and sea.

As the Giants disappeared, they left beings of strength and twisted form to rule their lands and fight their Long War. These old bloods were few and most bore a visage of madness which they used to cow the primitive men. Faces and bodies, half-twisted by the enormity of their blood, and minds with cunning intent.

As long ages passed, the old bloods waned until the blood was almost spent. They warred with the Great Race of Jekka and they warred with each other. Through the inexorable passage of time, mortals forgot about their masters.

The old bloods that remained bore children and the blood diluted until all that remained were abnormal remnants of deep time.

As the Jekkans left and men appeared, gaining their own power, naming their own lands, kingdoms and empires, the old bloods retreated to the darkness of the world. Some hid in forests, some in the deepest caves and some – those that could pass as men – walked paths of their own and kept alive the blood of Giants.

PROLOGUE

PRINCE ALEXANDER TIRIS could not sleep. He was resting against a thin bedroll, with his head on a rucksack and his back tormented by jagged rocks.

The weather was unrelenting. When it wasn't lashing down with rain, it was blowing a gale. If the One felt any sympathy for the family of Tiris, he wasn't showing it. Xander wished at least for a day of sunshine before he completely lost his faith.

The Duchy of Haran was barren and sparsely populated at the best of times. With the addition of a Karesian enchantress and the lack of a duke, the people were staying indoors. Those that lived on the rugged northern plains had, by decree from their duke, stayed clear of the city. The river men who fished the southern inlets rarely deigned to visit Haran anyway and had readily stayed away.

Xander was King Sebastian's younger brother and a former knight of the Red. He was a tough and jaded man with a temper that could fell an army and a wife that could fell any reinforcements that the army had. Lady Gwendolyn was from Hunter's Cross and nestled in Xander's arms as they huddled together in the cave, several days north of Ro Haran. She had insisted that they find somewhere indoors to sleep and had refused to consider another night under the stars. They'd have a more comfortable camp set-up tomorrow, but for tonight they were content to not be sleeping in the rain.

Xander had been the duke of Haran for twelve years, since he met Gwendolyn and left the Red. He had been an exile from his city for almost seven months, since a Karesian woman called Shilpa the Shadow of Lies had appeared.

3

He was approaching his fortieth year and had recently decided to shave his head to disguise the hereditary baldness that plagued the family of Tiris. A lifetime of wielding a sword and refusing to simply sit in his hall had gifted Xander with a strong and muscular physique, and a skill in combat that was brutal but efficient. He wore no beard, preferring to shave rather than weather the endless complaints of his wife, and the Red Prince of Haran was considered handsome by most.

His men were loyal and had accompanied him with no questions, leaving the city under the charge of watchmen. These five thousand soldiers camped nearby and had treated the time away as an extended military exercise; most had maintained a good humour about their absence from Ro Haran.

Gwendolyn shivered in her sleep and awoke. She grasped Xander's hand firmly.

"You need to sleep," she said wearily. "Thinking doesn't change anything."

"Neither does running away," he replied.

"I don't remember any running. I think we walked away."

Gwen had a way of puncturing his self-pity. It was not always gentle, but Xander had come to rely on her assessment of their situation. She was tougher and cleverer than him anyway.

He gazed at her for a moment. Gwendolyn had long black hair that was usually tied in a warrior's top knot. Now, it was spread out across her back and shimmered in the minimal light. Her eyes were angular and coloured a deep green. Xander thought her the most beautiful creature he had ever seen, though he knew that most men found her harsh and intimidating. Her two Dokkalfar leaf blades only added to her fearsome appearance and she had killed more than one man who had insulted her husband.

Gwen was the reason Xander was no longer a knight of the Red. He'd met her during his first excursion into the Dokkalfar woods of The Darkwald. She'd been trying to assist the forest dwellers in repulsing the knights and had shot him in the throat with a short bow. Several other men and women, allied with the Dokkalfar, had recognised his white eagle heraldry, identifying him as a member of the House of Tiris. They had taken him, dying and bloodied, into the woods where they'd slowly nursed him back to health. It was a month until they told him why they'd saved him and another two before he was healthy enough to leave.

Sir Alexander Tiris, knight of the Red, fell in love in those woods. He fell in love with a boisterous bitch of a woman who showed him the depths of his mistake. The Dokkalfar were not monsters. If it weren't for their healing arts, he would have died in the forest. He met their shamans, their warriors and their children, he saw a culture and a civilization beyond anything preached by the Purple clerics and he turned his back on the One God as a result. If it weren't for his older brother, Xander would have been executed for vow-breaking. Instead, Sebastian put him out of the way as duke of Ro Haran and tried to forget about him.

He leant over his wife and kissed her deeply. She grumbled against his lips, shoving him away.

"I'm trying to sleep... and you smell," she said with closed eyes and a contented smile.

"No sleep for me tonight," he whispered. "But don't let me disturb you." He didn't move and allowed Gwen to nuzzle closer to him. Their collective bodily warmth helped shut out the biting winds of Haran.

With his eyes wide open and his mind racing, the duke of Haran waited until morning.

*

The garrison of Ro Haran were known as the hawks of Ro and were the finest true fighting men in Tor Funweir. They were separate and distinct from the ranks of watchmen who policed the streets and they lived and worked as soldiers from the day they took their tabard. Each man wore chainmail armour and carried a large rectangular shield, displaying the heraldry of their duke – a rising red hawk with talons bared. They were arranged into cohorts of two hundred men, each with a lieutenant and an individual standard.

Xander had fostered a somewhat apathetic view of the gods amongst his men. Tribute was paid, as was the custom, but these men believed in what they could see, hear and fight, not what was told to them by men wearing the Purple of nobility. Because of this attitude, Xander preferred to be known as the general of Haran, rather than the duke.

Leaving the cave and venturing out into the morning mist, he cast a critical eye over the men camped under his banner across the rugged flats of Haran. Many cohorts were already awake, building cook fires, tending to horses and going about their daily duties.

Nearby, leading some lacklustre morning prayers, was Brother Daganay, Xander's confessor and his one concession to piety. When offered a cleric, the duke had dismissed talk of the Purple and insisted on a man of the Blue, a cleric of knowledge, to advise him. Dag was a man in his early fifties, but still healthy and tough, and more than capable of holding his own on the training grounds. He insisted on wearing his blue robes, eschewing armour, though he carried a heavy mace which Xander had, on more than one occasion, seen buried in a man's head.

As the duke approached, the Blue cleric raised his head and announced with a smile, "And, brothers, we must never forget the blessed house of Tiris, for they are the greatest gift bestowed upon us by The One."

His words were accompanied by a sly wink and the kneeling men in front of him all looked up to see why their cleric was being so formal.

"Oh, sorry, my lord," said Dag, pretending to see Xander for the first time. "You interrupted our usual morning blessing."

This got a laugh from the praying hawks.

"Yes, I'm sure you bless me and my house every morning,

brother," he said ironically. "As you bless the weather." He spread his arms wide and looked up into the drizzling rain. "While you're praying, you couldn't get the One to give us some sunshine could you."

Another ripple of good-humoured laughter from his men and Xander wandered away to inspect the camp.

There was no immediate danger, but he had insisted that they act as if there were. A stockade was built each night and hourly guard duties were still applied. That the hawks had accepted this, and not raised a single word of complaint, was testament to their dedication and the respect in which they held their general.

In his more contemplative moments, with only Gwen for company, Xander wondered how long he could remain on manoeuvres and when was the right time to take back his city. He knew little of the Seven Sisters, but was reliably informed by Daganay that they could enchant a man with but a glance. He was wary enough to stay clear of Haran as long as Shilpa the Shadow of Lies was in residence. The last thing he wanted was to unknowingly lead the hawks of Ro into a war instigated by the witches of Karesia. Sebastian, his elder brother, was already enthralled to one or other of the enchantresses and Xander was determined not to share the king's fate. Further to this, he had received disturbing reports from Tiris, Weir and Cozz. The hound occupation of Tor Funweir was proceeding unopposed.

But he was still free. For now at least.

His cousin, Archibald, was nominally in charge of the capital. An old friend, Knight Marshall Wesson, had been the protector of Cozz. Archibald was a fool, easily swayed and weak-willed, whereas Wesson was a soldier who'd died to protect the enclave. Wesson had been Xander's squire before his title forced him to other duties. If nothing else was accomplished, vengeance against the hound that killed Wesson would be enough for the Red Prince. Though he planned a much more obstinate and long-lasting campaign.

He kept his chin thrust out as he walked amongst his men. Tough faces and smiles greeted the general of Haran. He had trained many of them himself, sparring daily with sword and shield until each man was as tough as a soldier could get. The kind of bond forged when you see your general getting as bloody as his men was priceless. Xander was proud to command them.

He wandered past his men, enjoying the morning breeze, until he got to the smithy on the northern edge of their camp. Sergeant Ashwyn had been in possession of Xander's sword for a day or two, repairing the hilt, and he'd promised that it would be returned today. The duke felt strange without his bastard sword, the blade given to him by an old Black cleric called Alistair, and the scabbard hanging at his side was uncomfortably light.

"My lord," said Ashwyn as Xander entered the forging tent.

"At ease, Ash," he responded with a friendly salute. "Where's Peacekeeper."

"Finished last night, milord. As sharp as ever and as heavy as my wife," the blacksmith said with a wry grin. "You'd do better with a normal longsword. This thing will fuck up your arm one day."

Ashwyn rubbed his sweaty hands on his stained apron. He crossed the tent to a workbench set up next to a smouldering forge. He picked up the long blade and hefted it several times, feeling the weight. Peacekeeper was longer and wider than a traditional Ro longsword and could be used one- or two-handed, depending on the need. It was too heavy for most men and Xander used it as much to intimidate as to kill.

Ash handed the bastard sword back to Xander and pointed out where he'd repaired the hilt. The leather grip had split during a training exercise and the hardened walnut beneath had been damaged. The blacksmith had re-hardened the wood and added a fresh leather strap, making the hilt feel like new as the general held it.

"Are you going to be cracking some Karesian heads with that over-sized hunk of metal, milord? Soon, I mean... well, in the next year or so." Ashwyn was a good soldier and a master of steel, making him a well-liked and valuable member of the hawks.

"Find me a man that can kill Shilpa the Shadow of Lies and I'll kill as many hounds as you want, sergeant," replied Xander with a comradely smile. "But I need my city back first."

The general was about to sheath Peacekeeper and leave the tent, when Ashwyn spoke. "Two riders were sighted coming down the mountain road to the south, my lord. Captain Brenan went to see what they want. Apparently, one of them was a Kirin with a longbow."